OF FATE SO DARK

FOREVER AFTER: CRIMSON SNOW
BOOK THREE

SIERRA ROWAN

MOUNTAIN TREE PRESS

Proofreading: Happy Ever Author

eBook ISBN: 978-1-955991-08-7
Paperback ISBN: 978-1-955991-15-5
Hardcover ISBN: 978-1-955991-22-3

First published: March 2024
Urbana, IL, USA

v.0.1

AUTHOR'S NOTE

If you would like content guidance, please see the author's website at sierrarowan.com.

1

GWYNEIRA

Darkness writhed within me, trying to devour all I'd ever been. My mind. My memories.

My love for the men I'd just left behind.

Everything had been going well. My scholarly giant, Byron, had just cast a spell that gave me back something I hadn't possessed since I was turned into a vampire by my stepmother—the ability to walk in sunlight. My vampire lover, the Zeniryan king named Casimir, was able to use the spell on himself as well. With him and my giants, I'd watched my first sunrise in what felt like an eternity, even if it was actually only a short while since I'd been turned.

But then it all went wrong.

When we'd neared the border of my kingdom, Aneira, an earthquake shook everything, tearing fissures in the earth that weren't *just* products of the shaking. No, they'd been shredded open by magic, and that magic had somehow allowed creatures from the empty realms to ride the destruction into this world.

The Voidborn. They came in black smoke, writhing like eels with vicious metal teeth and multicolored eyes that glowed like a deranged rainbow in the darkness. Everything I'd learned from Byron and from the witches of the Jeweled Coven with whom we'd stayed for a short time said that the Voidborn shouldn't be able to enter this world. Reality itself repelled them. They couldn't survive in it.

Someone had obviously forgotten to tell *them* that.

They'd attacked, striking me and filling my mind with their darkness. Their touch had unleashed the worst aspects of the vampire I'd become. The hunger. The need to feed and kill, no matter who was my prey. Once upon a time, the Voidborn had been the creators of the vampires, and it was their plan for us to be a force of unmitigated destruction in this world.

My giants had saved me from that fate once. Their blood was one of the few things in existence that could break the hold of that rabid madness and bring a vampire back to their own humanity. But that had been when I was first turned, when my stepmother was the only one trying to draw out the ravenous predator within me. And that time, it had taken all seven of them working together to stop me from draining them dry.

This time, I'd been alone with Ozias, the scarred and secretive giant who I thought wanted nothing to do with me. No one could have reached us. No one could have saved him if I'd attacked.

Still he'd offered himself.

Right before he called me his *treluria*, a giant's fated mate.

His true love.

So I'd gathered the last of my sanity, and I fled from him. From all of them. It was that or kill everyone I could sink my fangs into, and I'd do anything to save those men.

Even if it cost me myself.

Half-mad with hunger and fear, I careened through the forest now, the smoke of the Voidborn pursuing my body while their whispers hounded me through my mind. I prayed the creatures had left Ozias be. That he was back there helping the others trapped on the other side of the earthquake's fissures now.

That he wasn't chasing me.

Because my vampire side was taking over, and my ravenous hunger was growing worse with every second. Already, I had no pulse. No breath. No warmth in my skin so pale it looked like snow. Soon, there'd be nothing left of me at all, and no thought in my mind but to feed.

Ozias's blood might save me, but I knew without question I'd kill him if I bit him now.

My body moved faster and faster, flashing between human form and something else I'd only seen but never experienced. As smoke and shadow, I left the ground behind in fits and starts, crashing back to the earth in human form and then taking off into the sky again.

Trying to escape what could not be escaped, and craving blood that would only damn me.

Because human blood, witch blood, *any* sentient creature's blood but that of a giant or a vampire would give this darkness even more of a foothold. To kill a human or witch would only mean surrendering fully to the madness of the creatures chasing me. But murdering my men to save myself would kill my soul.

I slammed into something hard and rebounded away. A tree, maybe. I couldn't tell. But the Voidborn pursuing me took the opening. Surging closer, they swept across my body with a feeling like cold, dead hands dragging over my skin.

I screamed.

Flinging myself away again, I took fully to the sky, skittering between a falling human form and a flying shadow one. But I could feel the Voidborn stronger now, their voices inside my mind like rushing water carrying the murmurs of the dead. I couldn't see the forest anymore. Couldn't hear anything but the sibilant whisper of their commands in my head.

To feed.

To kill.

To let the vampire rage.

I'd lost the war to reclaim myself.

And the Voidborn had won.

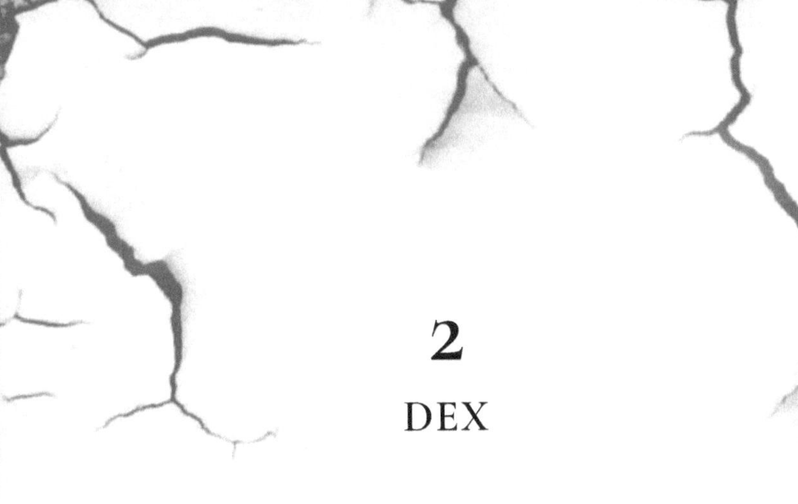

2

DEX

"On your left!"

I spun at Lars's shout, slashing at the Voidborn with the sword given to me by the witches of the Jeweled Coven. "Up top!" I shouted back.

The blond man yelled at his twin to move. As Clay ducked, Lars stabbed at the shadowy creature diving toward them both.

"Watch out!" Byron flung nuggets of ore at the Voidborn and called out a spell, making the small rocks burst like they'd been struck by lightning. The creatures fell back, but not far enough.

We were still surrounded.

But even as they lunged and dove, I suspected the Voidborn were just toying with us. Only vampires could survive contact with them—if going mad and turning into a rabid predator could be considered *surviving*. Everything else touched by the Voidborn only turned to ash and died.

Yet these creatures hadn't killed us. They'd trapped us within a circle of the fissures they'd torn through the earth, leaving only Ozias outside the cage. Black smoke poured up from the gaps, offering glimpses of the world beyond this maelstrom of monsters, but providing no way to reach it and survive. I'd spotted flashes of the forest, enough to see that more cracks riddled the terrain like some massive beast had shredded the ground with its claws. Every few moments, more Voidborn would surge up from the fissures to join their fellows in swooping and darting at us like snakes that had learned to fly.

And yet still we weren't dead.

"Anyone got a plan?" Lars called.

"How about not dying?" his brother Clay retorted dryly. Even now, the man couldn't resist making jokes.

I ignored him, slashing at one of the creatures and trying to catch another glimpse of the world beyond our churning cage. The princess was the Voidborn's true target. She was the one they'd gone after right from the start. But beyond the swirls of the Voidborn, I couldn't see her, and the brief sight of Ozias's face gave me a sinking feeling as to why.

If they'd touched her...

If she'd felt their power taking control...

"Go!" I shouted at Ozias. "Protect the princess!"

His massive axe gripped in both hands, the bearded giant ripped the blade through one of the Voidborn and then gave me a tight nod. Whirling, he slung the weapon onto his back with practiced ease and raced away into the woods.

Dozens of the creatures took off after him as if intent on chasing him down.

Fuck.

"That's not good," Niko said as if echoing my sentiment. Worry clung to the younger man's face as he stabbed at another Voidborn.

Clay scoffed. "Big guy can run for it. We're the ones who are screwed."

"Not helpful, brother," Lars protested tiredly.

"Fine," Clay retorted. "Anybody see a way out of this shit?"

I spun, searching for exactly that. In the seconds after the earth had started shaking and cracks had torn through the grass and dirt, there'd been precious little chance to evaluate our position. But now...

"There!" Niko pointed at a small stretch of solid ground between two fissures.

I nodded, backing toward the gap. "Pull in. Swords to the outside. We—"

Like a blanket of smoke, Voidborn smothered the opening. The rest raced in toward us, the yellowed winter grass beneath them turning to ash as they sped over it.

"Fuckers," Roan muttered tightly, his pale face even more bloodless than normal. He retreated from the creatures, but strangely, he kept his distance from us too, almost like he was as concerned about coming near his friends as he was about the Voidborn. "Next plan?"

I didn't answer immediately, watching him in between swift glances at our attackers. Something was off about Roan. Had *been* off ever since we entered the Wild Lands.

It made my skin crawl and I had no idea why.

"Yeah, *now* what?" Clay called.

Grunting a curse, I shoved my concerns about Roan back down, though that didn't stop me from keeping an eye on him too. "Circle up! We move forward as a unit, got it? Head for the—"

Casimir snarled viciously, and my heart hit my throat.

Oh, shit.

I threw a glance back at him. The king of the fallen kingdom of Zenirya was a vampire, turned when his country fell in the Witch War over three decades ago. He and our princess were the only two of their kind *possibly* in all of existence who still had their human side intact.

But if the Voidborn got to him...

Gods, I *knew* those creatures were toying with us for a reason.

Casimir stood motionless while his shadow wolf, Ruhl, flowed around him like an erratic tornado, attacking the Voidborn in an effort to hold them back from the vampire. A burned gash cut through Casimir's coat all the way down to the dark skin of his forearm, and I could see blood seeping from the wound. Nearby, one of the Voidborn hovered as if preparing to strike again, only to suddenly whirl away and dive back into a fissure like its tail was on fire instead.

What the hell?

"You okay there, buddy?" Clay called.

Casimir shuddered.

Not good. Tipped into madness, the king was easily as much of a threat as the Voidborn—and that was without taking into account the magic he possessed, courtesy of his decades of study and a heritage that apparently descended from angels. Against a predator with that much power, we'd be hard pressed to survive.

We did have one move to save ourselves, though...

"Clay. Lars." I nodded for the twins to cover the stretch of our defense that I was currently guarding. After so many years of fighting and running together, the two understood me immediately.

"You sure?" Clay asked. "He's not looking too friendly."

"Just go."

Seamlessly, we switched positions, the blond men watching the Voidborn while I headed for where Casimir stood. Gripping his sword tightly, the vampire king didn't react to my presence, barring the quivers that began racking him so hard, the long braids of his dark hair shook.

"Hey." I shoved up the sleeve of my coat and cut a quick slice across my forearm.

The vampire's eyes snapped up to the wound immediately. His lips peeled back, revealing his fangs. Sharp, low growls slipped from him like the sounds weren't entirely under his control.

Fuck...

Clay slashed at a Voidborn, holding the twisting smoke back. "Dex, maybe you shouldn't—"

Casimir moved so fast, I couldn't even flinch before his fangs sank into my arm.

I grunted. Once, Niko had hinted that being bitten by a vampire was intensely intimate, but even if Casimir and I had slept together in the past, there was nothing erotic about this. With vicious pulls, Casimir dragged on my vein, both his hands gripping my forearm hard, like a predator determined not to lose its prey.

Shifting my stance with effort, I fought to keep my feet beneath me and my attention on the Voidborn still trying to reach us. Feeding him my blood was a desperate gamble, considering that—if he was too far gone—he might try to drain me dry.

But there wasn't an alternative. Giant blood gave vampires their humanity back. Angel blood too, apparently, which meant Casimir had an innate advantage our princess didn't possess. It was part of why he'd retained his human side when he was first turned thirty years ago. But how effective his heritage alone would be against the Voidborn was anyone's guess.

So blood it was. After all, I didn't want us fighting a war on two fronts. Not if we could help it.

The Voidborn swirled around us faster.

"I don't think they like what you're doing there…" Clay called.

Shit.

With a snarl, Casimir broke away from me, his chest rising and falling in rapid gasps. He sealed the wound on my arm quickly and then released me to swipe the back of his hand across his mouth. "Thank you."

I nodded, striking out at another twisting creature of smoke. "You good?"

Tightly, he echoed the motion. "Oh, I'm marvelous." His voice dripped with irony as he cast a glance at the wound left by the Voidborn. The gash was smaller but not gone, and blood still dripped down to make his sword hand slick. With an ease born of years of training, he switched his weapon to his other hand and slashed at one of the creatures as it tried to reach us. "What a lovely way to spend my first day in sunlight in three decades, yes?"

I exhaled with relief my gamble had worked, while Clay just scoffed like he appreciated the vampire's sarcasm—because of course he would.

"We need a stage two for our plan, friends," Lars said, still striking out at the Voidborn.

I swung at the creatures as they darted toward me, my mind racing. We were surrounded, we had only our swords, and coming in contact with these things would likely be bad on a scale I didn't want to imagine, at least if the ashen terrain around us was any indication.

"I've got an idea." Byron ducked to stay clear of a Voidborn. "Remember the sunlight protective spell?" He threw a fast look at Casimir and the twins.

They nodded.

"Like that, on my mark."

I tossed a prayer up to the gods, even though I doubted it'd do too much good. I'd seen too many things in the war to trust any deities gave a damn about us. But whatever Byron was planning, it *had* to work. We needed something if we were going to make it out of here alive.

"One, two…"

A thud went through the air, like the pressure of a storm surging higher and then dissipating just as fast. A rush of light followed in its wake, ripping past me to slam into the Voidborn.

The creatures' screams nearly took my legs from under me, and my hands clasped my ears on pure instinct, desperately trying and failing to keep the sound out. It felt like razor blades on my brain. Like knives in my insides.

I was distantly amazed I was still alive when it finally faded away.

Shaking, I straightened.

The creatures were gone. We were still here.

Maybe the gods gave a shit about us after all.

"Everyone all right?" I asked, my voice rough to my own ears.

The others nodded. Everyone except Roan. For a moment, the pale man just stood there, his eyes squeezed shut and his body trembling.

Clay followed my gaze. "Hey, Roan. You all right?"

Seconds passed. Worried looks flew between the others.

"Fine," Roan said, not opening his eyes. The word came out gritted and strange, like a growl between his teeth.

My gut did *not* believe that response, and the nervous looks that still passed between the twins told me I wasn't alone in that. But after another heartbeat, Roan straightened, his breaths coming short and fast, and he opened his eyes. "Anyone hurt?"

He sounded like himself now, even if he still looked paler than normal.

Murmurs of confirmation that they were all right came from the others.

Niko bent quickly anyway, retrieving a strip of cloth from a roll in his bag. The witches had put the packs together for each of us, and on some level, it alarmed me how much they'd known about us to stock them as they had. Healing materials for Niko. Small nuggets of ore to focus Byron's magic. Food supplies for Lars to use with his replication spells. All those were just a few of the unique options they'd provided.

But then, they were witches. The gods only knew what they could detect about us.

"Casimir?" Niko asked. "Do you—"

"I'm fine, thank you." The vampire clasped a hand over the wound on his arm and muttered a spell under his breath.

Niko studied him with the sharp eyes of someone who'd spent all his life training to be a healer. "Okay. Let me know if you need anything."

The vampire king nodded once in return.

"So now what?" Lars asked from where he crouched over the shards of the magical glass coffin we'd used to carry the princess through the Wild Lands. The box had been enchanted to keep the sunlight away from her, but the Voidborn had shattered it within moments of their arrival, as if determined to keep us from protecting her in every way.

Only the spell Byron cast upon her last night could guard her from the sun now.

"We need to get after her," Clay responded. "Oz too. If those creatures drive her back into the Wild Lands..."

Sickened looks crossed the others' faces. We'd barely survived that cursed terrain. And while the princess was formidable and Ozias would stare down the gods themselves, that didn't mean I wanted them to face that on their own.

Roan made an irritated noise. "Then we should get going instead of standing around here talking."

Ruhl growled, and Roan's gaze snapped over to him with a glare. The wolf fell silent.

A cold feeling settled in my stomach. Something was *definitely* odd about my friend.

"Well," Clay said, strained levity in his tone. "Back into the woods we go. Fun times."

"Indeed," Casimir agreed far more seriously.

Clay's eyes slid in the direction of the Wild Lands, and his wry look faded into dread.

"She may not have gone that far," I said. "But if she did..." I drew a breath. "Stay close to each other. Trust nothing. We made it through there once. We can do it again."

The others nodded.

Keeping our weapons ready, we headed for the forest.

3
OZIAS

I darted between trees and leapt over fallen logs, and everything in me raged as if I was being torn in two. Ahead of me, Gwyneira was in danger. Behind me, the men I called friends were too. I couldn't save them both.

I might not be able to save any of them at all.

Anguish came from the beast inside me, spurring me to run faster. Dex had told me to find her, but he hadn't seen Gwyneira's face in the moments after those creatures rose from the cracks in the ground. Her horror. Her terror as they lunged at her.

The way her expression transformed into that of a rabid predator when they touched her.

Those Voidborn were trying to sap her humanity. They wanted to steal everything she'd fought so hard to hang onto after she was turned.

And for that, my beast roared with rage.

Leaping fallen logs and tearing past bushes stripped

leafless by the winter cold, I threw a swift glance back. Trails of black smoke sped between the trees behind me, turning everything they touched to ash. More tentacles of smoke rose from the fissures in the earth around me, twisting like snakes and lunging into my path, cutting me off.

The hell they would.

Skidding to a halt, I whipped my axe down from its strap on my back and slashed at the Voidborn, the ore-lined edge leaving burning trails in the air where it ripped through them. Their screams reached into my brain like claws, bypassing my ears entirely to grate at my mind.

But I didn't care. Let them scream. They were between me and Gwyneira, and for that, they would die.

I whirled, slashing through one that tried to whip around behind me, as I struggled to find any sign of where the princess had gone. She wasn't touching the ground any longer, which meant my power couldn't detect her. But surely she would come back down.

Gods, let her come back down...

At another slash from my blade, the Voidborn fell back for a moment. It was all I needed. I darted through the gap they left, slinging the axe back into place as I moved with practice born of decades of use. Screeching, the creatures dove after me.

They'd never be able to keep up.

Adrenaline and power poured into my muscles. My beast wasn't here yet, not fully, and there was no time to shift. But its strength fueled me, giving me greater speed. Branches tore at me like grasping claws when I whipped past them, and the smoke of the Voidborn twisted after me like vengeful snakes, hellbent on tearing me down, but still I ran.

I wouldn't lose her. Even if she hated me for all those weeks when I'd tried to drive her away, even if she never understood that I'd only done that to save us both pain, I still would never let her die.

Never let these bastards drain her humanity and keep only her body alive.

My beast snarled with fury in my mind, thoroughly in agreement.

Onward, I ran as the minutes ticked past and the forest refused to yield up my princess. But with every glance I threw back at the creatures chasing me, there were fewer. At first, I thought they were circling wide, perhaps planning to cut me off from either side again, but no attack ever came.

But then their serpentine bodies started to grow thin. As often as they sped after me, they crashed into the trees and bushes too, scarring the bark and branches with ash. They looked like drunken sailors stumbling on dry land for the first time, and while some veered off to the north as if suddenly trying to flee in that direction, others continued their erratic path after me.

And they were burning.

Alarmed, I slowed in spite of myself. Only one of the Voidborn remained now, twisting and thrashing far behind me as if it was fighting to push through mud rather than air. Tendrils of smoke were peeling away from its body like the creature was being shredded as it flew. The black wisps evaporated in the bright light of the morning when they left the creature's body.

Still, the Voidborn tried to rush at me, flashing its metallic teeth in a snarl. Amid the smoke, eyes glowed a pus-like shade of yellow and glared at me with so much hate, it was like the creature despised my very existence.

Which was probably the case. But before it came within a dozen feet of me, it could last no longer. With a thin, screeching sound, the Voidborn faded away into nothing.

A breath escaped me. So... sunlight killed them. Or this world did, considering the witches claimed none of those creatures could survive outside their endless void anyway.

Good.

But my princess was still out here somewhere, and while I knew there was a chance she'd also fled to the north and that was the reason the Voidborn sought to go that way, I refused to entertain the possibility Byron's spell to protect her against the sun had failed when the Voidborn touched her.

No, she would be alive. Mad, perhaps, but alive.

I'd shred the void itself if she was otherwise.

But where the hell *was* she?

Swiftly, I scanned the forest, using my magic to check on my friends. They were miles behind where I stood. Still alive and coming this way, yes, but at the speed of men, not monsters.

They'd never have to know about me.

I yanked my coat and sweater off and then removed my boots. Both went into the bag the Jeweled Coven had given me, stuffed down among the sharpening stones for my weapons and all the other supplies they'd provided.

And then I let the shift tear through my body.

At high speed, my bones twisted and my skin did too. My joints cracked, my knees bending backwards in brief, sharp points of pain, giving me the ability to run on four legs as well as two if I needed it. Fur erupted over my body, and my vision blurred for only a heartbeat as my skull lengthened and changed, shifting into that of a wolf but with sunken eyes and more bone than fur on my face. Claws came from my newly massive hands, long enough to skewer a man clean through, and more curved out from the elongated paws my feet had become. Gnarled antlers twisted up from my skull, and my tail shoved past the carefully concealed flap I'd stitched into these pants while the waistband stretched to accommodate my other form. Likewise, the straps of my weapons tightened across my chest, but I'd crafted my equipment well. They didn't snap or rip.

My gaze swept across the forest while hot poison dripped from my fangs, making the ground steam. To my prey, the venom would be like acid. To my mate, it would be something else entirely.

I had only to find her first.

Sniffing the air, I growled. In my ordinary form, my senses were heightened above any other Erenlian's, but they didn't hold a candle to this. In an instant, a flood of new information reached me, painting a rich tapestry across my mind of the forest and the earth and the directions in which all the creatures upon it had gone.

But I only cared about one.

A hint of sweet strawberries and tangy blood ghosted

across the breeze, as faint as the first blush of sunrise and then gone.

The princess.

I took off. Small creatures scattered, fleeing as they detected my scent on the wind. Deer leapt into a panicked run and birds took to the sky, but they couldn't move fast enough to escape me, had I cared to catch them. I was a monster in this form. Truly, I was a monster even when I hid in my Erenlian shape pretending to be a man. When I looked like that, I was simply better at making others believe I was not a wild animal inside. But my beast was another matter entirely.

The mere sight of me in this form had prompted everyone from strangers to my own mother to try to kill me just for existing.

I wished I could believe there was a chance Dex or the others wouldn't do the same. After all, they were good and noble, the best people I'd ever known. But I'd spent too many years roaming the wilds alone, chased from every scrap of civilization I found, to risk what little I had now on the fantasy that anyone who knew the truth about me would ever let me stay.

Ever let me have a home.

Because the *actual* truth was, I was an abomination, unfit for civilization, let alone friendship or love. It was only by keeping what I was a secret, by pretending to be an Erenlian, that I could have a home at all. But if the truth came out, that would shatter.

Any sane person who saw my beast would know they had to kill me. They sure as hell wouldn't risk me staying anywhere near someone as rare and incredible as Gwyneira.

And I knew they would be right.

I stretched out my magic, scanning the earth even as I searched the air to find her scent again. But there was nothing. No hint of her on the ground or in the air any longer, as if she'd just vanished from—

The bright sense of her touching the earth flared to life in my mind like a star peeking past clouds only to be swallowed by them again.

Gwyneira.

No one else shone like that to me, and as long as she was touching the earth, I'd always find her. But she was there only for an instant before vanishing, like she'd hit the ground and then left it again, becoming human only long enough for her presence to reach me.

A fanged snarl twisted my face. I veered right, leaping past fallen logs and gnarled underbrush. We were still outside the edge of the Wild Lands. But I was moving fast, and gods, she was too.

In her current state, would she make the mistake of heading back into that cursed territory?

I fought for more speed, flying through bushes and branches with none of my usual care for not leaving a trace of my passage. Boulders the size of houses barely managed to slow my pace. A ravine passed beneath me in a blur, the gap bridged by a fallen log, here and then gone. My claws tore gashes in the rough dirt and ripped through tangled branches that blocked my path, shredding the obstacles at high speed.

Gradually, Gwyneira's scent returned on the breeze

ahead, weaving through the forest and leading me onward like fragments of an invisible ribbon scattered over the terrain. Had she returned to human form even in the air? Perhaps. But the details didn't matter.

Only finding her did.

More endless minutes ticked past as I bounded up slopes and over broken boulders, speeding past small creatures so quickly, they didn't have time to bolt away. Forever, Gwyneira remained ahead of me, but with each passing moment her scent grew stronger. I was closing the distance between us.

And gods, somewhere past my fear, my beast was starting to *love* this chase.

Shame came on the heels of the realization, but my monstrous side had more control now. It pushed back against the pain, breathing deep of the crisp air and altering course instinctively to continue after her. That part of me had always wanted this—to chase my mate, bring her down, and pin her as I rutted her. That side of me was pure predator.

Hunting my mate felt as natural as breathing.

Of course, my Erenlian side knew *exactly* how contemptible that made me. When I was nothing more than a young teen, I'd seen a man chasing after a woman, pursuing her as she fled from him across the open field that bordered the forest where I lived at the time. Gods, I thought I'd never seen anything so erotic. Need and desire had overwhelmed me, and my cock grew hard in an instant, everything in me so aroused that I nearly came just watching them.

Until I realized how wrong I'd been about it all.

I thought it had been natural and welcome to chase a mate like that. That she was running, yes, and maybe afraid of being claimed by him in a way, but not that the woman was *truly* an unwilling participant. Yet when he grabbed her and threw her down, and she started shrieking with such terror and desperation in her voice, pleading in broken sobs for him to stop or for someone to save her...

I just reacted.

She hadn't thanked me.

But she'd gotten away. And he never got up again, his blood on my fangs and his gurgling breaths falling silent even as the woman ran.

From the monster.

A sharp huff left me, a protest from my beast side. It still couldn't fathom why we'd been wrong that day—about wanting to chase and claim a mate, if nothing else. But I knew this was the closest I'd ever get to running after the one I wanted. There was no one who would enjoy joining me in such a thing, no mate who would ever welcome being hunted. And after I found Gwyneira... after I shifted back *before* she could see me in this form and thereby kept her from ever knowing what I truly was...

That would be the end of it.

The beast threw indignation at me, along with the memory of her blushing face and the taste of her arousal on the air after Casimir had whispered to her in the cave this morning, his words so impossible they couldn't even make me outraged.

He'd hurt her.

She'd liked it.

And, the beast reminded me, that wasn't the first time I'd witnessed hints of how wrong I was about her. She'd taken Casimir and Dex together, even while the former fucked the latter. She'd let Niko bind her with his vines—a moment that should have been my first hint she wasn't the gentle innocent I'd mistaken her for.

No, she was more than I ever could have dreamed.

But that didn't mean she would want *this*. Want me to chase her, dominate her, rut her and knot her, just like the mate I dreamed she could be. I'd driven her away long before I learned I was wrong about her. I'd been cold and cruel, and I'd ruined everything before it had a chance to begin.

Her presence flared to life on the earth again, light and delicate and still moving so quickly.

I shoved my anguish back. She was on the ground once more and that was all that mattered. I was Erenlian enough for my blood to help bring her back to herself, same as it had on the cliff outside the Jeweled Coven's hideout. So I'd shift back before she could see me this way, I'd feed her my blood, and I'd save her from this madness.

I'd hide every bit of this monstrousness from her, and in that way too, I'd still be her protector.

No matter what it cost me.

Drawing on more speed, I fought to run faster. She'd come back down near a cave about a mile from here, which was good. Safer, just in case the magic shielding her from the sun could not sustain itself this far away from the others. It was untested, after all, and the idea that she might burn before I could reach her...

I skidded to a stop thirty feet from the cave, my claws digging into the dirt and weeds beneath me. Bushes and young trees hid me, but past gaps between the branches, I could see the cave opening.

Nothing inside it moved.

And nothing outside did either.

I eyed the bloodied carcass of a deer lying by the cave entrance. She'd taken it down hard and fast, making short work of the kill, and my beast side admired the swift ferocity. The deer's throat was gone, and blood soaked the dirt beneath it. Deep cuts lined its flank that I didn't need to guess the origin of.

After all, I had claws too.

But everything the Jeweled Coven claimed about vampires meant deer blood would likely accomplish little when it came to stopping this madness.

She still would need my help.

I glanced around, but there were no traces of the Void-born here. No one else either.

It would do.

I took a breath, summoning up the magic to shift, but my beast side resisted, holding me in this form. That part of me didn't want to change into an Erenlian again. It wanted to claim her now, just like this.

Apparently, madness was contagious.

Gritting my teeth, I tried to fight the beast back, and the barest whisper of a frustrated growl slipped from my elongated jaw as that side of me protested again.

Making a sound was a mistake.

In an instant, my sense of Gwyneira vanished from

the earth. A black streak of smoke and shadow shot from the cave. I had no time to move.

She slammed into me.

It was like being hit with a battering ram.

Before I could do a thing, my legs were out from under me. The earth tried to soften my fall but it couldn't adjust quickly enough, and air rushed from my lungs as my back crashed into the ground.

Lightning fast, she shifted back to her human-like form. Her eyes were insane; her expression feral. She wouldn't know this was me, not when I looked like the beast.

But even if she had known, it might not have mattered. Nothing of Gwyneira was in her beautiful dark eyes or the snarl on her luscious red lips. She was only a hungry animal, one I might die trying to stop.

Because even though my blood could bring her back to herself, in this state, I had no guarantee she'd return to sanity before she bled me dry.

She screeched, thrashing in my grip, flashing into shadow and then back into human form again.

So be it.

I released my princess.

Her fangs went for my throat.

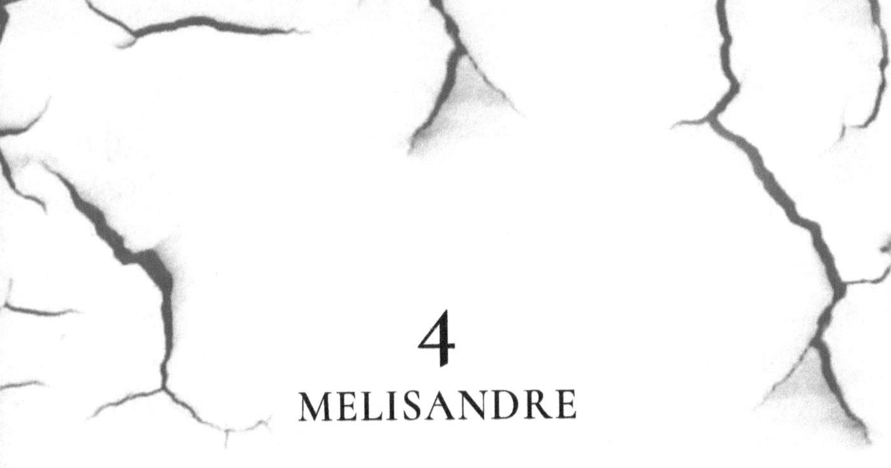

4
MELISANDRE

I was surrounded by an army of monsters, but none of them were mine.

And none of them were what they seemed.

Sheltered from the sun by a crude hovel with no door, I sat, watching them. The wind swept across the terrain ahead, making the dry winter grass roll like the sea. The shattered earth lay behind me while the Warden Wall that surrounded Aneira waited several miles beyond the horizon. But all around this insufferably pathetic hovel, monsters milled about in the grass, waiting for the burning light of day to end. Orcs and shifters and creatures with tentacles filled the horde now. Even a dragon lounged off to one side, its body so massive, it could be mistaken for a small hill if not for how its emerald scales gleamed like green metal in the overcast light. Alaric had raised them days ago, resurrecting them from the dirt and stone of the northern forests to serve as his army.

But the creatures themselves were hardly the true

threat. No, it was the Voidborn inside them that presented the real danger. Those sinuous, eel-like beings of smoke and nothingness that inhabited the empty realms, desperate to feast on reality and destroy it all, now watched from within the monsters' bodies, and the only sign of their presence was the unnatural glow in every creature's eyes. Alaric had cracked the barrier between this world and the empty realm itself, rending the earth with countless fissures to bring them here.

And he'd needed my power to do it.

Not that he would admit that part.

I exhaled slowly, keeping my face calm. The insufferable bastard currently seated beside me wanted me to believe I was merely his *pet*, as much a slave to his will as these monsters were to the Voidborn within them. He pretended to entertain my continued existence only because I was mildly useful for the moment. To hear him, I could no more break free of him than I could go without blood.

But I knew he was wrong. In the moments when he cracked reality open and allowed the Voidborn into this world, I'd come within seconds of shattering his hold on me. I'd felt the shape of the tether he'd tied to my essence. Had he been distracted for even a few more seconds, I could have broken free.

And he never noticed.

I suppressed a smile. Alaric thought he was so powerful, so unassailable. Sitting there on the boulder beside me like a king on his throne, his hands calmly folded atop his knee like he hadn't a care in the world, he deceived himself into thinking I presented no threat at all. Never sparing me a glance, he surveyed the plains before us as if he could see all his plans playing out across them, unquestionably destined to come to fruition just as he wished.

He was a fool.

Yes, he'd forced me to sit in the dirt exactly like the *pet* he proclaimed me to be. And yes, he'd crafted his body into everything I despised, his tall, slender form like that of an arrogant nobleman. Barely even glancing my way, he carried on with such an unrelenting audacity, he would rival the gods themselves, and he put so much faith in the magical tether with which he'd bound me that he believed he had nothing to fear from the vampire queen at his feet.

But the closer we came to Aneira, the closer we came to the seat of power I'd spent the better part of nineteen years building. Alaric schemed to shatter the nexus of ley lines beneath the capital city of Lumilia, but he never considered all the ways I could kill him before we ever reached it. I had my Huntsmen, the most elite of the soldiers and my own personal guard. They waited for me there. And I had the vampires I'd created over the years—everyone from annoying noblemen to servants who vexed me, now waiting for my return.

Most of all, though, I had the wall.

And that alone could destroy him.

I restrained a chuckle. All it would take was one second of distraction, and I would have him. I'd burn the contemptible leash he'd fastened around the innermost parts of my essence and I would scorch him from this realm entirely.

I knew this as certainly as I knew the sun would leave the sky tonight.

"Your emotions are intriguing, pet," Alaric commented, not turning from his study of the monsters beyond our hovel. "You find your situation amusing now?"

I kept my smile hidden inside. The intolerable fool fancied he could read my mind. And while, yes, the strange abilities he'd shown in that direction were disturbing, that had been *before* he brought the other Voidborn into this world. Before he drew on my power so strongly, it had let me see the nature of the tether with which he bound me.

And now, just as his leash was no longer as strong as he believed, so too was his window into my mind not as transparent as it had once been.

"Of course not," I replied.

"And now you lie."

But he could still pick up some things.

I made myself remain calm, no matter how much I wanted to rip the throat from his body right now. Survival was a matter of patience—and *that*, I had in spades. "I only find it entertaining to think what will happen when we return to Lumilia," I demurred.

He smiled, the sharp points of his metal teeth gleaming. No matter how much the rest of his body appeared human, his teeth and eyes had remained like the Voidborn. The sharp points looked like knives in his mouth, and his eyes had no whites around the pupils, only black spheres slit by a line of gold that made it hard to tell where he was looking.

"Destroying the nexus of power at Lumilia *will* be quite entertaining," he acknowledged.

I waited, but he said nothing more of what he intended once we reached the capital city. He almost never did, choosing only to explain himself when it suited him, and even then only speaking in vague generalities. "Might I know what happens then?"

He chuckled. "Patience."

I drew a slow breath, determined to continue remaining calm and not give him the satisfaction of driving me to violence that would only end in my own pain. His tether still kept me from physically attacking him, same as it kept me from straying too far from his side.

He would only find it pleasing to watch me writhe in pain. After all, he'd enjoyed killing my fellow vampire witch, Stelaruna, too much for me to think otherwise.

I remained still, refusing to shiver at the memory. I'd get to the wall. I'd tear him to pieces.

Nothing would stop me from being free of this contemptible simulacrum of a man.

"You remain so eager," he teased.

I kept my expression neutral. "I only wish to witness our plan's success."

His eyebrow arched as he turned his black eyes to me. "*Our* plan? It is *my* plan, pet. You are only a tool for my ends, nothing more."

I would watch him die screaming, whatever liquid passed for blood in his body pouring out onto the cold, dry earth.

He smiled at my silence. "But you are correct. Traveling this way is taking rather long. Your vampire nature is such a hindrance in this regard."

I bristled. My vampire nature was a *hindrance*? I, who was the only reason he could even exist on this plane of reality? How *dare* he... "You are not standing in the sunlight any more than I am."

My caution caught up to my outrage, but it was too slow to stop the words from passing my lips.

Alaric's brow arched, amusement flickering over his face.

I braced myself for him to step so far into the sun that his leash pulled me after him, making me burn alive. There was no telling what horrors he would inflict, merely because it entertained him to watch me suffer.

But he said nothing.

Distrustful confusion joined my caution. He was such a proud and insufferable creature. Why wouldn't he respond to my supposed insolence?

Was he unable to withstand the sunlight as well? But how could that be? All his fellow Voidborn were there.

Rising to his feet, Alaric merely craned his neck as if searching for something beyond the horde of monsters waiting outside the rough shelter. The skin of his throat stretched as he moved, the craning motion extending his neck several inches beyond what any human body would be able to accomplish.

I suppressed a shudder, turning my eyes away. Even when he tried to look human, he failed.

And then he made a satisfied sound as if he spotted something out there that pleased him.

My apprehension surged again. I climbed to my feet,

watching him warily while I brushed the dust from my dress. The fabric was becoming threadbare after so many days of travel—an insult to my station for which I would also make him pay. Likewise, my passage through the empty realms had sapped the cloth of some of its vibrancy. Only patches of the blue velvet still glimmered in the shadows of this hovel.

When I got back to Lumilia, I would have the thing burned, if only to keep it from ever reminding me I had endured such an indignity.

"What do you seek now?" I asked, adopting a bored tone, as if I couldn't care less what he was after.

Alaric didn't respond.

My teeth clenched. I forced them to relax, comforting myself by listing yet again the ways he would suffer before I was done with him.

On the horizon, a trail of black smoke suddenly surged up from a crack in the earth. At high speed, it zipped toward us like an eel swimming through the air.

I tensed. Another Voidborn, this time not inside a monster but instead on its own in the open. It darted across the field, wavering this way and that as if it was barely in control of itself, and yet it never stopped. Not even as it whipped between the monsters at the edge of the horde. Not even as it sped through the crowd like a dark arrow.

It was heading directly toward me.

Terror wrapped its cold hands around my throat. Surely Alaric didn't intend to let one of those creatures take *me* over?

The Voidborn sped closer. In spite of myself, I

retreated, but short of breaking through the rear wall of this gods-forsaken hovel and burning up in the sunlight, there was nowhere else to go.

"What..." I couldn't maintain my composure nor hide the fear in my voice. "Why is it coming toward—"

"No need to panic, pet."

I looked at him in alarm, but he didn't turn from watching the creature fly toward us. Closer. Closer. The Voidborn racing at us barely had a face, let alone anything resembling a body beyond the sinuous trail of smoke that was its form.

I swore I could see its gleaming eyes locked on me all the same.

My back bumped against the hovel wall. "Don't you dare try to make that thing take me over like—"

Alaric caught the Voidborn in one fist as it darted into the open doorway. Contorting in his grip like a snake, the creature didn't resist as Alaric reached his other hand between the shimmering suggestion of metal teeth and straight into its mouth.

"What are you doing?" I demanded.

Grinning, Alaric drew out his hand again. Blood glistened on his skin.

My nose twitched. The blood wasn't his. I could tell immediately the creature hadn't bitten him. But the blood did smell... odd. Not human. Yet not from a vampire either. Not exactly, anyway.

I resisted the urge to step closer with curiosity. When hunger required it, I'd bitten enough of my own minions back in Lumilia to know the scent of a vampire's blood with ease, and while this smelled *partially* of vampire, there was another indefinable quality that made it distinct.

Still smiling, Alaric lifted his hand and licked the blood from his skin.

A sharp shudder rolled through him, like a convulsion of disgust except his smile never changed. Under his breath, he made a hissing-clicking sound, and just as it had the night before, somehow my mind understood the noise was some sort of language. An incantation, perhaps, though I did not know for what purpose.

Again, he shuddered, harder this time, as if something hurt all over his body. In a strange, ghostly way, I could almost feel it, as if the leash passed the reaction on to me.

I recoiled from the feeling. It was abhorrent. Foul. I loathed having it anywhere near me, even if only as a ghost of sensation from that bastard.

As if noticing my revulsion, Alaric turned toward me, still gripping the Voidborn in his fist. His black eyes narrowed, scanning me and searching for the gods knew what. But after a moment, irritation passed over his face.

"What was that?" I asked.

Alaric didn't respond. He only started toward me.

My back pressed harder against the wall of the hovel. Wood creaked behind me, threatening to break and spill me out into the sunlight where I would die.

He extended his other hand to me, traces of blood still on his skin. "Taste it."

"I will do no such thing."

"We are linked, pet. Thus it is as if you already did. But I would have you allow yourself to taste it fully now." His metal teeth glinted in a grin. "Trust me."

He was mad. "I refuse to—"

His expression turned thunderous in an instant, his human-like skin shimmering toward that of an eel and his dark eyes flashing with rage. "Taste it!"

The tether of his magic tightened on me like a vise, crushing down on my insides and making me cry out with pain. I crumpled to the ground, my legs unable to hold me, and my vision swirled and danced with spots of darkness and light, making the world blur.

A cold hand took my chin, prying my mouth open. I couldn't pull away fast enough. Blood smeared my teeth and lips.

The grip vanished.

I choked as I tasted the blood. It was vile. *Wrong* in a way that burned, as if its owner had poisoned it.

Hissing sounds came from above me. The incantation again.

In an instant, the burning grew worse. Spread into my skin. Coated me from head to toe, setting every inch of me on fire.

I screamed.

And still I burned.

Drowning in a sea of agony, I writhed. I couldn't survive this. There was too much pain. Too much fire, even though I couldn't find evidence of a single flame. After a few agonizing heartbeats, I couldn't see anything at all. My vision turned kaleidoscopic, overrun by flares of red and white light all stemming from the torture.

It was an eternity before the pain faded.

And Alaric's chuckle was the first sound I heard.

Snarling, I struggled to my feet, letting my rage hide

any sign of my shock. But I could hardly believe I was still in this world. That much pain felt like it should have reduced me to dust on this grimy dirt floor.

At the entrance to the hovel, he stood watching me, amusement on his face like my pain was nothing but entertainment to him.

Which it was.

But I would endure him no longer.

I lunged, crossing the pathetic shelter in an instant. My hands wrapped around his throat. My fangs went for his vein. He fell back, still chuckling, barely even putting up a fight.

Sunlight poured over us both as we crashed to the ground outside.

I gasped, shoving away from him, but a creaking sound came from behind me. Before I could reach the hovel, the rickety structure collapsed, shoved down by one of the orcs. The green-skinned creature stood watching us, his Voidborn-possessed eyes glowing sickening yellow. No trace of an expression resided on his gruesome face.

Still chuckling to himself, Alaric climbed to his feet. "No place to retreat now."

I threw a panicked look around me, seeking any shelter at all, when suddenly the truth registered past my instinctive fear.

I wasn't burning.

"Now you see." Alaric walked over to me, his human appearance back in place with the continued exception of his black eyes and metal teeth.

"What is this?" I surveyed my hands, my arms, and

then patted my face, seeking any smoldering or stinging skin.

"Angel blood." Alaric idly brushed the dust from his gray jacket. "Or as close to it as this world possesses. Your stepdaughter apparently has discovered one of the last remaining descendants of an angelic line in this world, and he travels with her now. My brethren came upon them at the edge of a mountain range far south of here, and this one managed to draw his blood." He nodded to the Voidborn currently lying limp on the ground. Even as I watched, the creature's body was evaporating like mist fading in the light of day. "Seeing as how we need to travel faster and you are vulnerable to daylight, I employed a spell we learned from another realm to use that blood to give you protection against the sun."

My thoughts reeled. A spell from another realm? Angel blood protecting me from daylight? It was madness. Pure madness.

Yet the fact I stood beneath the sun for the first time in decades spoke for itself.

"What is happening to that one?" I jerked my chin toward the Voidborn on the ground. "Will that happen to me because of this 'angel blood'?"

Alaric glanced down at the creature, and I would swear a flicker of regret crossed his face. "That is a sacrifice, one willingly made for the cause. Carrying such foul blood through the abyss as this one did is no easy task, to say nothing of the fact there is a reason your kind die in the light of that damnable fireball. A reason the sun too will die when we are done."

The Voidborn's body vanished entirely.

I eyed Alaric warily. He would have me believe angel blood poisoned the creature, yet that bastard ingested it without problem. Forced *me* to ingest it, moreover.

What nonsense was he spinning, hoping I would buy his games?

My gaze turned, sweeping the monsters. Each of them sat in the sunlight. None of them were dying. His lies were so transparent as to be moronic.

But then the truth hit me.

Each Voidborn had sought shelter within a monster from the moment it broke through to this realm. Alaric had stayed in the hovel with me.

Only the Voidborn left exposed to the light had died.

My lips parted with shock. Just as vampires could not survive sunlight for long without burning, neither could the beings who created them. Thus they needed to inhabit dumb beasts such as these in order to hide from the light.

That did nothing for me—or for Alaric, who'd taken the form of a man to walk this world and who needed my power to accomplish his ends. Like the Voidborn in their form of smoke, sunlight presented a threat to us.

But with the aid of angel blood and magic...

Swiping his hands together as if to rid his skin of the last of the angel blood, Alaric straightened. "Come, pet. We have a nexus to destroy."

He started walking, and I said nothing as I followed him. I resented his treatment, yes. But that resentment had fallen into a distant second place compared to the ideas now spinning in my head.

In all the decades I'd been a vampire, I'd sought ways

to reduce the sun's ability to harm me, from the magical to the mundane. Spells I'd ripped from the books of old sorcerers. Umbrellas I used on days without a single raincloud. Even ridiculous hats and full-length coats on occasion, all to shield me through whatever absurd royal function I needed to attend. I dispelled questions about my avoidance of the sun by claiming I wanted to keep my skin looking youthful, yet even the most powerful of spells had only protected me for a short while.

But this...

As we walked through the waves of dry, yellowed grass, I turned my hand back and forth, marveling at the play of sunlight on my skin, the sight indescribably foreign to me after so many decades with only my night vision or candlelight to see by. I'd scarcely remembered how many *colors* flesh possessed when exposed to daylight. Each tiny hair or fleck of oil on my skin reflected the light like a crystal, shimmering and beautiful.

By the gods, I could go anywhere now. Conquer anything. Any*one*.

A smile pulled at my lips. Even if it was for his own reasons, Alaric had just given me an advantage beyond compare. My strength and skill, and my magic too, were no longer constrained by the ravages of the sun, and thus I could strike at my enemies, day or night, with impunity.

But he'd given me more than that.

My eyes slid to the south. He'd provided information.

Without the aid of magic to protect them, angel blood could prove fatal to his kind. Moreover, Gwyneira was out there somewhere, and knowing that irritating brat, she was probably headed for Lumilia too, caught up in some grand delusion of taking my throne from me. But she had a descendant of angels traveling with her. Likely those damned giants as well. And once I removed Alaric from being an insufferable thorn in my side, I could send my Huntsmen and the Aneiran army after them.

I'd capture her giants. Bleed her angel dry.

And then I would destroy her once and for all.

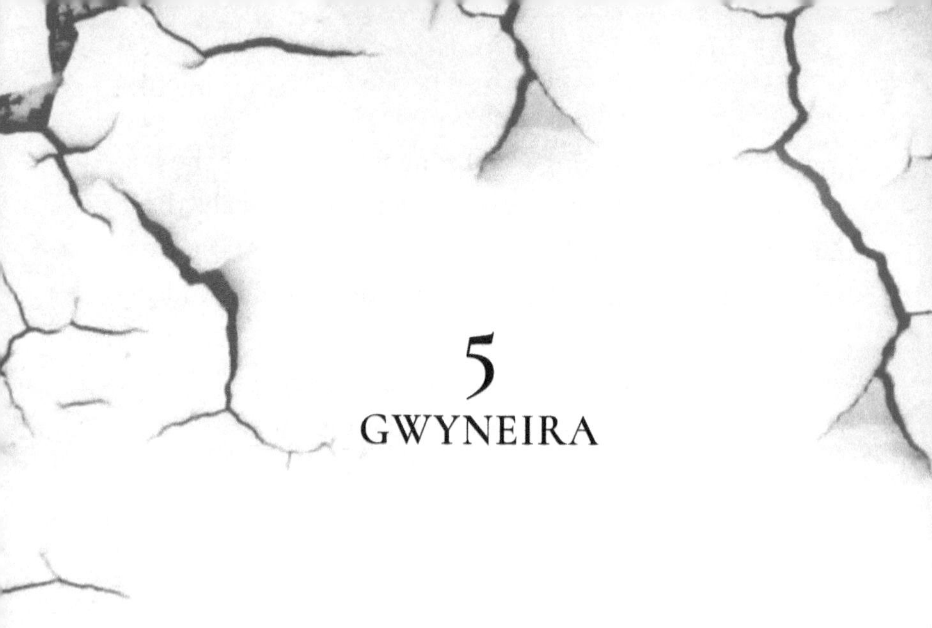

5
GWYNEIRA

I was trapped inside my own mind, screaming at myself without sound.

And the vampire I'd become was about to kill a creature unlike anything I'd ever seen.

The furred beast fell as I slammed into it, even its massive size unable to compensate for the strength and speed of my attack. The creature's head looked like a cross between a wolf and a horned deer, and it had a tail like a wolf too. But unlike those animals, this beast had walked on two legs, not four, with its body built as tall and broad as any of my men. Its enormous jaw and sharp cheeks showed edges of bone, and its body was pure muscle beneath its thick, gray fur, like the gods had thought the wolf that this beast resembled was too soft and gentle a creature to fully emulate.

No, it was more than a wolf. More than a horned deer. A forest god.

Fangs the length of my hand glinted in the sunlight. Its enormous hands bore claws like blades, as did its feet. When I struck, the creature grabbed at me, holding me back while I snapped my fangs at its throat. But already I could tell it wouldn't be able to stop me for long.

Nothing could. The vampire was fully in control now, shifting my body between human form and smoke effortlessly. Meanwhile, I was nothing but a speck of memory in the back of my mind, helpless to stop myself from killing this strange and beautiful beast that had—

Suddenly, the furred creature stopped fighting.

The vampire didn't hesitate, lunging down and sinking my fangs past the beast's fur into its throat. Blood flooded my mouth, hot and sweet and smoky.

And familiar.

Horror shot through me. Oh gods, I knew this creature. But it was impossible.

Ozias.

The vampire didn't give a damn. It was still hungry and that deer it had torn down in a desperate concession to stave off starvation hadn't satisfied.

But this was *Ozias*...

Gulping down his blood, the savage creature I'd become gripped his furry shoulders, holding his massive body in place even though he made no move to stop me. No, he'd actually surrendered the moment I landed on top of him, and anguish filled me at the possible reason why.

Ozias knew his blood could bring me back to sanity. The witches of the Jeweled Coven and my own experience had made that clear. And even though he'd given me a thousand signs he wanted nothing to do with me, he'd still come here as this beast.

And he'd let me bite him.

More blood poured down my throat, as delicious as an elixir from the gods themselves and more flavorful than the most exquisite meal. No matter how I wanted to stop, my body still drank it down like it was water in the desert, regardless of how I could feel his heart slowing with every second.

How I could feel him dying.

Frantically, I struggled to wrestle control of my body back from the ravenous monster I'd become. Nothing I'd done until this moment had worked, but now I had Ozias's blood in me.

Giant blood, no matter what he looked like right now.

A snarl escaped my lips, and blood spilled around my mouth to pour down his neck and soak his fur as the vampire fought back, determined to stay in control. Still trapped in the darkness in my mind, I marshaled every scrap of strength I could and tried to fling my body backward.

My hands ripped free of his shoulders. My back slammed down onto the dirt. I'd succeeded in breaking away from him, if only barely.

Please gods, let the blood he gave me be enough to cage the vampire inside me once again.

But the monster I'd become didn't want to go quietly. Need still pounded through me, demanding I return to the feast. Ragged shrieks tore from my throat as the dark flood of the vampire's will pushed at my control, shoving me into a sitting position and then trying to throw me back down upon him to create more bites upon which to feed.

Desperately, I gripped the tree roots below me like they were anchors and squeezed my eyes shut, drawing up every memory, every moment of care and compassion and gods-damned *humanity* I still possessed. I wasn't this monster. I wouldn't be. And I'd never kill Ozias or any of the men who'd saved me.

My chest spasmed, my heart and lungs starting and then stopping as the vampire tried to regain full control. It didn't want to be fucking *human*. It wanted to feed. One of my hands ripped free, taking a chunk of tree root with it as my arm reached for Ozias, my fingers curling like claws.

Grunting with effort, I forced my arm back and twisted, shoving to my feet and stumbling farther away across the clearing. I knew I likely looked insane. A girl staggering around a clearing, thrashing uncontrollably as she fought a battle no one else could see.

But gods, it truly was a war. At every turn, the vampire was there, looking for a weak point in my mind, my will. Endlessly, it sought some way to make me take the last of Ozias's blood.

Winning this fight when I first woke as a vampire had required the blood of all seven of my giants. Ozias was only one man, wounded, who wasn't making a single motion to save himself from me.

Who wasn't making any motions at all.

Tears leaked down my cheeks. I couldn't go closer to help him. I'd only bite him again. But the throb of his heartbeat drummed in my ears, slowing, weakening. His breaths were shallow, barely stirring the air.

He was almost dead anyway, the vampire whispered in my mind. I'd taken too much already for him to survive. So wouldn't it be better to put him out of his misery quickly? After all, it didn't matter whether I finished him off or left him there. The result would be the same.

Ozias would die.

A scream ripped from me, raw and agonized. The vampire surged up immediately, trying to take the opening. It was only a predator, nothing more, and to its eyes, I looked weak crying like this.

Like I was nothing.

Like I was *prey*.

The vampire smiled in my mind. Prey like him.

And that thought was the monster's mistake. Cold rage surged up inside me, the sensation so intense it felt like frost in my veins. Ozias was no victim. And I was no weak and broken thing. I'd survived my stepmother and the witches' tests and the gods-damned Wild Lands.

I wouldn't lose to the vampire inside me now.

Staggering across the clearing, I flung myself forward step after step, even as the vampire let out another scream from my throat in protest at being forced from its meal.

But I didn't stop. Every inch was a battleground, but one that I would fucking win. Because I was not prey. I was Princess Gwyneira of Aneira, daughter of a king.

And Ozias had given that back to me. His blood fueled my power.

My will.

Slowly, excruciatingly, the last of the vampire's

vicious hunger receded like a predator slinking back into the darkness, until only I was left standing half in light and half in shadow at the entrance of the cave, blood soaking my face and gasping breaths entering my lungs.

The vampire was back in its cage. Its needs ruled my body no longer. I was the one in control now.

My heart pounding, I looked back.

Ozias hadn't moved.

Oh, gods.

I raced over to him. Still in the form of this strange creature, he lay on the dirt while blood seeped from the savage bite in the side of his furry throat, the flow slower now. His broad chest barely moved as shallow breaths passed from him, and even those were fading.

The vampire hadn't lied. I'd taken too much. He really was dying.

Frantically, I bent down, licking the wound as I'd done with Niko ages ago at the Jeweled Coven's hideout. Somehow, it would make the injury seal up, that much I knew.

But even as the bite closed, he didn't stir. His breaths slowed until they were scarcely more than twitches of his massive, furred chest.

Oh gods...

"Help!" I cried. "Dex! Byron! Anybody!" Deep in the forest, birds scattered, chirping in panic as they fled. "Someone help!"

Nothing happened. No one came.

My eyes stung with tears as I scanned Ozias's body, searching for a hint of how to save him. Because surely, *surely*, there had to be a way to save him.

His breathing stilled. The whisper of his heartbeat went silent.

No.

"Ozias." I pressed my hands to his chest, praying I was wrong and that I would find a pulse after all. "Ozias, please. Please don't do this."

Nothing.

I couldn't breathe. "Please..."

Icy horror crept through me. I'd killed him. Oh, gods forgive me, I'd killed the man who came to save me.

My fingers curled in his thick, coarse fur as the frozen horror inside me grew stronger, like ice from the deepest winter rising up to swallow me whole. "Please," I whispered, my voice choked. "Please don't die. I'm so sorry. Please."

His fur grew cold in my grip.

And at the center of my chest, something suddenly burned my skin like frostbite.

I gasped, releasing him to grab at the source of the pain.

The diamond pendant given to me by the First Matron of the Jeweled Coven, ages ago before we left their home.

From beneath my sweater, I drew it out, confused. On the end of its silver chain, the diamond glinted in the sunlight.

A coating of rime ice overlaid its surface.

Confused, I looked back down. Ozias lay as I'd left him on the hard ground. His chest was still, his eyes closed.

Frost glinted on the tufts of his fur, exactly where my hands had been.

And then his chest twitched with a tiny breath.

A gasp escaped me. How...?

I shoved the thought aside. Yes, I'd tried over and over for weeks to reach my magic, and I'd failed every time, but who gave a damn about that? If I'd done something to help him, I needed to do it again.

But what the hell had I done?

I wrapped one hand around the diamond pendant, a hiss escaping me as the frigid surface burned my skin. Pressing my other palm to his chest, I closed my eyes and focused with everything I had on something, *anything* within me that maybe could bring him back to life.

"Please," I whispered. "Oh, gods..."

I opened my eyes again.

Nothing. His chest barely moved, the breaths so faint I worried I only imagined them.

Exhaling sharply, I squeezed my eyes shut again and crushed my grip around the pendant. The stone bit at my palm like a blade.

"*Please...*" I urged.

Seconds ticked past. The pendant remained the same, cold but without any other change.

I didn't open my eyes this time, trying desperately to focus harder. Because dammit, I wouldn't lose him. I couldn't. Even if he'd pushed me away over and over again. Even if he'd treated me like dirt only to turn around and call me his treluria. Even if the attraction I felt for him confused the hell out of me and made me question my own sense of self-preservation and sanity, I didn't care. I wasn't going to let him die.

Not when maybe, just maybe, I could do something to save him.

Ice shivered through my veins. Beneath my palm, his fur became colder.

"Yes," I begged. "Live. Please, Ozias. *Please* live."

The cold grew deeper. Harsher. I kept my eyes shut, focusing on him and not on how my entire body felt like it was freezing from the inside out, every second drawing me closer to when my strength would give out entirely. But I wouldn't let it, because I wouldn't fail him. Not now.

My sense of the clearing around us faded. Any awareness of daylight or the winter breeze did too. The whole world came down to his chest beneath my palm and my desperate entreaties for him to live.

I couldn't feel my fingers any longer. Air puffed from my lungs, cold as the breath of winter itself past numb lips that felt like they were made of clay.

Whispers niggled at my consciousness.

I shook my head, trying to dispel them. The tiny motion made my muscles creak as if I'd been frozen solid.

The noise faded. Seconds ticked past, marked by the slow, dull thud of my heartbeat resounding in my head like a clock.

At the edge of hearing, the whispers returned, distant and unintelligible like a voice from a far-off room saying words I couldn't quite hear.

I dug my fingers into Ozias's fur, fighting to concentrate past the distraction. Maybe I was on the verge of losing consciousness. Maybe the voice was my own mind, throwing out last-ditch attempts to get me to stop.

But I wouldn't. Not if it let Ozias live...

The noise grew louder, like the hiss of a wave rushing into the shore and then sweeping away.

Mirror, mirror...

Grunting with irritation, I kept my eyes closed, trying to ignore the voice. It was a woman's. Somehow familiar too, though it didn't sound like my stepmother or any of the witches I'd met on the other side of the Wild Lands.

Maybe it was the vampire trying to take control again.

Broken now it lies...

It didn't *feel* like the vampire, though. That creature was buried so deep right now, I could barely even detect its impulses.

Bold are the Nine...

Really, it didn't matter what this voice was. It was distracting me, and that made it a problem because if I stopped to listen to it now, I knew beyond a doubt I'd lose Ozias.

Who shatter the skies.

A chilly feeling ghosted over my cheek like a hand brushing my skin gently.

Alarm propelled my eyes open of their own accord, my heart in my throat.

No one else was here. The clearing was utterly still.

The whisper returned, so close it felt as if the woman's lips were only inches from my ear.

Careful now, my little one.

Ozias gasped, his eyes flying open.

A ragged sob of relief escaped me. It worked. Oh, gods, it worked.

My eyes rose to dart over the clearing, but no one was there. Yet in some strange way I couldn't define, I'd swear it felt like a presence in the clearing was fading, as if rather than the two of us here, there had been three.

And now one was gone.

Coughing, Ozias lurched away from the ground.

Refocusing quickly, I moved to help. His eyes snapped around and then landed on me as I grabbed his shoulders, supporting him.

He froze, staring at me, and I didn't know what to do. Yes, he still looked like a strange beast, his face like a wolf but with sharp, savagely carved edges of bone protruding amid the fur. Pale, gnarled horns extended from his head, and his hands and feet bore enormous claws. But everything in his eyes was still wholly *him*, and I refused to be afraid.

Because he was alive. Oh, thank the gods, he was alive.

He drew a sharp breath and then suddenly, his form rippled and shifted before my eyes. His fur receded. His skin returned. The massive twisted antlers atop his head shrank back into his skull, and his elongated jaw and viciously pronounced brow molded back into the bearded face of the man I knew.

"Gwyneira?" He stared at me like he was the one who couldn't believe I was still here.

"Hi." I smiled. "I'm back. And you're okay. You—"

My vision spun. I gasped, catching myself with one hand on the ground as a fresh bout of shivering poured through me like my blood had turned to ice in my veins.

The voice had been right. I wasn't careful enough. This cold was too much, and not even the blood Ozias had given me could warm me enough to withstand it.

"Princess?" He grabbed at me as I swayed.

But the light was fading, taking the world with it, and

sorrow sank over me, bittersweet. I didn't know what I'd done to save him, not really. Yet I couldn't be *truly* sad about it, not when it meant he lived.

But now the cost was due.

Ozias's shocked face was the last thing I saw before frozen darkness dragged me down.

6

BYRON

"Anything?" Dex called behind me.

"Not yet." My voice was steady. Even. Meticulously calm and not remotely over-wrought by fear. I was careful when I glanced down at the map in my hands, by no means crushing it regardless of how useless it currently was.

To be sure, the map hadn't failed us. Its magical surface was changing constantly while we walked through this gods-forsaken forest, and with every passing moment, it showed me countless new pieces of suppos-edly relevant information. Where we were in the woods. What rivers and chasms lay ahead. What damage the Voidborn had wrought upon the terrain when they broke through into this world. That was helpful, of course, but what the damn thing *didn't* show was a single detail related to the most important information of all.

Where in the name of all that was holy the princess had gone after the Voidborn attacked her.

"You sure we're heading the right way, man?" Clay asked.

I would not strangle my friends with my bare hands. I would not drive my fist through the map either.

I was calm.

"The map shows that this is the most direct path through the destruction left by the Voidborn. I would assume they followed her, and thus following their trail will lead us to her location."

Where she would be fine. Alive, in her way. *Not* driven mad with her humanity stripped away. *Not* burned to ash because the spell I cast had failed, leaving nothing of the beautiful woman whose body I touched with my magic only last night, guiding my power over every line and caressing every curve—

The map crinkled in my hands. I closed my eyes for a heartbeat, mentally summoning up a calming prayer out of desperation. My training as a monk in the Order of Berinlian had included hundreds of them, from poems to prose, all of them as familiar to me as breathing.

Since the princess joined us, I swore I'd needed them on an hourly basis.

"It still doesn't show her, though?" Lars asked.

I threw a look back at him. "You assume I'm simply not mentioning that I've already found her?"

He blanched. "No, I—"

"The map shows nothing. Not Gwyneira. Not Ozias. There are small woodland creatures, a deer, and a blur that might be a running wolf, but unless the princess has become a bunny rabbit, then none of that is helpful."

Silence followed.

I stopped, exhaling sharply. Closing my eyes, I pinched the bridge of my nose and drew a slow breath, repeating the prayers until my pulse slowed down. "Apologies. I am merely tired. I should not have spoken to you that way."

Another moment passed without sound.

"We'll find her," Niko said at last, kind and encouraging as always.

How he could be so *calm*...

The irony was painful. I may have been the monk, but he was Niko. He believed in the good of the world the way others believed the sun would always rise. Even during the war, he'd kept our spirits up with his optimism and his simple faith in each of us, and now he was doing the same here.

Of course, he also wasn't being torn in two by desire for a woman he could never have.

I shuddered, dropping my hand from my face. "Yes," I made myself say. "We will." I turned to Lars. "Again, my apologies."

"It's okay." Lars smiled. "It's been a rough morning for all of us."

He was too kind.

And *also* not being eviscerated by desire.

Settling for a nod in return, I took up the map again and started walking. I wasn't jealous that my friends could attend to their craving for Gwyneira whenever they liked. To be thus would only mean I resented my vows, and that would be nonsense.

The memory of the curve of her ass flashed through

my mind, as vivid as if I was touching her with my bare hand right now.

I shoved it down. Enduring temptation was part of being a monk. I would not falter. It had been the greatest honor of my life to join the ranks of the Order of Berinlian, and even after the Order fell, I refused to betray my oaths. Indeed, it had never felt like a loss not to join the twins or Dex when they went to taverns or found companionship for an evening. Not to study with Niko as he poured over books that taught how to please a lover and how to be a good romantic partner someday.

I had my own studies. My own mission. As a monk of the Order, I was sworn to the preservation and further-ance of magical knowledge. Those vows mandated that I be chaste, eschewing all romantic attachments and priori-ties that might conflict with that goal. Moreover, I'd spent my youth being told that the fact I was a *dwarf* meant I could never be worthy of taking those vows in the first place. That I couldn't possibly be strong enough or have enough character and integrity to hold true to that calling.

To give in to my longing for Gwyneira now would violate my vows and make myself a liar and a failure. It would prove every last one of those accusations right.

Thus, if anything, I should be *proud* of how I was conducting myself in the face of such temptation. Yes, my soul cried out she was my treluria. Yes, even now, my cock stiffened and wept at the memory of how she felt beneath my magic last night...

I scowled, adjusting my pants surreptitiously. None of that mattered. The memories would fade. My chants and prayers would soothe my longing. And jealousy that my friends could lie with her and I would never do the same was foolishness that I would not entertain.

"What does your magic tell you?" Casimir asked behind me.

I turned sharply. "What my magic did has nothing—"

He wasn't looking at me. Or, rather, he *hadn't* been, though now he appeared more than a little confused by my truncated outburst.

Because he'd been speaking to Niko. Which, of course, was logical.

"Yes," I amended, praying my voice didn't sound as stilted to the others as it did to my own ears. "What does nature say?"

Niko hesitated, eyeing us both. "Only that *something* came through here and scared all the plants and animals, but whether it's the Voidborn or something else entirely..." Discomfort flashed over his face. "I can't tell."

"So, uh, which way is everything the *most* scared, then?" Clay asked like he was bracing himself for the answer.

"West."

"Toward the Wild Lands," Roan spoke up from the rear of the group, his cold voice scarcely making it sound like a question. Not meeting any of our eyes, he looked out at the forest like it held more monsters than merely the ones we'd escaped this morning.

Niko nodded.

Dex sighed, and frustration lined the former soldier's face as he said, "That tracks with what I'm seeing, then. Broken branches. Scuffs in the dirt. *Something* went through here at high speed, heading that way, but I can't tell much else from the terrain."

"From what I can decipher of Ruhl's opinion," Casimir added with a nod to the cloud of smoke and darkness drifting along near his feet. "He concurs."

The vampire king hardly looked pleased by his own words. It chafed at him, I suspected, the fact he was traveling with us rather than racing on ahead to find her. But given what the Voidborn could do to a vampire—what they'd nearly done to him before Dex's blood brought him back to sanity—it wasn't safe for him or anyone else if he encountered those creatures on his own.

And he knew it.

"So how do we tell if those creepy bastards are still ahead of us?" Clay asked as if he was thinking the same thing.

Niko made a concerned sound. "I'm not sure. Their destruction ends in about another mile, though. But I can't tell where they've gone."

Casimir frowned as if debating whether that was sufficient for him to rush after her now.

"The Voidborn could still be hiding out there," Dex said, likely coming to the same conclusion about where his thoughts had ventured.

The vampire king's frown deepened, but he made no move to leave.

We continued onward, the minutes ticking into hours. The terrain ravaged by the Voidborn fell behind us, leaving only endless forest and the threat of the Wild Lands looming on the horizon. And no matter how much

I turned, twisted, or shook the map, no sign of the princess or even of Ozias appeared.

I'd thought crossing the Wild Lands was a form of hell.

It had nothing on this.

Niko suddenly straightened, peering ahead of us with his eyes narrowed. "There's a ravine ahead. Too big to cross."

"Great," Clay muttered. "Just fucking great."

Niko continued, ignoring the interruption. "About a half mile that way, though, a fallen tree forms a bridge." He turned to us. "If Ozias came this way, he must've used that to cross. Maybe the princess did too."

Dex nodded. "Good thinking."

At his motion, we adjusted course, our footsteps moving faster, and soon, the ravine came into view. The tree lying across it must have towered hundreds of feet into the sky once, and now it stretched across the wide ravine like exactly the natural bridge Niko said it was. Moss clung to its bark and mushrooms had sprouted from its sides, each one suspended over a ravine so deep and dark, when I peered over the side of the cliff, I could barely make out the churning water of a river rushing by far below.

"Any sign of those things?" Clay's fingers flexed around the hilt of his sword.

I shook my head. "None so far." I glanced at Casimir.

The vampire regarded the drop. "They'd have some distance to cover before they reached us, if they are there."

Clay gave him a dry look. "Not really comforting, man."

The vampire shrugged and started across the bridge. Ruhl flowed after him, only barely in the form of a wolf.

I tucked the map back into my bag as, one by one, the others started across the natural bridge, until only Dex and I remained on this side.

"After you," Dex said.

I regarded him. As our de facto leader, it made sense he would think it necessary that he bring up the rear. "You don't always have to watch out for us, friend."

He chuckled, simply twitching his chin toward the bridge again.

I started across. The moss on the dead tree trunk was slippery, but the bark around it was rough enough to provide my boots purchase. Every few feet, there were intermittent scrapes through the rot that appeared remarkably fresh. Some wild creature had likely run across this bridge not long ago.

The air began to tingle.

I stopped in the middle of the natural bridge, my eyes darting around. I made no sudden moves, keenly aware I was entirely too far from either end with only my balance to keep me from tipping over into the abyss. But a swift glance downward revealed no sign of the Voidborn. Likewise, nothing up ahead had changed.

"Byron?" Dex called from behind me. "Everything okay?"

It took me a moment to nod. "Yes."

I hoped.

Cautiously, I started forward again.

The sensation intensified. I gasped sharply, a chill

sweeping across me like a thousand bites of icy water swelling up and then rushing past like a river.

Frozen on the bridge, I didn't dare move, every magical sense I possessed suddenly on alert. What was this? This *power*, this intensity. It—

Gwyneira.

"What?" Dex demanded.

I hadn't realized I spoke my thought aloud, but I couldn't muster a breath to explain. The energy surging past me was too overwhelming.

And I recognized it. When I cast the spell to protect her against the sun, it wasn't only her body I'd touched with my power. It was her magic too. And that force had been... incredible. Matched to my own magic in a way I couldn't begin to explain, as if we were meant for one another down to a level I could scarcely imagine. She was the cold light of the stars and the fire in them too. Everything in me had resonated with that energy.

Now I could feel her again.

But something had changed.

The Nine...

A whisper drifted past me, fading in and out like a ghost on the breeze. The words felt like something I should recognize. Like the memory of a dream I didn't recall having, so familiar and yet alien, and if I only focused—

Hands caught me, snapping me back to reality. I realized with a lurch of my stomach that I'd started to lose my balance on the tree bridge.

Dex gripped my arms, shock on his face. "What's wrong?"

How could he not have felt that?

"Fuck, guys," Clay cried from the other side of the ravine. "Get off the damn bridge before you start chit-chatting!"

Dex cast him a tight look, but he nudged me to start walking.

My legs shook while I crossed the remainder of the tree trunk.

"Is Gwyneira all right?" Casimir asked the moment I stepped onto solid ground.

Clay threw him an alarmed look. "Wait, what?"

I glanced at the vampire in alarm before I realized he probably could hear better than the others around me, and thus he would know I blurted out her name on the bridge.

"What the hell happened?" Dex demanded.

I scrubbed a hand over my face, the prickle of beard growth scratching at my palm. What I wouldn't give for a razor and a moment's peace to restore order to my appearance.

A scowl rose up in me at the thought, and I fought to keep from letting it show. I was stalling out of fear, and that was beneath me. But the chill hadn't faded from the air, though none of the men around me gave any sign of feeling it.

"I... I detected what I believe is her magic," I admitted. "Only stronger than I've felt it before."

"She's doing magic?" Niko asked.

"And strong enough to reach here?" Lars threw the forest an alarmed look.

"You sure about that?" Clay argued. "I mean, we all knew she *could*, but..."

"Is she nearby?" Dex asked, ignoring them. "Is she in danger?"

I shook my head. "I don't know."

He let out a breath, turning away to scan the terrain. Nearby, Casimir looked ready to abandon human form and race onward to reach her, the fact the Voidborn might lurk out there be damned.

"Would, um..." Niko cast a worried look around, as if he didn't want to ask the question but felt he must. "What you felt... would that happen if someone killed her?"

The others stared at him.

My stomach churned. "I don't know."

From where he'd been standing silently at the back of our group, Roan suddenly turned and strode toward the forest.

"Roan!" Dex called.

The other man didn't stop. Shoving past the underbrush, he stalked off, disappearing from view a moment later.

"Dammit, man!" Clay yelled. "You don't even know if you're going the right way!" The blond giant threw us all a baffled look, as if seeking someone who could explain what in the world our friend was thinking.

I stared after Roan. He'd always been prickly. So focused on our safety and security that he worried more than seemed logical and caused all manner of undue stress for us over the years. But during the past several weeks, he'd changed. Prickly became sullen, became angry. He rarely spoke anymore, and he sulked on his own more often than not. While I struggled with being tempted by Gwyneira, he gave every sign of loathing her and resenting her presence, even taking it so far as to snarl insults at her on occasion.

In truth, it was a miracle he hadn't left us already, to say nothing of whether the others might secretly wish he was gone. No one had asked him to go yet, but gods, the man was steadily working toward driving a wedge between himself and the rest of us with how he behaved.

"Well, uh... I guess we should follow him, yeah?" Niko offered into the silence. "The forest *is* more disturbed in that direction, so something did go that way."

An unsettled feeling swirled in my gut. How could Roan have known that was the right direction...?

I shoved the thought aside. Only fools ascribed meaning to mere coincidence.

Yet still my skin crawled.

"Any sign of the Voidborn?" Dex asked Niko.

The younger man shook his head.

"What of Gwyneira?" Casimir asked.

Niko appeared worried. "I'm not sure."

Lars hoisted his pack higher. "All right, well, better get after Roan then, yes? Since apparently, he knows where he's going."

"And before something kills his dumb ass," Clay muttered.

I glanced at Dex, and I would swear the same thought went through his mind as went through my own. Whatever was going on with Roan, something killing him didn't seem like as much of a concern as it may once have been. In the time since we crossed the Wild Lands, my worried, prickly friend had transformed into someone I didn't quite recognize.

Now part of me only wondered what would befall anything that got in his way.

Weapons at their sides, the others started off, the vampire and shadow wolf following.

Resisting the urge to shake my head, I trailed after them. I was kidding myself. This journey was changing each of the others, not just Roan, to say nothing of what love for Gwyneira had done to some of them. In the face of that, all I could do was make sure I held as true to myself as possible.

I was a monk. A scholar. I would live every day proving I had the strength, the character, and the will to hold to my oaths, no matter how much some in the Order had once claimed a dwarf was doomed to fail.

Yes, I was drawn to that beautiful woman. Yes, her power resonated with the very soul of my own. But I was no liar. No failure.

What I felt for Gwyneira would never take me from my calling.

7
MELISANDRE

I would never tire of standing in the sun. Of watching the world dance with color, more vibrant than the finest painting.

Of seeing my enemies run from me, every line and twitch of their fear on brilliant display.

I smiled as the Voidborn-possessed monsters tore into the outpost, their actions punctuated by screams that danced on the air like music. Yes, the fort and its inhabitants were technically Aneiran citizens, even though we were still a few miles from the border and the Warden Wall. They were comprised of a smattering of soldiers who had been assigned here with their families to monitor the road to the wall and to provide authorized visitors with passage past the barrier.

But though I was the queen of Aneira, that hardly meant I needed to keep *all* its people alive.

I strolled through the shattered gate, and even the fact I still trailed Alaric couldn't dim my enjoyment at the scents of blood and fear on the air. The orcs had torn through the logs like they were paper, and the shifters had followed, while the tentacled creatures scaled the vertical extent of the crenelated walls with such ease, they may as well have been racing up a flight of stairs. The dragon circled overhead, roaring as if for the sheer enjoyment of watching people scream in terror. The scaled beast had already incinerated those who'd tried to flee the outpost.

It was truly beautiful.

A young man raced at us, screaming, his sword raised and his Aneiran armor gleaming in the daylight. Blood coated him like a glaze on roast meat, tempting me to bite down and taste all the delicious flavors inside.

Alaric caught him first, merely bending out of the way of the man's wild sword strike and then catching his wrist and breaking it in a single motion. While the young man screamed, Alaric whipped him around and sank his metallic fangs into the fool's neck.

A shiver rolled through me as I watched the fight drain from the young soldier along with his blood. I could practically taste it, that death. That delicious ending gushing out of him. My tongue licked my lips in spite of myself.

Alaric pulled back and grinned, his silver teeth coated in red. "Finish him off, pet."

He shoved the young man at me. I caught the soldier as he stumbled, and my brow rose.

The Voidborn bastard was sharing now?

Alaric mirrored my expression, a sardonic glint in his eye.

"You seek to trap me?" I asked accusingly.

He scoffed. "I seek to feed you. The spell to protect you against sunlight was draining and it does us no good if you collapse uselessly."

My eyes narrowed, noting the implication that my collapse *could* have use, if he thought the situation called for it.

But I was also hungry.

I bit down on the soldier's neck, swallowing instinctively as blood flooded my mouth, and a renewed shudder passed through me. Energy poured into my body with his blood, making my heartbeat accelerate and my limbs feel looser and more powerful. Gods, I *had* been hungry. Famished, in point of fact.

The sheer overwhelm of walking in daylight had distracted me.

But this was exquisite, like a feast beyond any mortal I'd bitten before. Was drinking blood in daylight more fulfilling? Or had Alaric done something to me?

Surely not. I would feel it. This was likely only the pleasure in finishing off a delicious meal after so long without sustenance.

As the young man's heart stopped, I let his body fall. When it hit the ground, his corpse began to crumble, turning to gray dust on the ground.

I paused. That wasn't right. My victims never did that.

"Our meals are escaping us, pet," Alaric called.

I glanced up at the bastard.

Bending idly, he retrieved the young man's sword from where it had fallen. A ludicrous blade, more ornate than any young soldier should have possessed, it glinted in the firelight with metalwork and engravings, along with chips of red gemstones in the hilt. It must have belonged to the dead young man's family, or else it had simply been stolen.

Twisting the weapon this way and that, Alaric grinned as if the idea of carrying such a thing entertained him. "Shall we catch our fleeing prey before they are gone?"

I did not bother to respond to the idiotic question, instead turning my attention to the chaos all around. Let the fool carry a sword. It only made him look like more of a vapid nobleman, good for nothing but show. And as for its former owner, well, perhaps the soldier turned to dust because Alaric bit him first. Regardless, it scarcely mattered.

I was still hungry.

Quickly, I scanned the village. Most of the humans were already dead, although a few still hid in their homes and screamed when monsters broke down the door. A fire had broken out in one of the buildings and was steadily spreading to more—not the dragon's work, but dangerous nonetheless. It would likely engulf the entire outpost soon.

By the outpost entrance, a woman was trying to slip away under the cover of the smoke, a small, crying bundle in her arms.

I grinned and started toward her.

Alaric matched my pace—and my smile. "Delicious choice." He strode past me, as if he intended to reach the woman and the infant first.

But then he came to an abrupt stop, and every other monster around us did too.

Pausing in confused alarm, I turned to him. "Why are you—"

His lips peeled back in a ravenous snarl, cutting me off. But his eyes weren't on me. Neither were the eyes of any of the Voidborn.

To a creature, they all stared to the south.

An icy shiver coursed over my skin.

Alarmed, I turned too, ignoring the villagers as they fled through the gate and ran into the field beyond. Even the dragon no longer paid them any mind.

That chill... I remembered something like this from long ago...

I snarled as the memory snapped into place. Eira. The dead queen. I'd killed her almost twenty years ago, striking her down right in front of her baby's crib only to turn around and convince her fool of a husband that giants had been the ones to crush every bone in his beloved wife's body.

But this chill couldn't be from Eira or her power. Yes, that bitch had been a diamond witch, the highest echelon of power among the insufferable Jeweled Coven. But the only trace of her remaining in the world resided in Gwyneira, and I'd made sure that brat would sooner fly to the moon than use magic. I'd filled her head with tales of madness, kept her from ever encountering the slightest bit of training, and I'd poisoned her with my blood from practically the day she was born. For pity's sake, I'd transformed her into a vampire.

If Eira's daughter ever felt any stirring of magic at all, it should have only fed into making Gwyneira more of a vampire. More of my pawn. That weak-willed child couldn't have changed the fate I set for her, not even with giant blood in her veins.

The Nine...

The words whispered like a distant voice carried on the breeze, and instantly, a growl rose from the Voidborn. Several of them lunged for the gate as if to chase down the source of the words, only to slow at a barked command from Alaric. His order was unintelligible, spoken in the language of those creatures and giving me only the barest suggestion of its meaning. But his tone was imperious, and its effect was immediate.

The monsters stopped. Only a few grumbling growls continued.

All around us, the chill faded from the air, allowing the heat of the blaze consuming the outpost to return.

"The Nine have come." A vicious grin split Alaric's face, the kind of expression a psychopathic executioner wore before the axe fell.

I hesitated. I could tell him he was mistaken, because of course he was. The Nine were a fairytale. This was the real world. There were no warriors spoken of in prophecy. No battle for the fate of the world itself. There was only power and those willing to claim it.

And the fact he said that when the chill on the air made me think of Eira and her brat...

I drew myself up straighter, refusing to tolerate such a ludicrous flight of fancy. Gwyneira was no witch, and she certainly was no warrior. She was a whiny, pathetic child. A leech. A shackle on my ankle that I'd been forced to drag around for nineteen years while I waited for her to become the ideal sacrifice to get these creatures off my back. And rather than serve that simple purpose, she'd run off like the selfish wretch she was and ended me up in this position.

But then, if Alaric would remove her from being an irritant who might try to claim my throne...

"So kill them," I replied. "Be rid of them now before we reach Aneira."

Alaric shook his head, that smile still in place.

"Why not?"

"Because they are exactly what we've been waiting for."

"What?"

"This realm thinks the Nine are such a boon. Warriors of legend, yes?" He chuckled, bending briefly to claim a sheath and belt from one of the fallen humans. Donning it, he stowed the sword inside. "They're hardly that."

"What does that mean?"

Ignoring me, he gave a small jerk of his chin, motioning for his brethren to leave the destruction.

Furious, I stalked after him. I would have answers for this.

Gwyneira was *nothing*.

"What do you mean?" I demanded again.

Still he ignored me, walking onward as if I wasn't even there.

"If there is a threat awaiting us," I snapped, "I would know its form before meeting it."

He threw me a glance over his shoulder, and his

amusement was so patronizing, so viscerally disdainful, it felt as tangible as a knife straight to my gut.

How *dare* this intolerable mockery of a man look down his nose at me that way? I was a queen. I was—

"Hush now, pet. We have every intention of destroying your stepdaughter."

I eyed him warily. "You do?"

"Eventually."

Rage surged inside me. "The girl needs to die."

"Not yet."

"*Why?*"

Alaric turned back to me, a condescendingly patient look on his face. "I already told you. Because this realm is mistaken. The Nine are not its saviors." He grinned, his vicious metal teeth glinting in the light of the fires. "They are the ones who will ensure its downfall."

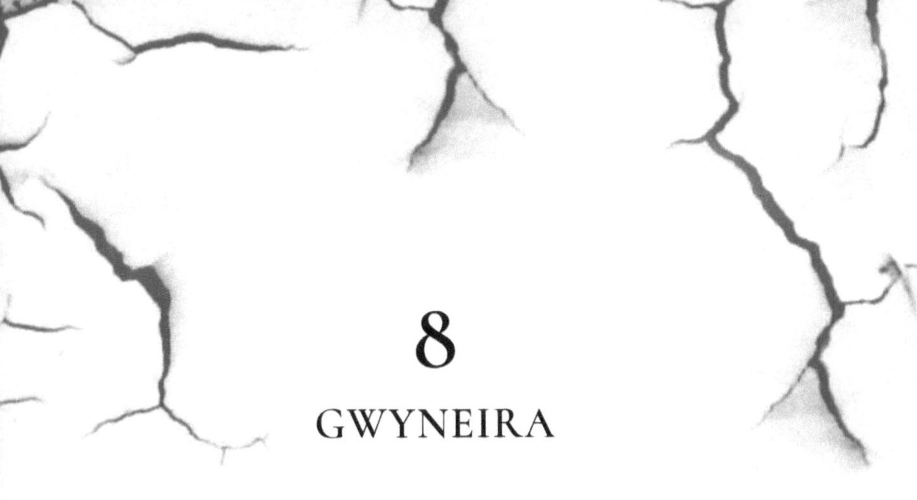

8

GWYNEIRA

Consciousness returned slowly in a wave of tiny sensations.

My heart beating steadily.

The scent of spice filling my lungs with every breath.

Warm skin against my cheek.

My eyes flew open.

Ozias held me. We were on the floor of the cave where I'd fled when the vampire still had control of my body. His weapons and bag were gone, as was his shirt. But he was in his Erenlian form again, once again looking like the man I'd known these past few weeks.

He tensed, caution flashing past the worry in his eyes. For a moment, I wasn't even sure if he breathed, but then, that suddenly made two of us.

I stayed motionless, staring up at him. This close, so many details I'd never had the chance to appreciate became clear. The intricate mix of brown shades flecked by green and blue in his irises. The way his scars ever so slightly interrupted his beard on his cheek and jaw, and how they continued down his neck to his muscled chest like gnarled rivers crisscrossing his skin. His hair was a complex mix of dark brown and gray, like the fur of his other form. I suddenly wanted to reach up and run my fingers through it to see what it felt like.

A short breath escaped him as if he saw my impulse, and it shattered the moment. Carefully, he sat me up and then eased away as if wanting to let me go but wary I might collapse again without his support.

Regret tangled through me. I had no idea what Ozias truly thought of me. He went back and forth so often with how he treated me, I swore I'd sooner solve the mysteries of the universe than make sense of him.

"Are you okay?" His voice was gruff.

I nodded. "Are you?"

His head twitched in a short nod.

Neither of us made a move to get up.

I swallowed hard, trying to strengthen my voice. "I'm sorry I—"

He made a sharp negating noise as if to dismiss my words before I could even speak them. "It's fine."

Silence prevailed once more.

I glanced around the cave, not sure what to do.

"Speak if you wish," he said shortly.

I looked back. His eyes were on the cave floor like it had answers for all this.

Maybe to him, it did.

"What was that?" I asked. "What did you—"

"I won't come near you. You don't need to worry."

He shoved away from the cave floor and strode toward the exit.

I stared after him, baffled. "I didn't say that."

"It's fine. I—"

"Ozias!"

He stopped.

Carefully, I pushed to my feet and followed him. My legs shook like I'd run for too long, and my heart thudded hard for a few moments before settling again. "I wasn't going to tell you to stay away."

His head turned, but not enough to meet my eyes.

"I..." I hesitated, unsure whether my words would be welcome. But then, even if they weren't, at least they'd be the truth. "I thought you were magnificent."

Now he turned to me fully, incredulity and shock in his gaze, like I might as well have said I thought a poisonous snake would make a pretty necklace.

But then his expression turned to outrage. "Do not lie to me."

"Lie?" I blinked. "I wasn't!"

He snarled, turning again and stalking out of the cave.

"Why would you think I was lying?" I went after him, tensing a bit as sunlight poured down on me once again. The spell was holding, though. I only felt warmth, not pain. "Ozias?"

He whirled, glaring at me. "Because the beast is hideous. It is repulsive. *I* am repulsive, and what good you think *lying* to me will do, I—"

"I'm not lying!"

His expression became scathing, his disbelief more than clear.

I scoffed. "Fine. Believe me or don't, but you aren't repulsive. Not to me."

Stalking past him, I headed for the forest. We needed to find the others, wherever the hell they were.

And I was tired of this argument already. This man no sooner went one direction than he switched and went another. Helping me, then snarling at me. Giving me his blanket to cover the bottom of the glass box where I'd been forced to rest, then treating me like I meant nothing to him at all.

Clearly this was just who he was, and no matter how stupidly I was drawn to him, I couldn't let that keep driving me to make a fool of myself. I had more self-respect than that.

"Why not?"

I stopped. His words were measured. Wary, even. When I turned, he was watching me like I might be something that would bite.

Which... I was. But I didn't intend to bite *him* again.

"What do you mean, why not?" I replied coldly.

"Why don't you find me repulsive?"

Did he seriously want me to make a fool of myself for him again? "I'm not going to argue about that with you."

I turned to leave.

"Everyone does. Always."

I paused and then looked back at him, alarmed in spite of myself. "Why?"

"Because I am a monster."

He said it like it was so straightforward, no one could possibly miss it.

And I wasn't sure how to respond. It hurt, and not just because he made it sound like I was an idiot.

"I suppose that means you think I'm repulsive too," I replied archly, drawing myself up to hide the pain. "Given that I'm clearly a monster as well. How kind of you to inform me of that."

Fury surged across his expression before I could turn away again. "No! You are—" He cut off, looking to the side sharply while his teeth bared in a snarl.

Damnable curiosity nibbled at me. I shouldn't give in, not when I'd had enough of his attitude to last me a lifetime.

But… "Did someone make you like this? Turn you into that?"

He looked back, his brow furrowing like he wasn't sure why I asked. "No."

"Then why did your people say you were repulsive?"

"My people are Erenlian."

Again, that tone. That look. Like I was asking obvious questions.

I struggled to keep my temper in check. "And that is supposed to mean what, exactly?"

He was silent.

I exhaled. Forget it. When I returned to Aneira, I'd take up talking to the walls. It'd be easier than trying to talk to him. "Either explain yourself or forgive me for how I'll simply ask someone else. But I will not keep going back and forth with you like this."

For another moment, he said nothing, his eyes locked on me. "Don't do that."

"Why?"

He was silent.

Shaking my head at myself, I started for the forest again.

"No one knows what I am. No one can."

I didn't bother asking why or turning around. But I did stop walking.

"They'll try to kill me."

That got me to turn. "Dex and the others wouldn't do that."

His jaw muscles moved beneath his beard. "They'd send me away. They'd have to. They wouldn't think I was safe for them." Again, a clenching of his jaw. "For you."

I eyed him cautiously.

"They might not be like other Erenlians," he admitted like the words were being pulled from him. "The ones who..." He gestured to himself like that answered something, and it took me a moment to place what it could be.

His scars.

Gods, *all* those scars. His people had done that?

"But what you saw," he continued, still not looking at me. "What I am..."

"You didn't try to hurt me," I said quietly when he trailed off.

"I could." His body shook with the tension of how still he was holding himself. "The things I want when I see you... when I'm near you..."

"What?"

A short huff left him like my confusion confirmed something for him, and he shook his head sharply as if dispelling what he'd said. "I'll stay away."

He turned and started into the forest.

Oh, for the gods' sakes. "Ozias." I crossed the distance between us with every bit of my vampiric speed, circling in front of him and bringing him to a halt before he could make it more than a few feet.

His brown marble eyes glared down at me.

"Do you think I'm an idiot?" I demanded.

Confused incredulity filled his expression.

I arched my brow. "No? Then do you think I get to decide what I believe for myself, and that I deserve to have you respect that?"

Silence. And then a short, small nod, though the incredulity never left his face.

I'd take it. "Okay. So then… do you want to kill me?"

His eyes widened.

"Do you?" I repeated.

Tension made his body shake. "No."

"Good. I don't want to kill you either." I started to step back. "So stop saying you're—"

His hand caught my arm. "I want to hunt you."

I froze.

His grip tightened until it was nearly painful. "I want to chase you down. I want to catch you and pin you to the earth and fuck you until you scream my name. I want to knot you and mate bond you so thoroughly, you'll never be apart from me, not in this life or the next. And when I'm done, I want you so limp and broken from all the pleasure I've given you that you'll be ruined for having any beast's cock but mine inside you ever again. I can share you with the ones you've chosen. But only them. Any other who tried to touch you would die with my fangs in their throat and their heart in my claws, and when they were gone, I would fuck you in their blood just to prove to their ghosts you're mine."

I stared, unable to even blink at the things he described. At the way my body caught up faster than my brain, slowly starting to burn with desire.

Which clearly meant I was mad. Utterly deranged. That shouldn't be arousing me, not like this. But when I tried to speak, all that emerged was a strangled squeak of, "What?"

He grunted again and released me, turning to go. "Don't."

He paused. A dry scoff left him. "See? Repulsive."

I grabbed his arm. "I *meant* you don't just leave after saying something like that. You don't."

Everything in me was shaking when he looked back.

"I-is that true?" I pressed. "What you said. Is that—"

The growl that left him sent a hot rush through my body, tingling through my breasts down to my core.

"You didn't..." I wetted my lips. His eyes flicked down, tracking the motion. "You never told me..."

"Because I am not a safe creature, princess. I never will be. But you..." He scowled.

I pulled back. "Me what?"

"You're the most beautiful thing I've ever seen. Only a monster would risk breaking that. And a monster isn't worthy of you."

He started to turn away again, and I tightened my grip, stopping him. My pulse was racing and my mind was too, a thousand impossible thoughts rattling through me. This was a man who'd gone hot and cold and spun my head around so many times, I was dizzy with it.

And yet...

"Apple."

His brow furrowed in confusion.

I swallowed hard. "My word. When I first..." I wetted my lips again. "When I agreed to sleep with Casimir the first time, he told me to pick one and to say that if it became too much. That it would be his cue to stop the kinds of things he wanted to do with me. So that's mine. Apple."

Ozias didn't even appear to be breathing.

"I know my own mind," I continued. "I decide what I want."

Carefully, I took a step closer to him and put my hand on his chest. Beneath my palm, his skin was warm, and at the small contact, another low growl left him, sending a thrill of need through me that turned my insides molten.

My eyes lifted to his. "And I want you."

His growl deepened.

And then his lips were on mine.

9
OZIAS

What little control I still possessed kept me from shifting and claiming her that instant. But only barely.

She tasted like what her scent had promised, sweet strawberries tinged with a hint of blood, and the combination was more intoxicating than the richest wine. The beast side of me would never get enough.

Neither would the man.

Growling, I lifted her, never letting her lips leave my own, and like the good girl she was, she came to me so willingly. Her legs wrapped around me, her hands raked into my hair, and she opened to me, letting me delve into her taste as deeply as I wished.

Gods, how had I resisted her this long?

I hadn't, that was the truth. Not fully. I'd only been a fool who hadn't dared to imagine such a gift as this could ever be set before him.

But now...

I growled as I kissed her, and to my amazement, the rich scent of her arousal grew stronger at the sound. She wanted that. This. Me.

Fuck, how was this possible? Even with everything I'd learned of her time with the others, for her to be turned on by *me*...

Shudders rolled through me as my beast clamored to strip her down and thrust into her now, and gods, my control was slipping fast. I knew the other men were out there, likely worried and wondering whether I'd found her. If she was safe and if I was too. It wasn't fair to keep them in suspense.

But they were still miles away from here, and the instinct to have her in every possible way was stronger than any guilt could hope to overcome.

She was my treluria. My mate.

And I'd delayed claiming her for too long.

She moaned as I gripped her ass tightly, holding her in place. The strength of her vampire side was clear in how she clung to me, in how she kissed me back every bit as strongly as I kissed her. There was a ferocity to her passion that only served to stoke the flames of my own, a need that made her seem like every bit as wild a creature as me. She devoured my mouth even as I did the same to her, and in a desperately instinctive motion, she rocked her hips against me as if she was already seeking her release in my arms.

But it wasn't time for that yet.

With my magic, I searched the terrain around us, checking for any threat that would impede what I wanted to do. But there was nothing. No humans. No predators of any kind.

Except us.

Roughly, I broke away from her, and breathlessly, she stared at me. Her pupils were blown out by desire, and her red lips were swollen from how hard I'd kissed her.

I'd leave more marks still.

"You won't shift," I told her, my voice thick with the growl of my beast. "I want you in this form when I catch you. Shift against my orders and I won't fuck you when I find you. Do you understand?"

Her eyes widened, but she nodded. "Yes, sir."

My cock grew even harder at that delicious obedience. "Good girl." I set her down on her feet again, a cold, hungry grin twisting across my face. "Now *run*."

She gasped, but in only another heartbeat, she spun and took off, sprinting out of the cave and toward the forest.

My cock ached, and I braced a hand on the wall, fighting the way my beast surged within me, demanding I go after her immediately. I could feel her on the earth, her small feet darting this way and that as she raced through the woods. My gifts hardly made it a fair chase, and someday when the world was safe for her and the Void-born were gone, I would let my princess shift when I went after her for a true hunt. But right now, I wanted her where I could get some glimpse of whether she was safe.

Yet it wouldn't be much of a pursuit if I didn't at least give her a tiny head start.

I grinned as I felt how she veered to one side only to double back as if laying a false trail. Gods, she was marvelous. A predator playing at being prey, all in the hope I would fuck her every bit as savagely as I'd told her I wanted to.

Marvelous didn't come close. She was a damned goddess, and I couldn't wait any longer.

I took off after my mate.

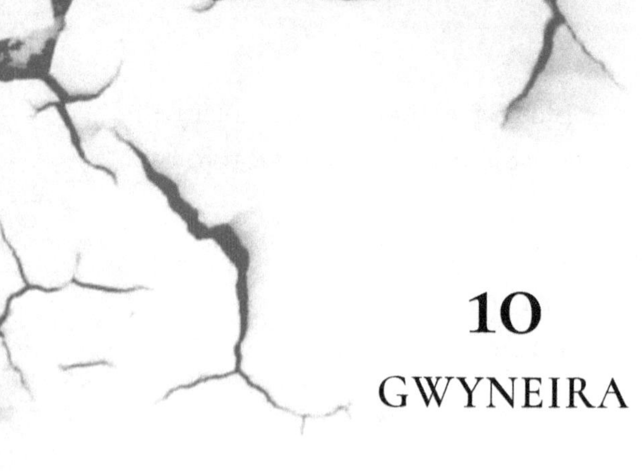

10

GWYNEIRA

Never in my life had I thought I'd find being chased by a vicious, beautiful beast *exciting*.

But it was more than that. Every nerve in my body thrummed with heightened awareness. Every sound and scent in the forest was amplified. Even the vampire side of me was on board with this, bizarrely doing nothing to fight me or try to take control as I fled through the woods.

No, it loved this just as much as I did, and with each passing second, the rush of running from Ozias only grew stronger, until I was fairly certain I'd come on the spot whenever he caught up to me.

I knew his powers were probably telling him where I was. That really, this was only a game.

But that didn't mean I wanted to make it easy on him.

Doubling back again, I cast a swift glance at the trees, wondering if climbing was against the rules. Would that stop him from feeling my presence on the earth?

A branch cracked in the distance, shattering my debate and making me freeze like a rabbit who'd suddenly detected the presence of a wolf. But Ozias wouldn't make a sound, that much I knew. He'd always been so quiet, even before I learned what he actually was.

Before he wanted to *hunt* me.

But what if he was trying to put me more on edge? Hint that he was coming for me now?

Turning, I cast a fast glance around and then took off again in the opposite direction from the noise I'd heard. Faster and faster, my legs moved, my vampire abilities lending me speed. After all, he never said I couldn't use those. He only said not to shift or else he wouldn't—

He was in front of me.

Gasping, I skidded to a stop. He was in human form, but the barest hint of a shimmer was fading from his skin, making me think he'd shifted to get here. Gods, how fast *was* his beast?

That low growl rumbled from him, making my core throb.

But he hadn't caught me yet.

A grin flashed over my face. I darted to the side, racing as fast as I could through the underbrush. A snarl came from behind me, but not one of rage. One of anticipation.

He was enjoying this too.

I ran, pouring every bit of my strength into gaining more speed. Adrenaline pounded through me, fueling ancient instincts that swore I really was his prey no matter how much I trusted this was a game. That a monster was after me, intent on bringing me down and doing the gods knew what with me. Over and over, branches snapped behind me, adding to the rush of a chase that felt less and less like fantasy and more like I was running for my life.

But gradually, the sound of snapping branches grew more distant the farther I ran. Was I truly outpacing him? I couldn't hear anything anymore.

Warily, I slowed, casting a glance back over my shoulder. Had something happened to him? This whole game was some measure of madness, after all, given that there could be all kinds of predators out here.

The gods-forsaken Voidborn, for example.

I stopped, breathing hard as I scanned the forest behind me. Gods, I was an idiot. What if those creatures came back? What if they were attacking him right—

A dark blur moved at the corner of my eye, and then suddenly he was on me. I slammed to the ground, the air rushing from my lungs as Ozias pinned me down. One of his hands took my wrists, trapping them above me, while his knees shoved my legs apart. I gasped, too stunned to do more than stare up at him.

His hair was wild. His teeth bared. He still looked like a man, but only until I met his eyes.

Those were as savage as any rabid beast.

Gods, I loved it.

The earth flowed around my wrists, imprisoning them. With rough motions, he ripped my clothes away, and I trembled with the urge to shift, to flee. But that'd be breaking the rules, and nothing in me wanted this game to end.

Cold bit at my bare skin as the last of my clothes vanished, but I scarcely had time to react to it. Swiftly, he pulled me from the ground and flipped me over, putting me on all fours on a nearby slab of stone so that I was at a good height for him and then shoving my legs apart again.

Like water, the rock flowed around my fingers, my wrists, my knees, swallowing them down and then hardening again.

Trapping me in position for him.

His deep growl came from behind me, making my pussy clench with need. I could shift in an instant and escape, I knew. But I didn't even breathe.

Fabric rustled, and then his pants and bag landed in a heap at the corner of my eye. Metal clanked as his weapons hit the ground too. The cold air moved across my backside, brushing across my soaked core. He was close, but I couldn't see him, and trembling, I started to glance over my shoulder, searching.

Roughly, his hand took the back of my head, stopping me, and he growled again, low and wild like an animal. The effect on me was immediate. Need trembled through my legs and my pussy wept, aching to be filled.

One hand still holding the back of my head, he bent over me and sniffed sharply as if he could smell my arousal on the air.

Which... gods, he probably could.

Slowly, his hand eased away and slid down my spine. But his growl continued, a wordless warning to stay still and let him do what he wished.

I barely breathed. His palm and fingertips were rough, a product of years outdoors. They traced along my skin with a delicious friction until they found a bundle of nerves at the base of my spine.

I gasped, bucking slightly in spite of myself.

His growl took on a pleased edge. His palm cupped my ass briefly, squeezing down as if he was testing the feel of me, and then he slipped his hand around to my front, covering my pussy.

I didn't move.

"So small for me." His words were thick and barely intelligible. "My little mate."

Every nerve of my body was on fire, and he hadn't even entered me yet.

One finger pushed inside me, then another. Slowly, he began pumping them in and out while the rough pad of his thumb circled my clit.

I was so close to the edge already. It only took a moment before my orgasm crested and crashed into me, making me cry out as my body sagged toward the stone. His other arm caught me around my middle, keeping me from collapsing while his fingers wrung out every last bit of my pleasure.

He didn't let me go as the wave receded. Bending closer so his mouth was right beside my ear, he rumbled, "Again."

My breath caught.

I could hear his dark smile in his voice, even if I couldn't see it. "Need you relaxed as possible to take this thick cock."

Oh gods.

Without another word, he resumed pumping his fingers into me, relentlessly making me come and come until my juices dripped down my legs and I could barely see the ground in front of me for how much pleasure had blurred my eyes. I was boneless in his grip. As limp with satisfaction as I'd ever been in my life. And that was when he leaned over me and murmured into my ear, "Good girl."

His fingers vanished, leaving my pussy bereft only for a moment.

And then his cock pushed into me.

I cried out, my eyes going wide. It felt like he was splitting me open. Like I'd rip in half from the size of him.

But after how many times he'd made me come, after the rush of running from him and all the adrenaline still coursing through me, that pain turned out to be exactly the tipping point I never knew I needed.

My muscles clenched around his length and my vision blacked out as another orgasm hit me like a hurricane. I was no longer in my body. I wasn't even on the earth. There was just me and the pleasure and the over-whelming sense of him stretching me in a way I never wanted to end.

But he wasn't done with me by far.

No sooner did I regain awareness of what was happening than he braced his massive body over me with one hand on the rock. Taking my hair roughly with his other hand, he looped the length of it around his fist in a swift motion and then pulled me back toward him.

My back arched as the restraints remained in place, holding my hands down even as he hauled me closer.

"Mine," he snarled in my ear.

I could only twitch my head in a tiny nod. "Yours."

He growled and rocked forward, thrusting himself deeper into me, never letting my hair go. "My mate. Mine. Mark you. Kill any fucker who touches you."

My vision swirled. I gasped, managing a tiny nod again. "Yes. Yours."

He thrust harder and only his grip on me kept me from collapsing. Wordless noises escaped me as my pussy stretched, and I swore somehow he was getting even larger inside me than he was already.

"Knot you," he snarled in my ear.

I rasped out my agreement, even if I had no idea what that meant. But gods, it felt amazing. Possibly like it would rip me apart from the inside, yes. Definitely like my body was struggling to take him without damage.

But *amazing*.

Grunting, he changed his thrusts, driving himself against me in short, hard jerks like he'd die if he didn't fill me with his cum soon. His growl became more ragged, more feral, and a shiver pulsed against my back, the strange sensation washing over me and then receding.

He wanted to shift. I didn't know how I knew, but I did. He wanted to and he was fighting it.

"Take me... as you," I gasped out. "All of you. Please."

His grip on my hair tightened painfully. "If I mate bond you..."

A thread of worry carried through his voice, even though he never stopped thrusting into me, hitting me so deep and hard.

I rocked beneath him, another orgasm building like a tingling wave inside my core, and though his hold on my hair made me wince, but I didn't try to escape it. I wasn't sure what he was talking about—mate bonds and knots and all that—but even though he sounded concerned, I couldn't find it in myself to be scared.

Gods help me, I wanted this. Him. All of it.

Because no matter what he thought might happen, I trusted him.

"Do it," I breathed. "Please. Oh, gods... please..."

Whimpering sounds of need overtook my ability to speak as pleasure began to blur the world again. He snarled, but the sound changed soon after, deepening as the shiver of his magic turned into a wave pouring over my skin. Beside me, his muscled arm suddenly rippled and transformed, becoming the enormous, furred arm of the beast.

A choked scream left me as his cock stretched me farther. He was going to break me apart. Shatter my bones. There was no way he wouldn't tear me to pieces with—

His hot breath puffed against my back. The stone released me as he suddenly hauled me upright by my hair.

And then his clawed hand was in front of me, moving so fast, I couldn't even gasp before it struck.

My eyes darted to the right. Four tightly grouped gashes welled with blood above my breast where his claws had torn my skin.

I trembled, the pain catching up to me. It wasn't much. Barely more than a sting, really, and the shock was the worst part.

But what did this have to do with a mate bond?

Huffing again, he leaned in close. At the edge of my

vision, his long jaw of bone and fur came into view over my shoulder.

A thrill of fear shot through me, the response primeval. Every instinct I possessed screamed that was a predator, a monster.

But what was he going to do? Surely he wouldn't lick the wounds? That wasn't safe, right? I was a vampire. He couldn't drink my blood and not end up turning into—

Steaming liquid dripped from his fangs onto the gashes.

Pleasure slammed into me so fast, all I could do was scream. My juices gushed around his cock as I came so hard, I lost all sight of the forest. The sky. The world itself. There was nothing but this blinding wave of ecstasy that erased all conscious thought.

Leaving only me. Only him.

So much of him.

I blinked, my vision swimming as awareness of my body slowly returned. I was on the ground now. I had no memory of moving. But my pussy was raw and aching from how hard I'd come, and Ozias was on top of me, his body still in his wolf-like form. His bony jaw was above my head. His hips were between my legs, spreading them wide. Thrusting with slow strokes, his cock still felt like it was splitting me in two.

But in the most amazing way.

Dazedly, I wrapped my legs around him and slid my hands up his furred chest, marveling at it while I rocked with him, my body moving on pure instinct.

A rumbling carried through his chest, making my hands vibrate, and I smiled, somehow knowing he was pleased at what I'd done. A strange thrumming sensation was coursing through my veins, making me match his pace without any conscious thought on my part. It was like we were together in a way that surpassed merely his cock inside my pussy. Like we were one being, one mind, unified by the desire to fuck and fuck and—

I choked on a gasp at the same time he suddenly grunted. My eyes flew wide, another orgasm taking me out of nowhere at the exact moment he came. His hot cum rushed into me, and I moaned, overwhelmed as much by an awareness of his relief as I was at the sensation of being filled. My pussy clenched around him as his claws dug into the dirt beside my head, as if both of our bodies needed to express this shared ecstasy in their own way.

He growled, wordless, but I could hear the claiming in that sound.

I could only nod. "Yes. Yours."

The growl changed, radiating satisfaction now.

Yet it wasn't only that sound that made his approval clear. I could feel it too. Feel *him*. Not just physically, but in my mind as well.

My mate.

A smile tugged at my lips. I hadn't known what he meant before, but now... gods, I could feel that. A craving for him. A need. A closeness that went beyond my body and my mind down into my soul, tying us together so powerfully even the gods themselves couldn't tear us apart. I'd drank his blood before and felt close to him, but *this...*

It was different. Intense in a way that should have

been driving me insane, but somehow, I wasn't drowning in it. No, instead of losing myself because I suddenly had more than my own sensations and feelings in my mind, I was just...

Safe. Calm. At peace in a way that made no sense but was real all the same. Deep inside, even the vampire was resting and sated, as if this claiming had appeased something for that part of me too.

For a long moment, Ozias and I lay on the ground, the only sound our breathing. His fur was warm, keeping away the winter breeze, and his claws lightly stroked up and down my arm, never breaking my skin.

Between my legs, the stretch of his cock eased.

Carefully, he slipped from within me and pushed up from where he'd been resting. I glanced down, curious, and then paused.

The base of his cock was... different. Thicker. Rounded, like something there had swelled up but now was receding.

I realized he'd stopped moving. I looked up to find his eyes watching me carefully from within the sunken pits of his wolf-skull face.

"Your... knot?" I asked, remembering the word he'd used.

His head nodded once. Before I could say anything else, a shudder rolled through him, and then a shiver of magic ghosted across the air as he shifted form.

Naked and crouched in the dirt between my bare legs, he stared at me, waiting.

"It felt incredible," I said.

Relief filled his eyes. Reaching out to me, he drew me

into his arms. I curled against him, resting my head on his broad chest as he gently brushed the bits of dirt and debris from my skin.

"My little mate," he murmured softly.

I nestled in closer as a lump formed in my throat. I could feel his contentment too. His peace. And I knew both were new to him, not just because he was somehow sharing these feelings with me, but because he'd never known anything quite like them before.

"Mine," I whispered back.

He pulled me closer, holding me to him like he'd never let go.

But then he froze.

I didn't move, confused and disoriented by the sudden blur of emotions coming from him. Protectiveness. Worry. Aggression. Dread.

"What is it?" I asked.

For a moment, he didn't respond, and then a slow breath left him. "The others. They're close. Heading this way."

That didn't explain his reaction. "But what's wrong?" I moved a bit so that I could see his face.

His eyes avoided mine. "They can't know about me. What I am."

"What? Why? Ozias, I swear, I can't imagine them trying to make you leave just because you're—"

"And if they do?" He looked at me solemnly, no doubt in his gaze despite the fact he'd asked the question. "If they decide you're not safe with me and they have to protect you?"

My lips parted, but I couldn't find the words to

respond. It seemed so impossible. Those men were his friends. They'd fought together and stayed together for years, and that was after growing up in a world that despised them just because of the way they'd been born. Surely given all of that, they wouldn't dream of driving Ozias away simply for being what he was.

"One of my first memories," he said quietly, "is when my mother tried to drown me."

I went still. Holy gods...

"I was an abomination to her. To our village. But after that, there were others. Villagers and merchants who tried to kill me or cage me for what I am. They gave me my scars. All of them. Nowhere was safe." He shuddered. "These men... *you*... are the only home and the only real family I've ever known. But if they think I'm a danger to you..."

His jaw muscles clenched beneath his beard, the tumult of fear and pain and dread inside him growing stronger.

It hurt so much, and yet to look at him, he was as stoic as I'd ever seen him.

Gods, the things he hid inside.

And I wanted to make it better. To tell him I wouldn't ever let them send him away, not on my account. But I also knew that solution wouldn't be good enough, not really. That wouldn't be acceptance or trust or any of the things he had with them now, for what was likely the first time in his whole life.

Even if it was based on a lie.

The dilemma of it all gnawed at me. I didn't want to lie either, not to the men I loved. But I also didn't have the right to tell them Ozias's truth when that was his to share. And now that I understood the dread that lay like a cold leaden ball within him...

Gods, after all he'd been through, who was I to decide how and when he revealed himself? If he thought telling the others the truth meant there was even a *chance* they wouldn't accept him or that he might lose the only real home he'd ever had, what right did I have to jeopardize his world and make that choice in his place?

I swallowed hard. "Your secret is safe with me."

At his silence, I glanced back. The tumult in him had changed, but I couldn't make sense of it. "What?"

"I'm sorry I ever doubted you. Who you are. *How* you are. Anything. You—" A ragged breath left him as he stared at me. "You're just..."

His hand gripped my head, drawing me to him. As his tongue plundered my mouth, his fingers curled into my hair and his beard scratched my cheeks, both giving delicious counterpoints of pinprick pain to how he devoured me. I already knew I'd never get enough of the combination, and my body thrummed with renewed need when he finally let me go. Even his kiss had me wet.

His nostrils flared, and a low growl full of carnal hunger rumbled from him. "I can smell how much you want more, little mate."

Gods, this man.

With a tiny whimper of desire, I rocked my hips against him, my clit aching.

He grinned.

That only made me crave him more. Ozias already looked like a rough and wild creature, but grinning like that, he was a sexual forest god. Still holding me with one arm, his other hand stole down my middle to delve into my wet folds. His fingers circled my clit, massaging it so perfectly, and I could feel his enjoyment thrumming through the strange new connection between us.

Which meant he could feel mine too.

Shock at the realization made my eyes go wide, but that couldn't last. Not against the incredible way he touched me, the rough pad of his fingertips playing over my clit like I was an instrument and he was a master. I clamped my lips shut against gasping moans as the tension built inside me, my hips jerking in his grasp. Shuddering hard, I gripped his bicep as I came again.

His grin widened as he withdrew his touch and licked my slick from his fingers. The sight was so erotic, I shivered. My lips parted to feel his hard length pressing at my hip.

I wanted to taste him too.

Wriggling a bit, I tried to reposition myself to reach his cock, but Ozias stilled my motions with one massive hand. A sigh left him, regret flashing over his face. "Your clothes. Before the others arrive, you should..." He frowned, glancing at the remains of my clothing scattered around us as if realizing how useless most of it had become for covering me. "Here."

He reached into his bag, tugging out his sweater a moment later.

I could have used it as a blanket, it was so large on me. Even bundling up the sleeves only left them bunched around my wrists, threatened to flop down at any moment, and the bottom hem hung past my backside.

Ozias was staring at me when I looked back up at him. He didn't move a muscle, save for the way his nose twitched.

"What?" I asked.

There was a hint of growl in his voice as he said, "Good to have my scent on you again."

I paused. Again? What did he—

Memory played back. "The blanket. The one in the glass box." Certainty settled over me as a tinge of embarrassment flitted through his eyes, there and then gone. "That was you... putting your scent on me?"

The words felt strange and yet erotic, and when he stepped closer and bent down low enough that his head was near mine, another quiver of desire rolled through me.

He inhaled like he was drawing me deep into his lungs. "Yes."

It took me a moment to find my voice. "I see."

His fingers took up a lock of my hair, brushing it back behind my shoulder.

The quivers grew stronger, even at that light touch. Because it *wasn't* just that. It was the desire I could feel from him. The way I knew he wanted to strip me naked again right now, covering me even more with his scent in the most natural way possible.

But then his gaze flicked to the side, and regret crossed his face.

A shaky breath left me as he stepped back again. The others were coming. Right.

Discomfort swirled in my chest as I pulled on the rest of what remained of my clothing. My shirt was a total loss, but while my pants were torn, they were still usable. I supposed I would need to ask Clay for help fixing them, considering I had no needle or thread. I only hoped he didn't press for too many details.

Which was *really* unlikely. This was Clay, after all.

I squeezed my eyes shut, the discomfort swirling up inside me again. Gods help me, I didn't want to keep secrets from my men. The thought of doing so left me feeling sick. And yet I didn't want to risk the seemingly impossible chance I was wrong about them either. I knew I trusted them completely, but Ozias knew them well too, and if his fear had even a *possibility* of being corroborated...

Besides, was it truly my secret to tell?

Raking my fingers through my hair in an effort to return it to something resembling order, I looked out at the forest. It was my secret and it wasn't, and I didn't have a clue how to sort out that mess. What I felt between Ozias and me was incredible and beautiful, and I didn't want to hide it.

But then, maybe I wouldn't have to. Not forever. Maybe somehow I could help determine if Ozias truly was in danger of being cast out. And then, with that fear assuaged, he could tell them the truth himself, knowing he'd still have his home and family afterward.

It wasn't a perfect answer, but it was something.

Ozias cleared his throat and I glanced over at him. His pants and boots back in place, he was watching me, and a wave of his concern and grim resolve rocked me. As much as I'd relished feeling what he felt during sex, I still wasn't anything *close* to adjusted to this new reality.

He twitched his head toward the forest. "Come on, little mate."

I nodded and then followed him, a warm feeling flickering through me for the sweet nickname he'd given me.

One he wouldn't be able to use once we were around the others.

The warmth faltered, but resolutely, I tried not to give in to despair. Keeping this secret was a temporary situation. It would only last for the hopefully short, *short* time it took for me to somehow figure out what the others thought of people like Ozias—all without letting on what he was.

Even if I had no idea how to do that.

11
MELISANDRE

I didn't care what Alaric wanted to do about Gwyneira. I would see that brat dead with all traces of her mother's magic erased from this world. I would show every last one of those elitist fools in the precious "Jeweled" Coven that their affiliation to gods-be-damned *rocks* meant nothing.

And the moment we reached the Warden Wall, I would absolutely kill that metal-toothed bastard.

My fingers clenched and unclenched while I trailed Alaric across the windswept terrain. We'd left the outpost behind and spent the past few hours picking off stragglers who'd escaped in this direction. Alaric seemed to think continuing to provide me blood would make me forget the indignity of my position or the injustice of the fact my stepdaughter would remain alive longer thanks to his idiotic beliefs about the so-called Nine.

But I'd spent too long under the thumbs of people who believed themselves better than me to be appeased so easily. From the beginning, my childhood had been one series of indignities to the next—from the village children who labeled me "Smelly Melly," all for being the daughter of impoverished farmers, to my own father who'd only ever seen me as a possession to barter away for something he believed more valuable. Being taken into the Jeweled Coven should have been an improvement, but when their flawed system decreed my magic wasn't significant enough to matter to them, they sentenced me to be nothing more than a servant to those they deemed more *worthy*. Even as queen of Aneira, nobles still whispered behind their hands at how I wasn't as good, as kind, as *strong* as their beloved, oh-so-dead Eira—or as her precious little Gwyneira would supposedly be when she took the throne.

No, I'd had a lifetime of being trapped and held down by others. I'd spent decades being labeled and dismissed due to their assumptions about their own supposed superiority.

And from it all, I'd learned one lesson.

People only thought they were better than you until you slit their throat and watched them die.

Then they understood. *Then* they looked at you with fear, which was infinitely better than respect or love any day. Respect was cheap. It got you nothing. Love was a drug for fools. *Fear* could move nations and topple kingdoms. And fear mixed with power?

That could reveal the truth of the world.

Leadership wasn't given by destiny or merit or some pure, inherent worth. It was taken by those with the strength to claim it and the focus to never be swayed from the pursuit of it, no matter the manipulation or lie or supposedly innocent sacrifice required. Only the weak crafted rules to say what was allowed and what was not, all in some desperate effort to convince each other they make the world safe. But in reality, no rules applied. There was what you wanted and what it took to get there.

Nothing more.

And now Alaric and his Voidborn would learn that too. The wall was my creation. Alaric would need me to give his beasts passage through it, which would require me to access its power.

I'd burn him from this entire realm before he knew what hit him.

We crested a rise in the rolling terrain, and the base of the Warden Wall finally came into sight. Anticipation boiled inside me, reaching a fever pitch. The wall shimmered like a massive soap bubble, one whose sides stretched away as far as the eye could see. Stone pillars stood at intervals along its edge, each taller than a grown human man and carved with warnings to let the unwary and the idiotic know they would encounter certain death if they came near.

Because this was no fragile membrane. Any giant, witch, or creature of magic who tried to touch it would burn alive, their bodies and their powers alike devoured in an instant. Even humans could only pass with the aid of talismans carried by the guides who inhabited the outposts along the border—or *had* in the case of the one we'd just left behind. To humans, they looked like mere medallions emblazoned with the crest of the queen of Aneira—an apple tree with roots spreading wide beneath the ground. But in truth I had imbued them with dark spells and the blood of those whose lives had been sacrificed to create the wall.

Not that the king or any of his precious little subjects knew that last part.

A secret smile lived inside me as we approached my creation. It had required enormous effort on my part to create this barrier. Hundreds upon hundreds of lives drained to fuel the magic—not, of course, that anyone missed them. No, I had been cautious, taking only from the poor and homeless, prisoners and farmers too far away from the major cities for their absences to be noticed.

And to be sure, some among the rabble had still questioned what was happening. But the beautiful thing about humans was that they were more likely to adapt to changes than to continue fighting them, especially once those changes were in place and protest began to appear pointless. Their inability to easily leave Aneira simply became a fact of life, one that only fools would question considering all the *threats* they'd been told existed beyond its borders. And that only those who received royal approval could cross the border became a measure of protection, not control, because surely their trusted king and queen would never deny *them* passage if they wished it. No, the limits were only meant for those who deserved to be forbidden to stay or go.

Thus the wall cemented me in the hearts of the populace as the queen who protected Aneira from any threat and who wanted nothing but to shield them from the dastardly murderers of their beloved former queen Eira.

When this was done, Aneira would be an engine of conquest controlled solely by my hand. No more pacifying a king still afflicted with some measure of conscience, regardless of how often I reminded him of his supposed enemies' crimes. No more convincing nobles through diplomacy or bribes to allow me to do what I wished. Anyone who tried to flee would be executed, and any who thought to fight me would find themselves facing a vampire whom even sunlight could not burn.

The people of Aneira would serve me or they would die.

Only to rise again as my servants anyway.

"You're smiling, pet," Alaric commented.

"Only enjoying the thought of what's to come," I answered, framing the truth in a way he might not question.

He made a considering noise while, around us, the monsters slowed. "Indeed." He continued on toward the Warden Wall, surveying it with a look on his face like a long-suffering parent observing a disappointing child's substandard handiwork. "Your little shield would be quite disastrous to creatures of this realm."

Fury singed the edges of my anticipation. *Little* shield?

Oh, the ways I would make him suffer before this was done.

"You killed so many to build this, didn't you?" he continued mildly. "Their screams echo just beyond what those in this petty little realm can hear."

I didn't respond. How he could make even a feat of *this* magnitude seem substandard, as if I'd crafted something barely adequate rather than created an instrument to control an entire nation... it boggled the mind.

I couldn't wait to watch him burn too.

He turned his back on the wall with a sigh, looking at me as if I'd failed him in some unidentifiable way. "I take it you plan to use this against me too?"

I froze. "What?"

Condescending patience met my eyes. "Did you believe it wouldn't occur to me that you would try to drain all this power—*your* power and the power of all these lives—and use it to try to shake my hold on you?" Pity radiated from his expression, but it couldn't fully cover the ever-present amusement.

Enough of this.

Spinning sharply, I flung my hand toward the Warden Wall.

The magic answered my silent command.

Pure power rushed at me like I'd opened a channel to the heart of a dark star. The air thundered as the magic around the entire nation ripped away from where it had been anchored. In a shimmering cascade, the surface of the wall roared toward me, flowing toward my hand like I was yanking a vast tapestry away.

And pulling it into myself.

All the light and power funneled to a single point. Me. My outstretched palm that had become the center of this vortex of magic. The energy of the wall surged through my body, through my mind—an entire nation's worth of defense flooding instantly from all across the land to return to me.

Alaric could never stand against this.

I whirled back, whipping my other hand toward him.

He was gone.

My eyes flashed over the monsters still spread all across the terrain, seeking that smiling bastard. But while the Voidborn were here, as was a clear space where Alaric had been standing, I couldn't find him anywhere.

Had he hidden himself from me? Run from me in terror, his verbal jabs be damned?

I grinned, but I also was too smart for him. I wouldn't let down my guard, not yet.

Slowly, I turned a small circle, cautiously searching.

"Trouble, pet?"

Alarm shot through me as I whirled back to face the horde. His voice came from the empty spot where he'd stood moments ago, as if he hadn't moved from where he'd been before I took in the power of the wall. Moreover, I could hear that same infuriating smile in his voice, like the metal-toothed bastard was amused by my discomfort.

"Not quite what you anticipated, is it?" he continued.

My heart raced. I extended my hand toward the monsters, taking aim. If I could not kill him, I would kill his fellow Voidborn and watch him reveal himself as they burned.

Alaric made a chiding noise. "Oh, I don't think we'll be putting up with any of that today."

The ground lurched.

Everything around me had changed. We stood on a small cliff overlooking a river, no trace of the Warden Wall markers in sight. The monsters were ahead of me now, fording the swiftly running water like a herd of cattle on their way to another pasture.

"Did you know that rivers often follow ley lines, pet?" Alaric asked as if he stood right at my ear. "But I don't think we'll stop to break this one. It's rather small and pathetic... like you."

I gasped, looking around, but he was nowhere to be seen. "What is this? What are you—"

He chuckled. "Indeed."

The ground lurched again.

I stood in a valley now with monsters all around. Late afternoon light turned the dry winter grass to gold, while a cold wind whipped over the horde, carrying scattered snowflakes that melted before they hit the ground.

And Alaric was standing in front of me, regarding me with a mild expression like he'd been there the entire time. "You made a little barrier around the capital city as well, didn't you? That will be fun to drain and hear the populace scream."

My hand came up instinctively, aiming at Alaric.

He winked at me.

Another lurch. We were on a hillside, the river and the valley gone, and the sunlight had nearly vanished from the sky. A small town lay ahead of us. Already, the monsters were descending on it, and the cries of the townsfolk carried on the breeze like a far-off melody.

"What is this?" I demanded, my heart racing. I turned a tight circle, but once again the bastard was nowhere to be seen.

"Oh, my silly, broken little pet."

I whirled back to face the village, but he wasn't there.

"What are you doing to me?" I shouted.

Alaric made an amused noise. He sounded like he was standing right beside me, and when he spoke, I could feel his breath on my skin as if he was whispering right into my ear. "You'll see."

12
ROAN

I'd lost any chance at the princess's heart by pushing her away.

Now I'd lost the princess herself.

And the demon was going to burn everything in sight if I didn't find her soon.

In the distance, I could hear my friends struggling to keep up, their voices calling out every so often to tell me to slow down. Be careful. To caution me that those Void-born bastards could still be out here, and that I couldn't possibly know if I was heading the right way.

But the demon had no doubts, and its strength fueled my speed. No, I couldn't feel her. Hear her. Smell her. I couldn't do a damn thing except stride through this gods-forsaken forest, heading back toward the cursed terrain that was the Wild Lands and praying she hadn't made the mistake of returning there.

The demon had vanquished that foe once. It would

scorch the earth itself to ash if that place tried to take her from us again.

If *anything* tried…

I shuddered. My eyes were burning. Patches of my skin might have been shifting toward gray, or maybe that was just fear making me jump at shadows. But I'd nearly lost control of this monster back at Casimir's castle, and I knew I'd been fooling myself to believe it had returned to sleep since then.

No, with every step, the demon fought harder to take control and break free of the chains I'd wrapped it in long ago. Once upon a time, it'd agreed to them. Even believed it deserved them for all the horrors we'd committed and the lives we'd taken.

But that was then. Before the Wild Lands. Before that arrogant bastard of a vampire king had stolen the only woman we ever wanted, no matter what his reasons for that had turned out to be in the end.

Before that strange winter's day, weeks before, when our treluria had first stumbled in barefoot from the bitter cold to curl up in my armchair like she was seeking the protection of us and us alone.

"Roan!" Dex shouted far in the distance behind me.

Branches slashed at me as I shoved past. Roots tried to trip my feet. But I needed to go faster. Stay ahead. Not slow down, not even for a moment.

A groan escaped my lips. The urge to shift rolled through my body, making every tendon and bone ache like they were being pulled apart. The demon was thrashing within me, determined to break free and bring an end to this pursuit. Gwyneira was ahead of us, it was sure. Thus we only had to find her, claim her as we should have on the very first day we laid eyes on her, and then everything would be all right.

And I knew without *question* that meant the demon was insane. None of that would happen.

Instead, she'd just die.

"Dammit, where the hell are you, man?"

Clay honestly expected me to slow down enough to answer?

I ripped past a tangle of vines, my nails too sharp, too long, and well on their way to claws that would tear flesh from bone. A patch of skin on my hand was *definitely* gray now, and if the others saw—

The demon didn't care about those men. Let them see us. Let them stare. It loathed the thought of hiding any longer. It was tired of staying bound inside me, locked down in the dark where I—like a fool—still believed it belonged. No, all those horrors we'd committed were *then*. This was *now*. Now was not then, and in this *infuriating* now, our mate was in danger.

Nothing else mattered.

Shudders rolled through me. Gods, I'd forgotten how alien that side of me truly was—and that was before this moment when I started to suspect it'd truly lost its mind. I'd buried the demon for so many years, there'd been times at the cabin when I could almost let myself pretend it no longer existed, this monster who both was and wasn't me. This *thing* that made me unlike any other living being in the world. I could pretend I wasn't a selfish bastard risking the lives of everyone around me, just so I could play at having some kind of family again. No, I was an ordinary man. A giant, not a monster, just like my friends.

I'd been a fool.

Irritation surged up from the demon. It was sick of how I fought it, of what I believed. Everything was simple in its mind. There were no shades of gray nor any question of what we should do now. We would find Gwyneira. We would mate her. And if that meant the death of everything in our path, then everything would simply have to die.

The end.

Everything including her? I snarled back silently, hurling at it the memories of what we'd done years ago. *Including my friends?*

The demon faltered.

Taking the opening, I forced my fingers to unfurl. Forced my eyes to return to normal. "If I *ever* have to bury her ashes because of you..." I growled under my breath.

The demon grumbled within me, wanting to reject the idea, but the creature knew the cost if it returned. It knew what would happen.

So did I.

And dammit, I *also* knew that meant I should have left months ago. *Years*, even. I shouldn't have risked these men, to say nothing of a beautiful, precious jewel like Gwyneira. Hell, I should have turned around and gone the other direction from the moment I first saw Dex and the others during the war, confining myself instead to the wastelands of Erenelle and wandering the empty salt flats until the day I finally died.

But no, I wouldn't give up the damned illusion of

family. Wouldn't stop pretending I could control this, hide this, and keep anyone from knowing. Of *course* my friends would never need to drive me away out of fear for their own safety. Of *course* I'd never need to bury their burned corpses like I'd buried so many others.

Even now, I couldn't quite stop believing that fantasy could be true. That the demon wouldn't return, not fully. That I'd win this fight and protect every fucking person who mattered to me.

No one would die. And no one would know.

I could keep this family, even if I'd lost the one before.

"Roan, please slow down!" Niko called, closer now. "It's not safe!"

A spike of panic shot through my veins. He wasn't just close, he was *too* gods-damned close. At any moment, that fucking vampire king could rush ahead of him and spot me struggling to get my body under control. He could overhear me and wonder what the fuck I was saying to myself.

We were perilously close to ruining everything.

The demon growled at me sullenly from the depths of my mind. Nothing was ruined. No one would come between us and our mate.

Damn you, she is not *our mate!* I snarled back silently.

The distant sound of a woman's scream carried on the wind, coming from somewhere ahead.

My head snapped up. I was running before I even realized what I was doing.

"Roan!" Dex shouted behind me.

"What the hell, man?" Clay yelled.

I didn't slow. Surges of energy shot through my

muscles as the forest blurred around the fiery red tinges in my vision. My skin burned, and I gritted my teeth as I held back the change. But the demon wanted out. Wanted to attack. That scream had been strange. Wrong.

Everything in me said it had come from Gwyneira.

A black blur of smoke rushed past, followed by another, and for a terrifying moment, I thought the Voidborn had returned. But green eyes flashed and a wolf's head formed in the smoke, its fangs like dark splinters of night. It swept onward, sparing me only a brief glance like it was welcoming me to join it in this chase.

Ruhl and that bastard Casimir. They'd heard her too.

I grunted out curses, fighting the monster within me even as I fought to run faster. I'd be damned if that vampire would be her only protector, but I also couldn't just rush to her only to lose control of my monster and kill her and everyone else here.

But every minute was too long. Every inch of distance between me and her too far. There were no more screams, and with each breath, I dreaded picking up the scent of her blood on the breeze.

The gods themselves would die if she'd been killed before I could save her.

On the far side of a clearing up ahead, Gwyneira suddenly stepped from the forest with Ozias at her side.

I staggered to a stop, relief hitting me like a solid wall just to see her alive. My eyes swept over her, taking in every detail, searching for the slightest injury or hint she was still under the Voidborn's spell. She was walking gingerly with some measure of discomfort, but I could see no wound to explain why. Her top was gone, replaced by one of Ozias's massive sweaters. Back in human form, that vampire asshole followed her with that same placid expression I loathed so much, while nearby, Ruhl calmly trailed them all in the smoky shape of a wolf.

A wave of her scent carried on the breeze.

My gut twisted hard. That wasn't blood.

That was sex.

My hands curled into fists, my body quaking as the demon instantly rioted to break free. Her scream... it'd sounded wrong because it wasn't pain. Not fully. And the way she was walking wasn't from a wound.

Everything realigned itself in my head. Ozias had found her. He'd fed her, returning her to sanity. And rather than bring her back to us immediately, rather than let anyone know she was safe...

He'd fucked her so hard she could barely walk.

A snarl peeled my lips from my teeth. My jaw ached, my bones quivering under my skin. I ducked my face away quickly, praying no one saw the reaction.

But the demon was furious.

So was I.

"Roan." Gwyneira's footsteps came toward me, and I recoiled immediately, trying not to breathe. The lingering scent of her arousal choked me while the demon surged and rained hell beneath my skin, demanding I take her to the ground and claim her now.

From the corner of my eye, I saw her stop, a flicker of hurt in her eyes. But it vanished quickly, and when she spoke again, her voice was tightly controlled with only a cool curiosity and not the concern it'd held only moments before. "Where are the others?"

The tone shouldn't have felt like a knife, but it did.

"They were not too far behind," the vampire bastard assured her calmly. "Though Roan had gone on ahead."

The need to snarl intensified. Was that some kind of criticism? That level, royal-ass tone he loved to use gave away nothing, but that didn't mean—

"Oh." Gwyneira's small sound of surprise cut my thoughts short. When I glanced at her, she was giving me a confused look, like she was trying to figure out why I would've done such a thing.

Fuck.

The thud of running footsteps saved me from needing to explain—not that I would've been able to anyway. The other men raced into the clearing, rushing past me to her side.

"Are you all right?" Dex demanded of her immediately.

"What happened?" Niko asked. "Nature couldn't tell me where either of you were or—"

"We're fine," Ozias cut in gruffly.

They were damn well more than that.

I turned away as the others kept talking, all of them checking if Gwyneira was okay and assuring her and Ozias of how relieved they all were that the two of them were alive. I was an asshole for not joining them—I was relieved too, dammit—but if I let her know that, she'd only ask questions about why I was suddenly acting like I cared.

And that didn't even bring into it the demon inside me currently raging over the fact one more person who was *not us* had fucked our mate.

I squeezed my eyes shut. She wasn't ours. *Wasn't*, for the love of the gods.

Maybe we should just leave.

The demon only got angrier. Like hell we were leaving her, and if I wouldn't stop opposing what it insisted was true—

"You sure you're okay there?" Lars asked.

I looked back sharply. His attention was on Gwyneira. The group had started east like they were planning on resuming the journey.

Of course they'd noticed she was walking strangely.

She blushed, not quite looking at Ozias. "Yes, I'm sure."

"Wait..." Clay chuckled, glancing between them. "Did you two have some fun while on the way back to all of us?"

I ground my teeth. She only blushed brighter.

"Enough," Ozias growled.

To my utter *lack* of surprise, that hardly deterred Clay. His brow shot up like the response confirmed everything. But it was Lars who said, "Well, good for you both!"

Always so fucking cheerful, that one. But then *he* hardly had a reason to be jealous. He could lie with her whenever he liked.

The demon pushed at my skin harder. We could too. She had only to see the truth and then she'd understand.

I bit back a snarl.

"But hold on now," Clay said, still sounding amused. "How the hell'd you get so far ahead of us so fast, man? We've been hiking at top speed for hours, and yet you managed to make it all the way here and still have time for some fun too?"

Sharp discomfort and alarm suddenly flashed over Gwyneira's face, but she ducked her head quickly, hiding the reaction behind a pretense of fussing with her hair.

I froze. That was odd.

"I track well," Ozias replied gruffly.

Bullshit.

The thought was as much the demon's as mine. Ozias may have been acting nearly the same as ever—curt and about as emotionally expressive as a boulder—but Gwyneira's reaction told another story. Even beyond that, Clay also had a point. No amount of skill at tracking should have given him *that* much of a lead on us.

No, Ozias was lying somehow. And Gwyneira knew it.

The others didn't call them on that, though, and for me to do so would only make me look like even more of an ass. But something was wrong here, and nothing in me could just stand by and let it—

A strange sound like a tide of branches rattling against one another interrupted my thoughts. With the others, I looked to the east.

The trees were rustling. And bending. And—

Oh, shit.

I spun, lunging for the princess while Dex shouted, "Everybody down!"

And then we were out of time.

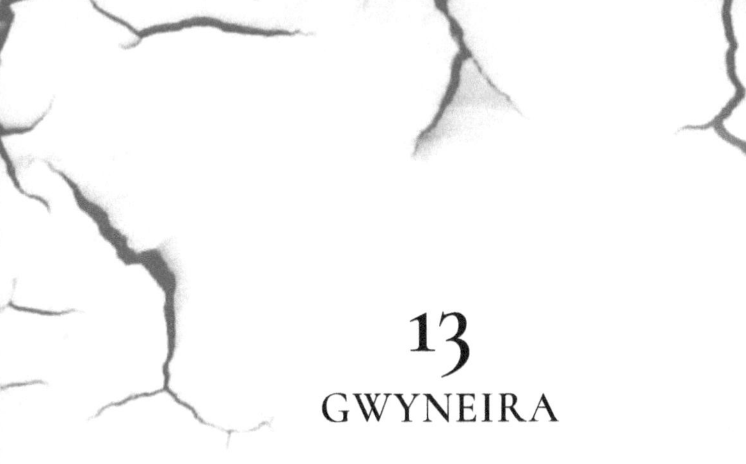

13
GWYNEIRA

With incredible speed, Roan lunged for me. Ripping me away from Ozias, he flung me to the ground, covering my body with his own.

Wind hit the clearing like a battering ram.

The blast howled like a wild thing, scouring over us and pelting us with branches and rocks and the gods knew what else as it ripped past. My instincts screamed in panic like everything awful in the world was flooding over me and there was nothing I could do to escape it. To flee would only be to get caught in it. To fight back would be to die. Tucking myself into as tiny a ball as possible, I wrapped my arms around my head and begged the gods to spare us from whatever this was.

It felt like an eternity until the wind finally eased.

Trembling, I started to straighten, only to have panic surge a second time when Roan didn't do the same. His body was shaking, proving he was alive, but his arms felt like restraints of iron around my body.

He wasn't letting me go.

I wriggled in his arms. I could feel Ozias somewhere nearby, still alive, and my thrill at our connection earlier had nothing on the gratitude I felt for it now.

But he was in pain. And I couldn't hear the others at all.

"Roan, let me go." I twisted my shoulders, trying to break free of his grasp.

His chest hitched in a sudden breath. Sharply, he released me and shoved to his feet, retreating quickly.

My eyes widened.

The back of his coat was peppered with bark and branches. Parts were shredded where larger pieces of debris had cut straight through.

Blood dripped from the wounds.

"You're hurt," I started. "You—"

Roan cast a short glance over his shoulder and then onward to me. His face was cold and as shut down as I'd ever seen it. "Yeah," was his only response.

Turning, he strode away. I stared after him for a moment, thrown by his icy attitude on the heels of literally putting himself between me and danger. The former, I was used to. But the latter...

With a tiny shake of my head, I turned and then froze, all my confusion about him falling away as my blood went cold at the sight of the clearing.

Or what was left of it.

My men were alive. A dirt-encrusted slab of stone reared up beside Ozias like it'd erupted straight from the earth. Several more dotted the clearing near a few of the men, along with tattered webs of vines that wrapped over the others like protective shields. Ruhl flowed away from where he'd been covering Casimir like a blanket, and Niko's hands shook as he extended his palms toward the earth and sent the vines retreating into the soil. But even with the rough shelters, not a single one of the men was without cuts or growing bruises.

And the clearing itself looked like a war zone. Branches were everywhere. Several trees had snapped, unable to withstand the blast. The ground looked like it'd been scoured, the winter grass either plastered to the soil or ripped away.

Ozias tossed a glare after Roan and then set to checking me for wounds, even though it was patently obvious he was far more injured than me.

"Everyone all right?" Dex asked, wincing as he gingerly touched his fingertips to a gash that was dripping trails of blood down his light-brown cheek.

Byron and Niko nodded.

"Quite," Casimir said tightly.

Lars said nothing, rubbing his wrist. Nearby Clay stared to the east, uncharacteristically silent too.

Worry tangled up inside me like one of Niko's vines. I'd never seen that look on the twins' faces before, and when Dex called their names, Lars flinched.

"What?" The blond giant didn't meet anyone's eyes.

"Are you okay?" Dex repeated.

"Yeah."

Dex studied him, obviously not convinced, but didn't press for more. "Clay?"

For a long moment, Clay was silent, and then he

answered in the flattest tone I'd ever heard from him. "I'm fine."

No way I believed that was true.

"Does anyone know what that was?" Niko's voice shook with adrenaline.

"The magic in it was..." Byron trailed off like he couldn't find the words.

"Horrifying," Casimir finished while Ruhl swirled around the clearing as if stalking anything that would bring that wind back again.

The scholar nodded tightly.

I shivered in agreement. I'd never felt anything like that before in my life, and I never wanted to again. But I couldn't take my eyes from the twins for long. While the others were regrouping and Roan was off by himself at the edge of the clearing, my blond giants were still visibly struggling to act like themselves again. Avoiding anyone's eyes, Lars rolled his shoulders and shuddered, while Clay hadn't moved from where he stood.

"Clay?" I started toward him. "Are you—"

"You know what that was?" Clay said, his voice distant. He didn't look away from the eastern stretch of woods. I gave the others a worried glance, but he didn't wait for anyone to respond. "The Warden Wall."

"What?" Niko appeared alarmed. "But... how? It's miles and *miles* from here."

"If it fell," Byron filled in, watching Clay. "If someone took it down the wrong way..."

"Or if they wanted it to kill all the giants still alive out here," Lars said, still rubbing his wrist.

A sickened feeling twisted in my gut as I realized what he was doing. That wrist bore scars from the first and only time the twins had encountered a smaller version of the wall.

I remembered the story they told me about it weeks ago. During the war, Lars and Clay had joined with a few other giants in an effort to break some of their people free. But when they came in contact with the smaller version of the Warden Wall around an Aneiran camp, everything went wrong. The magic *chewed* into them, trying to devour them both, while all the other giants around them died grisly and awful deaths. Only the fact they were dwarves seemed to buy them time enough to escape and survive.

But not without scars—both outside *and* inside.

I swallowed hard and walked over to Clay. His face was cold as he stared out at the forest, his jaw muscles jumping, but when I came up beside him, he flinched, blinking fast and trying to bury the expression.

"Are you okay?" I asked in a quiet voice.

He let out a breath, clearly struggling to push away the pain of his memories. "Fine, baby."

It wasn't his normal tone, but it was closer. Carefully, I reached out, putting my fingertips on his forearm to test whether he wanted to be touched and then leaning into him when he wrapped his arm around me and pulled me close.

My hand rested on his middle, where I knew he bore his scars from the camp wall. A shudder went through him, but he only tucked me tighter to his side.

"If that wall is down," Casimir said, "what does that

mean for our passage into Aneira? Are there any other obstacles to hinder us?"

I cast a glance back and saw Byron shake his head. "None that we knew of," the scholar said. "The wall was more than sufficient."

A quiet scoff left Clay like that was definitely an understatement.

"We need to head out," Dex said. "See what we're dealing with. If the wall really is gone and there's nothing else stopping us from entering Aneira again..." He shook his head. "Maybe whoever's in charge has decided to take a less monstrous approach to protecting the borders."

I felt Ozias tense at Dex's choice of descriptor, but across the clearing, I noticed Roan do the same.

Which was strange.

Yet no one argued as we set out again, although I could hardly say anyone seemed excited that the magical barrier that could have killed us was possibly gone. And I couldn't be either. Yes, it meant we could enter my nation without confronting a wall I'd had no idea how to pass. But for most of my life, the Warden Wall had always been there, surrounding the border of Aneira, while a smaller version encircled the capital city of Lumilia too.

For it to just fall like that...

Of course, there was always the chance it could be coincidence. Though the Jeweled Coven feared my step-mother might have survived being ripped from the world into the empty realms, neither they nor I had real proof she was alive. So if she *was* gone, perhaps the magic of the Warden Wall simply couldn't sustain itself any longer, and the fact it had fallen was nothing more than the last bits of flame dying after a candle wick ran out.

I wanted to believe that. It would be a stroke of luck in what otherwise had been a perilous mess of a journey. But I couldn't shake the fear she *was* alive somehow. That the destruction of the ley lines that had driven us from the Jeweled Coven's hideout and the cracks in the earth that had unleashed the Voidborn were both byproducts of her plans, as was the sudden destruction of the Warden Wall.

Except I couldn't fathom how taking *down* the wall could possibly help her in any way.

A night and another day passed as we traveled, and though the desire to explore my bond with Ozias more deeply pushed at me, there was no privacy to speak of and nothing I could figure out to say to the others besides. Likewise, I would have done what I could to comfort Clay and Lars, but they only seemed focused on keeping me close to them, nothing else. The memories of their last encounter with the magic of the wall haunted them. At night, they tucked me between them, wrapping me in their arms as if being protective of me somehow left them feeling safer too.

Another day later, the sun was sinking toward the horizon when we finally crossed a rise and saw the massive stone pillars that marked the edge of the Warden Wall on the plain ahead.

To a person, we stopped, speechless.

Every pillar had fallen. The carved stones lay scattered as if struck by a massive hand, their pieces hurled across the terrain like the toppled construction of a child's building blocks. Scorch marks scored the grass, stretching away along the line where the pillars once stood, and I realized with a sinking stomach that it was a minor miracle a wildfire hadn't started.

But there was no trace of the shimmer of the Warden Wall on the air.

"What could have done this?" Niko whispered.

Byron shook his head, looking dumbstruck. "I don't know."

A shaky breath left me. "Could the Voidborn?"

Both men gave me a worried look, and then Byron's head twitched in a tight nod. "Perhaps."

"How do we determine if it's safe to cross?" Niko asked. "If some measure of that magic remains..."

Nervousness like ants on my skin made me shiver. He had a point, one that meant there was no way I was letting any of my giants be the first across. But even if my stepmother had made the Warden Wall, that didn't necessarily mean it was safe for a vampire to cross either.

"I will test it," Casimir said solemnly.

I was already shaking my head. "If there's anything left and it reacts to what we are—"

"I'll be cautious," he assured me. "If there is any magic lingering, I should be able to detect it before I am close enough to be harmed, especially after what happened earlier. The feeling is quite... *memorable.*"

He said the final word with a tight expression, and I shuddered. It was that. Gods, how had I never noticed *how* horrible that magic felt before?

But then, I hadn't had access to my own power before either.

With a nod to the others, he started down the hill, Ruhl flowing along at his side. Despite the protests of the others, I trailed after him, ready to grab him and yank him back if anything started to go wrong.

But away from the forest, we were horribly exposed, and I glanced around as we walked, bracing for any sign of an attack. With the wall down like this, surely soldiers were patrolling the area or at *least* trying to determine what the hell happened.

Unless the soldiers already knew. Or unless something else had gone wrong and there were no soldiers left...

By the time we neared the fallen pillars, I was so on edge, I could barely breathe. But even as we passed the first of the scattered stones, there was no tingle of magic or whisper of a warning on the breeze.

The Warden Wall may as well have never been there at all.

"Are you picking up anything?" I asked Casimir when we came to a stop just short of the scorch marks on the grass. My words felt loud in the eerie quiet of the field, and the breeze stirred smells of ash and something vaguely sour that I couldn't place.

Casimir shook his head. "Whatever was here, it's not just drained. It's like it never existed in the first place. Like it was taken right out of the world."

His eyes met mine, and I could read between those lines. "The Voidborn," I whispered.

"Possibly."

"Anything?" Dex asked from several yards back.

"An absence that is chilling," Casimir replied. "But no

more so than the presence of this Warden Wall would have been, I'm sure."

The silence from the others was confirmation enough.

"So then," Clay prompted, gallows humor in his tone. "Who's going first across the big swath of death, eh?"

Again, there was silence.

"I will," Niko said.

I turned to protest—I didn't want any of them to risk this, though I knew there wasn't really much choice—but he was already walking forward.

Ozias muttered something about self-sacrificing fools under his breath and started to follow.

"Careful," Lars cautioned, looking as tense as I'd ever seen him.

Niko flashed them all a smile before turning the expression on me. Reaching out, he clasped my hand.

I didn't let him go. "I'm coming too."

Ozias's growl was hardly necessary to let me know how little he liked the idea. But I didn't care. I wasn't letting one of them get hurt because I was too far away to do anything.

Our footsteps on the burnt grass were the only sounds as we stepped onto the scorched swath of grass.

The strange smell on the air grew worse. I wrinkled my nose in disgust.

"Princess?" Niko tightened his grip on my hand. "Are you okay?"

"You don't smell that?" I asked, barely wanting to breathe. "It's—" I cleared my throat and then swallowed hard to keep my gorge from rising. "It's awful."

Niko gave Ozias a worried look.

"I smell nothing but ash," Ozias replied carefully.

Every bit of his alarm carried through my connection to him, and it sent chills through me.

How could I smell something he couldn't, especially something *this* awful? The smell was everywhere. It clung to my skin, my nostrils, even my eyes like a layer of sour grime I couldn't place and couldn't shake. I swore it was familiar somehow, but so suffocating I couldn't hope to—

Apples.

My chills grew stronger. That was it. The sour, sickly sweet smell of rotting apples, so strong I was gagging on it. But we were standing on a grassy plain without an apple tree in sight. How...?

Memories rose up as if in answer, but they only made it worse. I'd always loved apples. They were even part of the crest of the Queen of Aneira, a symbol that predated my stepmother, my mother, and countless others besides, all the way back to the creation of my country. I was certain that was why I'd chosen them as my word with Casimir and then Ozias.

But once, an apple had more or less killed me. Something about this smell—this *stench*—brought back the memory of that day like it was a foul creature rising from the grave.

My stepmother had been behind that magic too.

"Enough of this." Ozias suddenly gripped my arm, moving us faster across the last stretch of scorched earth and then continuing into the field beyond, scanning it all like he didn't trust a single blade of grass.

The stench faded as we put distance between us and the burned land.

"You all okay?" Clay called to us.

Niko gave me a worried look. "Are you?"

I made myself nod. "It's gone now." I braced myself as the others crossed the swath of land. "You all really didn't smell anything?"

Heads shook. Even Casimir looked perturbed.

I glanced up at Ozias in silent repetition of the question. His head gave a tiny shake.

"What was it, princess?" Niko asked.

"Like rotting apples. Thousands of them."

The concerned looks deepened.

"Maybe it's a reaction to the burned ground," Lars offered after a moment, as if trying to find an answer better than one where I was losing my mind. "Like the way some people detect a flavor they dislike in a dish while others don't pick up on anything displeasing at all."

"Yeah," Niko added. "That makes sense. Maybe it was just something in the grass or the dirt that you have a sensitivity too. That happens."

"Or it's a reaction to the magic that took down the wall," Byron countered in a much more somber tone, not meeting my eyes. "It was your stepmother's power that made it, after all. And that turned you."

If I'd been on edge before, that had nothing compared to now.

"So what, you're saying it's messing with the princess's head?" Clay replied incredulously. "And you all claim *I'm* the one with no tact."

"That *was* you having no tact," Lars pointed out to him.

Clay gave him a dryly exasperated look, though it turned embarrassed when he glanced back at me.

"Whatever it was," Dex interrupted before anyone could continue. "It's gone now, yes?"

I nodded.

"Then we keep it gone." He hoisted his bag higher on his shoulder. "Let's get the hell away from the ruins of the damned wall."

I wasn't sure what I'd expected upon returning to Aneira. That we'd likely need to avoid soldiers, yes, and probably anyone else besides.

But endless miles of utter silence and stillness had never crossed my mind. There were no travelers. What few people we saw at a great distance in the fields appeared to turn and run when they spotted us. All around, there was a strange feeling in the air.

Fear.

It hung over the terrain like an invisible cloud, covering everything from the grass to the sky itself, and it only grew stronger the farther we traveled. I didn't think it was just the product of my own nerves either. No, it was those instincts that had once told humans when a hungry beast was prowling near their tents and caves.

Something was very wrong in my home country. Given the fallen Warden Wall, it worried me for us, my people, and anyone else in the path of whatever lurked out there, waiting.

"Tell me," Casimir commented as we sat around a tiny

campfire one night. "Has Aneira been this sparsely populated for the past thirty years, or is this a more recent development?"

The giants glanced at me as if waiting to see what I wanted to say. Sitting with his back to us at the farthest reaches of the firelight, even Roan's head turned toward us slightly. He hadn't said a word to anyone in days, but clearly he was still listening if he seemed curious about my answer.

"This is new," I murmured. "At least as far as I know."

Casimir's eyebrow arched at me, curious.

"I rarely traveled before this," I admitted. "With the war and what happened to my mother, my father didn't like me leaving the castle, barring a few state visits here and there. My stepmother encouraged him to keep me close as well. For protection, she claimed."

The truth rankled. My *protection* had never mattered, at least not in any context my father or I would have supported. In reality, Melisandre only sought to control me. Control my father too, through his fears. All that time, she'd only actually wanted to turn me into this creature and sacrifice me to the Voidborn.

Of course she couldn't risk someone else killing me first.

"Royalty in a time of war would have been a tempting target," Casimir said kindly. "He was not mistaken."

I smiled, grateful for the attempt to make me feel better, even if it didn't change much. "What I saw of Aneira wasn't like this, though. People were still traveling from place to place. Farmers didn't run from the sight of strangers. This…" I shook my head. "Something's very wrong."

"Word has likely gotten out about the wall coming down," Dex said. "And if what destroyed it is here as well, it would make sense that people are staying home or hiding."

"Do we think it's the queen?" Niko asked with a questioning look to us all. "Could she still be alive?"

"Perhaps…" Byron nodded thoughtfully. "But why would the queen make people run? Assuming she hasn't revealed she's a vampire and all." He made a perturbed sound. "Even what we saw through the magic mirror at the cabin never showed a populace running at the mere sight of someone they didn't know—and when those strangers were still easily two miles or more away."

"No kidding," Clay said. "What the hell did they think we were going to do? Fly across that distance to attack them?"

Murmurs of disquieted agreement came from the others around the campfire. But my skin crawled, my eyes slipping toward the deep night beyond our little circle of light. We'd made camp in the lee of a large outcropping of stone, where rocks had long ago crested through the gently rolling hills. To one side, the granite sheltered us, while the other side was open to the broad expanse of grass and grain that we'd crossed today. Most of us were up near the rock, and only Roan lingered at the edge of the light like he was trying to put distance between himself and us all.

But although we had stone at our back to cut the wind and shelter the light of our flames—to say nothing of how we'd seen no one in my land for hours—suddenly I felt as if we were horribly exposed to the moonless night.

"Who wants to take first shift keeping watch, eh?" Clay said.

"Are you volunteering?" his brother countered.

Clay scoffed. "Hell, no."

Several of the others chuckled and shook their heads as if this was an old argument and it amused them to hear it again.

I watched my giants while Niko grew several long blades of grass from the ground and held them in his fist for the others to select in a prairie version of drawing straws. How many nights must they have spent just like this during the war, sneaking through their own country and then across mine as well?

"So now that we've made it past that wall," Casimir prompted when the drawing of proverbial straws was finished and Clay was indeed given first watch. "What is your plan from here?"

He directed the question to all of us, but my heart still sank because I had no answer. We weren't an army. We were a collection of people who for various reasons would be seen as a threat by my people, not allies, no matter what they now faced. And while the Voidborn were a danger beyond anything I could imagine—an enemy that wanted to eradicate all life from our world and crush reality itself—that wouldn't change what my people thought about us.

To the Aneirans, I was an assassin. A princess who had murdered her own father in cold blood, only to escape after being imprisoned for that crime. Moreover, they believed my giants were invaders whose people had killed my mother.

And all of us together...

Nausea stirred in my gut. Even if my people saw the Voidborn as a threat, they still might try to lock us away.

I was aware Casimir was waiting for an answer, never mind how I probably should have had one before he even asked. My tutors had trained me in strategy and tactics. I should have been better prepared for this. Yes, the Jeweled Coven had insisted we return to the capital city of Lumilia before the Voidborn could harm the magical nexus there—to say nothing of our own plans to retake my throne and free all the giants my father had locked away. But in reality, I'd only woken as a vampire a few days ago, I'd spent most of the journey across the Wild Lands sleeping in a glass box so the sun wouldn't kill me, and most of the time before that trying not to die, which meant how we'd accomplish *any* of those plans was something I hadn't had a single moment to figure out.

"I'm not sure," I admitted finally, ashamed of myself. "I need to find out what allies I might still have in the royal court, and what they now believe about the accusations against me, as well as determine who may have tried to claim power now that my father, stepmother, and I are no longer there."

I scanned the night, my skin crawling at moonless depths of darkness beyond the small circle of light cast by our fire. "From what I've seen, we might be in the southern province of Sinaria, which is the domain of one of my father's most loyal allies in the court. If we visit Lord Thomas here and I can convince him I'm not a murderer, he might be able to give me a better idea of what we'll be facing when we reach Lumilia."

"But what if he tries to arrest you instead?" Niko asked worriedly. "If he was so loyal to your father, and he thinks you killed him..."

I winced. There was that possibility.

"Then we do whatever it takes to get her out safely," Dex said, no debate in his voice.

The twins nodded, and I could feel the wave of agreement coming from Ozias too.

It hurt and it warmed me all at the same time because while my heart swelled at their unwavering love and support, it also terrified me that they might be harmed in their efforts to protect me.

"Indeed we will," Casimir said with a nod of his own. "But assuming he believes you are not the villain your stepmother claimed you to be, what will you tell him of your men here?"

I hesitated. And then there was that too.

Gods, how would we navigate this?

The problem wasn't only that most of the men with me were giants, even if they didn't look like the rest of their kind. No, my nation frowned heavily upon "non-traditional" relationships, and Lord Thomas was nothing if not traditional. He'd even put in a complaint when the palace staff tried to change the palace banners to satin rather than the silk we'd used for the previous fifty years. Never mind that the war had made silk hard to come by. It was tradition.

What would he think of me, of us, and of how we were about as unconventional a group as anyone could come by? The fact this was a consensual, respectful relationship where all members were aware of each other and welcomed each other would hardly matter. My people thought anything except one man and one woman together was immoral and abhorrent.

I never thought I would have something like this or meet men who would welcome something like this. Before I'd been driven away from my home, I'd never even considered the possibility it could exist for me.

And now, I didn't want to hide. I truly didn't, because I hated behaving as if I was ashamed of what we had and who we all were to one another.

"Tell them we are your allies," Dex said gently at my silence. "Everything else can wait."

Reluctantly, I nodded, though I still felt sickened by the need for the deception.

But then, I reminded myself, it wouldn't be forever. Once I had my throne and I could solidify the court behind me, I could start working to change things and help my people accept that relationships that didn't match what they were accustomed to could still be valid and beautiful and respectful to all members involved.

Because deriding the idea that people could love as we did served no one. We were not harming anybody. We were not deceiving each other or manipulating anyone so we could be together. We were all consenting adults who chose each other and chose to love this way. And in truth, I was also not so vain as to believe that I was the only one in all of Aneira who wished to love in this way, and yet who couldn't do so openly because of social rules dictating what love had to look like in order to be "good."

How many of my people were living and loving in secret, just as committed and loyal to each other as we were, and yet who were afraid every day that they'd be discovered and scorned—or worse? How many of them were suffering, unable to make the changes I could simply because of the position of privilege I'd been born to occupy?

I sighed. Gods, there were so many things I needed to change in my country, from this to the unjustly imprisoned giants, and so many other issues besides. And I *had* to change them. I couldn't back down. Not when I would be the one with the most power to do it.

Assuming I could succeed in claiming my throne.

"Will this lord have forces to aid us if we face opposition once we return to your capital?" Casimir asked.

And then there was *that*.

I winced. "All the provinces have standing militias to aid them in case of attack, as well as forces they contributed to the war with Erenelle. Most of those returned home when Erenelle fell and the Erenlian leadership erected their own version of the Warden Wall, sealing everyone out."

Casimir gave me a quizzical look. "The giants created their wall *after* the war, not during it for protection?"

I glanced at the others, not sure what to say since the only explanations *I'd* ever heard for that were disrespectful, to say the least. For years, my father and his generals claimed the reason the Erenlians hadn't built their own wall was simply that they were not as skilled with magic as us. That they didn't care as much about protecting their people. That they were corrupt and couldn't agree on even the most basic safeguards for their own citizens, let alone something as massive as creating their own version of the Warden Wall.

And so on, and so on.

But then, in the last days of the war, a magical wall suddenly rose around Erenelle, sealing the borders completely. Not even the Erenlian prisoners brought to the edge of it could cross, though the generals and prison keepers claimed they were simply refusing to do so.

As far as I knew, no one had entered or left that land ever since.

"Rumors in the Order of Berinlian spoke of the cost of crafting such a barrier," Byron said quietly. "I heard no details beyond the fact that it was so high, so terrible, no sane nation would ever pay it."

His eyes flitted toward me and away again, a flicker of apology passing over his face at the implication.

"But no one knows how it was made?" Casimir pressed.

The men shook their heads. He turned his curious look upon me.

I gave a small shrug. "Even my stepmother kept the details of her spell for the Warden Wall to herself. For our protection, my father said. Because knowing anything of how she crafted her magic could drive us mad."

I couldn't keep the bitterness from my tone as I finished. So many lies, and I'd never once questioned them. I'd simply trusted my father and by extension, my stepmother, and believed Melisandre had our best interests at heart.

How much *had* my father known of what she did, really? And how much had Melisandre used her magic to keep him complacent and prevent him from pressing for details?

Ones that clearly should have mattered to any king.

"However it was made, the wall around Erenelle isn't our most pressing concern," Dex said. "If Lord Thomas *isn't* on your side or was swayed by your stepmother before she died—"

"*Potentially* died," Byron murmured. "If the Voidborn are here, she may still be out there too."

"Before she potentially died," Dex persisted, "then there is the chance he'll try to arrest you or put you on trial for your father's murder. We need to have a backup plan in place to get you away from there, in case he—"

A screech came from above. Before I could move, blurred figures made of darkness broke from the night sky to dive straight at us.

Vampires.

Ruhl was there in an instant. Leaping high over the fire, he caught one of the amorphous forms of smoke in his fangs and ripped it from the air, landing on all fours and shaking the thing like a rag doll.

But more came after it. I lunged as one of them struck Niko and knocked him away from the flames. The creature shifted to the form of a man in an instant, trying to sink his fangs into Niko's throat.

I didn't think. I just struck, tearing him off of my giant and screaming in rage when he tried to fight me, his fangs snapping at me like a mad thing.

He looked familiar.

The shock cost me. Twisting in my grasp, the man tried to shift form and break free. Recovering as fast as I could, I shifted too, shoving him back against the wall again. Taking human form again, he snarled, thrashing. I hung on, pinning him to the rock wall and trying desperately to figure out how the hell I could stop a vampire.

One that I swore I'd seen in my father's castle, maybe as a servant, though it was hard to be sure when he was writhing and slashing at me with his fangs.

"Duck!"

I felt the order as much as heard it, and I flung myself down only a moment before the blade whistled through the air.

Ozias's axe cleaved the vampire's head away from his shoulders. As the man toppled away, the blade slammed into the stone, but only for a moment before the rock wall rippled and released it again.

As Ozias kicked the disintegrating body aside, I shuddered, staring at the fallen vampire for a moment. A cook. That's who he was. One who'd trained with the chefs of Gentresqua. He'd left in the middle of the night a few years ago, and everyone had assumed he was homesick. I remembered because Father lamented the loss of the Gentresquan delicacies he used to make.

Breathless, I turned, seeking any more attackers. Casimir had one of the vampires pinned to the ground, and I didn't recognize that one, but he was holding the man fast while Ruhl leapt at the creature to rip it apart. Dex and Lars had another held at bay with their swords— a servant from the laundry, one who'd vanished after being unable to clean a stain from my stepmother's favorite ballgown—and Clay was helping Byron and Niko stop a third who I swore might've once been a gardener on the castle grounds.

Roan stood alone far to the side of the group, a vampire I didn't recognize in his grasp, and I froze for a whole new reason. The skin of Roan's hand looked strange. Drained of color and oddly textured somehow, though maybe it was just a trick of the dancing firelight. But hanging from his grip, the creature thrashed, clawing at Roan's fist as if unable to shift or escape.

Swiftly, Roan braced his other hand on the snarling man's shoulder and then yanked his grip away. With a sickening sound, he tore the vampire's throat out before letting the creature fall to the ground.

The remaining vampires shrieked and took off across the field, fleeing Clay and Byron's blades and the rest of us alike.

"Ruhl," Casimir snapped.

The wolf didn't need encouragement. In a blur of high-speed smoke, he sped away after the creatures.

I barely took my eyes from Roan. How had he—

Roan caught sight of me across the camp, and he froze. The others were busy with the disintegrating vampires and protecting the camp. Even Ozias had his attention elsewhere, watching the sky for any further threats, though as he sensed my alarm, I could feel him turning back to me with concern.

Myriad emotions chased themselves over Roan's face as he stared at me, and every one of them was baffling. Pride. Disorientation. Confusion. Nauseating dread swallowed a moment later by anger.

Roan turned away as if annoyed by my staring, but

suddenly, the reaction struck me as artificial. I'd seen his face in the moment before that contemptuous anger took hold.

He'd been scared, and I'd swear it was somehow related to me. Never mind how that made no sense—he'd just ripped the throat from a vampire with his bare hands, for the gods' sakes, and there hadn't been a shred of fear on his face about that. Quite the opposite. But suddenly I had a sneaking suspicion that if I asked, not a single man in this group would tell me they'd known Roan possessed such a power.

And then there was how fast he'd crossed that clearing to shelter me from the blast when that wall came down...

Roan was scared that I saw what he'd done. I'd bet half my castle on it.

"Anybody spot any more of those fuckers?" Clay snarled, his hand gripping and re-gripping his sword.

"Don't think so." Niko sounded unsure.

The others said the same as they scanned the night. They hadn't seen what Roan did, and the body was turning to dust, hiding the evidence besides.

"Are you okay?" Ozias murmured to me, and I knew he didn't just mean about the vampires.

I nodded, but I didn't take my eyes from Roan. Crossing the clearing, I watched him grow more tense with every step I took nearer to him.

"Gwyneira?" Niko called, sounding confused.

I didn't respond, coming to a stop near Roan. "What was that?" I asked in a low voice.

"Is everything okay?" Dex pressed.

I hesitated. I could say something. I really could. But would that be fair? If I wasn't going to reveal Ozias's secrets until he was ready, was it right to put Roan on the spot and pressure him into telling everyone about whatever was going on with him?

Especially when I didn't even know what that was?

"I-I just thought I saw something," I said, still watching Roan. "I wanted to be sure he was all right."

Roan's dark eyes darted to me. He was so tense, I could see him trembling, but when he spoke, his voice was hard as stone. "I'm fine."

Without another word, he turned away, busying himself with his bag like I wasn't standing there at all.

Ozias came up beside me, putting a hand on my shoulder and gently drawing me back toward the fire with the others. A wave of support and love coursed into me from him, so intense it was like being engulfed in a warm hug by his furry beast form.

It made me melt inside. This bond was unlike anything I'd ever dreamed of feeling, but I'd be grateful for it every day simply for how it let me know the true depth of feelings this stoic mountain of a man hid inside.

I sank down by the fire, casting a worried glance at Roan in spite of everything. How was I supposed to ask him about what I'd seen? Whatever he was hiding, he'd probably *been* hiding it for years, considering no one here had ever said a word about him having abilities like that. I hated the way secrets were piling up, but was it my place to reveal his or Ozias's or anyone's?

He couldn't be a danger to us, right?

I stirred the fire with a stick, watching the embers

rising into the sky like maybe they'd have an answer. In the clearing, Roan had protected me. At the Jeweled Coven, he'd warned me to stay away.

When I was turned, he fed me his blood and whispered *not you too* as if begging me not to die.

It made my head spin.

Ruhl paced back into the circle of firelight, smugness radiating from his smoky wolf form and answering any question of whether the vampire he'd been chasing had survived.

"Looks like someone had a good hunting trip," Clay joked.

Ruhl settled beside the fire, looking satisfied as hell.

"So…" Niko began. "Do we stay put or should we move on?"

I glanced at Dex.

"It's too dangerous in the dark," he said. "Even if Ruhl caught that one, there could still be others out there. We've got a better chance of defending ourselves here than in the open fields."

The others nodded. Roan never looked away from his bag.

I poked at the fire again, and nothing in me could figure out what to say. When we fought my stepmother, I'd seen vampires who had once been part of the castle staff among those she brought to attack the Jeweled Coven. It should have occurred to me to wonder what had become of them after she was gone.

If she was gone…

I shivered, straining to hear any whisper of more vampires coming to attack our camp. I had to believe she'd kept control of them somehow while my father ruled. Otherwise, tales of monsters in the night would have certainly reached his ears and, eventually, mine. But with her gone, there was no telling how many were now out there, tearing apart the countryside.

No wonder my people were hiding. If they didn't know sunlight contained those creatures, if they couldn't tell where the threat was coming from, only that it looked like a human until it tried to sink fangs into their throats...

Of course they ran. Hid. Stayed out of sight as much as possible. They were just trying to stay alive against creatures who may even have once been their friends.

Dex sank down beside me and rested his sword across his knees, protectiveness practically radiating from him. I tried to give him a smile, but it was difficult to sustain the expression. My people had to be terrified, and terror could make people do horrible things. What was happening out there right now in my kingdom? What lines were being drawn and agreements being made out of the desperate desire for safety and protection?

And what would Lord Thomas or any of my people do when they discovered I was a vampire too?

14
GWYNEIRA

In all the days and nights that we trekked across the southern province, we saw no more vampires.

And almost no people either.

"So," Clay started one afternoon while the men packed up the remains of their lunch. "Anybody got a plan for what we do if nobody's home when we get to this place?"

Dex cast him a frustrated look, though I suspected it was more for saying the worry out loud than for the question itself. They all had to be wondering the same thing.

Gods knew I was.

If the vampires had killed everyone, what would we be walking into when we arrived? I could tell by Casimir's expression over the past few days that he was already imagining it, and given what happened when the Witch War destroyed his country and the vampire witch killed or turned everyone in his palace, he likely had plenty of awful memories to supply grisly detail. Similarly, Dex had only grown more quiet as we traveled, a grim set to his jaw that made me wonder what memories of the war he was reliving every time he closed his eyes. He never told me, not even when I asked, but he'd also taken to making me and several of the others rehearse sword-fighting maneuvers with him before we collapsed into sleep every night.

It was exhausting, but I was fairly certain reassuring himself we all knew how to fight was the only way he was keeping his own fears at bay.

Because none of this emptiness could be a good thing. Even when Aneira had been at war with Erenelle, we'd still been a thriving country with a population greater than many of our smaller neighbors.

Now, it felt like a land of ghosts.

Some of them with fangs.

By the time we crested the last rise before the stretch of prairie that led to the castle at Sinaria, I could barely breathe from tension. Given that it was now late afternoon, whatever vampires were nearby shouldn't be able to roam free yet—at least as long as none of them had figured out the same magic that protected me and Casimir from the sun's rays. What the two of us had was rare, a gift of his angelic heritage and my giants' magic combined.

But I couldn't help but worry I was wrong in thinking that the few humans we'd seen since arriving in Aneira simply didn't know vampires couldn't come outside during the day. Maybe they had a reason to fear, even in the daytime, and I just wasn't aware of it.

At least not yet.

The walls of the Sinarian city of Duteliera came into view. Air escaped me, and I heard the others give a similar reaction.

Everything still stood. No smoke rose from the city. No bodies littered the prairie. There were even people working on the grassy swaths close to the city and guards standing on the walls.

A *lot* of guards.

"Well, *that's* a problem," Dex muttered.

"Yeah," Clay scoffed. "Those fuckers look like they're getting ready for a damn war."

I shuddered. He wasn't wrong. Every able-bodied person in Duteliera looked like they'd been called to arms. They stood along the wall, some keeping watch, others marching to different locations. There were some at the base of the wall, digging what appeared to be a moat, moving fast like they were afraid they'd run out of time to get the watery trench in place. Still more were hurrying carts past the gates, barrels of supplies stacked precariously high and guarded by people who were watching from every angle for signs of an oncoming attack.

Which is when they spotted us on the hill.

Shouts went up, the thin sounds carrying over the distance even if the words were unintelligible. To a person, the citizens reacted like the occupants of a kicked-over anthill, scattering from their work and scrambling to retreat through the gate like they thought we would fly at them so quickly, they wouldn't have time to get inside.

Just like the handful of farmers we'd seen days ago, all of whom fled from us even though we were miles away.

"What the *hell* is going on in Aneira?" Lars murmured, clearly as baffled as I felt.

I couldn't respond. I'd never known my people to react like this, even in the war. I was sure the first few years after my mother died had been filled with fear, though I'd been nothing but a baby and thus I couldn't remember it. But by the time I was a young child, my people traveled easily through Aneira, trusting that my father and our soldiers had the war confined beyond our border with Erenelle and well in hand.

The last of the citizens disappeared behind the city walls and the gates slammed shut. Every guard aimed their weapon toward us, though we were so far away, there was no chance they could hit us with their bows and arrows, much less their swords.

"I suppose there's nothing for it but to approach, yes?" Casimir suggested.

"Princess stays to the rear of us," Dex replied, not taking his eyes from the city. "We keep our weapons sheathed, but Byron, you take point with me in case they try something with magic. Casimir, you stay close to Gwyneira. Get her out of here fast if anything goes wrong." He paused, his eyes flicking back to us for the first time. "Can Ruhl *not* look like that, by chance?"

Casimir glanced at Ruhl questioningly. "I've never seen him take such a—"

The shadow wolf made a sound that I swore was a grumble, and then a shudder went through his body. The smoke drifting up from him faded away, and the shifting clouds that only ever looked *sort of* like fur suddenly became a solid pelt. Even the glowing light of his eyes dimmed until his gaze only appeared like shimmering emeralds and not like brilliant green stars.

Dex regarded him for a moment before glancing at Casimir. "Someday, my friend, I'm going to want more of an explanation of what our ally here might actually be."

"Would that I knew," Casimir replied with sincerity.

Ruhl just turned and walked calmly to the rear of our group.

"Okay, then," Clay spoke up. "On that note, shall we go say hi to all the humans with weapons?"

Dex didn't respond but simply started down the slope toward the city. The others followed.

"Do not worry," Casimir said to me as he hung back, waiting until they'd gone ahead before twitching his head for me to accompany him. "We'll all get out of here safely should the humans decide to start a fight."

I nodded, hoping he was right.

Dull metal glinted in the sun as we walked toward the city wall, all the swords, knives, bows, and arrows catching the light. I could feel the pressure of dozens upon dozens of eyes trained on us, and the aura of fear that had permeated the air throughout our travels felt like a smothering blanket. The city wall wasn't as high as the one around Lumilia—roughly three times as tall as a human man—but it was well maintained and topped by embedded shards of glass that shone in the sunlight.

Most giants had stone-like skin, but they were hardly invulnerable. Even they would be hard-pressed to climb over that without cutting themselves to ribbons.

A *thwip* sound came from atop the wall, and then an arrow impaled the turf several yards shy of our feet.

Across the distance, I heard a man on the wall snarl some-thing about holding fire until ordered otherwise.

"Fucking Aneirans and their little weapons," Clay muttered.

"Quiet," Dex replied, not taking his eyes from the guards. Briefly, he gestured to the others.

My men stopped walking.

"We seek an audience with Lord Thomas," he contin-ued, pitching his voice loud enough that it would hope-fully carry to those atop the wall.

A number of the guards cast nervous looks to one another. Now that we were closer, it was easier to see that not all of them had been soldiers before this. They didn't have the rigid stance or solemn expressions of those who'd been trained for my father's armies.

No, they looked like farmers.

And they looked scared.

Several of them glanced back and then shuffled out of the way, still gripping their weapons. A gray-haired man with dark-brown skin and a stubborn tilt to his chin came into view.

Lord Thomas.

He regarded us all with a coolly appraising expression, saying nothing. His face was clean-shaven and his hair was cropped short. He wore a metal chest plate over his fine blue linen clothes, and though the combination might have looked foolish on another man, on him, it only reminded me of why Father had respected Thomas. Like many in his position, the lord had been born into his rank, but that hadn't stopped him from training to fight and defend Aneira.

When the war came, Thomas had been one of the last to call for an attack in response. Father had resented him for it at the time—my mother was dead, after all, and everyone thought the Erenlians were to blame—but eventually my father came to respect the man's reasons. Thomas was well acquainted with the pain of losing someone he loved. His own wife had died in childbirth years before. But he also knew the lives a war would cost, and unlike others in the court, the lord saw the soldiers as people rather than tools to be used and then discarded.

To him, sending soldiers to fight should always be a last resort.

Yet for all those principles, he was still a trained fighter, and he'd been relentless once engaged in battle with the Erenlians. More than one Aneiran victory had been brought back from the edge of defeat because of him.

And now I stood before him with seven giants and a Zeniryan vampire at my side.

This could go bad quickly.

Something in Dex's stance made me think he was aware of that too, and suddenly it occurred to me to wonder if he knew who Lord Thomas was as well.

And whether Lord Thomas had heard of *him*, the Erenlian who'd been part of the Aneiran army until he rebelled.

Oh gods, this could go *so* badly...

"We are here on behalf of Princess Gwyneira of Aneira," Dex called loudly. "We seek your assistance."

Casimir shifted his weight a bit at my side, and I glanced at him to see tension written all over his face.

Revealing my name was definitely a gamble, but better that Dex do that here where we could make a run for it than inside the city where we'd be trapped if something went wrong. Besides, the lord had likely recognized me when he saw me anyway.

At Dex's words, Lord Thomas said nothing, and I couldn't read a damn thing from his expression over the distance. But then he turned to a stern-looking woman with pale skin and a dark braid of hair beside him, murmuring something even my vampire senses couldn't pick up over the distance.

She nodded and then shouted, "Open the gate!"

A breath left Lars. "One problem down," he said optimistically.

"Maybe," Clay countered. He glanced at the rest of us. "You all are with me on the whole 'not setting foot in there till we know they're not going to stab us the second we're through the gate' plan, right?"

It was barely a question, but Dex nodded anyway. "Agreed. And princess, you still stay to the rear of us. Casimir—"

"We'll be miles away before they breathe the word to attack," Casimir cut in, utter certainty in his tone.

"I'm not leaving without you all," I countered.

None of my men responded, and my jaw clenched. Abandoning them was not happening. I didn't care what they thought they needed to do to protect me.

I'd damn well protect them too.

The sound of chains clanking accompanied the slow progress of the gate opening, and as the gap widened, it revealed more guards standing with their weapons clutched tightly in their fists. To a person, their eyes were trained on us like they expected at any second for us to lunge across the distance to them.

None of us moved.

The guards started forward, and I could feel the tension in my men rise. Through the connection between us, Ozias felt like a landslide waiting to fall, and all it would take would be one wrong move by the Aneirans for him to come crashing down on them and unleash hell. Clay and Lars stood shoulder to shoulder, nearly motionless save for the slight twitches of Clay's hand like he was fighting the urge to reach for his sword this instant. Byron's chest moved in slow, even motions like he was practicing some kind of calming technique, while beside him, I couldn't tell if Niko was breathing at all. Meanwhile, Dex's stance radiated careful control, and an alertness like even the slightest hitch of the Aneirans' footsteps or twitch of their eyes didn't escape his notice.

And Roan wasn't moving a muscle. His hands weren't anywhere near his weapons. His stance wasn't braced for a fight.

Somehow, everything about him still looked like death itself waiting to strike.

As the Aneirans came closer, Casimir carefully rested his hand on the small of my back, while on my opposite side, Ruhl shifted his weight, his furry flank pressing to my hip. If anything happened, those two were making it more than clear they were going to get me out of here, no matter what.

My teeth clenched in irritation. Gods save me from protective men who didn't think I would give the same protection to them. I was a vampire who could walk in sunlight, for pity's sake.

Anything that tried to touch my men would die.

A twinge of discomfort settled in my chest as the crowd parted and the woman who'd been with Lord Thomas came into view. I really hoped that *anything* didn't include the Aneirans.

Regarding us briefly, the woman gave a quick nod to a younger man at her side. In his arms, he gripped a carved wooden box like it was the most precious object in the entire city.

My eyes narrowed. That couldn't be good.

"If you wish to enter the safe haven of Duteliera," the woman called. "You must pass inspection. Understood?"

Clay gave a quiet scoff, muttering so softly, I doubted anyone else beyond our group could hear. "Uh, no?"

I was baffled too. Safe haven? Inspection?

What in the gods' names was going on in my country?

The woman's eyes narrowed like she could tell we weren't in agreement with her demand.

"What is this inspection?" Dex called back.

The woman didn't respond, but instead simply motioned sharply to the younger man and then started toward us. He and several armed guards followed her.

We tensed.

"Everyone here will handle the object inside this box," she said as they came closer. "If you have no reaction, you will be allowed into the city. If you *do* react, you will be killed instantly for the safety of all humanity."

"What the *fuck*?" Clay sputtered.

Her mouth tightened.

"Um, apologies, but..." Niko tried for a polite smile, though it couldn't hide his worry. "Might we know what you have in there?"

Not responding, the woman nodded to the young man. He opened the box and reached inside. I braced myself for magic to lash out at us.

He extended his hand. A bulb of garlic rested in his palm.

"Wait, what?" Clay laughed. "Garlic. You want us to touch... garlic."

"Oh, dear," Casimir murmured.

My eyes darted to him.

"Draw upon your magic," he continued to me in the same low voice, his lips barely moving and his gaze never leaving the Aneirans. "I will do the same to help us both."

I had a thousand questions, and I couldn't ask a single one, not without the woman and the guards noticing.

But I started scrambling inside myself for any trace of magic I could reach. It was too much to hope I could grip the diamond pendant that now rested beneath the sweater Clay had fashioned for me to replace the massive one belonging to Ozias. Such a motion would undoubtedly make the Aneirans think I was trying to get away with something.

One by one, the young man extended the garlic bulb to my men, who took it briefly and then returned it, each of them giving him a baffled or wary expression when they were done.

Except for Byron. He lifted the bulb and then returned it, and when the Aneirans approached me, every line of his body was tense.

Just as I feared, the woman caught it. "You worry the princess or her companion will fail this test?" At her words, several of the guards put their hands to their weapons. "Why?"

"I fear any test with such a seemingly subjective outcome." Byron's voice was cool and analytical, but even though I'd only known him a few weeks, something about his tightly controlled expression made me suspect his tone wasn't really the truth.

No, the scholar was as on edge as I'd ever seen him.

"Trust me when I say there is nothing *subjective* here," the woman replied.

She jerked her chin at me in a wordless motion for me to take the bulb. Nervously, I reached out for it, still struggling to draw up any magic inside, though what the hell I was supposed to do with it, I didn't know.

Casimir's fingers dug into my back. His grip was hard, nearly painful with his tension, but instantly a warm and soothing sensation spread from his touch like golden light shining just beyond the corners of my eyes. None of the Aneirans reacted, as if they couldn't see anything at all.

My hand closed around the bulb.

A biting sensation pricked at my palm like I'd wrapped my fingers around a ball of acid-laced thorns. But before I could react, the pain faded, swallowed up in that golden warmth like a balm of soothing honey had slipped between me and the bulb.

Carefully, I lifted my eyes to the woman and her companions. "Satisfied?" I asked, my voice meticulously calm.

The woman jerked her chin at Casimir. "Him next."

"Indeed." Casimir took the bulb from me, holding it and arching his eyebrow at the woman as if implying the same question I'd asked.

Her jaw clenched, and then she glanced at Ruhl. "Press it to the dog."

Silence reigned for a heartbeat.

"Ruhl," Casimir snapped without taking his hand from my back.

The wolf circled to his side. Casimir lowered the bulb down, resting it briefly on Ruhl's fur and then removing it.

"May I return the produce now?" he asked coldly.

The woman's expression hardened, but she nodded.

"I assume that means we passed your inspection," Dex said as Casimir placed the bulb back inside the wooden box.

Her eyes scanned us, and she gave no sign of noticing that even now, Casimir's magic still pulsed through the contact he maintained with my back. "You are permitted entry to Duteliera."

"Wonderful," Clay replied, and only a fool would have missed the sarcasm in his tone.

Her gaze snapped to him angrily. "That test has saved countless lives. It is the reason Duteliera still stands when numerous other cities have fallen. You would do well to respect our ways. They might just save your life too."

"What exactly does this test prove?" Lars asked.

The woman merely gestured for the guards to return to the city. "It is not safe to remain outside the walls for long."

With that, she turned and strode back toward the gate, leaving us to follow.

"Here," Byron said, pulling out a scrap of cloth from his bag. He headed immediately to me and Casimir, an urgent look on his face that, with his back turned, the Aneirans wouldn't see. Placing the rag on my palm, he clasped my hand briefly and murmured something under his breath.

A cool sensation swept my palm as he pulled the cloth away.

Casimir removed his hand from my back and took the cloth, waiting a heartbeat for the scholar to murmur the words again.

"Thank you," Casimir said, his voice soft but sincere.

Byron gave a small nod and then glanced at Ruhl. "If I may?"

I couldn't tell if he was asking Casimir or Ruhl himself, but the wolf paused long enough to allow Byron to wipe the rag over the place on his fur where the garlic had touched.

Ruhl gave a little shake when the scholar finished, but only as if he was rearranging his fur to his liking rather than experiencing any discomfort.

Quickly, Byron made his way around the group, offering the rag to all of the men and giving the Aneirans a tight smile when they glanced back.

"What?" Clay asked them. "You expect us to go around smelling like garlic all day?"

One of the guards' eyes narrowed. I held my breath, bracing myself—but for what, I wasn't sure. We'd passed. Whatever the hell this test was, we'd passed.

"Don't stall," the man warned. "You don't want to be out here if anything comes over those hills." Without another word, he hurried after the woman and the rest of the guards.

Uneasy looks passed between my men.

"Well," Clay said tightly. "That's ominous as fuck."

Dex twitched his chin in a motion for us to get going. "Best we listen to them." His eyes flicked back to where Byron was tucking away the rag, and then over to me and Casimir. "Just in case."

15
DEX

It had been years since I'd been surrounded by this many armed Aneirans, and back then, they'd all been debating whether to kill me. I'd just revealed myself as an Erenlian, even if I looked more like a human than one of my own kind. I'd tried to stop them from slaughtering a village of nothing but women and children, and the gods knew that had all gone horrifically.

I wasn't sure this would go any differently, not if these people learned the truth about us.

All of us.

I kept myself from glancing back toward the princess, if only to avoid heightening any suspicion in the Aneirans watching us. That they were not trained soldiers was clear. They didn't hold their weapons correctly, and their body language wasn't quite right. They were tense because they were nervous, not because they were readying themselves to strike.

Which wasn't to say I would let my guard down.

Frightened people with weapons could be infinitely more dangerous than a trained soldier any day. For the gods' sakes, one of the Aneirans on the wall had even shot at us by accident.

And now we were walking into a whole city full of them.

My teeth ground, and I stilled the reaction with effort. Gwyneira wasn't wrong that we needed help if we were going to take back her throne, stop the Voidborn and possibly her stepmother, and ultimately free the giants from their imprisonment too. Up against those odds, I wanted nothing short of a damned army.

But this... gods, it was not that.

My eyes flicked across the guards atop the wall as we started through the gate, and the pit in my stomach grew deeper. Old people with battered helmets. Young ones too, their grips bloodless on their swords and spears. There were no children to be seen, but I suspected everyone old enough to hold a weapon had been conscripted to fight.

What in the hell was going on in Aneira?

I kept walking, even though everything around me felt like a march to the hangman's noose. And that feeling only grew as the gates closed at our backs. These were the people you called up when all hope was lost. When there was no choice but to fight because everyone else who could have protected you was gone.

But I knew better than anyone the size and might of the Aneiran army. If they were not here, it could only be for a truly terrible reason, and I could think of precious few options for what that might be.

Another nation had chosen to invade in a perceived moment of weakness.

An internal uprising had swept the nation, tearing it to pieces.

Or the Voidborn.

I knew where I'd place my money.

The crowd parted ahead, revealing Lord Thomas as he approached. I remembered him—or at least the stories. The Lord of Sinaria had been late to join the war, and for a short time, that had caused private murmurs of derision among the ranks. But then he'd personally turned the tide of battle at the Azure Pass and ridden to the rescue of a hundred Aneiran soldiers trapped in the Elorian Gulch, to say nothing of the victories he'd racked up across great swaths of Erenelle itself.

The man was an Aneiran war hero. He should have a garrison supporting him, not this ragtag collection of civilians. And here we were, aiming to ask him and his army of farmers to help us retake Gwyneira's throne and free all the prisoners he'd helped lock away.

Gods, this was a mad and desperate plan.

For a long moment, the lord regarded us with an unreadable look in his dark eyes. I kept my expression calm and nonthreatening, though I knew how we must appear. Seven armed men who would rival the height of the tallest human males, with muscles built by mining and survival. Weapons upon every one of us and bearings like we could use them. Even Niko knew well how to defend himself—of that, I'd made damn sure over the years—and although Casimir wasn't as tall as us, the vampire radiated the cool calm of someone who knew down to his bones that you weren't a threat, because he could kill you before you could land a single blow.

And at the center of us stood the princess, every bit as regal and powerful as the queen she would rightfully be. There was an otherworldliness to her beauty. A stillness to her even when she breathed, like pristine snow lying on a steep mountainside.

Like that snow, if she unleashed her power, no one would stand in her way.

Whatever he saw, Lord Thomas's voice gave nothing away when he finally said, "What business does the disgraced princess of Aneira have with us today?"

Outrage rolled through me, along with the overwhelming urge to punch the man who spoke like that to my treluria, and I knew I wasn't alone. I could practically feel the fury pouring off my friends at my back. Only the fact I'd spent years among the Aneirans and honed the skill of not reacting to their offhand comments about my own people meant I had the control to restrain myself.

But I still gritted out, "There is nothing *disgraced* about Princess Gwyneira."

Lord Thomas's brow arched. The urge to punch him grew stronger, especially when he turned his attention back to the princess as if I hadn't spoken at all. "You are accused of murdering our beloved king," he said, his voice pitched so all the crowd could hear. "Of poisoning him like a coward and seeking to do the same to your stepmother too. What say you?"

I cast a quick look back at Gwyneira, checking on her reaction to this verbal assault, and then I paused. There was no fear in her eyes. No weakness or hurt in the face of his questions. She stood before the crowd and this arrogant bastard like every inch of the ground upon which our feet rested and even the air itself was hers, unquestionably.

But not in a vain or cruel way. Not as if we were usurpers breathing her air or pests upon her soil. No, only as if nothing the lord said or did could ever make her question her truth, her identity.

And gods, I loved her for that.

I'd never had a queen or king, I realized. Not truly. I'd served the King of Aneira as a soldier, yes, but not because I believed in him *personally*.

But Gwyneira was my queen. No other could come close. She would always hold that position, no matter the throne or the crown or our nationality.

I'd serve her and love her with all my heart and soul until the day I died.

Her voice was calm as she replied to Lord Thomas, "I say the same thing I have said since the first moment my stepmother falsely accused me. I am innocent. I would never have hurt my father, much less assassinated him. My stepmother was the one who killed him. She arranged his death and my imprisonment so that she could take the throne for herself."

Lord Thomas's gaze skimmed the crowd briefly. "You say Queen Melisandre is the guilty party?" he asked when his eyes returned to Gwyneira.

"I do."

"And your evidence?"

I would not have thought it possible, but somehow, she drew herself up even more regally. "I have my word as the daughter of the king. I have the fact she imprisoned me and ordered my execution without even a mockery of a trial. She sought to claim my father's throne and be rid of me before I could speak to any lord or lady who may have listened, and she used dark magic to silence any in the castle who might have come to my aid. It is only because these men found me after her Huntsman abandoned me in the wilderness that I am still alive to seek justice for my father, and that is what I plan to do. I *will* have justice for the king, for Aneira, and for all who have been harmed by my stepmother's actions. This I swear to you."

Her eyes never wavered from Lord Thomas, but I heard the implication nevertheless. We were included in that. Our people and all of Erenelle too.

I looked back at Lord Thomas, reading his every twitch and infinitesimal movement for his reaction. His gaze flicked across his people, a measuring look in his eyes, and suddenly, an intrigued sort of suspicion gripped me.

This had been intentional. All of it. Questioning her in front of the crowd, challenging her on precisely the questions everyone here would have. Like the skilled military leader he was, every second of this had been part of his plan.

But not necessarily to harm us, I suspected. He was a leader in a city under some unknown kind of siege, and whatever the threat they all faced that left them caged behind these walls, it was enough that every person felt the need to take up arms. Yet, between what Gwyneira had been accused of and what his people had likely heard she'd supposedly done, if he were to grant her sanctuary immediately, it would only raise questions of his commitment to their safety and thus breed more fear.

This public interrogation was a rational move on his part. I could almost respect that.

Except it still left us surrounded by hundreds of armed and terrified humans.

"You all have heard the stories," he said to the crowd. "You know why we are here. And you know that I will give my last breath to protect Aneira and every person within it." His gaze turned back to Gwyneira. "You will be given sanctuary within Duteliera. You and your allies." He offered a brief nod to me and the others. "Until such time as Aneira is safe and the Council of Lords can be convened to evaluate your claims of innocence and of your stepmother's guilt, just as they should have been granted the right to do when your father was killed." His chin rose as he called out, "This is my command. It will be obeyed."

Murmurs ran through the crowd, but numerous people nodded in agreement.

Lord Thomas surveyed them all a moment longer and then gave a brief nod to the guards around us. "Escort them to the castle. I will join them shortly."

Short responses of "yes, sir" came from the armed humans around us, and then the woman who'd led the so-called inspection gestured for us to start moving again. Lord Thomas started off into the crowd, clearing the way without making it appear as if he was actively yielding ground for us to proceed, and he never looked back once.

I could admire a fellow strategist. I could even respect

someone who clearly cared about the lives of those in his care.

It did little to reassure me of our safety, though. After all, he was still Aneiran. We were still Erenlian with a vampire princess in our care.

And I had bloody and terrible experience in how badly it could go when Aneirans discovered you were their enemy supposedly in disguise.

16

OZIAS

I stalked through the crowd, fighting the urge to bare my teeth at every armed human nearby. That they were watching us was a given.

That they dared threaten my mate was intolerable.

My beast paced restlessly within my mind, a sensation like tension ratcheting higher and higher beneath my skin, ready to explode at the slightest provocation. I hadn't felt this close to losing control in years, not since the last time someone thought to cage me.

And a cage this was. A city, yes, but that hardly made a difference. The walls, the people, the gate that had closed at our backs.

It was all just another kind of cage, and this time, I was trapped inside it with my mate.

A new sensation suddenly passed through me, like a cool and comforting hand stroking the beast in my mind, calming it, murmuring words without sound to reduce its rage. I tensed, startled, and at my reaction, the sensation paused as well.

My eyes darted to Gwyneira. At my glance, a flicker of fear passed through her gaze for the first time since we set foot in this place.

The mate bond.

At the realization, gratitude and wonder and a white-hot burning feeling filled me—the last of which took me a moment to place.

Love.

Love for her, for this, for what she'd been doing even though, of the two of us, reaching through that bond should have been more natural for me than it ever could have felt for her. But nevertheless, here she was, surrounded by potential enemies and countless humans filled with fear, and still she sought to comfort *me*.

A tiny smile lifted the corner of her lips. She'd picked up what I was feeling now, and her pleasure at it was like a brush of sunlight across my mind.

The cool, comforting sensation of a calming hand upon my beast's fur returned.

A shudder rolled through me as my tension eased. It was by no means gone—it wouldn't be until we were far from this place and my mate was safe somewhere, prefer-ably with my cock buried deep inside her—but I could think more clearly now than I had in quite some time.

Gods, I would never cease to be filled by awe at this. At her. At the bond she'd accepted between us and at the reality of how it felt to be connected to her in this way. None of the stories I'd heard did it justice, when they weren't just flat-out wrong. No, I wasn't a shifter like those in the tales I'd managed to overhear on my travels. Humans around campfires made shifters sound like people who donned animal skins and howled at the moon because they were insane. Meanwhile, on one of the rare occasions when a traveling merchant had managed to cage me for a short time, he'd only spun tales of horror, rhapsodizing to the crowds who came to see the "monster" about all the madness and nightmarish torments I'd inflict upon a mate.

Yet deep inside, my instincts had whispered something else. Something that turned to a roar of need when I met Gwyneira. Something that swore the bond wasn't terrible, no matter what those people claimed.

I'd been just enough of a bastard not to resist that call, and now, I'd worship my beautiful mate every day in gratitude that she gave me this wondrous gift.

Her smile remained as she turned her attention back to the crowds and the castle we now approached, and resolutely, I did the same. The structure wasn't as large as the one in Aneira, but in the eyes of humans who enjoyed building stone boxes to live within, I supposed it was grand. It stood inside a smaller wall of its own, a last line of defense against anyone who breached the outer wall of the city. Enormous blocks of granite formed its sides, stretching up three stories with vertical slits for windows higher up, likely so as to offer opportunities to shoot at invaders along with some measure of air circulation and daylight. The roof was gray slate barely darker than the stone itself, and all the color came from the bright blue banners hanging on the walls. White thread embroidery gleamed in the sunlight on each, the patterns alternating between the royal tree of Aneira and a scythe and shepherd's crook that were likely the symbols of this rural province.

That the latter two were also weapons didn't escape my notice.

The dark wooden gates of the castle swung open as we approached, and servants hurried outside, eyeing us curiously but with remarkably less fear than I'd seen on most of the armed people in the city. Perhaps they assumed that, since we'd made it this far with an escort, we were meant to be here.

Perhaps it was a trick to get us to let down our guard.

Although the soothing sensations from Gwyneira continued, I could tell she was on edge too as we trailed the servants into the castle. How this would all go was unknown, from whether this Lord Thomas would actually help her on down to what aid a bunch of scared humans could even be against anyone who tried to stop Gwyneira from taking back her throne.

My beast pushed at me again, determined to handle any threat against my mate with my claws and my fangs. And gods, it was tempting.

Except even that wasn't enough to stop the Voidborn.

Another shudder passed through me. There were too many threats to her. Too many, and alone, I wouldn't be enough to stop them all. Even with the help of these men with whom my beast and I shared her, we couldn't fight a war on two fronts.

We needed the humans.

Gods, how that rankled.

"This way, please," said an elderly man with short-cropped white hair and wrinkled skin so pale as to be nearly translucent. He wore black livery trimmed in the same shade of bright blue as on the banners, and though his back was stooped by age, he still bore an aura of command, as if he was the alpha of this domain.

He cast short glances back at us as we followed him through the dark entryway. I bit back the urge to snarl when it took a moment for my eyes to adjust to the shadowy interior of the castle after the bright daylight outside.

"My name is Forian," he said as he walked. "Head of household matters. I've served his lordship's family for over seventy-five years. Anything you require, please ask and, as long as it is within the realm of his lordship's wishes, I'll see it done."

"Thank you," Gwyneira replied.

He bowed his head without ever breaking stride. "You will wait for his lordship in the south library. Lord Thomas recalled you enjoyed reading, Princess Gwyneira. He thought it would be a pleasant place to speak privately."

My eyes narrowed. Was this another trick to make us relax our guard? Take us unawares?

Never mind that I wasn't comfortable with books. Or reading. Or all the squiggly shapes like spiders on a page.

I didn't care for spiders, and thus I didn't care for books.

But she did.

Discomfort tangled like a thorny ball in my chest as we continued into the damnable library and even the worried curiosity coming from my mate couldn't dissipate it. It wasn't that I disliked stories. Quite the opposite. I'd crept close to campfires specifically because I enjoyed the tales people wove for one another while they sat around the flames at night. Even if I knew they'd run in terror if they ever actually saw me near their fires, just listening to them tell each other stories had made me feel less alone.

Hell, it was why I was here. I'd snuck near to the fire Dex and the others set one night, not realizing they had magic that would whisper I was there.

I wouldn't have these friends if not for stories.

But that wasn't the same as *reading*.

"There are refreshments on the table and drinks at the bar along the wall," Forian said, gesturing to each respectively. "If you need anything, please ring the bell by the door and I'll return promptly."

With a nod and a precisely polite smile, he stepped backward out the door and then turned to leave as another servant swung it closed behind him.

Leaving us all alone in here.

"So, um…" Niko back at the door nervously, keeping his voice low. "You all saw how there's only a few *actual* soldiers here, right?"

Dex's jaw muscles jumped, and I didn't bother to respond. The answer was obvious.

"They could be fighting the Voidborn," Lars offered.

"Dying because of the Voidborn, you mean," Clay replied.

Lars cast him an exasperated look, and Clay made a confused gesture in response.

"Would Lord Thomas have stayed behind if his

soldiers were sent to war?" Casimir asked, directing the question primarily to Gwyneira.

Her brow rose and fell. "I-I wouldn't have thought so, but if the threat was here as well as wherever the soldiers might be... Perhaps yes?"

"He may have wanted to coordinate the defense here while his soldiers aid whatever battle is happening elsewhere," Dex added.

That didn't bode well, and I was obviously not the only one who thought so. Uneasy looks flashed over more than a few faces.

"Well, on that cheery note," Clay said. "Anyone want a drink?"

Without waiting for an answer, he started for the bar only to pause when he reached it, not moving to take up any of the bottles. My eyes narrowed, but my confusion cleared a moment later when he turned away from the drinks with a muttered comment of, "Or you could stay focused, idiot," that was so soft, only my ears and possibly the vampires' could have picked it up.

The strain of all this was not only getting to me.

I felt Gwyneira moving behind me a moment before her delicate hand took mine and squeezed briefly before slipping away again. A wave of reassurance came from her, and my tension melted at it. But remorse filled me soon after. I should be comforting and supporting her, not the other way around.

Confusion flickered over her face when I turned to her. "What?" she whispered.

I searched for a way to explain that wouldn't give away hints of the bond we now shared.

And the door opened before the words presented themselves.

Propriety fell like a mask over my mate's face and without a trace of anything but polite patience in her body language, she turned as Lord Thomas walked through the doorway, the woman who'd conducted the so-called *inspection* on his heels. Even Gwyneira's scent was calm as she watched them—a feat that would have thrown me if not for the years of royal training I suspected were at play.

Gods, she was born to be a queen.

"Apologies for the delay, princess," Lord Thomas said when the door closed behind him, leaving him in the room with only the brunette woman at his side. "This is Valeria, my personal bodyguard."

My nose twitched. No, she was more than that. Not a mate, exactly. But his scent was too pervasive on her for the woman to be merely a bodyguard.

"No need to apologize," Gwyneira replied. "We were simply admiring your library."

He smiled as if pleased by the praise. "If there's time, I'll have to show you the northern library as well. It has several volumes your father gifted to me."

Pain radiated through my connection to Gwyneira, though she only smiled calmly in return. "I would like that," she said evenly. "And may I introduce my allies?" One by one, she went around, giving our names calmly, as if we were no more than acquaintances she'd met along the road. The tone would have worried me, had I not understood why she used it.

She was protecting us. Herself as well. Tension

tangled deep inside her no matter how outwardly calm she appeared. And despite even her best efforts, I could still see the assessing way Lord Thomas and his supposed bodyguard eyed us the entire time.

They likely wondered what she'd needed to do in order to secure the assistance of eight male strangers such as ourselves, but they were too tied by their Aneiran sensibilities to ask.

I was glad. I wouldn't tolerate them looking down upon my mate for making her own choices, even if they didn't agree with them. No one would put *her* in a cage.

This gods-damned place aside.

Valeria's gaze snapped to me, though I knew I hadn't made a sound. She'd noticed my tension, I suspected. I met her eyes, knowing that to do so was a challenge.

I didn't care. I wouldn't back down. Human or not, a predator was still a predator.

"It's a pleasure to meet you all," Lord Thomas said when Gwyneira was finished with the introductions. "Thank you for assisting our princess."

A few of the others nodded. I didn't, and neither did Roan nor Clay. The former lurked as far from the humans and everyone else as he could, while the latter looked like he couldn't decide whether to crack a joke or demand we leave.

Clay clearly couldn't relax here. And Roan...

I pulled my attention back to the humans. Roan was a question mark. I just wasn't sure what the actual question was yet.

"It was our honor," Casimir replied to the lord, the regal etiquette with which he carried himself even more in evidence now. I hadn't realized until this moment how much he'd relaxed around us since we first met him. "And may I express our gratitude for the shelter you offer the princess and ourselves as well?"

Lord Thomas inclined his head slightly, a measured bit of body language like one would give to a stranger who was also a subordinate.

Human perceptions were so strange. Even setting aside Casimir's actual rank as king of Zenirya—not that the lord knew that—the vampire's bearing alone should have made his station clear. But humans rarely comprehended such things, if they even saw them at all.

"Why *did* you give us shelter, Lord Thomas?" Gwyneira asked carefully. "Truly?"

He was quiet for a moment, as if weighing his words, and I could hear I wasn't the only one who ceased breathing while we waited for what he would say.

"I've lived long enough to know that people can surprise you, princess," he said. "That they are sometimes capable of wrongs you would have never imagined they'd commit. But even with that in mind, I have also known you since you were an infant, and I haven't maintained my position all these years without being a decent judge of character. I saw the love you had for your father. It would defy my very understanding of sanity itself if you had actually killed him."

Gwyneira swallowed hard, but that slight crack in her composure was nothing compared to the anguished tumult of emotion I could feel through my connection to my mate. She'd never let on how much it pained her, the fact her own people might truly believe she killed her father. That they thought she hadn't loved him but instead had only seen him as a step between herself and a throne she hadn't been patient enough to wait to ascend.

Gods, I wanted to reach for her now. From a few of the faces around the room, I suspected several of my friends felt the same.

"Moreover," Lord Thomas continued. "The events following your father's death never sat right with me. If you had escaped like the queen claimed, then why in the world would you flee to the mountains where, rumor has it, she sent her Huntsmen to search? Your father was determined that you learn strategy and tactics. By all accounts, you learned them well. Yet rather than seek aid from me or any other lord who might have been your ally, you chose to escape to the barren wilderness in the depths of winter?" His head shook. "That is not where someone goes who is seeking to survive. That's where someone is *sent* if you wish to be rid of them."

My mate's head twitched in a small nod. "Indeed."

"I meant what I said to my people. I will see there be a trial, if for no other reason than to put to rest any doubts that you are wholly innocent. The people will need that, princess. The other lords will too."

Casimir gave the man a coolly appraising look. "I take it not all of your brethren believe she is innocent, then."

It was hardly a question, and the grim expression on Lord Thomas's face was more than enough answer besides. "There are those who are more opportunistic than what is perhaps in the best interests of their people."

"They want the throne for themselves," Casimir filled in dryly.

"So it would seem."

My jaw clenched. Humans talked around things rather than cutting right to the core of them, which meant his answer could be interpreted any number of ways. But I, on the other hand, didn't give a damn.

My mate deserved the throne, not only because she'd been born to have it but because she would be the kind of ruler Aneira needed if this damned nation ever wanted to reclaim its soul. They'd been a crazed and rabid predator for years. She could help them heal and find a different road.

But not if power-hungry lords got there first.

"Lord Thomas," Gwyneira asked, and I could feel how her words were meticulously chosen. "What is happening here? Is there a coup? An invasion? Every person we've encountered on our travels has run from us, and long before they could have identified who we were. From what we've seen, all your people are seeking sanctuary behind the city walls. And we needed to pass inspection with *garlic* to enter? What in the world has become of Sinaria?"

The lord's mouth tightened. "It is not just Sinaria, princess."

Dread filled my mate. She had feared that. So had I.

"For several weeks now, we've had reports of attacks at night by forces unseen. Shepherds and farmers found dead in the fields, drained of blood with barely a mark on them. Messages received from other parts of Aneira suggested we were not the only province with this strange issue. I ordered a curfew and sent word to the capital requesting aid in addressing whatever was threatening my people, and for a time, this seemed to stem the tide of the issue.

"But the response I received from Lumilia meant things were worse than I imagined. Reports from the lords at the capital said it appeared an army was approaching from the north, but one unlike anything we've ever seen. The forces were, for lack of a better term... not human."

Uneasy looks passed between several of my friends.

"Out of an abundance of caution, the lords asked all the provinces to send their soldiers to stop what they assumed was the source of the attacks we'd suffered. Preliminary efforts to destabilize Aneira ahead of an invasion and all that. And while we hoped the Warden Wall would stop their main force, given the attacks on the populace and the fact these enemies were not like ones we'd faced before, the lords could not be sure the creatures hadn't found a way to breach the wall already. Thus, every able-bodied soldier was needed."

Lord Thomas sighed. "Of course, Sinaria complied. I sent my soldiers north with great haste, and I fully intended to join them after putting precautions in place to protect my people while I was gone. It seemed the best plan to end what may well have been the origin of these strange attacks. But then the wall fell."

Valeria made a small movement beside him, like a repressed shudder at the words.

"Word of the destruction of the wall was followed shortly by tales of some new threat. People weren't simply being drained of blood anymore. Now they were vanishing entirely with only piles of dust and crumbling bones left where they'd stood, if anything remained at all. Soon after that, even stranger reports reached me. Farmers and shepherds were returning to their villages *changed.* Colder. Crueler. They would walk back to their homes without a word to anyone, and then the screams would begin. Villagers who escaped said those people would emerge from their homes covered in blood, sometimes with all their family dead behind them, sometimes with only a few killed. But whoever they spared within their homes had become like them—cold and strange and every bit as vicious. And then the killing would spread."

Lord Thomas shook his head, clearly disturbed even to recount the stories. "No one knows what creature or infection is causing this. Some speak of a magical curse. Others fear that the queen herself might be infected because she hasn't come forward to stop it. I cannot even be certain any longer that the messengers I send to the lords at Lumilia or our own soldiers are making it through without being killed. To make matters worse, the stories we've received from survivors are jumbled and confusing. Some tell of seeing an eerie glow in the attackers' eyes, as if they were taken over by magic. Others say they saw a shifting shadow pass over the attackers' skin when they would touch someone, and then that next person would become like them, as if whatever had been inside the first person now possessed another as well. But among the few survivors, a handful brought us a tale of fleeing through a market, chased by the possessed, and witnessing them recoil from a scattered cart of garlic as if burned."

He chuckled humorlessly. "It seemed absurd, to be

honest, but to comfort the populace, I ordered inspections. And to my great shock, it worked. A pair of travelers came to us two days later, and the moment the inspectors approached, the man changed. His eyes glowed as bright yellow as a bumblebee. His body convulsed as if something within him was trying to escape." A grim look crossed the lord's face. "He killed two of my people before he was put down. The guards swear they heard something *unnatural* in his screams as he died."

"Like metal in your brain," Valeria murmured, speaking up for the first time. A sickened look tinged her reserved expression.

Lord Thomas nodded. "Whatever poison or curse has been inflicted upon our land, it is allowing the infected to spread it to anyone they touch—if they don't just kill you outright. This is why you saw people in the fields running from you. This is why every person within the city walls is armed to defend themselves." The grim look on his face deepened. "I'm sorry, princess, but no one you might encounter beyond these walls is safe now."

17
GWYNEIRA

I stared at Lord Thomas, my mind racing as I tried to figure out what to say. This was the Voidborn. It had to be. Even if I didn't know what the glowing eyes meant, the shadows on people's skin were too similar to those creatures' presences in this world to be mere coincidence.

But how could I tell him that and not give away everything else that was too dangerous for him to know?

Like what I was now.

What my men were.

"Holy shit," Clay whispered.

Murmurs of agreement passed through my men.

I couldn't bring myself to make a sound. *Not* telling Lord Thomas about the Voidborn was dangerous too. In the absence of information, people were infinitely more likely to create explanations of their own. Every sentient being used stories to make sense of the world. Even at times when we didn't have all the information, we'd still make up a story of our own to explain the situation we found ourselves in.

My stepmother knew that. To explain away murdering my mother, she'd crafted a story about Erenlian assassins. To prevent me from learning magic, she'd concocted a story to claim how proximity to it would drive me insane.

We clung to stories. And without knowledge of the Voidborn, how long would it take Lord Thomas's people to seek out some other story, one that would ultimately only pin an innocent party with the blame?

"The enemy you face is called the Voidborn," I said.

Lord Thomas gave me an alarmed look. At his side, Valeria appeared equally startled. He'd called her a bodyguard, but for some reason, I suspected she was more. I didn't miss the way her body turned slightly toward him with her reaction, as if she was seeking to comfort him as much as protect him.

"They come from a place known as the empty realms," I continued. "It is a region that lies beyond this or any other reality, and their sole goal is to destroy reality itself."

"How do you know this?" Lord Thomas asked.

I tensed, but the only way around the answer was to lie, and that would only cause more problems.

But I couldn't yet trust that he would continue offering me sanctuary if I told him too many impossible things. That I hadn't killed my father was one thing.

That my stepmother was a vampire and had turned me into one too? Entirely something else.

"Because," I said carefully, "after these men saved me,

my stepmother chased us. We fled deeper into the moun-tains, where we were saved." I braced myself. "By witches."

"*Witches*?" Valeria snapped incredulously.

"Princess..." Lord Thomas started in a doubtful tone.

I hid a grimace. My people had such a strange rela-tionship with magic. Yes, they let my stepmother's power protect them with the wall and the various weapons and tools she'd helped fashion in the war and beyond. But that didn't mean they trusted magic or anyone who used it—besides my stepmother, anyway, and only because my father ordered it. The Witch War had created the Wild Lands, and Melisandre's story that madness would affect my father and I if we saw her spellwork had spread far beyond the castle, until many of my people believed that the entire enterprise was suspect at best—and that most witches were too.

"They helped us," I said. "Protected us at great risk to themselves. But it's not only because of their stories that I know this. It's because we've encountered the Voidborn too."

"Did you happen to receive reports of earthquakes approximately a week ago?" Casimir asked.

Lord Thomas nodded carefully. "A few farmers to the west said there were tremors, though we assumed they were a precursor to the wall falling." He eyed us all. "Were those caused by these Voidborn you speak of?"

I nodded. "The Voidborn briefly succeeded in forcing their way into our world. We managed to escape them, but only barely."

Distrust flashed across Valeria's face and she shifted

her weight slightly as if preparing to put herself between us and Lord Thomas. At the motion, the lord glanced her way.

"They passed the inspection," he reminded her, more gently than one would normally speak to a subordinate.

She barely seemed mollified.

"At the time we saw them," Casimir continued, "very nearly anything they touched turned to ash. Plants, animals. It scarcely seemed to make a difference to those creatures."

I held myself still, keeping my eyes on Lord Thomas and Valeria. I wouldn't let on that there was an important exception to what Casimir said about creatures with which the Voidborn came into contact.

Namely, vampires.

"Clearly, they've gained a new skill then," Lord Thomas replied grimly, giving no indication he noticed anything amiss from me.

"How do we kill them?" Valeria asked coldly.

I glanced at my men, all of whom looked uncomfortable. Barring Clay's small outburst, not a single one of the giants had said a word this entire time, and I could only assume it was out of a desire not to draw undue attention to themselves.

Or raise questions about exactly who—or what—they were.

"Thus far," Casimir said, continuing the pattern of being the one to speak for them. "We have only found sunlight to be effective. When we were fleeing them, they could not last long in the sun." He paused for a moment.

"This may be why they've taken to sheltering inside humans."

"Protection so they can continue their invasion," Lord Thomas filled in.

Casimir nodded.

I suppressed a shiver as silence took up residence in the room. Humans possessed by the Voidborn became vicious killers. And when I was touched by those creatures, I'd become much the same.

But I'd come back. And thus, what of the possessed humans? Could we save them too somehow?

Gods, how many were out there now, possessed by these creatures and committing who knew what kinds of atrocities?

"It's getting late," Lord Thomas said, "and undoubtedly you wish to rest after your travels. I've asked Forian to prepare rooms for you all. I trust you'll understand if I have dinner sent to you rather than hosting you in the grand hall as would befit your station, princess."

I could hear all the layers of complications his polite words covered. Not only was his city under siege, but his people were likely stressed by our presence and the crimes of which I'd been accused. Hosting us for a formal dinner was not only inappropriate in general but would make his words about a trial to determine my guilt appear only for show.

And that wasn't even bringing into it all the issues he didn't know about, like the fact I didn't exactly eat *food* anymore.

"Of course," I replied.

A measure of tension eased from his face. "Thank you, princess."

I nodded.

"Forian should be outside waiting to take you to your rooms, then. Additionally, it may comfort you to know that we have guards patrolling both the city streets and the halls of the castle at night. They each carry a small inspection kit of their own and are under instructions to test anyone they see moving about at night."

Dread sank over me. I worked to give no sign. "What a relief."

Lord Thomas nodded. "Nothing touched by those Voidborn creatures will stay safe for long in Duteliera, princess. On that, you have my word."

I made myself smile and nod in return, silently praying that—at least where Casimir and I were concerned—that wasn't *entirely* true.

18

MELISANDRE

I had never doubted my own perception of the world. Until now.

Places came and went in flashes, interspersed by Alaric's taunting. Faces appeared in front of me like swiftly turning pages in an illuminated book—screaming villagers became dying soldiers, became a weeping old woman, became a farmer coming to find out what caused a ruckus among his livestock. I smelled their blood. Tasted the barest hint of it.

And then they would vanish and something else would take their place.

I refused to keep demanding an explanation. I was no frightened child begging for answers in the dark. I was a queen, and I would see Alaric writhe and die in screaming torment for doing this to me.

As soon as I determined what exactly he'd done.

I staggered as the ground lurched beneath my feet again. My limbs ached, and swaths of dried bloodstains now marred the faded blue velvet of my dress. None of it had been present seconds ago—though from the fact the sun was currently sinking below the horizon, the time that just passed had been much longer than mere seconds. An entire day, at a minimum. Possibly more.

An eye-blink ago, the world had been swallowed in the depths of night, and yet now the sun was setting.

Shudders coursed through me, and I suppressed them ruthlessly. Alaric was nowhere to be seen, not that *that* meant anything. But the monsters were still everywhere, lounging in the tall grass or drinking from the river nearby. I wagered there were fewer than before, but now human soldiers were among them too—an alarming sight. Their eyes glowed like the Voidborn and their expressions were twisted with a cruelty that matched those vicious creatures too. Beyond them all, mountains lurked on the horizon like jagged teeth, so far away they were barely more than a shadow against the edge of the evening sky.

I couldn't tell at this distance, but they may have been the ones near Lumilia.

My heart began pounding harder. The closer we came to the capital, the more chance I might get to stop this madness. Alaric wanted to shatter the nexus there, yet every time he'd done that previously, he had needed my power—which had offered me a brief moment where his grip upon me weakened. And that had been when we stood in places I didn't control.

But Lumilia was *my* territory. My Huntsmen waited there. My vampires too. The castle itself would try to resist me, just as that damned stone edifice always had.

Its stones had once been soaked by Queen Eira's dying blood, and it had spent the nearly twenty years since trying to warn its precious little Gwyneira about me—not that she ever realized what it was doing. But perhaps that damned pile of rocks would see Alaric's presence as an even greater threat.

I was not above twisting its self-righteous intentions to my own end, especially when it would mean I could escape this wretched situation.

"See something you like, pet?"

I did not flinch at the sudden sound of Alaric's voice. I did not gasp or retreat. That foul bastard would not see me react with terror.

Though when I turned, none of my self-control stopped him from grinning at me like he'd won a victory anyway.

By the gods, I would relish watching him die.

"I take it you wish to converse now," I said coldly.

His brow arched. "Angry, pet?"

I refused to dignify that with a response.

Alaric chuckled. "Considering you tried to destroy me —and after all I've done for you, I might add—I find it amusing that you think *you* have the moral high ground."

Death was too good for him.

"Where are we?" I demanded.

He shrugged like it made no difference. "In your silly little nation, same as before. We've been enjoying ourselves for several days now. Seems your people possessed an army they thought to use to stop us. It's been quite entertaining to destroy them and then burn every village in our path to the ground."

That was what the flashes had been, then. And why the humans were here too.

Unease stirred within me, and I squashed it down. The villagers I cared nothing about. Peasants were nearly useless beyond being a marginally satisfying meal. But the army gave me pause.

I should have known those idiotic lords would send soldiers when word reached them of this horde. Never mind that those had been *my* soldiers, and I'd planned quite another purpose for them besides dying at the claws of monsters or being possessed by the Voidborn.

Fools.

There was nothing for it now, though. I would simply need to conscript more soldiers. I'd had years to convince the humans they needed to raise arms against a far-off threat, and the immediacy of what the Voidborn had just done would only make it easier to gather up humans ready to fight.

I just needed to reach the capital and reclaim my throne first.

Locking my eyes on the horizon, I adopted a tone of boredom, as if my words meant little to me. "You realize every second we delay grants my stepdaughter a greater chance of returning to Lumilia ahead of us."

Alaric scoffed.

"She may even be planning to take control of the nexus herself," I persisted in the same tone. "She was surrounded by witches, last I saw her. They may have instructed her to do such a thing, and she would likely obey, simpering little follower that she is."

Never mind that the thought of coming near magic would have likely scared her witless.

Or that it *should* have, anyway.

I exhaled slowly, maintaining my neutral expression. Gwyneira was not a witch. Whatever power I'd felt on the breeze days ago, whatever whispers of *the Nine* that had carried on it, I refused to believe that girl was anything but an insufferable brat I would happily kill for putting me in this position instead of dying when I'd intended her to.

"You wish me to hurry onward to your city, pet? I didn't realize you relished the thought of its destruction this much."

Lumilia wouldn't burn or fall. Alaric would die first.

And thus I merely arched an eyebrow at him. "I wish to see my stepdaughter destroyed. You know this."

His lip twitched. "Indeed, I do."

Seconds crept by. The ground did not lurch and the sun did not jump in the sky. Instead, the great ball of flame merely continued its descent below the horizon, slowly plunging the world into darkness.

My teeth ground, and I stilled them with effort. He was doing this on purpose. He wanted to keep me on edge. To make me ask why he hadn't yet tried to toy with my awareness again.

Something stirred in the dark field beyond where the monsters rested. My night vision traced the tall blades of grass in silver as they moved in a way they wouldn't if the wind were solely responsible.

"Ah, at last," Alaric said. "They really are so slow, these creations of yours."

That drew my eyes to him. "*My* creations?"

"Well, *ours*, obviously." He nodded to the monsters, clearly including the Voidborn within them in that term, not me. "But you had a minor hand in it too, considering you chose these from among the rabble to be the ones you turned."

Four vampires shifted into solid form in front of us. They all dropped to a knee before me and bowed their heads.

I glanced from them to Alaric and back. They *were* four of mine. A maid who'd failed to choose a flattering dress for me one morning, two stablehands who'd been too slow to stop a horse from panicking in my presence —nearly resulting in the disgusting creature kicking me —and a nobleman I'd once heard mumble something that might have been an insult when he left my presence.

The vampires looked quite well fed, considering I'd left these four at the castle when I went after Gwyneira.

Trepidation rose on the heels of that observation, and it wasn't solely for the fact I had not summoned these creatures here. If they had drained everyone in the castle, that could present a problem for filling the ranks of my own vampire army, considering the humans I would have turned would now be dead.

"Why are you here?" I demanded. "How did you find us?"

At their silence, Alaric chuckled. "Tell us why you're here, worms."

"Mistressss," the nobleman hissed. "We have found them."

My eyes darted from the vampires to Alaric again. Why did that one say—

"How lovely," Alaric responded.

"Found who?" I demanded. "Gwyneira?"

The vampires didn't answer me.

"I trust she's coming this way, yes?" Alaric continued.

"Indeed, Mistress," the maid replied.

My heart pounded, driven by confusion as much as rage. "Why are you—"

"Perfect," Alaric said as if I wasn't speaking at all.

Panic drummed in my chest, but I wouldn't bend to it. I let rage take its place. "You will cease this game at once!"

Ignoring me, he took a step toward my vampires.

I grabbed his elbow. "I said, you will stop—"

My hand was not visible. My arm wasn't either. I cut off with a strangled cry, looking down in alarm.

And finding nothing but empty air.

"What is this?" I demanded of Alaric. "What have you done to me?"

He ignored me completely. "Does she still only have her giants and angel with her?" he asked the vampires.

"And a wolf," one of the stablehands said. "A strange creature of smoke with eyes that glow."

"How interesting."

I started toward him, clinging to my outrage with all my might. "You will answer me!"

"What would you have us do?" the maid asked.

She wasn't looking at me.

"Stop this!" I snapped at the girl. "How dare you address him rather than your maker! You will pay with your life for this. *Again.*"

The maid never took her eyes from Alaric. "We could kill them for you."

"True." Alaric looked at the orcs. Four of them rose to their feet. "But I have something else in mind."

The orcs' bodies suddenly jerked like they'd been hit by lightning. Dark smoke erupted from them to rush across the space between the monsters and us.

My vampires didn't even have time to scream.

The smoke struck, flooding into them and making them convulse. Swiftly, the darkness vanished into their bodies, and when the last of it was gone, their shaking stilled. Gracefully, they straightened. Their eyes shone with vibrant, unnatural colors—pink like the flush of a fever, yellow like puss, putrescent green like mold. Proud, disdainful sneers now lived on their faces.

Behind them, the orcs staggered and looked around with terrified, confused expressions, like dreamers suddenly jolted from a nightmare.

The nobleman hiss-clicked something at Alaric, who chuckled again. "Oh, most definitely."

Without hesitation, the four vampires spun and tore out the orcs' throats.

Horror filled the monsters' eyes, but it was too late. Grasping at their throats as if to stop the escape of their life's blood, the monsters collapsed.

Smirking, the vampires turned back to Alaric, ignoring the monsters as they died in the dirt behind them.

Alaric tilted his head in a small nod. "Take the winged ones with you. They'll travel fastest."

"Of course." The maid's unnaturally pink gaze suddenly slid from Alaric to land on me. "*Mistress.*"

She chuckled and turned to smoke, flowing away.

I didn't move as the other three followed her. "What have you done to me?"

Alaric gave me a pitying look. "You still haven't figured it out?"

I refused to tremble. Refused to show fear. This was another one of his games. Another ploy to taunt and destabilize me, and I would not succumb to it.

"You're so proud, my pet. So determined." He gave me a condescending smile. "So delusional."

I rewarded his asinine words with a scathing look.

His pity only deepened. "You didn't survive the empty realms, pet. Not in the way you've made yourself believe. But your mind could not handle that, so you concocted this fantasy that your mind, your body, your entire being was still your own."

Never taking his eyes from me, he drew the ludicrous sword he'd taken from that young soldier we killed at the Warden Wall outpost days before. "See the truth. Your mind won't hold out much longer against these games you've made it play anyhow."

He turned the sword in his grip until the flat of the blade lay across the palm of his hand. Idly, he glanced down, and though I did not move, my vision somehow turned as if I was peering downward too.

My reflection stared back at me from the glistening surface of the blade.

Quivers shook me, radiating from deep inside, but I curled my lip in disdain all the same. "I see an illusion of a reflection that *you* must have created, for I cannot—"

"The *truth*, pet." His words echoed in my ears. "Your pretty fiction is at its end."

My head shook. I wouldn't believe his lies and twisted words. I refused. I was Queen Melisandre. I was the most powerful witch and vampire in the—

A stronger shudder coursed through me and suddenly, my reflection in the blade changed. It was still my face. Still my blond hair and flawless skin untouched by age for decades.

But sickening gold light glowed from my eyes.

19
GWYNEIRA

A city under siege was eerily silent.

One where the enemy could be anyone was even more so.

I shifted position uncomfortably on the bed. Even after bathing and changing into the nightclothes the servants had provided, I hadn't been able to stay lying down for long. The room was too cavernous, too empty. So now I sat with my legs crossed and my back to my pillows on this massive bed in the room Lord Thomas had given me, unable to sleep and silently hating everything around me.

Because none of my men were here. There'd been no way to ask if any of them could stay. Not without causing a scandal that would be certain to make every socially proper eyebrow in a hundred miles rise.

My eyes darted to the door as the whisper of footsteps came and went yet again, the guards passing by on their rotations. Thank the gods thus far none of them had tried to check on me. Without Casimir's help, I didn't want to think what would happen if they brought those garlic bulbs anywhere nearby.

But the truth was, it wasn't merely the threat of failing an inspection that worried me. I hadn't realized it until the door shut, sealing me in here, but this was the first time I'd been alone at night since I was turned into a vampire.

And I *loathed* it.

The absence of the men's warmth. The silence devoid of the soft sounds they made as they slept. The sheer emptiness of not having them with me. Every second felt like a chasm opening wider and wider all around, swallowing me in nothingness where my tiny breaths and quiet heartbeat were nearly the only sounds.

If I returned to Lumilia, would this be every night for me?

The thought was terrible. It was also likely correct. My father and stepmother had not shared a room, after all—though I wondered on some level if Melisandre had purposefully taken steps to make sure of that. I no longer had any illusions that she'd actually loved my father.

But even before that, I had no memory of hearing anyone mention whether my mother and father shared a room. There'd always just been the queen's chambers and the king's.

And that was its own problem, really. My people wouldn't accept me having multiple Erenlian lovers as well as a Zeniryan one in the first place. They'd expect me to marry some prince or duke from a politically advantageous nation. And even if I could argue that my men *were* politically advantageous, it wouldn't solve anything.

They'd still expect me to pick just one.

I rolled my shoulders with discomfort. I could find ways around that—ways that, by their very definition, would mean courting scandal rather than living out in the open with the men I loved. It would likely take years to change things enough to avoid that, though. Or an edict that would cause all manner of trouble with public opinion.

No, until I could work to shift public sentiment and gradually bring my country around to accepting different ways of loving, this cold, awful emptiness and silence might be my only bedmate for a long time.

A shadow stirred in the corner of the room. I tensed, my gaze snapping to it.

Ruhl rose from the darkness, his green eyes glowing at me.

I froze.

Even a few hours ago, the sudden appearance of the wolf wouldn't have sent the quiver of trepidation through me that it gave me now. Ruhl had saved my life enough times that I had come to accept he meant me no harm.

But that'd been before I heard Lord Thomas's description of the people possessed by the Voidborn. How their eyes glowed. How shadows like smoke moved over their skin.

Ruhl couldn't be like them... could he?

The wolf started to turn toward the wall only to pause, almost as if he'd spotted my tension and it confused him.

"Why are you here?" I asked softly, holding my voice steady by willpower alone. I wanted to believe it was impossible that Ruhl was like the Voidborn. After all, I'd come in contact with him and never felt any draining of my humanity. Quite the opposite. He'd been calming in some strange way.

But... still.

Ruhl's head cocked curiously. He paced closer.

I didn't relax a bit.

In a single leap, he jumped up onto the bed, and his landing did nothing to make the mattress move in the slightest. It was like he wasn't really there. Like I was watching him in a dream, except I could feel the cold air around me and hear the soft footsteps of the guards patrolling the hall, so I doubted I was asleep.

"What are you, Ruhl?" I whispered. "Really?"

The massive wolf paused again as if thinking how to respond. And then he sank down onto his haunches, still watching me with those eerie green eyes.

Carefully, he stretched out one massive paw. Amid the shadows of his form, his claws glimmered like moonlight on black stone. I didn't dare move as he gently placed the pad of his paw upon my knee.

I gasped.

Images flashed through my mind in a blur of sight and emotion. Fire everywhere, but I wasn't afraid. Darkness but it only meant home. A longing. A command. A passage away from the comforting fire and darkness into bitter cold and light, and gods, I hated them, yet there was no choice.

But the one I longed for—that *we* longed for—wasn't

here.

My throat ached with the memory of our anguished howl at that realization. Just as bad, the object of the command was nowhere to be found either. At least, not at first. And now—

The images and emotions vanished as Ruhl suddenly drew back and disappeared into darkness that flowed away like smoke in a breeze, vanishing into the shadows beside the bed.

I stared after him. Gods, his sorrow made my throat tight and tears burn my eyes. His longing, the loss when it wasn't fulfilled... all of it was agonizing.

Worry filtered through my connection to Ozias. He'd felt this too through me, and quickly, I tried to focus on reassuring him. It was strange to do this when we weren't actually physically together. It felt like *wishing*. Like just hoping he'd feel something that existed only in my body and mind, except it worked and his wary acceptance spread through me a moment later.

If I "said" I was okay, he believed it. For now.

Shakily, I hugged my arms to my middle, searching the shadows. "Ruhl?"

Nothing.

Why had he pulled back? Were the memories too painful? And what had that last impression been? He'd been commanded to find something, and it seemed as if maybe he had, but the flood of emotions and ideas had ended before I could understand what exactly he'd been sent to—

A click came from the wall.

I flinched, adrenaline racing through me and pushing

me to the brink of letting my fangs descend. In the shadows, my night vision picked out the edge of a wall panel swinging outward.

Casimir leaned his head around the opening.

My breath rushed out in shock and relief.

He cast a glance at the shadows, and Ruhl rose from the darkness a moment later. "You were supposed to let us know if the way was clear," Casimir chided pointedly.

The wolf didn't look remotely abashed. I'd swear his shoulder even twitched as if he was shrugging. Ignoring Casimir, he strolled to the door, but just as he reached it, he paused.

His head turned and his green eyes met mine. Even though he was a wolf, even though he didn't have facial expressions like me, and of course he never said a word, I still felt like he was asking me not to say anything about what he'd just shared.

Before I could move a muscle, the wolf turned away again. Shifting to smoke, he flowed beneath the door and out of the room.

Casimir shook his head but said nothing else as he pushed the panel in the wall aside farther.

Dex, Clay, and Lars followed him into the room.

I stared at them. "What is this? Is everything okay?"

"It's fine," Dex assured me.

"Now," Lars added.

I gave him a confused look.

"I don't know about you, baby." Clay crossed the room to the bedside. "But we weren't okay leaving you in here alone."

My mouth moved, but I couldn't find words.

"Casimir swore there'd be a way between rooms in this place," Lars said with an acknowledging twitch of his head toward the vampire. "Security measures, he claimed. Something about the architecture being influenced by Zenirya. Sure enough, he was right. There's a passage linking this one and the next two, and, well..." He grinned.

"Are you okay with us staying in here with you, princess?" Dex asked, coming over to the opposite side of the bed from Clay.

I nodded quickly. "Yes. Absolutely. I..."

The urge to pull them into the bed with me was overwhelming but I wasn't sure how to voice it and not sound desperate.

But gods, I'd missed them.

With a smile, Dex sank down onto the bed and drew me into his arms. I melted against him, overwhelmed with relief that he was here and the others were too. That, at least for this one night, I could still have them with me.

No matter what the future held.

On the other side of the bed, Clay grinned and then bounded onto the mattress, jostling us.

I clamped a hand to my mouth, stifling a laugh. We couldn't risk making too much sound, lest the guards hear.

"Take it easy," Lars cautioned his brother as if thinking the same thing. He sat down on the edge of the bed, drawing my feet toward him and then rubbing them gently.

Clay scoffed, pulling me into his arms when Dex relaxed his hold. "And waste one more second away from our girl?" He made a rude noise. "Never."

My cheeks warmed. Turning slightly, I reached over to Dex, taking his hand and squeezing it. I didn't want to lose contact with any of them, not for one second.

Not when I might have a lifetime where nights like this were only a memory.

Casimir made a pleased sound, drawing my attention back to this moment. I looked down at the foot of the bed to find him studying us, one eyebrow arched like a master painter considering the composition of an art piece.

And liking what he saw.

"You appear lonely tonight, princess," he said, a wealth of implication in his voice. "Like perhaps you missed being filled up by your men. Is that true?"

I hesitated and then gave a small nod.

He made a considering noise. "Then do you need us to show you what happens to little toys who go too long without submitting to a good fucking? Should we remind you to whom you belong?"

Speech failed me, but my body had no such trouble. My core began throbbing with need, becoming more soaked with every word he spoke, and my breasts suddenly seemed hyperaware of the men only a short distance away.

"Answer me, princess," Casimir ordered.

"Yes," I whispered.

His eyes narrowed with a dominant edge.

"Yes, sir," I added.

"Good girl."

His attention flicked to Dex, and the giant met the vampire's considering gaze with one of his own. A silent exchange passed between them, and then Dex glanced at the twins.

Clay smirked like there was no question that he was up for anything. Lars nodded.

"Take her nightclothes off," Dex said to Clay.

The blond giant's smirk grew positively devilish. A tingling sensation rushed over my body, and I barely had time to gasp before everything I was wearing simply disappeared, leaving me utterly naked.

"Well, that's a marvelous trick," Casimir commented, sounding impressed.

Clay made a satisfied sound and traced a fingertip beneath my breast before pinching my nipple. I flinched, my pussy clenching.

He chuckled. "You all remember that place near where we hid for a while? The, uh, *interesting* one?"

I looked between the men, confused, but no one explained. Instead, Lars's blue eyes only grew hotter, while Dex nodded.

"I do." Dex's fingertips tipped my chin up, and he smiled at me before glancing at the twins again. "Get the curtain ties."

Oh holy gods.

Lars climbed from the bed and headed for the window. Following suit, Dex walked over to the door. Pressing his hand to the surface, he closed his eyes.

The wood panel expanded and merged with the frame until they were one, sealing us in completely. There'd be no chance of the guards opening the door now, much less interrupting whatever we did.

But we'd still need to be quiet, and the men seemed to

know it. While Lars brought back the decorative ropes meant for holding the curtains open, Clay held out his hands and conjured a red satin sash.

"Now," he warned, a wicked light in his blue eyes. "You promise you'll shift if you run into trouble, baby? You'll take a way out if you need it?"

"Okay," I breathed.

"Good girl. Now open."

My lips parted.

He slipped the sash between my teeth and then tied it behind my head. "Gotta keep you quiet when you don't have a cock filling up that naughty mouth of yours."

My pussy throbbed.

Clay's smirk remained, like he could see how the words affected me, but then motion caught my eye.

Dex was looping one of the decorative curtain ropes through his hands, and with every pass, the rope grew longer. "We learned this in a small village where we hid for a time after the war." He nodded once at me. "Hands behind your back. Lift your ankles too."

I moved around to do as he said, but the vulnerability of being so exposed between them all had me twisting a bit, trying to keep him in view as he circled behind me. I had no idea what they all planned, but gods, my insides quivered, overcome with anticipation.

"And *now*..." he said from behind me. "Stay still."

I barely breathed as he began looping the rope around my wrists, winding it between each arm and then back again until it formed a sheath partway up my forearms, binding them together.

But he wasn't done. My ankles followed, each one

pinned to his rope construction between my wrists in such a way that it left my knees spread, my back arched, and my core exposed.

"Doing okay, princess?" Lars asked. He trailed a finger across my shoulders, making my breath catch.

I nodded.

"Hmm. Let's see about that." His fingertip trailed down my sternum and onward, his blue eyes never leaving me.

I trembled. Even if I didn't want to stop him, even if I knew I could shift and escape if I truly needed to, it was still overwhelmingly vulnerable to be bound like this.

His finger slipped between my slick folds, and he smiled. Lifting it to his lips, he licked away my wetness.

My core clenched.

"She's delicious, friends. Beautifully ready."

"Nah." Clay grinned. "Those breasts need attention first, don't they, baby?" He took a length of rope from Dex and then slipped it around my ribs. "Here you go."

I gasped around the satin in my mouth as he continued twisting and winding it around me. Though he crafted the knots by hand, they looked like magic by the time he was done. The knotted rope wrapped beneath my breasts and above them, as well as down the center of my chest in a ladder of knots. The restraint pinched the soft flesh of my breasts, forcing them outward as if for easier access. I swore my nipples felt more sensitive by the second.

"Stunning," Casimir commented, studying me again like I was a work of art. "I've read of this, but the books truly didn't do it justice."

Bound and exposed between them all, I waited, breathless, while the men ran their eyes over me. What they planned from here, I wasn't sure, but gods, I wanted them in me soon.

Dex smiled like he could see my desire growing. "You need to be filled up, good girl?"

I nodded.

He made a considering noise. "All right." He gave the twins a pointed look.

Lars and Clay grinned like mirror images of wickedness. Stripping down quickly, they shared a brief look, and then Lars climbed onto the bed. As he lay down, Clay came closer and his warm hands slid over my sensitive skin.

"You ready for this, baby?"

I could only nod.

He lifted me up and then eased me down onto Lars's cock.

I gasped around the satin sash, the stretch of taking him intense and yet comforting all at the same time. Still holding onto me, Clay tipped me forward until his brother's hands supported my weight.

I was suspended between them, unable to move myself, waiting to see what they'd do.

"I got that sweet pussy last time," Clay murmured in my ear. "It's only fair we trade, and I take that luscious ass of yours tonight instead."

Around my gag, I moaned as Lars rocked beneath me.

With a pleased noise, Clay grinned and then spat on his fingers, slowly working them into me one by one by one.

My eyes rolled back into my head. Lars had barely started moving yet, and already I was soaking him. When Clay finally eased his fingers away only to return with his slick cock, I shuddered hard, damn near ready to come.

And then they started moving me between them.

Muffled begging sounds slipped from me. I couldn't hold the noises back, and I thanked the gods for Clay's foresight in giving me a way to stay quiet. Because held between the twins like this, I was helpless to do anything but feel.

Gods, just *feel*.

Every nerve was sensitive. Every brush of their hot skin was pure fire. They moved in tandem below and above me, rocking me against them in just the right way. I didn't want to think about how they knew this. What it must have taken to learn what they were doing to me. None of that mattered, because they were here with me now. Their skillful movements were making a tingling build in my core and pulse out through my body in waves that grew higher and higher and—

I clamped my lips shut as best I could around the gag, fighting not to scream as I came.

"That's it," Clay crooned into my ear. "That's it. That's our... gods, baby. That's our good... good... oh *fuck*."

His hands clenched down as he filled me with his cum. Beneath me, Lars groaned softly as he did the same.

For a moment, I lay pinned between them, both men breathing hard from their release. My eyes slid to one side, finding Dex and Casimir.

They were watching me like hawks. Casimir's fangs glinted in the moonlight.

"Our turn," the vampire said with a grin.

Dex stripped off his pants. "Bring her here. Put her on her stomach."

The twins lifted and repositioned me on the bed so that I lay with pillows beneath my torso. Breathless, I stared up at Dex, wondering what he had planned.

A hungry light in his eyes, he took my chin and tilted my face up toward him. "Remember our first night together? How you wanted to taste me? How I told you someday I'd fuck that mouth of yours?" His other hand undid the satin gag and tossed it to one side. "Open, princess."

My lips parted with a tiny gasp.

His thumb pressed down on my chin, opening my mouth farther. "You're going to take this cock like a good girl, aren't you?"

I nodded.

He grinned and guided his dick between my lips. I tried to relax my throat and breathe through my nose, but suddenly, I wondered if I could do this.

Dex was huge.

His hand left my chin and slid into my hair, his fingers curling into the strands and holding my head in place. Rocking his hips back, he pulled out only to thrust back again, over and over. Every motion was controlled. Every plunge into my throat just deep enough to please him without risking me. He knew how big he was, and though I choked on him, I never felt in danger from his size.

The bed rocked a bit, and hands suddenly slid along my bound sides, startling me.

"Relax, princess," Casimir said, bending over me to

murmur sinfully in my ear. "I only wish to enjoy you with Dex."

Gods, yes, please.

His hands slipped back down, taking my hips and holding me in position. I closed my eyes, trying to focus on not choking on Dex, only to moan sharply as Casimir began easing inside of me.

"That's it, my little fucktoy. You can't do anything but lie there and take our cocks, can you?"

Gods, that vampire and his mouth.

Casimir chuckled and began moving, matching Dex's pace. Sliding a hand beneath me, he massaged my clit in time with his thrusts as well, steadily setting every part of my body on fire.

Dex leaned forward, one hand still gripping my hair while the other reached out. I heard a grunt from Casimir, quickly muffled, and then followed by the sound of a rough kiss breaking apart.

"Bite her," Dex ordered. "Make her come."

My eyes flew wide. I barely had time to gasp.

Casimir's fangs sank into my neck.

I choked on Dex's cock as ecstasy crashed into me, making everything blur into a dark wave of pleasure that I never wanted to escape. Casimir's mouth moved against my throat while Dex's grip on my hair tightened, control-ling my motion and adding pinpricks of pain to the rush of my orgasm.

Gods, I would never get enough of them. Not now, not for all of time.

Dex grunted. His thrusts started to turn ragged, only barely controlled.

A stifled moan escaped him as his release flooded my throat. Behind me, Casimir sealed the wound on my neck and then groaned. His hands dug into my hips, and a heartbeat later, he was filling me with his cum too.

Shuddering hard, I swallowed Dex's seed down, gasping a bit when he finally eased from between my lips.

He stroked my face gently and then tilted my chin up to look at him. "Good job, princess."

I flushed with pride at the admiration in his eyes.

He moved his forearm in front of my lips. "Feed."

My fangs descended immediately. I moaned as his blood rushed into my mouth as well.

The ropes loosened on me. I broke away from Dex, sealing the wound quickly, and looked back as my nerves hummed with heightened awareness from the sudden rush of blood flow.

"Any numbness, baby?" Clay asked as he ran his hands up and down my limbs. At his side, Lars was undoing my restraints one by one. "Tingling or pain?"

I shook my head.

Clay made a pleased sound, his hands never stopping their gentle motions while his brother continued unknotting the ropes. "Let's get you cleaned up then, yeah? Keep our girl nice and taken care of for next—"

Casimir suddenly stiffened with a short gasp, cutting him off. The vampire's face was a picture of wary alarm.

"What is it?" I asked. "What's wrong?"

"Get dressed," was Casimir's only response. He looked at Dex, his expression tense. "We need that door open again. Now."

20

ROAN

I hadn't actually been tortured before, but I was fairly certain it couldn't be worse than this.

Cursing myself silently, I adjusted my position on the couch. It was my own damn fault. I was a madman in here, trapped by Aneiran propriety in this bedroom across from Gwyneira's, hounded relentlessly by a monster who wouldn't let me sleep and who could kill everyone in this castle if I lost control.

I was a bastard for being here at all.

Grinding my teeth, I glared up at the ceiling. Gwyneira had seen something days ago when vampires attacked our camp. How much, I wasn't sure, and the fact she hadn't immediately told the others was a confusing miracle.

Monsters like me didn't get miracles, confusing or otherwise.

Every day since that moment, I'd been bracing for my whole life to come crashing down. For her to decide she needed to tell the others how I'd ripped a vampire's throat out with my bare hands. For the mere discussion of what I'd done to bring the demon roaring back.

For the demon to finally escape my control and destroy them all.

So for every one of those days, I promised myself I'd leave. This was too dangerous. The demon was too close to breaking free. Truth be told, I probably should have left ages ago, because every morning I woke up and felt the monster inside me rage at seeing her snuggled between Clay and Lars instead of curled up with me, I knew I was being a fool not to go.

One moment of the demon slipping my control and taking over, and everyone would die. That's all it would take. Yet here I was, lying on a *couch* in a fucking *castle,* across the hall from the woman I'd kill when that happened.

And still, I couldn't leave her.

I adjusted my position, loathing everything about myself, the cushions, and the gods-damned world besides. Of all of us, Gwyneira was the only one sleeping alone tonight—because of course she was. The rest of us had been split up between various rooms, leaving Niko in here with me, and Ozias and Byron next door, while the others were across the hall.

Just a bunch of bachelors bunking together as guests of Lord Thomas, because Aneiran sensibilities wouldn't *dream* of putting any of us in a bedroom with their pretty little supposedly-still-a-virgin princess. There was her virtue to consider and all, not to mention her value to royal suitors. Those fuckers viewed her sweet cunt as nothing more than a political *commodity*.

Rage shuddered through me, and my hands shook. I'd claw the eyeballs from the skull of anyone who looked at her that way. I'd slice off those suitors' gods-damned cocks and feed them to the bastards before I let them get anywhere near her.

Mine...

My hands curled into fists. No. Not because she was mine. Because...

Just *because*, dammit.

The demon's scorn for me was like acid coursing beneath my skin, and furiously, I fought to shove it back into its cage, not that the monster had the slightest intention of cooperating with that any longer. If anything, it wanted *me* in the damn cage. I was getting in the way. Stopping it from—

From being a fool, gods-dammit.

I dug my fingers into my scalp, trying to focus past its rampaging and remember how to think like a man, not a monster. But the silence of this room grated on my ears, and these damned cushions were like a squishy grave, wrapping around me, trapping me here. And through it all, Gwyneira was all the way across the hall, alone, unprotected, a wanted fugitive in her own country and—

Fuck it.

I shoved away from the couch. Moving quietly so as to avoid waking Niko, I crept across the room and opened the door.

The corridor was empty and still.

Like I'd trust that.

Snarling under my breath and glaring at the shadows, I stalked across the hall. I wouldn't say much to her. I definitely wouldn't answer questions. I'd just demand she keep the door cracked so that all of us—not just me, of course, because dammit, I wouldn't let on I cared—*all of us* could hear if she was in trouble.

I lifted my fist to knock.

A muffled moan came from beyond the door.

I stopped, my hand hovering in midair just an inch shy of rapping on the wood. That hadn't sounded like a noise of pain.

Wait...

Carefully, I leaned closer. My ear rested on the heavy wooden door.

Quiet grunts. Another moan. A short, rhythmic rocking sound.

I staggered back, blood rushing to my face and my cock in equal measure. Raking a hand through my hair, I floundered, my eyes darting around the hall.

That had to be my friends in there with her. Probably that vampire too. They'd decided not to leave her alone after all, even if it meant the risk of running afoul of damned Aneiran propriety.

And they were fucking her. All of them.

Shudders rocked me. My lips curled back, my bones aching. The demon wanted out. *Needed* out, because she was *right the fuck there* and whatever those men were doing, it wouldn't be anything compared to what we could—

Shadows stirred at the corner of my eye.

I reacted without thinking.

Lunging at the darkness, my hands sank into the shadows and landed on something that gave like flesh and fur, even if it actually had no form. I yanked the shadows toward me, my teeth bared. I'd tear this thing's throat out. I'd feast on whatever the hell thought it could—

The darkness melted from my grasp, flowing around my hands like water and rushing away from me. Twisting in midair several yards farther down the hall, the dark cloud transformed into Ruhl.

I lunged again. The wolf tensed like he was alarmed, but that only gave me an advantage. The creature shifted back into shadows, trying to evade, but I was ready.

My hands wrapped around the darkness and hauled it closer. My lips peeled back from my teeth again and rage flooded my veins. This soot-ridden mongrel had been watching us lust after our mate. Worse, it had interrupted us. If not for him, we would've gone in there and claimed the princess. The others had her ready, after all, and we wouldn't have let them interfere. She would've been nice and relaxed to take our thick cock when we shifted and—

What the fuck was I doing?

Horrified, I fell back from the wolf, collapsing onto my ass on the carpet.

Ruhl flowed away and reformed several yards down the hall, his stance clearly ready for a fight this time. His black fur was like a darker swath of shadow in the middle of the unlit corridor. His green eyes never blinked as he watched me cautiously.

I didn't move. The impact had jolted me, but it didn't stop the demon's fantasies still pounding through my brain.

They were all blurry, of course. I'd never actually shared such intimacy with anyone, because the gods knew I couldn't risk the demon taking control and killing my bed partner.

But that didn't mean I wasn't more than capable of dreaming up how it would feel to have my hands on Gwyneira's skin... my mouth on hers... her silky softness wrapped around every inch of my cock as I—

"Roan?" Niko whispered behind me.

I froze. Carefully, Ruhl eased out of the aggressive posture he'd adopted, his eerie green eyes going between me and where Niko stood.

I didn't turn around. There was a chance Niko hadn't seen me fighting with the wolf. It was dark in the hallway, after all, and my friend had been asleep only a little while ago.

"H-how were you doing that?"

Fuck.

Trembling coursed through me, born of adrenaline and a shit-ton of dread. But I made myself clamber back to my feet and adjust my cock to keep it from tenting my damn pants. Made my expression become as neutral as I could too, and when I turned, I twitched my shoulder in a shrug and held my voice steady. "Doing what?"

"Holding onto Ruhl in his shadow form."

Fuck, fuck, fuck.

I forced my expression to reflect disinterest. "I don't know. It was something the wolf was doing."

Ruhl growled.

I spun before I could stop myself, rage surging through me.

The wolf's teeth bared.

I'd kill him.

"Why is he reacting to you like that?"

I blinked, jarred by the sound of the younger one's voice. No, my *friend's* voice. Niko.

"I-I don't know," I lied, turning back to him.

Niko didn't look convinced.

I shuddered. Fuck, I needed to get out of this hallway. Much more of this and Gwyneira might hear. She might come out here, all sex-mussed and awash with arousal and—

I strode back into the bedroom. "Close the damn door."

Niko didn't react to my rudeness, which only went to show he *wasn't* a bastard, even if I was. The door shut. He was still standing in front of it when I turned around, and Ruhl hadn't followed—though I had no idea how I knew that.

But... good.

"What's going on?" Niko asked softly, his dark eyes wary. He had his arms crossed, and he stood like he was willing to fight to keep me in here until I answered him.

I could kill him before he drew his next breath.

Shuddering hard, I turned away sharply. Fuck, fuck, *fuck* me. Fuck this. I had to get out of this fucking—

"Are you okay?"

The genuine concern in his voice brought me up short, and just about broke me besides. Gods damn me, Niko cared. He *always* cared, and he didn't have a fucking clue about the danger he was in. None of them did. They had no idea I was the sick bastard who'd risked every last one of them all these years.

The sick bastard who *still* didn't want to leave, even though he damn well should.

Because it would mean leaving her.

"I'm fine." I shoved the words out. "Sorry to worry you."

Silence followed for a heartbeat. "Can I ask you something?"

Gods, no.

"Is there anything we should know about you?"

My breath stopped. Carefully, I looked back at him. "What?"

"It's just..." Niko frowned. "Whenever I'm around you lately, nature keeps saying something is... off."

Blood rushed in my ears. My skin felt too tight and hot and cold, all at the same time. This was it. The moment I knew might come, and of course it was Niko who asked. Stupid, fucking nature would know I wasn't anything remotely natural. It'd make sure he knew that.

I could tell him the truth.

It was hard not to scoff in disgust at the insane thought. Right. And then I could see the horror on his face, and on all my friends' faces when he told them too.

I could lose control.

"Roan?" That wary concern grew stronger in his eyes.

"No." I forced the lie from my clenched throat. "I don't know what you're talking about."

His brow drew down. "Then why—"

A shout came from beyond the castle, thin and reedy over the distance but unmistakable, and my head snapped toward the sound. On its heels, more cries arose, and by the time I reached the sliver of a window that was all the room possessed, an orange glow was flaring to life near the city walls.

"What is it?" Niko asked.

"We're under attack."

I whirled and headed for the door. Niko retreated fast when I yanked it open, everything in me snarling to get to Gwyneira and destroy whatever thought it could take my mate from me.

Something in my head tried to argue she wasn't mine. Something tried to say we needed to be careful. Those men were our friends. And if we burst in there and found her naked with them, their cocks buried in her, we needed to *not* kill them for daring to touch—

I staggered to a stop, my mind reeling. *I* was the one arguing that, dammit. *I was*. I—

Her door opened. The scent of sex clung to her, and my vision blurred, the edges of everything before me suddenly becoming tinged by flames. My fingers curled, my nails digging their sharp points into my palms.

"Roan?" Gwyneira started toward me, concern on her face.

I stumbled backward, and it took every last shred of my willpower to make myself turn aside.

"Are you okay, man?" Clay asked, his voice far away down a tunnel of screaming, of darkness, of death. Other voices came—Lars, Dex, Niko—but I couldn't make out their words. Byron swam briefly into focus, and then Ozias too, both of them now standing in the hallway but also drowning in the fire all around.

Fire... so much fire... I was losing this fight.

I was winning.

I was...

A screech tore the air, and my eyes snapped toward the sound. Something was barreling toward the narrow window at the end of the corridor. For a heartbeat, I thought it was a large bird, but it had arms attached to its wings. Breasts and clawed hands and a woman's face, and when she screamed, it was like a wild animal trying to tear through my ears straight into my brain. She hit the slit of a window, her arm thrashing in the opening in an effort to reach us. Her talons ripped at the air, and when she peered through the gap, her eyes glowed red like a burning flower from hell.

A crash came from the princess's room. Clay swore and grabbed for the door handle. I caught a glimpse of another winged woman with dark gray feathers and bright pink eyes. She shredded the bedding beneath her claws as she raced at us, and then Clay yanked the door closed.

Dark talons pierced the wood from the opposite side, and furious cries rose.

The first creature screamed again, shoving her shoulder through the narrow gap of the corridor window and twisting madly to make headway. Bones cracked. The scent of blood filled the air. She was breaking her own body just to get inside.

"Go!" Dex ordered. He grabbed Gwyneira, moving her ahead of him as he retreated. "Stay away from the windows!"

"They're the Voidborn, aren't they?" Niko cried.

"They've possessed those creatures like they did Lord Thomas's people."

"Fucking monsters is what they are," Clay snapped back.

I snarled at the description, and Ozias's eyes darted to me. I fought to keep from baring the fangs I didn't have.

Yet.

"They're harpies," Byron called. "I think."

"*Harpies*?" Niko threw him an alarmed and confused look.

"Those are myths!" Lars sounded incredulous too.

Casimir made a sound so wry, it practically could have come from Clay. "Rather like that lovely dragon in the Wild Lands, yes?"

Grim looks crossed the other men's faces, and I gritted my teeth, holding back another snarl. Gods only knew how or *why* that enormous beast had burst from the depths of a mountain in the Wild Lands, but the demon had known it was there. I'd felt the beast stirring deep beneath the dirt and stone even before Ozias had picked up on it.

And damn if *that* didn't scare the shit out of me.

I shook my head hard, my thoughts blurring so much, it was difficult to even see the hallway.

Except, no, now we were on stairs instead.

And now we were in the hall again, but on a different floor. Servants were running ahead of us, all of them moving like they knew where they were going, even if I didn't have a clue. But Lord Thomas had probably put plans in place for if the castle came under attack. The servants were just following them.

They were fools. We could fix this.

We'd kill them all.

I gasped. Cold sweat clung to my skin. I was hanging onto the demon with everything I had, but with each passing step, it felt like the monster inside me grew larger. Stronger.

"—then use whatever you can find, dammit!"

The lord's voice came from beyond the corner of the hall, and I staggered to a stop at the sound. The humans were a threat to my mate. They needed to die.

No, we couldn't kill them. The princess wouldn't want us to—

"Roan." Gwyneira suddenly appeared in front of me. In the blur of fire and darkness that was crowding my vision, she shone like a star, the one bright spot in my world.

Anguish choked me. I didn't want to kill her. Gods help me, I was losing control, but I didn't want to—

She put her hand to my cheek.

Everything went still. The demon. Me. The whole damn universe froze like a crystalline moment of perfection at the heart of winter.

"Breathe," she urged me, and her voice was the only thing I could hear in the world. "Whatever it is, just breathe, okay? We're going to be all right."

Air entered my lungs on her command.

A smile crossed her face. "Good."

She lowered her hand, looking back at the others.

I blinked, dazed. My friends were staring at us. Most looked confused.

Niko didn't. That wariness was back—a hundred-fold.

"Get the people to any stone building you can find, understand?" Lord Thomas's voice carried past the turn, breaking the moment. "These things are tearing through wood and burning it down."

"Come on," Gwyneira said, directing the words to all of us.

With a last careful look at me, she turned and headed for the corner.

Avoiding everyone's eyes, I hurried after her, reeling inside. How had she done that? I'd been about to lose control. I'd been seconds away from murdering everyone in this castle and probably half the city besides. But she'd calmed that. Quieted the demon enough that I could think again.

And all she'd done was *touch* me.

On shaking legs, I came around the corner. Lord Thomas stood in the open castle gateway, shouting orders at the guards in the courtyard. Valeria was at his side, sweeping the crossbow in her hands across the sky and then firing. The guards were doing the same with their bows, and screeching harpies plummeted to the cobble-stones every few moments, speared through by arrows. Beyond the castle wall, fires blazed in the city, the orange glow stark and terrible against the night sky.

With every harpy that fell, twists of smoke rose from their chests, weaving through the air like snakes seeking a target. Guards rushed at them, stabbing each one as quickly as they could. Screams that were more sensation than sound followed like metal grating against my brain.

"Lord Thomas!" Gwyneira rushed toward him.

The lord threw a glance back at her. He wore his armor over his bedclothes, but nothing about him said he gave a damn how that looked. He was a leader in the midst of a war. Fashion could wait.

"Princess." He scanned us all swiftly. "My guards didn't find you?"

"We saw no guards," Gwyneira said. "I'm sorry."

His mouth tightened, and I could guess why. The people he sent had run or they were dead.

Either was a bad option.

"How are your people striking those things down?" Dex asked.

"Garlic tincture," the lord replied. "Valeria's idea. We dipped the arrows and swords in it."

He stepped back seamlessly as Valeria swung her crossbow around and fired at an oncoming harpy diving for his opposite side. The creature tumbled out of the sky, and the moment it hit the ground, a guard was there to stab the smoke rising from its chest.

The horrible screech of the Voidborn came and then faded. But screams still rose in the city beyond the walls.

"Princess," Lord Thomas said. "Please go to the cellar. It should protect you while we deal with these—"

"Incoming!" Dex shouted.

Screeches came from behind us. A tumbling flood of feathers and talons surged down the corridor. A servant screamed, trying to duck into another room to escape them.

The man was too slow.

Snagging him with their talons, the harpies ripped

him away from the ground. Blood splattered the walls as they tore into the human like they were starved and rabid beasts.

"Open fire!" Lord Thomas ordered. "Protect the princess!"

Valeria spun, doing as ordered. The harpies lunged away from their dead victim and flew at us, their faces soaked in blood. Arrows tore down one creature after another, but still the horde kept coming.

I drew my sword, and a smile tugged at my lips. My hands were steady. My skin wasn't shifting anymore. The demon was still stunned by what Gwyneira had done, leaving me feeling more stable than I'd been in an age.

I could do this. Protect her. Stay in control. Keeping my distance from her had never been the answer. No, the truth was the exact opposite.

And now for her, *because* of her, I could do anything.

Something suddenly stirred at the edge of my mind, rumbling strangely through my elation.

I tensed. That wasn't the demon. Not exactly. It was familiar but not, and I couldn't place—

"Get ready!" the lord shouted.

The harpies struck.

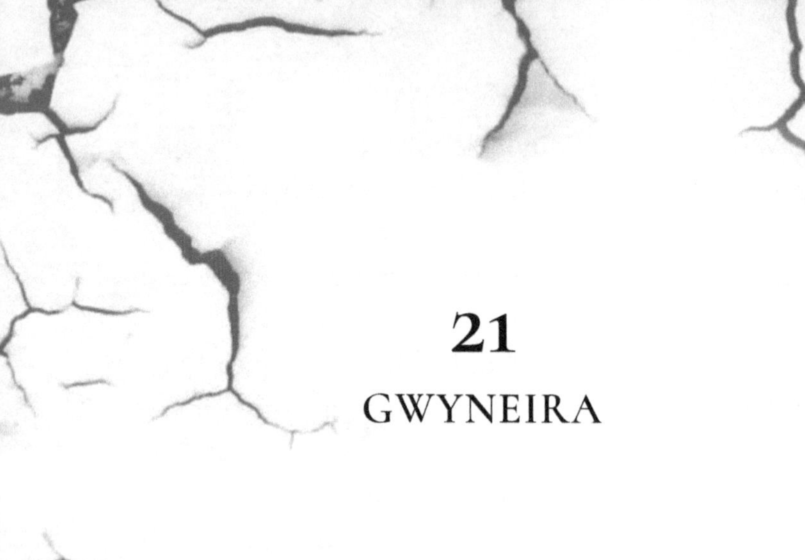

21

GWYNEIRA

I'd never seen a harpy.

I never wanted to see one again.

Talons whipped past my face, missing me by inches. Feathers sharp as knives cut the air only a hair's breadth from my skin, and eyes glowing like evil suns glared at me only to vanish when their owners were knocked aside. Somewhere beyond the throng of attacking monsters, Lord Thomas was shouting, but I couldn't make out his words.

It was all I could do to avoid getting killed.

The creatures drove us back, out of the castle and into the courtyard, but the greater space around us meant they had more angles from which to attack. And for every harpy that fell, the Voidborn inside them lunged out to strike at the guards, overwhelming them by sheer numbers, possessing them and then forcing them to turn on their allies.

It was a bloodbath.

But my men moved like they'd been training for this all their lives. They drove back the possessed guards. They slashed through the harpies and the Voidborn that erupted from them. They stabbed at any dying creatures who lunged up at us from the ground.

They were magnificent.

But we were surrounded with nowhere to go.

"Watch out!" Niko shouted.

I whirled. Beyond the throng of screaming harpies and attacking guards, I caught sight of half a dozen of the creatures flying directly above us, a massive shape supported between them.

My eyes went wide. That was a block of stone from the castle itself. They'd torn it from the roof or walls.

And then they dropped it.

The stone hurtled down toward us, and there was no time to move. But before it struck, Ozias was there, and a gut-dropping feeling thudded through me as he flung his hand upward.

Cracks spread through the stone so quickly, it was there one moment and then dust the next.

The harpies screamed with rage. Several spun, taking off for the castle roof again. Others dove for Ozias as if intent on killing him, and there were too many. Their claws sank into his shoulders, trying to rip him from the ground. Pain roared through my connection to him.

"Cover your eyes!" Byron shouted.

He flung his hand out. Small objects sailed through the air as he shouted something in a language that felt strange in my ears, like it had texture and weight as well as sound.

Light burst from the little objects in midair, flooding the night with a glare so blinding, it was as if every one of them had become a miniature sun. Instinctively, I did as he'd said and threw an arm across my eyes to shield myself from the blast.

Screeches like metal being torn in two filled the courtyard. But they drained quickly as if being pulled away down a long tunnel.

Leaving only silence.

The light faded. I lowered my arm, trembling. My skin ached like I'd just gotten an instantaneous sunburn, and I blinked hard, trying to clear the spots from my vision because I hadn't shielded my eyes quite fast enough.

All the Voidborn were gone. The guards and harpies they'd possessed had fallen to the ground, vicious scorch marks across their skin with wisps of smoke drifting up from each burn, like the Voidborn had been blasted straight out of their bodies.

None moved again.

Regret tangled in me for the dead, and when I looked over at Byron, I could see the same reflected on his face. There was no way to know if the possessed could have been saved. But now we didn't have that chance, and neither did they.

"You had no choice," Dex told him. "It was us or them."

Byron turned away. "Doesn't make it easier."

Dex nodded with an expression like he understood

that more than he could ever put into words. "Never does," he replied quietly.

"Princess…"

Lord Thomas's voice came from behind me, and I tensed.

Oh hell.

I turned.

With only a few of his guards still at his side, Lord Thomas stood thirty feet away across the courtyard, staring at me. At my men too. His bodyguard, Valeria, was doing the same.

And her crossbow was aimed right at Byron.

"Don't." I held up my hands. "Please. He's not your enemy, I swear."

"What was that?" Lord Thomas demanded coldly. "What did he do?"

Ruhl swirled into the form of a wolf behind the lord and his guards. His green eyes went between Lord Thomas and Valeria, and I could see the evaluations running there.

He could tear the woman down before she could fire. The lord would be next.

My heart hit my throat. "Please," I begged, hoping the wolf understood I was talking to him too. "No one needs to attack anybody here."

Dex carefully lowered his sword to the ground, drawing Lord Thomas and Valeria's attention. "We're not your enemies. Not if you aren't ours."

"What are you?" Lord Thomas demanded.

Dex's eyes went to me, questioning.

"They're the men who saved my life," I said. "And I'm... me. But the rest is complicated."

Screams came from the town. A burst of fire rose above the rest of the flames like something had just fallen.

"Please," I persisted. "Those people need help. You have my word we mean you no harm." I looked back at my men. "But we've got to help them."

There was a question in the statement, and the giants heard it. Grimness filled their eyes, but reluctant acceptance was there too, and it broke my heart all over again. Each man knew how badly this would go once the truth was out.

But none of them were willing to let people die.

"Lars." Dex lifted an eyebrow. "Take point?"

The blond man nodded.

"Byron, back him up," he continued. "Clay, do what you can but don't risk the buildings falling. The rest of us'll shore things up and save as many as possible. Got it?" He turned to me. "You should stay back."

I was already shaking my head before he finished. "I'm not leaving them. Or you."

He scowled but didn't argue.

Bracing myself, I turned to Lord Thomas. His brow had drawn down and a questioning sort of wariness now filled his eyes. "When this is over," he said. "We're going to talk. All of us. Understood?"

There was no compromise in his tone, and even though I wasn't his soldier, I knew that didn't matter right now.

This moment was balanced on a knife's edge.

And meanwhile people were dying.

I nodded. "Agreed."

His head twitched in a short nod as well.

"Move out," Dex ordered.

We ran for the city.

I'd had nightmares nicer than this.

No matter where we went, buildings were burning, and smoke poured from windows and doors, while harpies dove and slashed at anyone they could reach. The humans who lived here were trying to evade them, frantic to reach people still screaming within their homes, but the flames and monsters stopped them every time.

But whenever we reached a new blaze, Lars was there. Niko too. While my blond giant flung out his arms at the flames, making the fires fall back and vanish like snuffed out candles, Niko was right behind him. He sent thick roots erupting from beneath the cobblestones to climb the crumbling walls, keeping them from collapsing completely once the flames were gone. Over and over, Ozias and Casimir lunged into the fray, slashing and stabbing any harpies they could find. Ruhl swept around Byron like a vortex of smoke, guarding the scholar while he murmured spells over the nuggets of ore in his hands and then flung them at the dying harpies.

The Voidborn thrashed, burning up in flares of light that burst out everywhere the nuggets of ore fell.

Everywhere we went, the human guards seemed torn

on whether to attack. But Dex and Clay ignored them, racing into the houses and returning shortly with injured people from within, and soon, the leaders among the guards were shouting orders for their subordinates to help my men.

It gave me hope. Maybe the humans wouldn't automatically attack us when this was over. Maybe my men being forced to reveal their powers hadn't destroyed any chance of keeping Lord Thomas as an ally.

A screech came from above.

"Gwyneira!" Niko shouted.

A harpy crashed through the wall at my side, its chest impaled by an arrow. Bringing the wall down with it, the creature careened toward me, claws flailing as it fell.

There was no time to run.

My body instinctively flashed into shadow, and I whipped to the side, whirling out of the path of the monster and the falling stones.

With a sickening sound, the harpy slammed into the cobblestone road and didn't move again.

Reaching the sidewalk, I shifted back. My pulse raced. My eyes darted around, seeking another threat, another ballistic monster, anything.

Standing at the street corner, Lord Thomas stared at me.

My hope faltered. Accepting the giants was one thing, but what I'd just done...

A desperate cry tore my focus away from him. It sounded like it came from a burning house farther down the road.

And it sounded like a child.

I ran.

"Gwyneira!" Lars shouted behind me.

I kept going. Fire poured from the windows of the one-story house, and snapped and snarled from holes it had chewed into the roof. But when I reached the doorway, the flames suddenly fell back, and I threw a glance over my shoulder to see Lars staring after me in shock, one arm outstretched.

I nodded my thanks and started inside. On the far end of the room, two little boys were yanking frantically on a fallen ceiling beam. A woman lay beneath it, unconscious and pinned by the heavy wood. More beams crisscrossed the space, creating an unstable barricade, while tiles from the roof were suspended precariously overhead. Based on the charred rubble all around, it was clear the three of them had been trapped in the only spot in the room that hadn't been engulfed in flames only a moment ago.

But they'd had no way out.

I smiled, trying to look friendly and nonthreatening. "Hi." Carefully, I picked my way between the fallen beams. "I'm here to help."

A screech came from overhead, and the little boys gasped.

"It's all right." I kept myself from looking upward. "Just stay focused on me, okay?"

The boys trembled. They were like mirror images of each another, with short-cropped dark hair, round faces, and wide brown eyes. The boy on the left was taller by a few inches than his sibling, and he held himself like a child trying with all his might to appear unafraid. Their clothes were made of rough fabric but neatly stitched, though now soot smudged them both.

"What are your names?" I asked.

The taller boy swallowed hard. "Teos." His head twitched toward his brother. "This is Dorn."

"Hi." I clambered between two beams. "I'm Gwyneira. Is that your mother?"

Teos nodded.

"Okay, so—" Footsteps crunched on gravel behind me. I threw a glance over my shoulder.

Roan was there.

I blinked, shocked that of everyone, he'd been the one to follow me. He didn't look disgusted with me either.

Just very, *very* concerned.

"I need to get them out of here," I said, trying to preempt any snide comments.

He only nodded. "Agreed." Without another word, he started picking his way through the rubble toward me.

I stared. This... was odd.

A whimper from one of the boys snapped me back to the situation at hand. Turning, I forced my smile back in place. "It's okay. This is my, uh... my friend. Roan. He's here to help too."

Shockingly.

I tried to keep my thoughts from my expression while I ducked beneath another beam. "Now, I want you both to do something for me. You see how I just crawled through here? Can you do the same beneath those beams near you?"

Dorn's wide eyes grew rounder. "What about Momma?"

"I'll help your momma. Just crawl this way and—"

Another screech came, closer, followed by a crash that shook the house. The beams creaked. Ash rained down and a chunk of roof tile fell, shattering only a few inches away from me.

Roan was moving before the crumbling pieces hit the ground. Despite the fact he was over six and a half feet tall, he maneuvered agilely between the fallen beams without disturbing any of them, ending up at my side with incredible speed. "You good?"

My mouth moved. "Uh, yeah."

Except for being dumbstruck because he gave a damn.

He nodded as if my confirmation reassured him. "Back wall."

I regrouped, following his gaze. Past the boys, a crack had formed between the stones of the wall, spilling a trace of light into the room. It didn't look like fire, but rather like the glow of dawn.

And that was more than good enough.

"Right." I slipped past the last beam and crouched down by the boys. "Don't be scared, okay? We're getting you out of here."

I glanced at the woman, drawing on my heightened senses. Her heart was still beating. She might just have been knocked out by the impact.

I hoped.

Burying the worry, I aimed a reassuring look at the children again. "And we're going to save your mother."

Roan crouched down by the beam, running his hands along the charred wood for a moment before a smile tugged at his lips.

"What?" I asked.

"Nothing. It's just... my power's on its own again."

Confused, I started to ask what he meant, but before I could, he pressed his hands to the beam and closed his eyes.

Around his palms, the wood rippled and began flowing like water. There was something beautiful to the way it separated and then reformed into two new beams on either side of the woman, even the soot and charred patches twisting with the unburned woodgrain until the two new pieces of wood were like a striated and intricate tapestry.

I looked over at Roan, speechless. I'd seen his carvings at the cabin, and the others had mentioned his gifts with wood. But I hadn't actually watched his powers in action before.

It was breathtaking. But even though a smile still hovered on his lips, a hint of wariness showed around his eyes in a strange way. He kept glancing up and to the right like something was distracting him, only to pull his attention back to the wood again.

"What is it?" I asked. "Is something wrong?"

"No. It's just..." His eyes darted up again and then returned to the wood. "It's nothing."

I couldn't quite believe that. Not with the tension on his face.

A creak came from overhead. A chittering sound followed, and I looked up quickly.

Talons gripping the edge of the roof, a harpy glared down at us. Her eyes glowed a vicious shade of red, and blood splattered her claws and chin. She grinned at my alarmed gasp, revealing teeth stained with blood too.

"Shit," Roan swore under his breath. "We're going to need to move fast. Can you carry one of the kids?"

"I can take both," I said.

He paused, but no derisive remark ever came. "Stay close."

Gods, this was strange.

Ordering myself to stay focused, I looked back at the boys. "I'm going to do something a bit... odd, but I promise you're safe with me, okay?"

With eyes as round as the moon, Teos and Dorn nodded.

"Okay." Roan kept his eyes on the harpy. "One... two... go!"

I shifted form and grabbed the boys while Roan hefted the woman up and threw himself backward against the wall, breaking through it.

The harpy screeched, diving after us.

It was a mistake.

In a pile of stone, tile, and wood, the house collapsed on top of the creature.

Retreating fast, I set the boys down and shifted back to human form, coughing a bit at the soot and dust. "Are you okay?" I asked the children.

They gaped at me and didn't say a word.

Hopefully that meant they were fine.

Frowning, I looked around quickly. The sun had started to rise while we were inside, painting the indigo sky with shades of pink and gold, and casting dark purple shadows from the buildings around us. Like many houses in Aneira, the one we'd just fled had backed up onto a patch of communal land shared by all the homes that surrounded it. Gardens lay fallow throughout the space, waiting to provide vegetables in the next season. The land was nearly entirely enclosed by the houses, except for two narrow paths for cart access on either end. Right now, residents who hadn't escaped through the fronts of their homes were hastening toward those paths in desperate attempts to flee the harpies still spiraling and screeching overhead.

In Roan's arms, the woman groaned. Her eyelids fluttered briefly. "Teos? Dorn?" Confusion crossed her face as her eyes focused on Roan. "Wh-who are you?"

"Momma!" Little Dorn flung himself at Roan and his mother alike.

Shifting her around gently, Roan bent so that the boy could reach her. "We're, um—" He looked over at me, that hint of a smile on his lips again. "Friends. Here to help."

There was an odd note to his voice, like his words amazed him. Like he'd never thought he'd say them, somehow.

And it thrilled him that he could.

Not sure what to make of that, I just returned the smile and then put a hand to the woman's shoulder when she tried to move. "Stay still," I told her gently. "You were knocked out and you could have internal injuries. Let us get you and your boys to safety."

She stilled. "What happened? There was a fire, and these strange noises—"

Screeches cut her off. Harpies dipped and dove overhead only to dart back into the sky again, cackling like they were toying with us.

She gasped. "What...?"

Watching the harpies carefully, Roan lifted her again. "Just stay still and hang on." He twitched his chin toward the nearest path out of the open space. "Can you boys run?"

The two children nodded wordlessly.

"Okay." He glanced at me. "We need to get her to Niko, so when I say go—"

The harpies suddenly shrieked louder, but they didn't dive for us. Their attention went to the northern horizon.

And their cries sounded *victorious*.

Screams rose in the distance, near the edge of the city.

Oh, gods, this couldn't be good.

Roan's dread-filled expression said he agreed. "Run."

I grabbed the boys' hands and took off. The nearest path out of the communal garden lay twenty yards ahead, and every inch of that felt too far. But if I changed form, I didn't think I could carry everyone even with my vampire powers. I'd end up outdistancing Roan, leaving him on his own against whatever the hell excited the harpies.

He clearly didn't care. "Shift!" he shouted at me. "Just get out of—"

A deafening roar shook the air. Dorn stumbled, crying out in terror.

I threw a look over my shoulder.

Oh... *gods*.

Silhouetted against the rising sun, the dragon rose in the sky like a monster straight from hell.

"What is that?" Teos cried.

I couldn't find the words to answer because my mind couldn't wrap itself around what I was seeing. I knew what my men had said. They'd seen a dragon in the Wild Lands. And of course I hadn't thought they were lying.

But holy *gods*. I'd only ever seen dragons in paintings and tapestries, and every book claimed the creatures had gone extinct centuries ago, if they'd even existed at all.

Clearly, the books were wrong.

The dragon opened its massive jaw, its long and brutal fangs promising death to any who came near. A fountain of flame erupted from its throat like a battering ram of fire, slamming down to the earth and then raking across the city. The blast snapped and snarled like a monster of its own, and the heat reached us even here, making me wince as my skin tightened like I'd come too close to a raging bonfire.

But an oily, oozing sensation carried on the heat too, making me want to flee and yet bite something, all at the same time. The feeling wasn't like it'd been in the forest days ago, but I still recognized the effect.

That was the power of the Voidborn.

Beating its wings so powerfully the air made great walloping sounds, the dragon cut off the torrent of flame. Smoke billowed from the edge of the city, choking the sunrise and curling in the wind stirred up by the dragon's wings.

The creature swung its massive head toward us.

Oh *hell*.

Instinct drove me to shift. Stretching as far as I could, I tried to grab Roan, the woman, and her boys alike, determined to get us all out of here *now*.

But Roan only released the woman and then stumbled away from me.

And he stopped running.

Horrified and confused, I set the boys down and then shifted back to human form. "What are you doing?"

He didn't respond. He wasn't looking at me. At *anyone*, not even the dragon. His unfocused gaze lived somewhere in the middle space between us and the burning edge of the city. Slowly, his head shook back and forth as if in denial of something.

"Roan, what's wrong?" I threw a frantic glance at the dragon. The creature was almost on top of us. "We have to go!"

He didn't move, and when he spoke, his voice was as distant as his gaze, like he was speaking from someplace infinitely far away. "You have to get away from me, Gwyneira. As fast and as far as you can. Don't come back."

"What? I'm not leaving you!"

He didn't react at all.

At a loss, I floundered. Why would he say this?

Unless...

Cold fear stole my breath. The fire. That oily, oozing sensation. What if that strange feeling hadn't been *just* the Voidborn's power?

It was actually one of them.

And now they had Roan.

"Fight," I urged, terrified. "Please, you have to—"

The dragon slammed down onto the houses behind us, crushing the stone and wood and sending clouds of soot and dust into the air. Its roar bellowed out over the communal garden, shaking the walls of the houses and making me clamp my hands to my ears instinctively.

With a scream, the woman scrambled up and took off running, her two little boys in tow. She stumbled and wavered on her feet from her injuries, but adrenaline and the need to protect her children was clearly a powerful fuel, propelling her forward until she disappeared beyond the houses.

I couldn't move. "Roan, *please*. Fight."

A growl rumbled out over the gardens, and my eyes slid back to the dragon. Its emerald scales gleamed in the light of the burning city, and its eyes radiated a sickening shade of yellow, like puss and disease but lit up like the sun. While the harpies screamed and shrieked with joy above it, an orange glow started behind the green scales of the dragon's belly, the promise of another blast of flame none of us would escape.

But its eyes weren't on me.

"Gwyneira..." Roan's voice was agonized. He still stared at nothing like he didn't notice the dragon or the harpies at all. "Run. Get away. I... I don't want you to die."

Anguish flooded me like hot metal in my chest. Dammit, he'd just started acting like a *person* instead of an asshole, and now the Voidborn were trying to take that away.

I couldn't let them have him, but I didn't know what to do.

Desperate, I reached for him.

My hand landed on his arm, and he jolted like I'd struck him with a branding iron. A choked cry ripped from him and he tore free of my grasp, his body shaking so hard I swore he'd shatter his own bones.

Stumbling to a stop several feet away, Roan turned his head. His eyes found mine, and they were full of anguish like his heart was breaking. "Not her. Please don't destroy her too."

Horror stole my breath. He was begging the *Voidborn* now. Oh gods. "Please, Roan. No. Don't give up."

A red glow began to burn around the edges of his eyes. His expression was filled with such pain and regret, it made me want to cry. "Run," he begged me.

The dragon drew a deep breath.

A scream ripped from Roan like the world was dying. With a lurch, he threw his head back, his spine arching and his body going rigid like he was being stretched to the brink.

Even the dragon paused.

Just as sharply, Roan's body snapped forward again, his scream coming to an end. His dark hair fell around his face. Everything about him hung limp, as still as a puppet with his strings cut.

"No," came his soft, pleading whisper.

Overhead, the harpies fell silent, and a low growl rumbled from the dragon. But it didn't seem pleased or victorious.

That was the growl of a predator who suddenly saw something it *really* didn't like.

A terrifying new possibility suddenly filled me with dread. Had Roan been taken over by a *worse* Voidborn than whatever was in that dragon?

Roan drew himself up again. Every trace of fear and

pain melted from his face like it'd never been. A regal sort of amusement took its place, colder and more callous than anything I'd ever seen, even from him. His dark eyes swept the dragon, and he regarded the giant monster like it was an impetuous kitten trying to convince him it was a tiger.

Anguish joined my dread in a dark wave. Gods, please, no. Roan couldn't be gone. The Voidborn couldn't just—

"I said..." Roan's brow arched like a king eyeing the pathetic fool who'd thought to touch what belonged to him. "No."

The red glow in his eyes became fire. In a rush, it spread in a jagged pattern from the corners of his eyes through his temples, down into his cheeks and jaw like flames cracking through the surface of the earth. Around each fissure, his skin turned gray like it'd been burned to ash.

And suddenly, he transformed.

I stumbled back, shocked. His bones shifted and his body grew larger, until he towered as tall as Ozias's massive beast in height. Enormous wings ripped from his back. His clothes ripped and burned as all of his skin charred from deathly pale to the dark gray color of ash, though a glow like fire still showed through jagged cracks around his eyes. His cheeks and jaw became sharply pronounced, like a savage mask that only barely looked like the man I knew. A thick, sinuous tail whipped out behind him, lashing the air like a weapon unto itself, and his wings were tipped by curved points of bone that looked ready to tear flesh. Thick black horns rose from his head, their glossy surface reflecting the firelight, and on his massive hands, his fingers were tipped by dark claws that appeared as vicious as knives. When he grinned, his teeth were chipped to jagged points, interrupted by two long fangs.

He was also totally naked. His thick cock hung free between his legs, his length ridged and not remotely like a human or Erenlian's.

But he clearly didn't give a damn that he was naked. Or that he looked like every bit as much of a monster as any of the creatures around us. The full extent of that alien gleam I'd sometimes seen in his eyes was present now.

Holy gods... this might not be the Voidborn. This could be *Roan* or whatever had been inside him, whatever he'd warned me about all those days ago.

And it had just fully taken control.

Gone was the way he shrunk into the shadows and the way he avoided everyone's gaze. Gone was any trace of reticence at all. He stared the dragon down like he already knew he'd won, his lips curling into a smile that promised death, dark and bloody.

The dragon took a step backward, stones and wooden beams crunching under its enormous clawed feet. Inhaling deeply, it opened its maw to blast us with fire.

Roan chuckled.

Flames surged around his body like a blaze inside him had only been waiting for an invitation to emerge. In a blur of burning light and beating wings, he surged forward and slammed into the dragon, sending the massive creature tumbling backward into the street.

The harpies screamed and dove after them.

Gasping, I ran, trying to keep Roan in sight. Beyond the gap torn by the dragon's landing in the ring of houses around me, the city was an inferno, but that didn't matter to Roan. It was like he didn't feel the flames at all.

"Gwyneira!" Dex's shout rang out behind me.

I turned. He and the rest of my men raced through the gap between the houses at the other end of the gardens. Byron had a vicious burn on his shoulder, and Clay bore a gash on his head with dried blood trails dripping down his temple, but none of them delayed rushing in my direction across the wide space.

At least until they caught sight of Roan and the dragon fighting past the gap in the houses ahead of me.

Eyes wide, Clay gaped at the battle. "What the *fuck* is that?"

I was almost *entirely* certain he didn't mean the dragon. "It's Roan."

The way he turned his stare on me told me I was right.

Niko's head shook. "That's not... He isn't..." His mouth moved as he seemed to run out of words.

Another roar came from the dragon, yanking my attention back. Swinging its fanged jaw, the creature slammed the side of its snout into Roan, succeeding briefly in knocking him aside.

But even the dragon had apparently concluded it was outmatched. Beating its wings hard, it took the small victory as an opening and launched into the sky in what looked like a desperate attempt to flee.

Roan wouldn't allow that.

Leaping upward, he caught the air with his own wings and raced after the creature, colliding with it at high speed and sending it careening wildly through the air. Harpies screeched and circled, darting at him like an angry flock of birds trying to drive away a predator. But none could get close enough to the fire all around him to stop him slashing at the dragon.

"I take it none of you knew your friend was a... whatever that is," Casimir said carefully behind me.

Everyone's silence was answer enough. Even Ozias radiated shock, and I got the feeling that, whether or not he'd suspected something was different about Roan, he definitely had never imagined *this*.

The dragon's movements began to slow, turning sluggish and fitful. Its wings flapped erratically, fighting to keep it aloft, but it was losing height fast and Roan never let up.

"Watch out!" Dex shouted as it careened through the sky, tumbling straight toward us.

At the last moment, Roan slammed into its side again, propelling it past us.

The earth shook as the dragon crashed down onto the gardens. Dozens of gashes leaked blood all across its emerald scales. Its neck and head sprawled across the rubble of a house, while its body crushed the fallow plots of garden land. In fits and starts, its sides jerked as if the creature was fighting to breathe.

A twist of black smoke rushed out of its side where no fire should be.

I tensed. The Voidborn.

Roan dove toward it, and a strangled sound of shocked protest left Niko, as if he couldn't believe Roan would try attacking that thing too. But before Roan could reach it, the Voidborn took off, racing into the city like it was fleeing for its life.

Groaning, the dragon sagged to the ground.

I didn't move. I'd forgotten to breathe an untold amount of time ago, and I couldn't hear a sound from any of my men either.

His wings beating steadily, Roan hovered above the fallen dragon for a moment, surveying it like a knight observing a vanquished foe. The creature was still breathing—barely—but it made no attempt to attack or defend itself.

With a contemptuous jerk of his head, Roan left the fallen dragon behind and flew toward us.

I couldn't find words. But then, what was I supposed to say? Thanks for saving me? Us? Yes, of course, that much was obvious.

What *wasn't* obvious was whether I was still talking to the man I knew.

Gracefully, he descended to the ground only a few yards ahead of me, landing so easily it was like he'd been flying forever. But his gaze never touched the others. It was as if they didn't exist at all.

He only looked at me.

Shivers coursed through me out of nowhere. There was something so hungry in that gaze. So wild.

Not to mention it was rather obvious he was getting hard.

Swallowing dryly, I stayed where I was, unsure what the hell I should do. The air stirred as Ozias stepped closer to me, his footsteps utterly silent. Caution radiated through my connection to him, and from the corner of my eye, I could see his gaze locked on the winged creature that was hopefully still his friend.

But I remembered how Roan had acted right before he transformed. How scared he'd been. How he'd begged me to run. Even if he *hadn't* been taken over by a Voidborn, whatever the hell lived inside him clearly wasn't something he trusted.

His fiery eyes darted to Ozias as my mate's hand landed on my shoulder. This close, I could see they weren't just made of fire but had a black center like the depths of night, with only a few flecks of light where an iris would have been, glinting like stars struggling not to die in the dark.

Studying Ozias, Roan's head twisted to one side as if he was considering unleashing the fire again.

"Don't," I said.

His gaze snapped back to me for a heartbeat, and then it flashed over to Casimir as the vampire came up to my other side, Ruhl pacing along with him in wolf form.

At the sight of the wolf, Roan's lips pulled back. It was a grin, but gods, it looked threatening with all those pointed teeth.

But there was a certain odd familiarity in his fiery eyes too. Like whatever he was now recognized something about the shadow wolf.

"Is that you, Roan?" I asked carefully.

His gaze returned to me. Cold hunger glinted in his eyes. "No." His grin spread, taking on an edge like a predator looking at prey. "Mine."

Before I could say a word, he lunged. I recoiled in

shock, but Ozias and Casimir didn't hesitate, moving immediately to intercept him.

They didn't make it far.

Snarling, Roan shoved Ozias hard and sent him hurtling through the air to crash into the debris of a burnt house. Whirling, he slashed at Casimir with his claws. The vampire fell back, burned gashes torn across his chest. Ruhl surged forward, but even the wolf wasn't fast enough.

Wrapping his arms around me, Roan shot into the air, taking me with him.

22

THE DEMON

ine.

We had *mine.*

No one would take her from us now.

On the ground, the giant men and the vampire regrouped, while the shadow wolf spun and snarled, torn between chasing me and protecting his wounded charge. In my grip, our treluria twisted.

A memory from the broken one told me how she could try to escape us as smoke and shadow.

"Don't shift," I growled. "Won't hurt them more if you don't shift."

She stilled in understanding.

I sped over the burning city and out onto the open plains, leaving the giants and the vampire behind. Threatening those men didn't satisfy the way it should have. Neither did wounding that vampire. Our treluria would be upset if I needed to fight them. She wouldn't trust us if I harmed them more than I had already. I knew this, and the broken one was sure of it. But she was *ours*. Nothing and no one would stand in the way of that.

In my arms, she was breathing in a fast but steady rhythm, which pleased me. Not only because it meant she was keeping herself calm, but because it meant she'd fed enough recently. She would need strength for when I mated her.

Irritation rose then, but not from me. The broken one wasn't fully asleep. Hints of him came from the depths of my mind, drifting up like the murmurs of an angry dreamer on the edge of waking. I'd ripped control away from him in order to protect her, locked him away for his own good so he wouldn't interfere and risk her. But still he was fighting me.

And he didn't like the idea of taking her. Not unless she wanted that.

Yet that was nonsense. Of course we wouldn't take her if she wasn't willing. We would kill anyone who dared try such a thing. But our treluria *would* be willing. More than willing. Didn't he understand that?

He doubted me. Emphatically.

My teeth ground, the jagged points scraping against one another. The broken one was foolish. Our treluria only needed to understand and then she would agree.

She was ours.

Theirs too, the broken one whispered.

I pushed him down harder, just as he so often tried to push me away.

And he went. After all, I was stronger than him. I always had been. I allowed him to push me down only because I chose to tolerate his needs.

But now we needed to mate our treluria and complete our bond with her. Only then would she be truly safe.

Far away, he murmured again of how the strange one named Ozias had bonded her too.

My irritation grew. I did not wish to tolerate his words any longer, and thus, I pushed him so deep down, no whisper of him remained.

Up ahead, a crumbling tower of stone stood atop a hillside. An outpost long abandoned and left to rot in the elements. But it was tall, with only one spiral stairway up its side, most of which had eroded to nothing now, and gave a view of the terrain for miles around. No one would approach without me seeing them nor be able to reach us at the top.

Except perhaps that vampire.

I dismissed the thought. The vampire was wounded. Even if he could find us, he would not dare confront me if he wished to survive, and thus he did not matter.

Here, our mate would be safe.

I landed on the flat top of the tower. The center of the roof had long ago crumbled down into the levels below and stunted plants grew in the cracks between the stones, but most of the ground was still secure. Walls like broken teeth surrounded the edge, shielding my mate from the view of anything that dared approach from below, and nothing could come from above without me seeing it from miles away.

Once I was in position to keep her from falling into the gaping hole, I released her.

She retreated from me, eyes wide. "I want to speak to Roan. The other version of Roan."

A vexed noise escaped my lips.

Her expression turned insistent. "Now."

"No."

"Why not?"

She questioned me?

Her eyes narrowed like she caught something of my thoughts in my expression, and the reaction was enough to dim my irritation, if only slightly. My treluria was attuned to me. She simply didn't realize it yet.

"Who are you, then?" she asked. "Do I call you Roan too?"

My annoyance faded, but I couldn't define the strange feeling that took its place. It wasn't confusion. I was never confused. It was only that her question implied a need to explain myself. Identify myself, when I was nothing *but* myself. I needed no definition.

"I am the demon."

"Roan's demon?"

I huffed with indignation. "I belong to no one."

She gave a careful nod like she was accepting the answer because I spoke it, not because she believed.

But the acceptance still pleased me, if only by a small amount.

Her eyes darted to the open air and then down to my cock before returning to my face. "Why have you brought me here?"

I grinned. She saw how good I would be for her. How no one would interrupt us when I brought her pleasure. To be sure, her smaller body would need time to adjust to me. To take me fully, if she even could. But I would be patient. I would go slowly, until she ached to be filled by me again and again. "Because you are mine."

Rather than appear pleased, she tensed and her head lifted with an air of regal alarm, as if I had crossed a boundary between us.

But that was preposterous. No such thing should have existed.

She was being foolish too.

"I don't belong to you," she replied.

I snarled, taking a step forward before I caught myself. "You are *mine*."

Her head shook, absolutely no doubt or fear in her eyes. "I belong to me. I choose to share myself with certain others. You are not one of them."

The words were ludicrous. Insane. They made heat warp the air around my body, and I would not tolerate them. "You are my treluria!"

She froze.

Satisfaction surged in me. Now she understood. She would stop this foolishness and—

"I'm not sure you know what that means. Or, at least, what it means to me and those I love."

I stared, aghast at her mad words. "It means you are *mine!*"

Her eyebrow arched, every inch of her a queen. "And that proves it. Because if you did know, then you'd realize you can't treat your true love like an object you control, regardless of what they want. Like something you *own*, just because you say so. You don't rip them away from the men they love, injure those men, and then expect that person to be yours just because you demand it. That's not true love." She ran her eyes over me like she was peering past me to the broken one inside. "And whatever *you* might be, I hope Roan, at least, knows that."

I took a step back, as shocked as I would have been if she'd stabbed a blade into my chest. How could she believe the broken one surpassed me? I, who only entertained his existence because if I did not, he would have no one. He would break fully if I was gone, with nothing left at all. But he did not compare to me.

Nothing in her eyes hinted she understood that.

Shudders rolled through me, cold and strange. No. This wasn't right. This wasn't how it was supposed to go.

"Is that why he never told us about you?" she continued. "Why he told me to stay away? To run when you started to appear? Because he knew you couldn't live among us without tearing everything apart?"

My body shook, every word like a knife chipping away at something in my chest. And it hurt. It hurt like death because this was all wrong. All broken, when it should have been fine now that I was the one in control. Now that the broken one was mostly asleep and she could see what I—

"Give me Roan back," she said. "Now."

But she didn't see.

She didn't know.

I drew in on myself, cold horror making the world hurt too much to withstand.

The broken one had been right. We were not worthy of a treluria. Not in her eyes. The only woman we both wanted, the one we knew throughout our entire being was *ours...*

Didn't want us.

The cold shivers grew worse. No, not *us*. That wasn't it. She tolerated the broken one, even if she didn't want him the way he wanted her. But he wasn't the one she rejected. The one she looked upon with such disdain. I was, and that made the truth more than clear.

She was my treluria.

And she hated me.

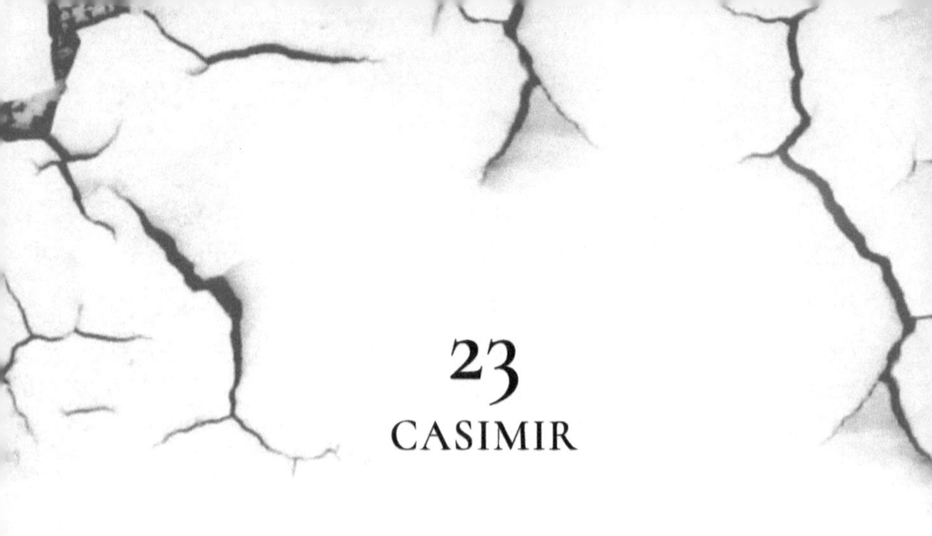

23
CASIMIR

The creature disappeared into the sky with Princess Gwyneira, and I could do nothing to stop it.

I had not felt this much rage since the day my kingdom fell.

"What the fuck was *that*?" Clay spun, staring at his friends as if they would have an answer.

Ozias snarled as he shoved out of the charred debris where the creature had thrown him. Soot smeared the man from head to toe, lending him an even more wild air, as did the vicious fury in his eyes. He stalked toward the pathway leading from this odd communal garden space, only to retreat when the flames burning in the city street beyond proved too hot for him to continue.

At which point he began pacing along the perimeter of the houses like an animal in a cage seeking the slightest weakness to give him a way out.

It reminded me of my shadow wolves when they

chafed at the need to remain in place for any length of time.

And that was only one of the many questions surrounding that man. I had not yet isolated the reason for why Ozias seemed so different from his companions, but I also had not missed how Ruhl reacted to him nor how something had shifted between Ozias and Gwyneira in the time they were gone.

Given what just happened a moment ago, it made me wonder if Roan wasn't the only one hiding something.

But first things first.

"Stay here," I said to Ruhl. The wolf's body was more of a churning smoke cloud than any solid form at this point, moving fitfully in his frustration. At my words, his head emerged from the smoke, and he growled. His green eyes skipped down to the wound on my chest and then back to me.

Ruhl never spoke, though I could never fully suppress the flight of fancy that made me think he simply chose not to. Yet he still communicated quite clearly, and right now, it was obvious he did not want me changing form nor flying with this wound.

But needs must.

I shifted into my smoke and shadow, rising to follow the creature that had taken Gwyneira.

Or I tried to.

A burning sensation lanced through me, like I wasn't just smoke but had been set on fire. I crashed back to the earth, returning to solid form out of pure desperation.

But it only barely helped. The claw wounds still burned like a particularly aggressive brand had been scorched in my skin. My heart stuttered at the agony, and my hands gripped the grass as if that could somehow stabilize me against the pain.

"Whoa, what just happened?" Dex strode over to me.

I shuddered, trying to find words. The pain was receding, but that did nothing for my rage. What the hell had that creature done to me?

"You good, Cas?" Clay called.

The nickname pulled my attention to him, though my chest still rose and fell in ragged breaths from the residual pain. No one in my former life in Zenirya would have dared give me a nickname, much less use it in my presence. Yet the fact the blond giant had done so did not offend me.

It was a sign of belonging, and I found myself unexpectedly pleased by that.

Dex reached down, offering his hand—another gesture of acceptance.

I took it gratefully.

"It appears," I said while he helped me to my feet, "the effect of this wound is more pervasive than I anticipated."

"There might be a reason for that," Byron said, studying the sky like he was piecing together a puzzle in his mind. By his side, Niko carefully tied off a bandage on the scholar's burned shoulder before turning his attention to the gash on Clay's forehead.

"And that would be?" Dex prompted.

"Stygiaterros," Byron replied.

Understanding hit me, followed by a rush of irritation

aimed entirely at myself. I was a fool. Of course. Though how the hell one of those was here…

"Stidgy what now?" Clay gave his friend a baffled look.

Not answering, Byron grimaced in pain as he adjusted the bandage on his wound.

"Leave that alone," Niko called without looking away from his examination of Clay's injury.

Byron frowned at him and then grunted as he shifted the bandage again slightly. Shaking his head, Niko rolled his eyes like he expected nothing less.

"Stygi-a-terros," I answered in the scholar's place, pronouncing the word more carefully for the other giants' benefit.

Dex's eyes narrowed. "What does that mean?"

"Is that a spell or something?" Lars asked.

I shook my head. "It is a creature. One of the many species of beings found within the demonic realm."

A new thought occurred to me. There were countless creatures in that realm, but precious few ever crossed over to this one.

Few was not none.

I looked at Ruhl.

His green eyes glowing the same as ever, the wolf met my silent question with a bland and indecipherable stare, revealing nothing.

"So, okay, wait." Clay's face was a picture of incredulity. "You're saying Roan's a *demon*?"

I marveled that he questioned it, given how that creature appeared. "Well, yes."

"Roan is our friend," Niko countered, but his tone

made it sound like he was trying to convince himself as much as me, and he didn't meet anyone's eyes as he spoke.

The young man was a gentle sort, I knew. He rarely argued, seeming content to let the others take the lead in any dispute. But I'd seen enough to learn he was a fighter and not to be underestimated in his fierce loyalty to the princess or his friends.

Right now, he looked like that faith had been shaken. *Hard.*

Thus, I merely gave a measured nod and said, "Indeed. I meant no offense, and I doubt your scholar did either. But several aspects of Roan's form match those I've seen in books I studied over the years, and the possessive behaviors he exhibited in his... *altered* state would also tend toward that explanation."

To say nothing of the wounds on my chest.

Gods, if that demon hurt the princess...

Rage snarled through my veins again, demanding I take off after her right now, never mind that I could not do so. No, that creature had trapped me quite well, constraining me to a form that couldn't pursue him easily. And it would be no simple matter to correct that. Demonic wounds were problematic at best. Healing them would be complicated and take time.

Would he tear into her too if she tried to escape him? Would he trap her with him, as unable to shift or fly as I currently was, and thus leave her entirely at his mercy?

A shudder rolled through me as old memories ghosted through my mind. They were my constant companions, these horrific nightmares that waited to assault me at any moment even when I was awake. And I would never forget them, not if I lived to be a thousand. The cries and screams of the final days of my kingdom echoed forever in my ears. The sight of ordinary people turned into vampires was burned indelibly behind my eyes. How there'd been nothing of their former selves in their eyes. How they'd torn into their loved ones with no care for who their victims had once been to them. Friends. Family. Children. None of it mattered. They fed on them all and laughed with glee as the innocents died.

Nothing of Roan had been in those demonic eyes.

"Roan is Erenlian," Lars said, drawing my attention back to the present moment. "He was raised Erenlian, and he lost his family in the war. He told us that."

Gods, I longed for the days when I might have believed such a thing could matter to a monster.

I did not rebuke him, though. I could not afford to alienate these men, not when I would likely need their help to save Gwyneira. Instead, I only made a level sound of acknowledgement. "Perhaps he is only half."

By the wall of flame, Ozias looked back at me, his eyes sharp in his soot-smeared face. I could not read the way he studied me, but it piqued my curiosity even as it deepened my suspicion.

Now why would *that* statement have prompted him to turn when nothing else had?

"We'll ask Roan when we find him." With his sword in hand, Dex started toward the gap between houses that led to the street. "When we find them both. Lars?" He jerked his chin at the fire between the houses ahead and then stalked forward when his friend used magic to quell the blaze.

I followed immediately. I appreciated many things about that man, and his focus was definitely one of them —especially seeing as, right now, it was mine too.

My gaze tracked across the sky. I could see no sign of that monster, but it was no matter. We would find the princess. We would stop Roan from hurting her, no matter *what* he truly was. And if for any reason we were too late, if he'd already harmed her in any way...

Even demons could die.

24
DEX

The heat of the fires parched my skin, the smoke burned my lungs, and everywhere I turned, the destruction looked like what I saw in the war.

Except this time monsters were responsible, and my treluria had just been taken by one of them.

The one I'd called *friend*.

I reached the street, and my innate sense of direction sent me to the right immediately. The gate lay this way, and beyond it, the open terrain where maybe we'd get a better idea of which way Roan had gone.

I didn't want to think of what I'd do if we lost him— and her—entirely.

Exhaling sharply, I kept moving. Debris crunched under my feet and the lingering smoke seared my lungs, bringing back too many memories of other cities, other days when I'd marched through the aftermath of destruction with other men who would eventually betray me.

My hand tightened on the hilt of my sword. I couldn't have loosened my grip on it if I tried.

I rounded a corner, and the gate came into sight ahead. It was only partially standing, one side of the massive barricade charred and smoldering. Burned grassland lay beyond the opening, but like the rest of the city, the harpies were long gone.

They'd taken off the moment that demon appeared, and given what Roan did to the dragon, I didn't want to consider what that meant he was capable of.

What those monsters somehow knew, even if we didn't.

Striding faster down the street toward the gate, I ground my teeth in rage. Years of living around someone. *Years.* And they turned out to be a gods-damned monster, and I never had a clue.

Until they took the woman I loved.

My grip shook on the sword. I wanted to believe Gwyneira would be okay. That, yes, Roan had attacked Ozias and Casimir, wounding the vampire and somehow trapping him in human form, but that didn't mean he'd do the same to her.

Gods, I wanted to believe that. But gambling that someone's better nature would prevent them from doing the unthinkable was a weakness the war had *more* than beaten out of my soul.

"Hold!" came a shout from behind me.

I threw a glance over my shoulder. Lord Thomas strode down the street with his bodyguard, Valeria, at his side and at least twenty armed humans following in his wake.

My grip worked on the sword hilt while my mind ran the angles and came up with *fighting equaled fucked*. Not so much because we couldn't take them. I suspected we could. But because we needed to get after Gwyneira and not waste time trying to stay ahead of an angry human army at our backs.

The lord took one look at us all and seemed to read the situation in its entirety. "Where is the princess?"

Now wasn't *that* the damn question.

My jaw clenched. Thus far, Gwyneira had taken the lead in speaking to the lord and his cohort, with Casimir filling in the gaps as needed. For all our sakes, I'd been willing to let that continue, considering that even the slightest slip-up could have risked her and us alike.

But things had changed. We'd left the castle grounds. We'd revealed ourselves as something other than humans. And yeah, we'd saved dozens of people in this city, maybe more. But even if there wasn't anything about us that specifically said *giant*—and even if there were male witches in the world too—Aneira had never been particularly comfortable with magic even when they were using it to raze my country to the ground.

There was no telling what the lord and his people were going to do now.

I glanced at Casimir. The vampire and I may have only known each other a short while, but I didn't think it was my imagination that we understood one another some-how. We'd both had the lives we thought were ours stolen from us. We'd both trained well in the military arts, and we were both committed to using everything we knew, everything we had, to protect the people in our charge.

And for Gwyneira, we'd cross hell and the empty realms itself.

"Taken," Casimir replied smoothly, turning back to the lord as if there'd never been any question that he would remain the group spokesperson.

"By whom?" Lord Thomas demanded. "Those creatures?"

"Not precisely. It is a rather complicated situation at the moment, but we intend to pursue her now." The vampire's eyes skimmed over the remainder of the lord's guards, all of whom looked like they'd like nothing more than to lock us up—or worse. "Alone."

That didn't go over well. "Why don't you want anybody with you?" one of the guards snapped, his surly tone clearly meant to disguise his fear—not that it was working.

"Because the creature who took her will understandably view you as quite the threat," Casimir replied in a grave tone. "It may not think the same of us."

It was utter bullshit, and I thanked the gods none of my friends—and specifically Clay—laughed.

The guard, however, was an idiot. Never mind the gashes on Casimir's chest that would have felled a human. Never mind the fact that demon just took out a fucking *dragon*. The guard still drew himself up like he was glad someone noticed his brilliance.

Lord Thomas's brow rose. Distrust flashed over Valeria's face.

Those two weren't fooled.

"See to the guard stations and the gate," Lord Thomas

said, turning his attention to his people. "I would speak to these men alone."

Several of the guards hesitated. "But sir…" one began, his eyes darting to us and then back to his leader.

"Valeria will remain with me. Surely no one doubts her prowess in battle nor her ability to defend me if required."

The guy blanched, which was answer enough. Hurriedly, the guards retreated.

A wry look flitted through Valeria's gaze—one she aimed at the lord as much as the other humans.

Lord Thomas met her eyes mildly, his brow arching again, before he returned his attention to us. "You have a way with words," he commented to Casimir.

The vampire didn't respond.

His sharp eyes scanned over us. "You are not witches or sorcerers. I saw enough magic in the war to know that. But I do believe you are worried about the princess, and that this is because you care for her as a person, not merely as an asset in some scheme. Also, I suspect you are alarmed by her disappearance, though perhaps for a different reason than us. So I would have the truth of what you are." Tension flickered through his controlled expression. "And what she is."

Fuck.

Lord Thomas's mouth tightened briefly at our silence. "I saw her at the beginning of the battle. What she did." He turned to Casimir. "And you are like her. Like… whatever she has become."

Casimir held his silence, but this time his gaze flicked over to me. I suspected I could read the question.

Now what?

I let out a slow breath. *Now*, we were burning time. Now there was only one card remaining that I had to play, short of the one that left us fleeing an army while chasing the monster who used to be our friend.

"You are loyal to Aneira?" I asked the lord, watching carefully for the first hint the man intended to call for his guards. "Both you and your bodyguard? You swear this on the royal tree in Lumilia, vowing your lifeblood to the apple and the crown for now and all time?"

"Yes. Without question." Lord Thomas regarded me curiously for a moment. "You speak as if you are a soldier of the crown."

Here went nothing... "I was. I serve Princess Gwyneira. We all do. We would die to save her. But to do this, we need to leave. Now."

Valeria spoke up, a shrewd expression on her face. "You're not Aneiran, are you?"

There wasn't much *question* in that question.

I drew a breath. "We—"

"We're Erenlian," Niko interrupted before I could thread that needle as carefully as I planned.

Shit.

Lord Thomas froze. Valeria's hand went for her sword.

Magic surged on the air, coming from my friends, but the lord caught Valeria's wrist before she could draw the blade. "No."

He held up a hand to us too with a cautious expression. "We need no more battles today."

Now, *that* was unexpected...

"Stand down," I said to the others, watching him.

The magic faded behind me.

"What the fuck, Niko?" Clay demanded.

"Lies serve no one," the younger man replied, his voice tight. Controlled. He wouldn't meet my eyes.

My jaw clenched with the urge to tell him suicide didn't either, but there was nothing for it. The truth was out now, and we were still burning time.

"We're not your enemies," I said. "Not unless you endanger the princess."

Lord Thomas's eyes scanned the others and then returned to me, a trace of suspicion coming into his gaze.

My stomach sank. He was putting the pieces together. The ones that probably would have occurred to him anyway, but thanks to Niko's honesty, I couldn't steer their arrangement.

"And the one who took the princess?" he asked.

I paused. "We're not sure what happened there."

The words weren't a lie. More like half a truth. Because I sure as hell didn't want to add *demon* to the conversation.

Thank the gods Niko apparently didn't either.

The lord gave a measured nod. "But you and the princess," he continued to Casimir. "You are both something else entirely."

Countless scenarios raced through my mind. Tactics and strategies and a thousand different outcomes. But then Casimir glanced at me, a confidence in his eyes that promised *we* wouldn't be the ones to suffer if anything went wrong.

Fair enough. I tilted my head in a gesture for him to go ahead.

A regal expression coming onto his face, the vampire turned back to Lord Thomas. "I am King Casimir zel Elric ver Altreya, ruler of Zenirya." A precise smile touched his lips, not too friendly, not too cold. "I was turned into a vampire at the onset of the Witch War, and recently, I was reclaimed from my self-imposed exile by Princess Gwyneira. I too am loyal to the princess. Any who threaten her or her allies will answer to me."

His fangs crept into his smile when he finished.

Lord Thomas recoiled slightly. Valeria's hand flinched toward her blade again.

"King Casimir is a rarity among his kind," Byron spoke up. "A vampire who retained the conscience and compassion he possessed as a human. And after she was turned by her stepmother, Princess Gwyneira was able to do the same. But most do not—including Queen Melisandre. She chose to become a vampire decades ago, and she turned the princess with the intent of sacrificing the girl to the Voidborn."

Silence followed after Byron finished, and when Lord Thomas finally spoke, his tone held the caution one used when conversing with madmen. "You realize this story is scarcely credible, yes?"

It was hard not to scoff at the obvious. "Yes," I replied. "But we would also hope the hero of the Azure Pass and the savior of the Elorian Gulch would be familiar with facing that which seems impossible."

Lord Thomas's eyes flicked back to me, a hint of wry estimation entering his gaze. "You're the so-called traitor of Orlindria, aren't you?"

"I am the loyal ally of Princess Gwyneira," I replied.

He made a thoughtful sound.

I braced myself.

"I can't say I support a soldier lying about their identity," he replied. "And the fact that an Erenlian infiltrated our ranks certainly didn't help with morale or trust among our remaining troops after you were discovered. The king and queen instituted all manner of safeguards after that, some of them quite... unsavory." His mouth tightened briefly. "But what those soldiers did in Orlindria was a disgrace. You have my respect for trying to stop it."

I couldn't have been more shocked than if he'd revealed he was Erenlian too. An Aneiran general—a hero of their fucking war—*respected* what most of their side considered treason.

Holy shit.

I cleared my throat, realizing I hadn't said a word, and old training rose fast, burying my shock beneath the neutral tone I'd used for years in the army. "Thank you, sir."

Lord Thomas tilted his head in a brief nod. "Over the years, many have called me an idealist. Perhaps I am. But where some would see a princess allied with traitors and foreign powers, I see a woman who has managed to draw together forces who have every reason to hate her or use her, but who've devoted themselves to her with unwavering loyalty instead, even at a cost to themselves." His gaze ran across us all. "Vampire or not, Gwyneira possesses the soul of what Aneira once was. A connector of countless nations, welcoming all and seeking peace not war. Gods willing, with her help that's what this country will be again."

I was speechless. Gwyneira had been right when she said we should come here. More than I could have expected or known.

Gods help us, maybe there was hope for this country yet.

The lord glanced over at Valeria. "Have the guards gather horses for these men. Bring one for Princess Gwyneira too. And give them any supplies they need." His face turned somber. "Go save the princess, gentlemen. Whatever it takes."

25
MELISANDRE

The ground lurched. The sun returned to the sky.

I barely noticed.

What Alaric claimed, the glowing-eyed reflection he showed me in that sword blade... it could not be true. None of it.

I would never believe his lies.

I'd seen him standing on the shore of that distant northern sea when I first came back to this world. His face had been like an eel, and his words were limited and sibilant. I'd witnessed how he transformed more and more into a man with every passing hour, until he'd taken on the despicable appearance of a nobleman that he wore now.

"Merely your fiction, pet." The world faded, not flickering into somewhere else, but merely descending into the darkness of oblivion. Through it, his voice slid around me like an invisible snake. "Shapes your mind crafted to shield you from my intrusion."

My head shook, the sensation distant in the dark.

"I learned this realm's speech from *you*, and your mind tried to explain it away by transforming me from a mere monster into an image of something you hated. You invented it all to give yourself the illusion of being apart from me. To offer the false hope that you might escape."

No. No, that wasn't true. Humans had reacted to him too. They'd run, they'd screamed. Even Stelaruna had—

The world appeared again, bringing the mountains closer, only to vanish into oblivion once more. "See it again, pet."

Images played out around me, memories but as visceral as if they were happening now. Humans pled with me to spare their lives. My hands grasped them, yanked them closer. Stelaruna stared with horror not at Alaric, but straight into my eyes.

"You lie," I whispered. "She spoke to us both."

"Well, yes." His pitying tone slithered across me. "It was amusing to see her plead for you to overthrow my hold on your body, as if you could do anything of the sort."

I refused to tremble, even as the memories flashed through my mind. He'd somehow prevented me from speaking when we faced her, closing my throat without even touching me and keeping it that way until he willed my voice to return.

"Now you see. It was always you. Your body. My control."

"The blood." I threw the words back at him. "The angelic blood. You held my face. You forced me to ingest it."

"Another illusion. You were hiding in your mind, trying to keep it from affecting you. I forced you to let it in."

The memory flickered. *My* fist held the Voidborn. *My* hand reached into its throat. My face was the one that twisted in irritation when she—no, when *I*—fought in vain to hide from the spells I—*he, dammit*—cast upon my body. The body.

No. *Mine.*

Panic began to swell, and no amount of willing it to recede would stop the waves from surging. My thoughts were blurry, but the *wrong* version, the *lie* version felt more real with every passing second.

And that couldn't be. It *couldn't.* I wouldn't let it. I was Queen Melisandre...

Fleeing the memories, I retreated in the darkness. Alaric laughed, but the sound was distant, as if I'd withdrawn from him.

Unless that was an illusion too.

"Of course it is." His voice felt as if it was right beside my ear.

I shrieked as I hadn't since I was a small girl, when the cruel village children would find my hiding place after chasing me with the intention of throwing me into the pigsty. I thrashed in the midst of oblivion like I was no witch queen but a frightened, pathetic child who knew nothing of fighting, not with magic or even with her fists.

Alaric's laughter rang in the dark.

I trembled without a body. I wanted to cry even though I could feel no tears. Reality returned in fits and starts, as if he was letting me see the world for the pure joy of torturing me with it. The mountains jumped closer and closer, until they reared like titanic barricades of stone so high, they speared the sky.

And below them, Lumilia gleamed in torchlight and pale stone.

We'd come to my city. The heart of what should be my empire.

But I could only see it from the other end of a dark tunnel, as unable to reach out and touch it as if I stood at the bottom of the sea.

The castle rose from the heart of the city, massive and imposing, while the rest of Lumilia crowded around its base like children seeking shelter from the great wide world beyond. My banners still hung from the towers, and more of my symbols hung on the outer wall surrounding the city itself, as if Lumilia had been waiting this entire time to welcome me back to my throne.

Now they would only welcome *him*.

I screamed in rage, and the sound echoed uselessly, drowning in oblivion and never reaching the outside world. I strained to escape the dark only to collapse in upon myself like a mountain robbed of its core. Even now, his Voidborn descended upon the city. *My* city. The monsters they inhabited tore into the populace, slaughtering the ones who should have been my servants if only they'd been turned. With every useless body that hit the ground never to rise again, my future army that was going to roll across the world and bend it to my will became nothing but corpses and smears of blood on the pale stone walls.

And I could do nothing.

"It was always going to end like this," Alaric chided. "You kidded yourself to believe it would be any different."

The castle gates reared in front of me... him... us... and in desperation, I strained to stop him from reaching the door. But with a sensation like the back of a hand striking my cheek, Alaric drove me back into the darkness.

"You chose this, pet. You chose it from the moment you offered yourself to us in exchange for the petty thing you call power. It's only because you're a coward that you fight me now."

At the top of the broad castle steps, the door swung open. The old castle steward, Harran, stood there, and he blinked in alarm. "M-my queen."

I had no opportunity to fight for a chance to speak. The world blurred. The castle hallway was around me now, and the building shook in protest of my presence.

Alaric's presence.

Ours.

But even that changed nothing. Servants bowed and hid their gazes from mine. They jolted with alarm and then screamed as monsters flooded through the gate behind me.

I couldn't stop it. Couldn't change anything as they died.

But they were supposed to die to serve *me*. They should have risen again as *my* servants, my army...

"You've seen enough, pet." The darkness grew thicker, taking on weight like a suffocating blanket drawing between me and the world. "There's nothing left for you now."

The pressure of the dark was familiar. Was this what

he had done to make time skip? It was like a thousand pounds of black cotton smothering me and stealing away the world. I couldn't rail against it. Couldn't shove it away.

Light faded, my tunnel view of the world becoming only darkness. Screams whisked away as if blown by a breeze, leaving echoing silence.

I would not disappear.

No, I refused.

I...

Any sense of my body faded away. My mind slowly forgot even the memories of sensation. Of expression. Of existence beyond this dark, empty world of horror.

Because horror it was. Not mere nothingness or petty cruelty. No, this was the essence of the worst moments of my life made manifest. This was the day my father thought I wasn't worth keeping, only for trading to get him a cow. The day the Jeweled Coven's testing proclaimed I was too weak to ever become a *real* witch.

The days when others thought I was nothing.

No one.

Just the greasy, unwashed daughter of a drunken farmer, all alone in the dark.

And Alaric had finally won.

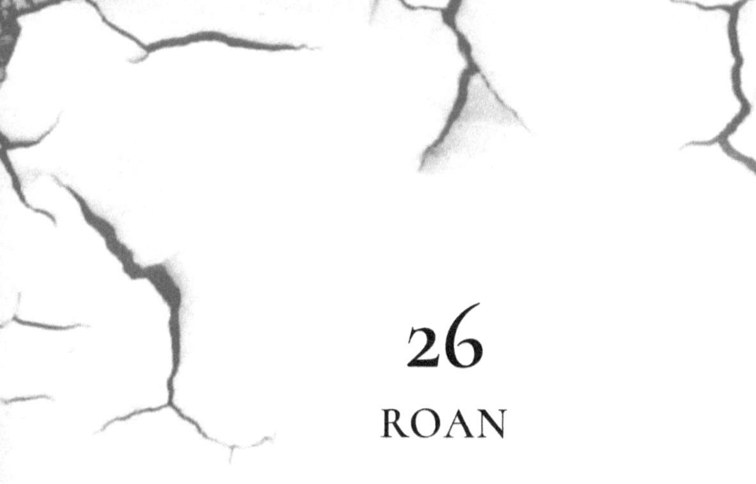

26

ROAN

One moment, I was in a city trying not to kill everyone while a dragon did its best to burn the whole place down, and then suddenly I was standing naked on a stone tower hundreds of feet in the air, freezing my damn dick off in the winter breeze with no idea how I'd gotten here or where *here* even was.

And Gwyneira was glaring at me.

Every other consideration vanished. Oh gods, what had I done?

Fragmented memories flickered past. Gwyneira trying to save that woman and the kids. The dragon landing in front of us, clearly intent on killing everyone. Me begging the princess to run, to save herself.

And then...

Horror gripped me, making my insides roll with nausea. Then the demon took over, and before I could stop myself, I'd shifted.

Right in front of her.

I couldn't breathe as I strained to remember what came next, but everything after that moment was blurry. I knew I'd tried to stop the demon from taking control. Tried to protect Gwyneira from the thing I was. But the demon wasn't about to let some fire-breathing lizard murder the woman we loved, and when it saw the danger she was in, I hadn't stood a chance. It attacked the dragon and won—because of course it had—and then…

Then…

The blank blur of my memories made me want to howl, and inside my mind, the demon huddled, giving me nothing. But the closer I came to the present moment in my efforts to remember, the more pain and anguish and confusion came from the monster inside.

Gods help me, clearly *something* terrible had happened. The demon was upset in a way I hadn't felt from it in well over a decade, since the last time every-thing went so horribly wrong.

And given the way Gwyneira was glaring at me…

"What is it?" I whispered, my voice tight with dread for what I knew was coming.

Confusion flickered through her angry expression.

"What did the demon do?"

The anger returned. "It took me from the others."

Agonized certainty shivered through my veins. That was it, then. The demon had killed them after it finished with the dragon. I wouldn't have wanted that, but the gods knew what I *wanted* had never changed a damned thing. But based on how upset the demon was now, we must have killed them and then—

Images suddenly pelted me hard and fast as if the

demon was hurling them at me. The others standing in the garden commons, staring up as we flew away with our mate. Their rage and horror. The way Gwyneira struggled and then stilled when I—no, the demon—promised not to hurt them, and her regal expression when she told us she wasn't ours.

I staggered backward as the images faded, barely stopping myself from going over the edge of the tower. We hadn't killed them? Oh gods, we actually *hadn't*? Gwyneira's reactions hurt like hell, yes, but that thing also hadn't touched her.

This was better news than I could've dreamed.

Unless the demon was deceiving me. Telling me some story to hide the horrific reality of what we'd done to my friends and the princess, all because it didn't want to feel my pain over it.

Cold dread returned. Fuck me, it *would* do that.

"Did it touch you?" I asked her. "Hurt you?"

Gwyneira's eyes narrowed warily.

Shit, I'd overstepped. Asked too much, too soon. If the demon hurt her, then I definitely shouldn't push her to talk about it until she was ready.

I squeezed my eyes shut, regrouping. "I'm sorry. For whatever it did to you and—" Gods, I wanted to throw up and howl and hurl myself from this tower all at once. "For the others. For what the demon did to them. I'm so sorry."

Her silence was horrible.

"Okay," she said carefully.

My eyes opened. Okay? Just okay? "What?"

Her confused look came back, and I couldn't breathe. That expression could mean anything. Bafflement that I couldn't remember killing them, for instance. Alarm that I would ever forget such a thing. "What do *you* think happened, Roan?"

Why would she ask that?

At my silence, she continued carefully, "The demon saved us. It threw Ozias into a house, and it hurt Casimir, but that's all."

No, that couldn't be true.

Nothing on her face said she was lying.

"It... it didn't kill them?" I could barely get the words out. "It..."

Her head shook. "No."

A choked noise left me. My body was ice, my blood tingling in every limb. But not like I was about to shift or because I was still buck-naked in this gods-damned winter cold. No, I was torn between extremes, unable to breathe and wanting to scream, because the hope and the relief and the sheer question of how the *hell* the demon could have managed that were all too overwhelming.

But... it hadn't killed them. It hadn't burned them. Okay, so the demon might've injured Ozias and I hated that. Definitely injured the vampire too, for which I supposed some part of me was sorry, even if I couldn't stand that bastard.

But no one was dead.

No one... was dead.

"Roan?"

I looked back up at her, reeling, and her beautiful face brought me back to the reality of the present moment. "The demon hurt you, though. You don't have to tell me details. Just please know I'm *so* gods-damned sorry. I never intended for it to—"

"It didn't hurt me."

I froze.

"It *infuriated* me. But it didn't hurt me."

I couldn't keep up. "What? But then why…" I shook my head, trying to dislodge a coherent thought and coming up with nothing. "What happened?"

Somewhere in all of this, her anger had faded, and now she was studying me like she wasn't quite sure who she was looking at anymore. "What are you, Roan? And what's the demon? *Really?* Because it wouldn't give me a straight answer."

I floundered, amazed the demon had managed to carry on a conversation long enough to spark her temper and not her fear.

Though from the look of it, the creature had still made a wreck of things.

Her brow rose, waiting and questioning.

I didn't know what to say, and the fact I was standing here naked hardly helped the situation. What were we? A monster. Or, really, a monster and a man who couldn't protect anyone, least of all from himself. There wasn't anything more to us than that. No name to define whatever the hell we were.

Yet here I was, learning that the creature who was only good for destroying everything and everyone we loved had just *talked* to her.

"Roan? Please, just tell me. What are you?"

My mouth moved. "I-I don't know."

She blinked. "But surely you—"

I turned away, though it only brought me to the edge of a tower I couldn't begin to imagine how we were going to get down. The stairs along the decaying wall looked so unstable, I'd never risk her on them. Whatever roof access had once existed to the tower interior had obviously fallen when the center of the roof collapsed.

We were trapped.

Maybe the demon wanted it that way.

Anger began to boil inside me, making my heart pound harder and harder until my veins felt like ropes tightening around my neck, choking me. That damned demon *would* do that. Give me hope, only to turn around and pick a place where any *decent* man wouldn't take her —and where, if not for the fact she was a vampire, Gwyneira would've been trapped with it. No, it hadn't killed the others. Hadn't burned the city to the ground. But with every gods-damned choice that creature made, it still only ground home the fact that we weren't worthy of her.

We were just a fucking monster.

My eyes landed on a collection of stunted weeds and bushes that had taken root between stones of the parapet nearby. I wasn't remotely as good as Clay at conjuring clothes from thin air, nor as talented as Niko at manipulating nature, but wood responded to me and those scraggly limbs were close enough.

Gwyneira said nothing while I extended a hand over the branches, weaving them together and making them grow by magic until they became a rough blanket to wrap around my shoulders and cover my nakedness.

"Roan."

I didn't turn. Gods, I thought I might actually hate hearing my name on her lips. I truly did. It hurt like hell itself was carving red-hot knives into my flesh.

Because I wanted her screaming it. Moaning it. Crying it out while I thrust into her and made her writhe with pleasure. I wanted her gasping it as I caressed her soft breasts and every inch of her beautiful naked—

I shuddered, shaking my head hard to dispel that disastrous wish.

"I'm sorry."

Alarm froze me. "What?" When I turned, she was studying me, and the gods only knew why. "What the hell do you have to be sorry for?" I demanded.

Her brow drew down, a cautiously curious look spreading over her face. "You never let on how scared of it you are."

I tensed, thrown by the shift in topic.

"You're terrified of the demon, aren't you?"

I recoiled. How the fuck *dare* she just—

A breath left her at my reaction. She turned away, her curiosity vanishing into tired frustration.

Somehow, that small action brought everything in me to a halt.

Damn me, I was driving her away. Punishing her for my own problems and treating her like she was my enemy.

Again.

And all for a battle I'd already lost.

Gods, I truly was the world's biggest moron, wasn't I? What was there to hide now? The demon? Too late there. My past? She already didn't want me. Nothing I said could make this any worse, and yet here I stood, letting my temper act like a shield when the parts of myself I was protecting had already been ripped open and displayed for her to see.

I couldn't be any more despicable in her eyes than I was now.

"You shouldn't be alive." I was distantly surprised my voice didn't shake, given how my lungs felt like they were in a vise. "No one in that city should be."

She turned back, wary confusion on her face that made me think she knew where I was going.

It only further confirmed how hopeless hiding from her had been from the start.

"Everyone dies when it... when *I* lose control. When the monster takes over." Shudders rolled through me. "I thought I could contain it. I *did*, for years. Nobody knew it was there, and nobody needed to know. But then you came into our life, and..."

I grimaced. I was making just as much of a wreck of things as the demon had, making it sound like she was to blame. "It's not your fault. It's mine. I should have left weeks ago because it was getting more and more difficult to keep the demon from breaking free. But when you touched my face in the castle, it helped. It calmed things somehow. So I thought I could contain it again. But I was wrong. When I saw that dragon coming for you, the demon just forced its way out and..."

"You thought the demon was going to kill us all," she said quietly.

I nodded, unable to meet her eyes any longer.

A moment passed before she spoke again. "Who did it kill before?"

My eyes closed. "My family."

A tiny breath left her. She made no other sound.

It pulled the words from me all the same.

"We lived in a village in the Velusian mountains. It's a range in the north of Erenelle. Far from anyone. Not much there. Just goats and old mines, neither of which were good for anything." My eyes squeezed shut tighter. I was only stalling in an effort to delay the inevitable. "I was out hunting with my father and brothers when the Aneirans came. We saw the smoke and heard the screaming and..."

My fingers curled into fists. The demon wasn't reacting to the memory, though. No, this was just me trying to hide from the past, while the monster inside me had buried itself so deep, I could almost let myself pretend it was gone.

"The soldiers had already killed most of the adults by the time we got back. Just cut them down in their houses with weapons made specifically to pierce giant skin. But they'd chained up my mother and some of the other women. And the kids, they..." Nausea rolled through me, same as it always did. "The younger ones were small enough that the soldiers thought they could take them and... and *use* them and..."

I couldn't finish. Even after all these years, the memories still made my gorge rise, each one as raw as a brand burned into my skin. My mother in chains, screaming as she strained against the enchanted locks to reach my sisters and brothers. The children struggling and crying while those bastards laughed.

Just *laughed.*

"That's horrible." Gwyneira's voice was barely a whisper.

I nodded tightly. "We tried to save them. But the soldiers saw us coming. They stabbed my mother right there, grinning like they just wanted us to watch her die. Other soldiers shot at us with crossbows, and when the bolts hit me, I shifted. But the pain was too much and—" I pushed out a sharp breath, making myself continue. "And I lost control. I burned... everything. Every*one.*"

She was silent. I risked a glance over at her, bracing myself for what I would see.

But there was only sorrow.

"Had you ever changed like that before?" she asked softly.

Why would that matter? "A few times. Only at home where no one in the village could see. My parents, they... they knew how to calm me down."

"Were they like you?"

I shook my head. "My family adopted me when I was an infant. My... my *mother* was a girl from another village. Young. No family to speak of. Scared of raising a baby on her own. So she gave me to them. My parents said I didn't start showing what *else* I was until a few years later, and by that time, no one could find the girl again. But..." An ache throbbed in my chest for my parents. For all they'd been, back before I destroyed them. "My mother and father didn't care. Even if none of us ever knew what the hell I was, I was still their son. That's what they always told me. That it didn't matter what I was. They still loved me."

I fell silent, my past whispering on the wind like the far-off, agonized cries of the dead.

"How old were you when they died?" Gwyneira asked.

"Thirteen. Old enough that I should never have let that happen."

"*Let* it happen? You're talking like you were the monster that day."

A pained scoff escaped me. Now she got it. She finally understood. "Exactly."

Gwyneira took a step closer, and when she spoke, her voice was firm. "No. Roan, dammit, *no*. You were barely more than a child, and you saw something horrific happening to the people you loved. You weren't the one who created that nightmare. Those soldiers did. And the fact you reacted when they *shot* you... It's awful. But it doesn't make *you* the monster."

I looked away, despairing. Dammit, I didn't want to hurt her. I'd done that enough. But how much more would it take to make her understand she was wrong about me?

"Roan." She reached for my hand.

I pulled back. "I was awake."

She stopped, but when I turned, all I saw was confusion.

I shuddered. "The demon and I... we were different back then. When I was a kid, we were more *one*, I guess. But it's not like that anymore. And I'm glad of that. I am. I don't want to be this... thing. I *hate* even being the way we are now. But back then, when it—when *we*—lost control, I saw it. All of it. My father and mother, my brothers and sisters. Even the people in chains. My fire took them all so fast, but they still screamed and screamed, and I couldn't stop it."

My chest ached, self-loathing surging as hard and fast as it ever did when I remembered that day. "My little brother was only seven when I killed him. My youngest sister was eight. I watched them burn alive because of me. Because of this *thing* that I am, the thing I just call a demon because what the fuck other description is there for something like that? And when it was over, the soldiers at the edge of the blast tried to run, and I... I just..."

"What?" she whispered.

"I chased them. Even with everything I'd just done, I wanted them to suffer. To pay. I burned those Aneirans to death nice and slow, and I relished every fucking second of it. And by the time I was finished, I was the only thing left alive in that village." My head shook, the motion tight and jerky. "The Aneirans might've been the ones to attack us that day, but I was the one who killed everybody. So you tell me, how does that make me anything but a monster?"

Silence reigned, and somewhere along the line, everything had gone cold. My skin beneath my makeshift cloak. The air in my lungs. I was shaking so deep down, it was like my insides had turned to ice, and no amount of demonic fire could ever make me warm.

Because now, at last, she'd see. She'd know every reason I hated myself, and because of it all, she'd do the same.

I *was* a monster. Her kindness would never last in the face of the nightmare of what I'd done.

For the longest moment, Gwyneira didn't move. She only watched me, saying nothing, until the silence was so deafening that I wanted to scream for her to just leave already. We both knew she had to. I wasn't worthy of anyone not hating me, let alone showing me the slightest care.

Or love.

Deep inside, the demon ached, echoing the truth we both knew to the core of our mangled souls. We'd only ever tried to drive her away to spare her. Spare ourselves too. She was our torture.

And this moment was the worst torture of all.

"Good," she whispered.

Everything stopped. "What?"

"Good." She walked up to me, taking one of my hands, and I was so numbed by shock that I let her. "When it comes to those soldiers, *good*. Those bastards deserved death for what they planned to do to those kids. For stabbing your mother and for killing all those innocent people in your village. Your people weren't warriors. That wasn't about the war. That was a massacre and those soldiers deserved every fucking *second* of what you gave them for it, and so much more besides." Her grip quivered, and her voice was tight with fury. "I'm glad you killed them. I'm glad you made it hurt. You did the world a favor."

What was happening?

Her mouth compressed as she dropped her gaze to where she held my hand in both of her own. "But I'm so sorry for what happened to your family and friends. More sorry than I can ever say. What you did to the people you loved was an accident, though. A horrible, tragic accident that you *never* would have chosen or wanted, and I hope to the gods that your family would tell you that too if they could. That they'd let you know they forgive you because *you* weren't the monster that day, and you still aren't one now." Her fingers tightened on my hand as she looked back up, her dark eyes so beautifully earnest and intense, they were like a black sun burning into me. "You kill the monsters."

I stared at her. "But..." Words failed me. I'd tried over and over to make her see what I truly was, and yet she still didn't understand. Instead she said these things that hurt so much because they couldn't possibly be true. Not for something like me. "I... I'm not..."

"You're the one who made things right. And the one who made a terrible mistake. You're both. But you were also a child, and you were trying to do something good before it went wrong." Her lips curved into a sad, kind smile. "Maybe it's time to forgive yourself."

I couldn't breathe. Something in my chest felt like it'd cracked, and although the breaking was painful, somehow the broken parts were melting too, becoming both open and full at the same time.

It was the strangest sensation.

But I couldn't do what she said. Couldn't be this good person she saw, not only because of that day, but because at every opportunity, I'd hurt her. I knew that.

And all out of my own contemptible fear.

"I'm sorry," I whispered.

Her brow drew down, questioning.

"For everything. What I've said to you. How I've been. How I..." A breath left me. "I kept pushing you away and treating you horribly, and it was never what you deserved. I just..."

"You thought you were protecting me," she filled in when I trailed off. "Didn't you?"

I closed my eyes, ashamed. "And myself."

She was silent, but she didn't pull her hands away from mine, and when I looked up, she was nodding to herself. "It hurt," she acknowledged, and something inside me shriveled and died at that truth. "And it wasn't fair."

"I know."

She nodded again.

"Tell me how to make it up to you," I begged. "Please."

Her gaze returned to mine, thoughtful. "No more secrets?"

I flinched inside. Of all she could have asked me, to stop hiding was the most risky of all.

But then, she'd already seen the demon. She already knew what I'd done. The only secret left was the truth of how much I wanted her. Craved her.

It felt like laying myself bare for her to burn.

"No more." I pushed the words out. "But in that case, you should know..."

Oh gods, the truth was like standing at the top of a cliff, knowing I had to take the fall even if there was no way I'd survive. But I had to fling myself over that prover-bial ledge. For her. For me and the demon both too. Because she'd asked us to do it, and so, even if we'd fucked everything up so much it was insurmountable, we would.

Because deep inside beyond all the bullshit, all the

demon and I had *actually* ever wanted was to make her happy.

"You should know I've wanted you since the moment I laid eyes on you," I said. "Since we all found you asleep at the cabin, curled up in my chair and half frozen from the snow. I've wanted you for every second, and I've hated myself for how I treated you. I never meant any of those horrible things I said. Not one. I *did* want to protect you from the thing inside me, and I thought if I made you hate me, that would keep you safe. That it would make wanting you hurt less. I thought driving you away would make this better for both of us. But I was a fool and a coward, and I am so, so sorry."

The horrible silence returned, yet still her hands stayed around my own.

It was a lifeline, and if it snapped...

One of her hands slipped away. I closed my eyes, waiting for the other to disappear.

But her soft palm only came to rest on my cheek.

My breath caught. I looked down at her again.

"Thank you," she said quietly.

I didn't move. Didn't breathe. Was this real?

Something soft and sad came into her eyes.

Panic shot through me. "What? What's wrong?"

"Is this who you really are, Roan? Someone this... kind?"

She thought I was *kind*?

My mouth moved, searching for an answer. "I-I don't know."

She nodded, seeming a bit concerned.

Panic pushed more words from me. "All I know is that

if you let me, I would spend the rest of my life trying to make everything up to you. I'd try to fix every second of making you feel like you weren't the most precious, valuable treasure in the whole fucking world. I'd take back every cruel word, and I'd *show* you what you meant to me, not just say it. I'd never make you doubt how much I wanted you again."

Her brow twitched down.

Oh, fuck, I'd gone too far. I knew it. The sheer fact she'd let me get to this point, to tell her this much without pulling away was a miracle. Hell, it *all* was.

And then I'd screwed it up again.

I smiled, trying to hide the way it hurt, and started to step back.

Her hand tightened on mine, stopping me. "And the demon?"

I tensed. "What do you mean?"

"It has very specific ideas about being the only one who gets to be with me."

The creature rumbled inside me for the first time in a while, pain and confusion rising from it. Disjointed thoughts came too, muttering of how she was ours. How it didn't understand why *she* didn't understand that.

I winced. "I'm sorry. I—"

Her hand tightened on mine. "Stop."

I looked back at her.

"Is that also how you feel? That you want me only to yourself?"

My mouth moved, and the truth emerged, as disjointed as the monster's thoughts. "I want you, but...

like an Erenlian. Sharing with the others. Living as a man. As a part of that group. And the demon..."

Years of hating it, of hating myself, suddenly felt like a thousand pounds of stone bearing down on my shoulders —a weight I'd always carried. The weight I deserved.

And yet...

"It wants you too. It..." The creature ached inside me and burrowed deeper as if to escape the admission. "I don't think it understands how to deal with that." Certainty shivered up from the demon. "But it would do anything for you. Die for you, if that's what you wanted. If that's what it took to keep you safe."

She stared at me, and I couldn't read her expression. Confused but pained, but... something that made no sense.

Then she stepped closer. Her hand caressed my cheek. "And am I your treluria?" she whispered.

My hand slid around her side carefully, cautiously, praying she didn't pull away, while agony and ecstasy tangled in me, an exquisite torture. "You always have been."

She smiled, and I couldn't hold back any longer.

I kissed her.

27

GWYNEIRA

I met Roan's lips with mine, at a loss for how this was even happening. I'd thought I was crazy for being attracted to him, this surly, glowering giant who looked more like a shadow than a man half the time. Even when he shifted back from being the demon, I hadn't expected more than cold distance with a small chance of an apology for kidnapping me.

But instead, everything changed, as if, when the demon disappeared, it took all his armor with it, leaving only him. A man so broken by all the horrors of his past, he thought cruelty was the only way to keep anyone safe. A man so scared of the monster inside, he'd do anything to keep it away from me. Seeing his pain and self-hatred laid bare was like suddenly discovering a raw wound he'd spent all this time trying to hide. But as visceral and real as that agony was, it had nothing on the desperate openness in his eyes when he revealed he craved me every bit as much as I wanted him.

And now he was *kissing* me.

If this was a dream, I prayed I didn't wake up.

As ever, he wasn't what I expected, though. Not savage or forceful. His lips were gentle on my own, and a bit hesitant, almost like he was afraid I'd vanish too. Slowly, his hands slid farther around my body, holding me to him like I was as fragile as a snowflake that might melt in his grasp.

Was he still afraid of the demon? Of losing control and hurting me?

His hard length came into contact with my middle. He groaned against my lips, and heat tangled through my core as a needy sound escaped me involuntarily in response. I parted my lips, inviting him to explore me, even as my body ached to take this to farther. To strip down and pull his rough blanket of branches and weeds aside so that I could feel all of his body against mine.

But he delved into me carefully, his hands still only lightly touching me. His hips jerked toward me when I rocked into him, but immediately he pulled back again, staying focused on kissing me.

My hunger and need for him began to clamor higher, but worry nibbled at the edges of my mind. Why was he being so cautious? Was he afraid he might make some mistake?

Did he think *this* was a mistake?

I broke away from his lips, looking up at him. "What is it? What's wrong?"

Worry flashed over his face. "Nothing. I just..."

"Is it the demon?"

His head shook.

I hesitated and then drew closer, pressing myself against his hard length again. "Then what?"

A quiver rolled through his muscles.

"I want you too, Roan. I swear to you that I do."

He let out a breath, but his tension didn't fade. Instead, his gaze only slipped away like he was embarrassed to look at me. "You... you should know, though, I've never actually..." He grimaced like he couldn't bring himself to say the words. "I don't..."

I blinked, surprised in spite of myself. Wait, was this cold, cocky, sometimes-asshole of a man trying to tell me what I *thought* he was trying to tell me? "Roan, are you saying you've never lain with anyone before?"

He shook his head in a short, tight motion. "Couldn't risk it. If the demon—if *I* lost control—" His eyes squeezed shut briefly. "I just don't want you to be... disappointed. If I'm not... If it's too fast, or if I can't give you what the others..."

Oh my gods.

I hesitated and then reached up, putting a hand to his cheek.

A shuddering breath escaped him.

"I promise you," I said firmly. "Disappointment is not a possibility here."

He winced like he thought I was just being kind.

"Are you calling me a liar, Roan?"

His dark eyes flicked to mine with alarm.

"You're here with me," I continued. "We get to share this with each other. That is..." I searched for a word that could possibly encompass it. "*Breathtaking* to me. I could never be disappointed in something as special as that."

He didn't move. Didn't say a word. And then air left him and his head tilted in a nod. "Okay."

I smiled. Stepping back from him, I lifted the hem of my sweater, stripping it and my underclothes off, leaving my breasts bare.

His lips parted like the sight of me stole his breath.

And gods, to see him react like that after everything he'd said and done...

It was incredible.

My hands dropped to the hem of my pants, but a choked sound escaped him, stopping me. Carefully, he moved closer. His fingers teased along the fabric, playing lightly at my skin and pausing at every tiny hitch of my chest. His attention was all-encompassing, like in this moment, I was the only thing that existed in the universe, and his life depended upon understanding me completely.

It was arousing and overwhelming, all at the same time.

Slowly—*agonizingly* slowly—he slid the fabric down my legs and then finally pulled my pants away.

Crouched before me, he was frozen for a heartbeat. The warm puff of his breath danced over my bare skin. A sort of calm came over his face, like whatever nervousness had gripped him before was finally fading.

Need was taking its place.

Carefully he drew his fingertips up my legs and past my hips, until his hands encircled my sides as he stood again.

Naked before him on the tower rooftop, I trembled, not from cold but only from the look coming into his eyes.

Hungry. *Ravenous*, even. His mere gaze devoured me whole.

"I want to learn every single thing that will make you scream my name, princess." He traced a fingertip down my sternum, and I shivered. "Every way to make you come so hard you can't even move after I'm done."

A tiny breath left me. The corners of his lips curled at the sound.

With a slight shrug, he dropped the blanket around his shoulders, leaving himself bare before me. His hand returned, drifting down my middle until it slipped between my legs and into my folds.

"Fuck," he groaned. "You're so soft and wet for me."

I nodded. "For you."

His smile returned. He slipped his fingers deeper into my folds until he teased at my opening. His other hand rose, taking my breast and carefully squeezing down.

My core clenched. He made a pleased sound, pinching my nipple between his thumb and forefinger while he began pumping his fingers in and out of me slowly.

I rocked toward him involuntarily. "Please."

"Please, what, beautiful? Tell me what you want me to do."

"My clit. My..." I gasped as his fingers bent inside me. "Oh gods, like that too."

I reached down, guiding his hand so that his thumb was on my sensitive flesh. My body lurched again as he slowly began massaging circles across it, crooking his fingers with every pass.

My heart sped up. My hands fumbled up to grab his elbows, steadying me as my body quaked from the pleasure building in my core. In his grasp, my hips rocked with him, pressing my clit harder against his thumb in a desperate effort to find my release.

"You like riding my hand like this?" he asked in a devilish tone. "You like me making your soft, wet pussy need me so badly?"

Gods, where had he learned to talk like that?

"Use your words, beautiful. Let me know what you want."

I nodded jerkily. "Yes. Yes, I... Gods, deeper. More."

He adjusted his hold, dipping his fingers into me deeper and hitting an even more sensitive spot there over and over. "You like how it hurts so good to crave my cock?"

Incoherent little gasps came from me as pleasure began to blind me to the world. "Yes, I do... I like... please, oh gods..."

He bent his head and murmured, "Come for me."

His other hand pinched my nipple hard, sending a jolt of pleasure straight to my core. I cried out as I came hard, gushing around his hand.

Roan's grin was the first thing I saw when I opened my eyes.

It took my breath away. I didn't think I'd ever seen him wearing that expression. So happy. So relaxed and open, no sign of hiding himself.

Gods, it was beautiful.

His grin spread, and that's when I realized I'd said the last part out loud. "You're the beautiful one, princess. Watching you come..." His head shook. "I've never seen anything so magnificent."

My insides quivered. Gingerly, I reached out and trailed a finger up his hard cock, teasing at the thick vein beneath the silken skin, lifting away the bead of moisture on its head.

He tensed, a tiny gasp escaping him.

A smile pulled at my lips. "And are we done?"

His black eyes somehow grew darker, as if heat and smoke had suddenly cloaked the stars in a midnight sky. But a hint of nervous tension returned too. "If I can't last…"

My hand came to rest on his cheek. "I'm with *you.* That's what I want. That's what matters to me. Sharing this with you."

He leaned into my touch, but the nervousness melted away, bringing the hunger back to the fore. His hands took my hips, his grip trembling.

"Fuck me, Roan," I whispered.

And just like that, his restraint snapped. He hoisted me up, and instinctively, my legs wrapped around him, bracing me as he slammed me down onto his cock. His lips crashed into my own, and then my back hit the crenelated stone wall. The rough surface scratched my skin, painful little counterpoints to the passion of Roan's mouth devouring me.

How had I ever thought him cold? He burned against me, not with fire but with need. His fingers gripped my ass, holding me to him, grinding my clit against his body. His cock stretched me, huge and bordering on painful, but hitting me so deeply I saw stars.

He broke away from my lips with a gasp, and his muscles shook as he thrust into me desperately, like he wanted to fill me with his cum this instant. "So... good," he grunted in rhythm with his thrusts. "So... good."

My head fell back. My eyes fluttered closed. "You too."

His hands tightened on my ass, and I moaned as it stimulated my nerves down there. My pussy clenched harder around him, the tingling of an orgasm starting to build.

I rocked against him harder, chasing that high.

A choked sound escaped him. His motions became more erratic, more desperate. I cried out, my orgasm surging through me. I clutched at his shoulders, quaking with pleasure as he threw his head back.

Roan roared with ecstasy as he came.

My legs shook as he gripped me tightly, his cock still twitching inside my body. "Gods..." he murmured. "I want to do that with you every day. Five times a day. Holy shit."

I choked on a startled laugh. "Is that so?"

He leaned back to grin down at me. "Give me a minute. We could get started again right now."

I laughed. "I take it you weren't disappointed either, then?"

His expression turned serious. Carefully, he lifted me down, and my legs trembled when he set me on the tower rooftop again. "Princess, I swear to you on every twisted piece of my soul..." His hand took my chin, tilting my face upward so he could meet my gaze firmly. "I could *never* be disappointed by you."

Tears gathered in my eyes.

His expression turned worried. "Did I say something wrong?"

I shook my head. "Something perfect."

Rising on my tiptoes, I met his lips as he bent closer. My hands tightened on his sides, holding him to me as I tried to pour every bit of my care, compassion, and love into kissing him, praying he'd understand.

His hand raked into my hair. His grip held me close, keeping me with him as he devoured me.

This was better than a dream.

He broke away, breathless as he stared down at me, and a tiny smile filled with wonder tugged at his lips.

Gods, I loved the sight of it.

But after a heartbeat, a tinge of regret flitted through his dark eyes.

"What?" I asked.

"I want to keep you here, but..."

Confused, I waited.

"The others. I shouldn't have..." He shook his head. "We ought to get back. They have to be terrified that I've... done something horrible."

I wasn't sure how to respond. My connection to Ozias meant he'd long since known I was okay.

Not that I could share that information.

Roan exhaled, scrubbing a hand over his face. Turning away, he retrieved my clothes, offering them to me before reclaiming the rough blanket he'd fashioned.

"Maybe it won't be as bad as all that?" I offered while I got dressed.

He didn't look like he believed me.

"Honestly. Perhaps they'll be more understanding than you think."

"It's just..." He shook his head. "They didn't know. But now they do and..."

"You mean about you?"

"Yeah."

I bit my lip. "But maybe they won't react badly once you explain it to them."

"I literally attacked them and kidnapped you. I've been lying to them for years about who and what I am. At any moment, I could've lost control and accidentally killed them all because I have a gods-damned *monster* inside." He scoffed like the outcome had to be obvious.

I looked away. If I said anything about Ozias, I'd be breaking my promise to him. But all these secrets, all this fear that he and Roan had about others not accepting them... Gods, I just couldn't believe their friends would have driven them away. So if the two of them had only shared the truth years ago, how much pain might they have saved themselves?

And was I a hypocrite for even thinking that, considering I was helping to hide the truth too?

"Still." I shrugged, not meeting his eyes. "Maybe it won't go how you think."

He was quiet. I risked a glance up at him.

His brow knit thoughtfully, as if he was at least considering the idea.

"Just try," I urged. "Please."

After a moment, he gave a small nod. "Okay."

"Thank you."

He pulled me closer, holding me to his warm chest. The wind was picking up around us, and everywhere his skin didn't touch, the cool air washed over me like an icy river, tangling through my hair and trying to rock me toward the tower's edge as if to protest the fact it couldn't freeze a vampire.

"Do you have a plan for getting down?" I asked after a moment.

He made a hedging noise. "Not really. I don't think the demon considered that part."

Or the fact Roan might be the one to deal with it, his tone seemed to say.

"I could help?" I offered with a small shrug.

He hesitated.

"Or not," I amended quickly. "If that's—"

"Oh, I have no objection. I was just..." He chuckled. "Well, thinking about what it would be like, having you so close to me in that form."

I swallowed hard as his implication became clear. "Oh."

He smiled, stepping closer, and his arms slipped around my sides. "So is there anything in particular you need me to do to hang onto you like that?" His hands slid down farther, cupping my ass. "Something like this, maybe?"

He tugged me against his leg, and I gasped.

"That, uh..." Instinctively, I pressed my core into his muscles. "That should be—"

An icy shiver suddenly coursed over me like fingertips of pure darkness dragging across my skin.

I froze.

"What is it?" Roan's grip loosened. "Did I hurt you or—"

"Do you feel that?" My words came out as a whisper as I scanned the horizon. Every instinct I possessed was clamoring that something had just gone horribly wrong. That the ground was shaking, even if it didn't move at all. That the world had been plunged into darkness, no matter that my eyes swore the sun still hung in the sky.

But Ozias was okay, and due to the fact he was not fighting or raging at a threat right now, I could believe the others were all right too. The landscape was unchanged beneath the bright sun, and there weren't even birds in the cloudless blue sky.

Not a single one…

"Gwyneira?" Roan stepped away from me, and from the corner of my eye, I could see him scanning our surroundings too. "You look scared. What's happening?"

My head shook, and I couldn't find the words to explain. Birds hid when a dangerous storm was on the rise.

Right now, I'd swear the apocalypse itself was swelling on the horizon.

"Princess?"

Roan took my arm, and I gasped, startled.

His dark eyes narrowed, but his concern had a dangerous edge, like he was waiting for me to point out the threat so that he could kill it. "Are you okay?"

I shivered. "We need to get back to the others. Now."

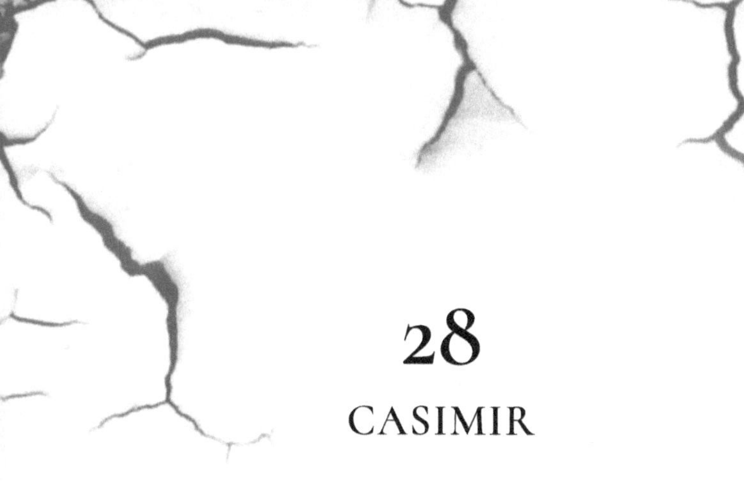

28

CASIMIR

In the thirty-odd years since I was turned, I'd never considered how much I'd started to take the ability to shift and fly where I wished for granted. But gods, I missed it now.

No, *missed* wasn't a strong enough word. I seethed at the loss of it. Raged at being trapped in one form, slowed to the pace of any other human or Erenlian, even as the predator inside me screamed for me to go faster. Ozias's gifts told him the princess was ahead. That the creature was too. But beyond that, he said nothing, and thus I was left plodding along, helpless to intervene should a new horror unfold.

It was enough to drive one to madness.

Every mile grated, just as I knew it did for each man behind me. Every minute that ticked by with no answer for what that bastard planned for her gnawed at my control and made visions of all the horrors I'd seen when my country fell dance like flickering flames behind my eyes. And the fact we had horses to help us move faster scarcely alleviated the torture.

After all, the beasts were anything but comfortable with us, and they couldn't move nearly as fast as I would have.

If only I could have fucking *shifted*.

Adjusting my position as my mount danced a bit beneath me, I drew a slow breath and attempted to project calm. I'd been trained in the equestrian arts since I was a child, and I knew how sensitive horses could be—and that was without having a vampire seated upon their back. In all these interminable hours, I'd learned well that if I allowed myself to spiral into rage, the buckskin gelding would only become even more skittish.

It had already tried to throw me off three times and to bolt at least half a dozen. As a result, I'd ended up riding at the front of our little group, if only for safety's sake and because I was tired of slowing the creature enough to rejoin the others time and again.

Or slowing down at all.

A grunt came from behind me. Ozias's horse suddenly galloped him beyond me only to slow when the large man hauled on the reins.

I was far from the only one whose mount was reacting poorly to its rider. The massive chestnut-colored horse he rode tried to bolt nearly as often as my own, which was strange indeed. But it hadn't taken long for me to see that he, like most of his companions, were unfamiliar with riding. Chances were, they'd probably never sat astride a horse before. After all, the equestrian arts likely weren't common in Erenelle, considering most giants were so huge they would crush even the largest horse. With the exception of Dex who'd trained as a soldier and Niko who seemed able to soothe the animals with a touch, the men perched atop their horses rigidly, clutching the reins with white-knuckled fists and tensing at every change of pace as if expecting the beasts to lunge into a stampede.

It made for infuriatingly sluggish progress.

I adjusted my seat, waiting to make space for Ozias to steer his horse back to the others.

He made no such move, sitting instead like the stone that was his power, motionless but for short breaths that made his shoulders rise and fall quickly.

My eyes narrowed. He hadn't seemed *this* afraid of the creature's skittish reactions before.

Adjusting my posture and leg tension, I urged my mount speed up until I reached his side.

Ozias's eyes were locked on the horizon. His expression was tight and his nostrils flared. Yet again, it reminded me of my shadow wolves when they sensed something in the distance.

A spasm went through his upper lip, as if it was on the verge of peeling back into a growl. But as quickly as it had come, the reaction faded. His eyes squeezed shut for a moment, and then a huff left him that sounded more like an animal than a man.

His posture eased. He opened his eyes, glancing at me and then locking his gaze on the rolling grasslands ahead, though his irritation at my proximity was like a pressure on the air, silently insisting I should go away.

I didn't retreat, etiquette and my desire to maintain a cordial relationship with these men be damned. I was uncertain what just occurred, but it had not been my imagination that he reminded me of my wolves. No, the reason for *that* was becoming as plain as if he had sprouted fur in front of me.

And given the way he'd behaved around Gwyneira when the two of them returned earlier...

A growl gathered at the back of my throat.

Quickly, I swallowed the reaction down. The wilder parts of me were certain I was facing a fellow predator, but it was not for nothing that I had survived for three decades as a vampire without losing control. "What do you sense of her?" I murmured, my lips barely moving and my voice so low, anyone more than an inch away from me would struggle to hear.

Ozias's eyes snapped to me all the same.

"It is not your gift with the earth that tells you she's ahead," I pressed. "You possess a mate bond to her, do you not? Because you're at least part shifter, and you bonded her. So, what does your connection tell you? Is she injured? Has that creature harmed her?"

Rage flared in his gaze, and yes, oh yes, a hefty tinge of fear. For him to be able to keep the others in the dark this long—which I suspected he'd done quite well considering none of them were asking the kinds of questions they should if they knew about the link he and Gwyneira likely shared—he must ordinarily be meticulous about his reactions.

Thus he was *truly* on edge to have reacted to my words at all.

Hoofbeats accelerated toward us. I glanced back to see

Dex riding closer. "What is it?" he asked. "Why'd you rush ahead?"

"Did the earth tell you something, Oz?" Clay called from behind us.

The bearded giant didn't turn. "No."

"What?" Niko asked, confusion in his voice. "You've never reacted like that if it's nothing."

"Horse bolted." Ozias's voice was tight, but he made it sound like that was the extent of it.

All without *technically* ever saying as much.

The men cast wary glances at each other. They trusted the bearded giant, that much was obvious. But they had also trusted Roan and now the princess was gone.

Were any of them now wondering who *else* might not be what they seemed?

A shriek rose in the distance.

"Fuck." Clay twisted on his horse's back, searching for the source of the sound.

Lars did the same. "You all see anything?"

The men turned their attention to the horizon. While they discussed whether the far-off, dark specks in the sky could be harpies or hawks, I kept my focus on the bearded giant, waiting.

It only took a few moments before Ozias's gaze darted to me once again. "Say nothing," he growled under his breath.

"Very well."

His eyes narrowed.

"Trust me when I say I wish to find her too," I told him. "But I must know what prompted your reaction just now."

His teeth ground, making the hairs of his beard ripple as he visibly debated whether to acknowledge what I now knew. But after a moment, his words emerged, grudging and barely audible even to my ears. "She's with him."

"With—"

The implication sunk in.

Rage surged within me so hot and fast I couldn't keep my fangs from descending. Beneath me, the horse danced and bucked, whinnying with fear.

With effort, I pulled my mount—and myself—back under control again. "Is that *creature* forcing himself on—"

"No."

I froze.

Ozias scowled and then cast a quick look over his shoulder at the others. Frustration on his face, he snarled under his breath, "She wanted him. *Wants* him." His face twitched, and when he continued, his voice was tight in a strange way. "Roan's not..." He cleared his throat and adjusted his pants surreptitiously. "He's not *hurting* her."

With another glance at his friends, he tapped his heels to his horse's sides, sending it onward faster.

I didn't follow. I couldn't. I was too shocked to move.

Because Gwyneira was having sex with that monster.

Willingly.

With enough pleasure that it aroused her mate all these miles away.

I didn't react to the others while they rode past and eyed me with curiosity. No, I was too busy reeling from the sudden realignment of absolutely everything I thought had occurred. Dispelled were the images of my kingdom as it crumbled, of the mangled bodies of the innocent and the blood-soaked vampires feeding on the ones they'd previously sworn to protect and love. Fading were the agonized cries of their victims, helpless to stop what was happening to them.

Now I had no idea what was going on.

"You coming?" Clay called back.

I shuddered. "Of course."

My voice was steady, and my grip on the reins was too.

Neither hinted at how much I was reeling inside.

"What did Ozias say to you?" Niko asked when I rode closer.

I hesitated, my mouth opening but no words emerging, and the gods only knew what they would have been. "Nothing."

That answer would scarcely satisfy anyone, but it was all I could say.

Because, gods help me, Gwyneira was currently having sex with that creature, never mind that it had *kidnapped* her from us all.

My thoughts slowed. Realization sank through me like ice water, washing everything else away and leaving only crystalline clarity.

Never mind that it had...

Oh, the gods had a vicious sense of irony.

Was this what her men felt when *I* took her?

My eyes swept over the giants anew. When I took her, yes, I'd *asked* her if I could feed from her, sleep with her. I had not simply stolen her away and done what I wished while she slept, her consent be damned. Such a thing would have been heinous and reprehensible. Utterly beneath any creature with the barest shred of a conscience or decency.

Except that for all those hours in the vault, these men hadn't known that. And if she *had* consented to be with me before seeing them and explaining the situation, they never would have known I'd asked her permission first. No, to them, she was simply gone, ripped away from them, with untold horrors possibly happening to her for all the hours they'd been apart.

Because of a monster.

"Hey."

I glanced to my right.

Niko rode beside me, his face somber. "Whatever it is," he said, a hard note to his voice that I hadn't heard from him before. "We'll find her."

I watched him, curious. He was young and beautiful with dark eyes and hair like Roan but with olive skin and a gentleness wholly unlike that man. Smaller than the others and thus closer to the size of a grown human male, he had always carried an air of trustworthiness and compassion. I estimated that he was someone I would have been honored to name a friend of the crown in my life before Zenirya fell.

But now it was clear he was in pain—from the loss of Gwyneira, of his trust in Roan, or perhaps just both. Yet even though he barely knew me as anything more than the vampire king who'd also once kidnapped his princess, still he offered comfort to me.

When he had to be as worried as any of them that his princess could be dying.

My head moved in a tiny nod. "Thank you. I…"

Hesitating, I did not allow myself to look onward to where Ozias rode, though I suspected the man could hear us all the same. But his true nature remained his secret to tell the others—if only because I suspected he would never dream of presenting a threat to Gwyneira. Quite the opposite.

And as for Roan…

Tightly, I returned the young man's smile. "I believe you're right. She will be fine."

Niko's expression turned grateful, as if we were friends and he appreciated my offer of comfort too. Echoing my nod, he kept going.

I started after him, feeling vaguely dumbstruck. Gods help me, after thirty years of isolation, this was certainly not what I envisioned it would be like when I left my castle behind. Crossing the Aneiran prairie with six Erenlians, pursuing a seventh who currently reminded me too much of myself for comfort.

All for a woman who defied description entirely.

But that was just it, wasn't it? Never in any version of my life—human or vampire—could I have foreseen *her*.

For Gwyneira, I'd fallen harder than my angelic ancestors must have when they crashed down from their celestial realm. I'd been overcome by wonder at this impossible Aneiran beauty who'd not only survived becoming a vampire with her humanity intact, but whose sheer presence could somehow make *me* feel more human than I had in decades.

When I was with Gwyneira, I wasn't a fading ghost clinging to the shadows of his former life. I wasn't some gods-forsaken amalgam of human and monster, a pathetic creature pretending to be a man even as he forgot more of what that meant with the passing of each dreary day.

No, I was Casimir zel Elric ver Altreya, King of Zenirya, ruler on the opalescent throne of my ancestors and last surviving descendant of the royal angelic line. I was a living, breathing man capable of making her laugh and smile and moan with pleasure.

I was me.

And in a thousand ways, Gwyneira made it clear that above all else, that last part was more than enough.

No matter how much I enjoyed her submission or her incredible willingness to be claimed and dominated by me and by all the powerful men who shared her, the truth was that Gwyneira was the one who had claimed me. Body, mind, and soul, I would belong to her until the end of time.

Perhaps she was working the same magic on Roan.

Absently, I stroked my hand along my buckskin mount's neck, attempting to soothe the beast while I regarded the men ahead of me. It was truly so strange, this unexpected situation I'd found myself in with them. Had my life gone the way it was planned, I would have been crowned King of Zenirya decades ago, elevated by ceremony and tradition rather than the mere default of being the only one of the royal line—or the entire nation—still alive. I would have been expected to marry, my prospects dictated by whoever provided the best political alliance at the time. And the idea of sharing that partner with others? Oh, that would have never crossed my mind, let alone come up for discussion.

Yet I found I didn't mind the prospect. Quite the opposite, actually. It was comforting to know Gwyneira's needs would always be met. That she had support and protection in everything, no matter what it might be. Equally surprising was the fact she didn't mind if I partook of intimacy with her companions either, if they chose to share that with me.

She even enjoyed it too.

It was odd, sometimes, how life gave you things you never suspected you were lacking, and once you had them, you couldn't imagine feeling as fulfilled any other way.

Up ahead, Lars's mount danced a bit and Clay poked fun at him in a brotherly way. The others chuckled as if trying to let the brief levity ease their own tension, even if it couldn't dispel it entirely.

I smiled at them all, but the amusement was accompanied by a small ache in my chest. Even now, something inside couldn't let me forget that nothing about this was as simple as I wished. These men were good and strong and kind. Gwyneira loved them, and given time, I suspected I could do the same.

But I wondered if it had yet occurred to my vampiric Aneiran beauty that, because of what she'd become, she would outlive them all.

"Creek up ahead," Clay called back. "We stopping?"

Dex nodded. "Just long enough to let the horses drink. I don't want to waste daylight if we can avoid it."

The others offered their agreement, and when Dex

glanced back, I nodded, keeping any trace of my thoughts from my expression. Sharp-eyed leader that he was, he still paused, waiting a moment longer as if to confirm I was fine before turning once again to face the prairie.

There was much to like about that man, and not just that he'd proven to be a fine partner in bed. It hurt to think he too would be gone someday.

I let out a breath, attempting to push the pain aside. I would be there for Gwyneira at that hopefully far-off time when the last of her other lovers drifted into their eternal sleep. Until then, I'd support and defend them all however I could, not only because they were worthy of it, but because of how much she loved them and they loved her.

And because maybe, after all it had taken from me, life had provided me a place to belong again, even if only for a while.

The creek came into view and sounds of relief arose among the men ahead of me. More than a few stumbled when they clambered down from their mounts, their legs undoubtedly aching and wobbly after so long on horse-back with no prior experience.

I swung off the horse and began leading it toward the water. Several of the others tried to do the same, only to struggle when their animals balked. "Look where you want to go, not at the horse," I called.

Questioning expressions met my words, but in short order the men were having more success than before.

"Is the water okay?" Dex asked Clay.

The blond giant extended his hand over the creek and then nodded.

With that confirmed, I changed my grip on the reins, letting the horse drink. The water in the narrow creek drifted along quietly, slow enough that the horses could likely cross it with ease. It would not stop us for long.

The plodding sound of hoofs and boots came from behind me, and a moment later Ozias appeared, leading his horse to the water as well. "Thank you," he murmured without looking my way.

I knew he wasn't solely referring to the advice about the horses.

"Of course," I replied just as softly.

Dex came up beside us. For a long moment, he didn't speak, his attention on his horse.

Discomfort flashed across Ozias's face. Without a word, he started to lead his animal elsewhere.

"I trust you'll tell me what the hell is up soon," Dex said to the bearded giant, giving me a short glance to include me in the statement. "We've had too many surprises to keep hiding things from one another."

Ozias stopped, not quite looking at his friend. Silence hung between us all, broken only by the sounds of the others still struggling with their horses several yards away.

"I would not presume to know your friends better than you," I said to him. "But I would imagine if these men can accept me, they can accept anything—and that they possess enough compassion to know not everyone would do what Roan has done."

Ozias's gaze landed on me. I couldn't hope to guess what decisions raced behind his eyes.

"I... am not fully Erenlian either," he admitted to his friend, his voice tight and low.

Dex tensed but didn't say a word.

Ozias pressed onward, almost as if forcing himself to continue speaking. "But I am not like Roan."

Slowly, Dex nodded. "What are you?"

Ozias closed his eyes briefly, his expression tense like he was bracing himself for something. "I—"

He cut off, his attention snapping to the horizon beyond the creek.

Cold alarm shot through me at the look on his face. "What is it?"

"Gwyneira."

Without another word, Ozias dropped the horse's reins and took off running.

29

MELISANDRE

With my last scrap of awareness, I fled. I retreated with every fiber that remained of my being, fleeing as hard and fast as I could from that nightmare and seeking something, anything to offer me refuge and stability against Alaric's lies.

That I was nothing.

That I was gone.

That my every goal, my great plans, were over.

He didn't care to chase me any longer. The darkness was all that was left. But still I raced onward, burrowing deeper and deeper to get away from what *couldn't* be real.

And just as I had throughout my whole life, I found it burning like a dark star at the core of the universe. Hate.

Pure.

Beautiful.

Hate.

It blazed within me, down below all the cruelty and disrespect. It glowed like an absence of light so profound, no star in the sky could compare. Because of its brilliance, because of its cold and hard embrace, I'd found the Void-born and become a vampire. I'd overthrown the Jeweled Coven and claimed Eira's throne. I'd even returned to my father's pathetic little village and personally ended every one of my tormentors' lives.

Monster, they'd screamed. Please, they'd begged.

Oh, how I relished those sounds.

Down beneath the magic and the fangs, *this* was my true power. This was why Alaric *still* could not erase or control me. Not because I was broken or because I couldn't handle his presence.

Because I was a more profound expression of this beauty than he would ever be.

Deep below the suffocating pressure of Alaric's power in my mind, I wrapped myself around that cold, black star and let it fill me, flood me, until I drew every ounce of it in. I *was* the darkness. *This* darkness.

And I'd never hated anyone in my life as much as I hated him.

Like flashes of light through thick fog, fleeting images of the world returned. Rough walls. Torches. A tunnel of crudely chiseled stone where the shadows moved in unnatural ways.

We were in the deepest, oldest parts of the castle. The place my vampires stayed. Even now, I caught glimpses of them in their human forms.

Alaric stood before them all, his arms—my arms— extended, palms down. The magic within me rushed to his call just as it had in the forest with Stelaruna. My power surged down into the earth, racing past the dirt and rock toward the nexus far below it all.

But though he drew upon my magic, he didn't possess the full extent of what I was. He didn't control the truth that lived at the core of my soul. Of my own will, I rode that blast of magic toward the nexus below Lumilia. I could not feel my body. I was only distantly aware of the castle groaning and quaking in its terror. But I didn't care.

I was the pure dark star that would take this nexus for myself, and Alaric would not stop me.

A ripple passed through the darkness—Alaric's surprise. "You're still here?" He sounded amused. "What a stubborn little creature you are."

I paid him no mind. In the forest, his hold on me had weakened when he destroyed the nexus. It'd only been for a moment, just a flash.

Even if he had control of my body, even if some things I'd experienced had been a lie, that moment could still be his undoing.

The brilliant glow of the nexus spread through the darkness ahead, a bright core where numerous ley lines all met and crossed. A thousand frail threads spread from each ley line, reaching out into the world, but if they were like thin roots holding reality together, then the nexus was the seed from which the supports grew.

And the energy of reality pulsed through it in waves of light, like the throbbing heart of the universe was pushing the force of life itself out from it to the roots beyond.

"You think to take this from me, pet?"

His words meant nothing.

"You think you're strong enough to survive what I could do to you?"

Alaric's hunger surged around me, his essence shedding any pretense at civility until he became nothing but the single-minded relentlessness of a predator so starved, so rabid, it would race itself straight off a cliff in pursuit of its prey.

He wanted to destroy that light out of pure offense that it could exist.

He wanted to consume it even though his hunger would never be satisfied.

And he wanted me to fear that he'd do the same to me.

The fool understood nothing.

My power and his struck the nexus at the same moment. Our darkness shattered the glowing surface of that tangled crisscross of light like a battering ram of pure night.

Ley lines snapped. Thrashed. Their energy spilled out into the earth like blood from torn veins.

A savagely hungry sound rolled through the darkness. Alaric's power lashed out, intent upon catching the closest ley lines and draining them dry.

And ever so slightly, the crushing power of his presence around me *slipped*.

I lunged for the closest ley line. My essence wrapped around it.

And my entire self, everything I was or had ever been, screamed.

Existence came to an end. Entire realities lived and

died. Realms burned, and whole civilizations passed in the blink of an eye.

Alaric's voice returned, as sibilant and hissing as it'd been when first I heard him on that seashore. "You're pathetic. You can't even survive *this*."

His dark power clawed through the blinding light of the ley line. He was nothingness. Emptiness. His essence wanted only to devour that light and me alike, erasing us both once and for all.

But I had advantages greater than he could dream.

He hated reality, but I was born of it. He longed to consume this power, but I'd already claimed it.

I'd reshaped the world while he was still trying to find a way through its door.

And I'd spent *nineteen fucking years* bending this place to my will.

The pure energy of reality poured through me, and my darkness tangled with its power. The hate that lived forever inside me erupted out to twist through the light like thorny, black vines, piercing the ley lines I'd claimed and sinking back into them, until both bent and coiled together, inseparable.

Alaric didn't stand a chance.

He screamed as a wave of tangled darkness and light swept over him, swallowing him.

Drowning him.

Twisting him into my tangled tapestry of hate and creation until he became a part of me as well.

Distantly, I felt my lips curl up into a smile. Felt my arms drift down to my sides. Through the earth, my awareness rose on a wave of power, every sensation from my body growing stronger and more vivid until at last I surged up past the surface of the world and into my own body again.

Dust fell like snowflakes on my cheeks. Quivers rolled through the stones beneath my feet, only to go still when I opened my eyes.

As if even the castle was terrified of me now.

My vampires cowered in the shadows, the old steward Harran pinned between them. When I turned, the orcs possessed by the Voidborn stared.

I stared back. It wasn't just the orcs with their glowing eyes I saw before me any longer. It was the Voidborn themselves, like the orcs were a shell and I could see through to the shadowy eels twisting inside. Their eyes burned from within those monsters, the colors glowing with the light of the realms they'd consumed and destroyed. A rustling whisper passed through my mind, echoing from farther away than merely the short distance between myself and the creatures here.

I could hear them. Not just the ones before me, but all of them, like the rush of a wave across the seashore.

No wonder Alaric had always known where the others like him were. When they were coming. What they had planned.

I chuckled. The Voidborn were connected to one another.

And now, they were mine too.

Rage surged across the orcs' faces. I was not Alaric, and they knew it. With a roar, the closest one lunged at me.

My hand came up. My wrist twisted in a sharp, short motion.

The orc howled as his limbs suddenly bent in all the wrong directions. Like a broken doll, he fell, turning to dust before he hit the ground.

Wisps of smoke drifted up from his remains, evaporating into nothing as the Voidborn inside him died too.

Hissing-clicking noises came from the other Voidborn monsters as they recoiled.

Curses. Exclamations of horror. I understood them all.

"That's enough from you," I said. "You answer to me now."

The creatures tensed.

But they didn't say a word.

I smiled, turning my attention to my body. A silver sheen clung to my skin, and when I looked closer, infinitesimally small scales glinted in the torchlight. I drew the sword from where it hung at my waist—where it had hung since Alaric took it from the young soldier, though I'd never been aware of its weight on my hip before now —and carefully, I turned the flat of the blade toward myself, half-expecting no reflection to appear at all.

But my own image was there. The silvery cast to my skin darkened beneath my cheekbones like a cold, metallic blushing powder, and the yellow gleam to my pale eyes had become a twisting tangle of gold through the blue.

Interesting.

A flicker of motion caught the corner of my eye. On the hilt, at the center of where the blade met the crossguard, the intricately shaped metal had been formed into the grotesque visage of a monster, its mouth open in a silent scream.

But just for a moment, I swore the metal countenance writhed.

My brow rose. How—

A whimper came from behind me, choked and terrified, drawing my attention. I glanced over my shoulder. Harran remained on the ground, and even though he was pinned down by two vampires, the horror in his eyes belonged wholly to me.

"Release him," I ordered.

The steward trembled as the vampires did as I ordered. "M-my queen? What—"

"Enough."

He clamped his mouth shut, clearly bracing for me to turn him to dust too.

And perhaps that time would come. But first...

I sheathed the sword, pushing my flight of fancy regarding its grotesque design aside. "I offer you a choice, steward. Run and you'll be dead before you make it to the stairs. Serve me, and you'll live... for now."

Another whimper escaped him. "Wh-what would you have me do, my queen?"

I smiled. In the distance, I could feel the Voidborn spread throughout Aneira. They twisted through monsters and humans alike, destabilizing cities and towns, spreading fear and death.

And seeking the Nine.

Find them... capture them... watch reality burn...

I shook my head, flinching back from the whisper that

carried through my mind. That hiss-click voice was familiar. I didn't want to hear it again.

Alaric was *dead,* after all.

But regardless of the so-called "Nine" and whether
they even existed, the Voidborn *had* found my stepdaughter in a city south of here. There'd been a battle.
Lovely fire and death that filled these creatures with glee.
But then a monster of a different kind had appeared, stopping the Voidborn on the verge of victory.

And oh, how they raged at that, but they weren't
deterred. The dragon was no longer ours, yes, and the
Voidborn inside it had been forced to flee. But it'd found
another host to occupy before the sun could burn it away.

My smile grew when I realized which one it'd claimed.
That was *perfect.*

"My queen?" Harran begged.

I looked back down at the pathetic little man.
"Summon my Huntsmen. I have a new mission for them."

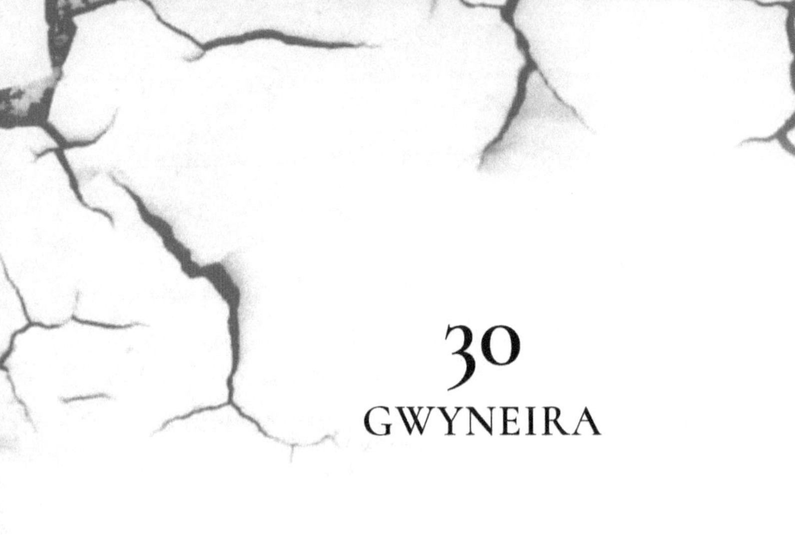

30
GWYNEIRA

Turning to shadow and smoke had never made me feel as vulnerable as it did now. Wrapped around Roan, I raced over grasslands and forests, rivers and creeks, while the bright sun bore down on me like it would burn me up at any moment. Even with my protection against it, the light still hurt like hell in this form.

But that pain was nothing compared to this growing sense of terror I couldn't explain.

Something was wrong. *So* wrong. Something was coming or had come, except I couldn't see it anywhere. Meanwhile, Roan didn't seem to feel it, but he also hadn't said a word since we left the tower, and for that I was grateful.

I was prey out in the open beneath the blazing sun. A rabbit with no choice but to run, because from this predator, there was nowhere on earth I could hide.

And the predator was coming closer...

Closer...

No matter how fast I flew, it didn't matter, because something was rushing toward me and I couldn't—

A stabbing sensation shot through me, cold and hard and dark as a moonless night without a single star. I crashed down into a forest clearing, narrowly missing sharp tree branches and barely able to shield Roan from the fall. As I tumbled to the earth, my body shifted back to solid form as if on some instinct that maybe this would alleviate the pain.

It didn't.

My vision blurred, warped by agony. I grasped my middle, my body curling up on itself as if to hide. I swore I was bleeding out, even if I couldn't feel a wound.

Cold death clutched at me. Wrapped its hands around my throat, choking out any chance of breathing air. My heart stuttered and faltered while the darkness grinned and prepared to sink its fangs into me once and for all.

A roar shattered my consciousness, fracturing the darkness like it was a breaking mirror. Some shards remained dark. Others showed the world as it'd been moments ago—blue sky, wintry forest, dried grass. Everything was a kaleidoscope of fragmented reality.

Arms scooped me up from the grass. A broad chest pressed to my cheek.

Fierce love and rage poured through my connection to Ozias, hitting the fragments of the broken world like a raging river and washing them all away.

Leaving only him.

"Gwyneira." His voice was a growl, and he held me so

close, it felt like the end of the universe itself wouldn't take me from his arms.

I blinked, looking around wide-eyed. We were in the clearing where I'd crash-landed. The forest close by, and the sky was blue and bright above me, not a cloud to be seen. The dread that had been building in me felt like a wave that had crested, pulling me under only for Ozias's love to yank me back up and stop me from drowning.

But the feeling wasn't gone. No, I'd found a safe harbor in Ozias's arms and our connection stabilized me like a rocky island in the sea. But without that, there would be nothing to stop me from getting dragged back beneath the invisible ocean of this ever-present horror.

"Is she okay?" Lars called from somewhere behind Ozias.

"Yes." Ozias's response was terse, but his arms tightened around me as if to belie his coldly certain tone. Bending his head, he nuzzled the top of my hair, inhaling deeply as he did, like he was drawing my scent into the farthest reaches of his lungs. A rumbling vibration carried through his chest, so deep it wasn't quite a sound. It was soothing somehow, like a growling purr that instantly reached down into some deep and ancient part of my mind, calming my innate survival fears. But as much as it was acting upon me, the reaction also seemed instinctive for him, as if he was reassuring himself I was truly here.

"I really am okay. I promise." I twisted a little bit, searching. "Is Roan—"

The rumbling turned darker. Deadlier and yet filled with a hunger that surged through the link between us.

"*That* one is the only reason I'm not dragging you away from here right now."

"What?" I looked up at him.

The heat in his eyes made an answering need suddenly twist in my core, like my body was more attuned to him than it was to my confusion at his words.

"You torture me, little mate," he murmured. "First I feel your time with the others in the castle, then with that one... and then..." Worry joined the hunger, and his grip on me shuddered like he was holding himself back from something.

Perhaps howling out the emotions roiling inside him like a building storm.

My mouth moved. "I-I'm sorry." My chest ached from the torrent coming from him. "I didn't think you'd... I mean—"

"Oz," Clay called. "What's going on, man?"

Ignoring him, Ozias murmured, "It isn't your pleasure I mind. It's that then you were afraid and in so much pain..."

His jaw clenched with growing rage, and before I could think what to say, he turned so the others came into view.

My words died. The men were several yards away.

Roan was on the ground between them, held at sword point.

"Wait." I struggled to get down. "Don't hurt him!"

"He hurt *you*," Ozias growled back as if that was more than enough cause for ripping Roan apart.

I grunted as I shoved at him, too scared of the chance the pain would return to simply shift and slip free.

Ozias scowled, but he put me down.

My legs wobbled, threatening to send me plopping back to the ground. "This wasn't Roan's fault," I insisted, settling for gripping Ozias's arm for stability. "He didn't hurt me, I swear."

Wary looks passed between the twins, while Byron's head tilted back a bit, his expression considering, as if my words confirmed what he already suspected. With his grip adjusting and readjusting on his sword, Dex appeared to be running a dozen scenarios through his mind, while Casimir stood to one side, his expression thoughtful. His chest still bore the gashes from where the demon's claws struck him, but he gave no sign of pain. Around his feet, Ruhl swirled, a low-lying tumble of dark clouds without any hint of a wolf inside.

Behind the others, Niko didn't take his eyes from Roan. He seemed so tense, I swore he was shaking.

"It's okay," I pressed. "*I'm* okay. Please."

Dex's jaw muscles jumped briefly, and then he asked Roan, "What version of you are we dealing with, friend? Assuming you *are* still our friend."

"Just me." Even though he sat on the ground surrounded by swords held by his friends, Roan sounded entirely calm.

I swore I could still hear pain beneath his tone.

"The demon..." His jaw muscles jumped. "It's asleep."

"You planning on it staying that way?" Clay asked coldly.

Roan's eyes flicked to me. He nodded once.

"Why didn't you tell us you were part—" Dex's gaze

went to the side, though I couldn't figure out who he was looking at. "Part stygiaterros?"

Confusion hit me, and for the first time, the careful shield of control Roan had around himself cracked. A hint of uncertainty entered his voice when he asked, "Part what?"

"Stygiaterros," Byron said.

"I-I'm not—"

"The *demon*, man," Clay snapped.

Roan's head shook. "I don't..." I could see his chest beginning to rise and fall faster. "I've never heard that word."

None of the men appeared to believe that.

"He doesn't know what he is." I started forward, and Ozias gave a short growl. "I'm safe with him," I insisted. "I swear."

His teeth ground, but he didn't protest again as I walked closer.

"Roan was adopted," I continued. "No one in his family ever knew what the demon was." I glanced at him. "It doesn't even have a name."

The other men were silent for a moment.

"Why didn't you tell us?" Dex asked him again.

I tensed, wanting to help and not sure what to say.

"Because..." Roan pushed to his feet, and the others took a step backward, their swords at the ready.

Roan's eyes went to me again, his pain so clear that I knew this was the moment he expected them all to loathe him just as much as he loathed himself. "I'm a coward," he said like it was the only explanation needed.

"What?" I protested. "No, you're not." I turned to the

others. "He had a good reason. Truly. Can't we just leave it at that?"

Only Dex reacted to the words, looking at me with a hint of apology.

My heart sank.

Closing his eyes briefly, Roan said, "I killed everyone I loved. My family. My village."

The silence felt like glass on the verge of shattering.

A breath left Lars. "You said they were killed in the war."

"By me."

I floundered, shocked he wasn't even trying to save himself. "It was an *accident*, though. He was just a child. He never meant for that to happen."

"It's what I am," Roan said like I hadn't even spoken. "When I lose control, people die. That... That's what I believed. I lost control when the Aneirans came, and I killed everyone, and I couldn't stop it. But I never told any of you because..." He scowled at himself.

Casimir's voice came from the edge of the group. "Because you didn't want to be alone." He stepped closer, his eyes on Roan. "Because even though you feared what you were, your life with your friends let you feel like a man, not a monster. Like you were part of something." His brow rose and his head twitched in my direction. "And so did she."

Roan stared at him, so still I wasn't sure he breathed. "How could you know that?" he whispered.

A soft chuckle left Casimir, sad irony in the sound. "Because you and I have something in common in that respect." His brow rose and fell, his eyes skimming across the giants but not landing on any one of them in particular. "I suspect several of us do."

My breath caught. He knew about Ozias. I had no question of it.

"You still lied to us, man," Clay persisted tightly. "I thought we were like family. You don't lie to family."

Roan winced, clearly pained.

"You should have trusted us," Lars added. "Like we trusted you."

"I'm sorry. I..." Roan shook his head as if words were failing him. "I was too scared to risk it."

Silence fell again.

"So you risked us, then," Niko spat out in a tight, angry tone I'd never heard from him before. "You risked her." He jerked his head in my direction.

Dread crushed down on me. Niko was the one who was always so understanding. So compassionate. Of all of them, I'd felt sure he would be the one to give Roan the benefit of the doubt.

But he was shaking so hard, I could see his hair quivering.

"Nature knew you had a secret," he said, his voice shaking too. "Something you weren't sharing. But I trusted you. I *never* thought you'd hide something that could hurt us. Hurt *Gwyneira*. But you cared more about your secrets and yourself than you did about keeping her safe, and even now, you... you're still..." His eyes raked up and down Roan like he'd suddenly realized he never knew the man at all.

"He's still what?" Clay prompted sharply.

Niko shook his head, watching Roan with such distrust it broke my heart. "I don't know."

Dex's jaw muscles jumped beneath the scruff on his light brown cheeks. "So what was today?"

Roan swallowed hard. "I lost control again."

The twins shifted their weight, clearly uncomfortable at the revelation. With aching disgust in his eyes, Niko looked away.

"I notice we are not dead, though," Casimir pointed out. "A few injuries notwithstanding." His chin twitched toward the gashes on his chest as if they were hardly worth mentioning.

"You controlled it," Ozias added, his deep voice measured.

Roan's head shook. "I didn't. It just…"

Byron spoke up for the first time. "Then the demon chose not to kill us." When no one responded, he continued. "And if that is the case, then it would stand to reason that it has gained some measure of control since what happened with your family, would it not?"

Roan didn't respond.

"The stygiaterros are protective by nature," Byron continued. "Fiercely possessive and aggressive too. Many demons are. Yet when faced with those who would keep it from Gwyneira, the demon exerted precisely the amount of force necessary to disable our group without mortally wounding anyone." He glanced at Dex and the rest. "I do not know whether it is trustworthy. And I do not know what passed between the demon and Gwyneira in the time she was gone. But I will note it is *Roan* standing here before us, not a demon, and that he is admitting to horrors in his past that anyone would wish to hide."

"He still put her in danger," Niko insisted, and it was like a knife in my heart to hear that furious tone coming from him. "And he's not the only one hiding things."

His eyes landed on Ozias.

My blood went cold. "This isn't about—"

A choked sound left Niko as he spun toward me in alarm.

"Take a moment, Niko," Dex cautioned. "Don't—"

"You were keeping secrets from us too?" Niko demanded of me, ignoring Dex and looking at me with so much hurt in his eyes, I wanted to cry. "You're our treluria and you—"

"Don't you turn this on her," Roan snapped, a snarl in his voice like maybe the demon wasn't entirely asleep after all.

Clay scoffed. "Yeah? How about you stay out of it, since you're so good at keeping your damn mouth shut about—"

"Enough!" Ozias roared.

In a surge of magic, his bones and skin warped, dark fur rushing out to cover his body, and suddenly the beastly form of my mate stood before us, fangs bared and a growl rumbling from his throat.

No one moved.

A shudder rolled through Ozias as his fur vanished and he became his Erenlian form once again. "Not all of us had homes before this, boy." Cold fury showed in his eyes as he glared at Niko. "And this?" He gestured sharply to the group at large. "This is why."

Without another word, he stalked away.

Silence fell. Uncomfortable looks passed between Clay and Lars, while Byron regarded the ground as if it might hold answers to this mess. Roan stared after Ozias, motionless, and Casimir said nothing, watching him. Pain in his eyes, Dex looked around at the others, and I wondered if he could see even better than I did all the cracks that had just been torn in the foundations of their friendships.

I searched for something to say. Anything to make it better. "Niko, I—"

Before I could finish, he'd already turned and walked away.

31
NIKO

I could have lost everyone. My friends. My only family.

Gwyneira.

At high speed, I strode away from the others and headed into the forest. Branches and vines twisted, moving quickly out of my path, but I didn't see them. Didn't care. I just wanted it to stop hurting, this horrible way everything was falling apart.

Because of secrets. Because of lies.

"Niko!" Gwyneira called behind me.

I bit back a cry of pain and fury, everything in me feeling like a wounded animal in a trap, flailing around and lashing out wildly. She didn't deserve what I'd said to her. How I behaved. But I couldn't be near her right now for fear of spewing more of my rage her way.

Because dammit, I'd *trusted* Roan. Trusted Ozias too. I never for one *second* believed they'd put our treluria in danger, no matter how uncertain about them nature had seemed.

And it still was. Not about Ozias. The reason for his strangeness had finally become clear. But with Roan...

I raked my hands into my hair, my fists clenching on the strands like maybe I could rip clarity out of my mind by sheer force of will. Nature was still telling me *something* about Roan, but the feeling only made my head hurt. I couldn't figure the message out. It was like an echo somehow, similar to what I'd felt from him in the past but different too. Some insane part of me still wanted to think he wasn't a threat to us, but given how wrong I was about that before...

Except he *hadn't* killed us. Or her.

An angry sound escaped me at my own thoughts. Yes, but he still *took* her. He'd still been hiding something so heinous, it could have cost every one of us our lives.

And he knew that. He'd actually known! He lived every day hiding this horrible secret, hiding the fact he could lose control at any moment, and never once did he admit that we were risking our lives being around him. Risking Gwyneira's life! Gods, with one wrong move, he could've accidentally *killed* the only people any of us had left in the world.

Ozias's words burned in my ears. *Not all of us had homes before this, boy.*

Yes, but we'd all lost ours, hadn't we? Lost the people we loved. The people we'd sworn to protect. My home before the Aneirans burnt it to the ground had been a tiny cabin in the forest, and my only family was Marnira, the old healer woman who found me as an infant and raised me as her son. The two of us hid in the forest for years while the war raged on, and every day she swore we'd be safe.

But Marnira's magic had been failing. Her health too. She hid that from me, using her skills with herbs and medicines to disguise it all because she didn't want me to worry. By the time I learned how bad off she really was, it'd been too late for me to help her, and then the Aneirans came...

I bit back a furious cry. Some secrets shouldn't be kept, especially the ones that could kill people. And whatever Ozias thought, those men and Gwyneira *were* the only family and the only home I still had.

Roan had risked that. Ozias too.

But so had I.

My feet stopped and my breaths slowed to ragged gasps, the truth hitting like ice in my veins. Dammit, that was it, wasn't it? Yes, when our treluria came along, those men kept their silence about what they were, but in the end, I helped them do it. I was as guilty as they were because even with how oddly nature reacted to them, even with every strange impression the world around me sent, I never said a word. I'd been so sure they would never risk us. So trusting that I... I'd just...

Failed.

Raking another hand through my hair, I looked around the forest, my heart aching. I was north of the clearing where I'd left the others. There were no predators nearby. Nothing but rocks and trees and one useless giant so horrified by the lies, the secrets, and the sheer fact I'd trusted Roan and Ozias despite everything I *should* have seen that I'd failed the people who mattered to me most.

Because this time, *I'd* been the one who should have said something but didn't. Not Dex. Not Byron or the twins. No, it was me. I was the one nature spoke to, and instead of watching out for my friends or being a worthy protector for my treluria...

My head shook, fury at myself now burning in my veins. Gods, Gwyneira even *asked* me about Roan, back at the Jeweled Coven. She'd been worried about him, but had I let that concern outweigh my faith in my friend? No. I'd reassured her that even if they had their secrets, Roan and Ozias wouldn't dream of hurting us. I let her believe she could trust my word. That I would never risk her and would always make sure she was safe.

And I... *I* failed her.

The weight of it all settled on me like a mountain, and in desperation, I stared up at the blue sky like it could answer any of this. Why hadn't Gwyneira told me when she learned the truth about them? Had I done something, said something, that made her think *I* wasn't trustworthy? Or was it about protecting them, when she should have been protecting herself?

Gods help me, didn't she understand how *important* she was to us? She was our treluria, for the gods' sakes! She was our beautiful, precious, vital heart of everything, and if anything happened to her, I didn't think any of us would survive. Why hadn't she kept herself safe, when at any moment, we could have lost her?

"Niko!" Gwyneira called in the distance.

I could have.

The truth felt like my heart was ripping from my chest, and before I knew it, I'd spun and was striding back toward the sound of her voice. I failed her, yes. Undoubtedly hurt her too by losing my temper and lashing out at her today. With all of that, I didn't know what I'd do when I reached her. Not really.

Except... I did know.

I'd tell her I was sorry. I'd beg her to forgive me for how I treated her and how I failed. And if she did, then by all the gods, I'd tie her down with every vine in this forest, kiss her breathless because I needed her lips on mine, and make love to her until she screamed from pleasure at being with me. I may not have been as skilled a lover as the others—and, gods, I was only a regular mortal man, not a demon or beast—but right now, I desperately needed to fill her, to feel her, and to remind every part of my body that I *hadn't* lost her today, no matter what horrible secrets anyone held.

And then I'd ask her why in the hell she never told me about these things she—

The ground suddenly shifted, ripping away from the forest floor and yanking me upward. I tumbled to the side, one hand catching on a rough rope while the other shot out into the open air.

Finding nothing.

"Well, isn't that a treat?" A cruel voice came from below me. I twisted, trying to find its source.

A burly man strolled into view from behind a tree, and he had a long stick with a hook on the end in his grasp. His face was a mottled mess of pockmarks and discolored skin, like an old peach that had been tossed around too many times. Contempt showed in his cold gaze, and his nose was bulbous above his sneering mouth. A smaller guy followed him, skinny with a weasel-like look to his pale face and no trace of emotion in his eyes. A pair of manacles hung from the smaller man's belt, the metal lashed tightly to him so it made no sound when he moved, and he gripped a strange tubelike device in his fist.

But both wore chest plates and helmets that glinted in the dappled light of the forest.

My blood went cold at the symbol embossed above their hearts on the metal. Aneirans. Aneiran *soldiers,* moreover. But what they were doing in the middle of nowhere or how they'd gotten this close without me knowing, I had no—

Horror stole my breath as the truth hit me.

Nature was saying nothing about them. Nor did it reflect any trace of the net in which I was trapped. To the natural world around me, there was no reason at all I should be dangling a dozen feet up like a caught fish in midair. No, as far as everything I could feel was concerned, the forest nearby was empty save for ordinary woodland creatures too small to do any good.

Chuckling to themselves, a dozen more soldiers sauntered out from behind the trees. Most held spears while a few had crossbows.

And not a single one of them made an impression on the world around me.

This wasn't possible.

"Looks like we got ourselves a baby stoneskin here." The first man jabbed at me with the hooked stick, and I flinched. "Or..." He cocked his head as if curious. "Damn thing looks like a grown man."

"Charms don't work on humans," the smaller man sniped, affront in his voice. "Nets don't trigger for 'em either. It's a giant. Doesn't matter what it looks like."

I stretched my free hand down toward the forest floor. The net was spinning slowly in place, propelled by his jabs, and the ground itself was easily a dozen feet below me, but that didn't matter. My power could still reach it.

Except it didn't. Nothing responded. Not a vine or a branch or a single weed. I could feel them down there, but for the first time in my life, they weren't reacting to me at all.

The first guy chuckled. "Oh, yeah, look at him. He's acting like a stoneskin, all right."

Heart pounding, I abandoned my efforts and turned my attention to the forest, straining to feel where Gwyneira and the others might be. I couldn't just shout for help, though. She might come running alone. No, I needed to know that Dex and the others were in the forest first, because the princess had been the only one I'd heard, and if I called out and she rushed to me...

My gut twisted. The Aneirans still thought Gwyneira was an assassin. If these soldiers caught her, there was *every* chance they would try to hurt her.

Or worse.

"Fucking animals," another soldier muttered, jabbing his spear at me. "You think they're forcing humans to make them half-breeds now?"

The first soldier made a contemptuous noise.

"Wouldn't put it past them." He jerked his chin at his shorter companion.

In the distance, nature whispered that Roan was in the forest now. He still felt strange. So odd in a way that made my head hurt.

But gods damn me, my options were a nightmare, and he was better than these Aneirans.

I opened my mouth to shout.

Something struck my neck. I flinched back, trying to smack it away, only to see the smaller man grin at me. He lowered the tube device from his lips.

And just for a moment, his eyes flashed bright orange.

A dart fell from my neck, dropping to the forest floor far below. The world blurred in front of me, turning into a smear of greenery that descended into shadows and wrapped me like a smothering blanket. My body became thick and numb. I couldn't feel nature or even the net around me anymore.

From far away, the first man's voice reached my ears. "Let's finish with this one quick. We've got a busy day."

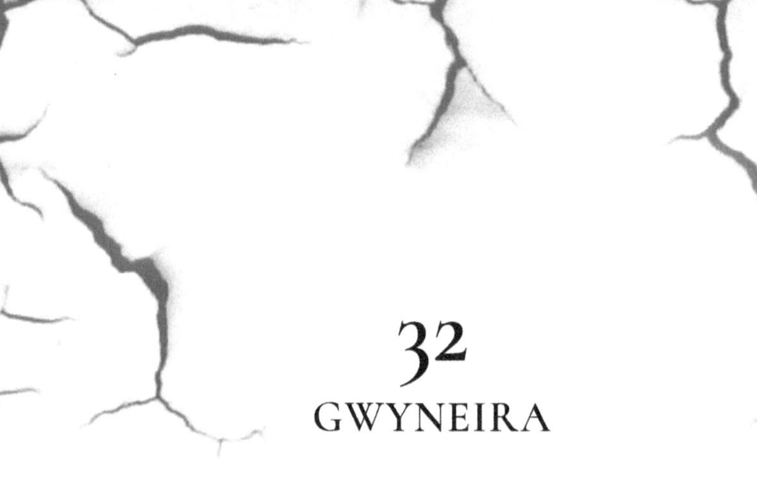

32

GWYNEIRA

"Niko!" I shouted, scanning the forest desperately. Everywhere I looked, there was no sign of him. Not a broken branch. Not a footprint in the dirt.

Nothing.

Exhaling roughly, I turned a circle, wishing I had his ability to speak to nature or Ozias's power to hear the earth telling him which way to go. I could feel my mate to the south of me, and I could tell enough to know he was okay—albeit angry at how this all had gone. Of all the ways for his friends to find out what he was, this had to be near the bottom of his list. But he wanted space right now. I felt that too. Which left me chasing Niko, even though, yes, given Niko's abilities, he was probably fine too.

But he'd been so furious. I'd never seen him like that before, and it hurt my heart to think he blamed me for part of this mess—especially when I knew he had a point.

I had learned what Ozias was, but I hadn't said anything. True, I'd wanted to help Ozias find a way to tell his friends *himself*, but Niko didn't know that.

To him, it probably looked like I'd been lying to them all.

Just like I feared.

"Niko!" I shouted again.

Gods, where the hell was he? Surely I should have come across him by now. Unless he was ignoring me, which maybe he—

Something rustled softly in the distance to my right.

I froze, my attention snapping toward the sound. It was far away. Barely audible above the ordinary noises of the forest, even to my vampire hearing. The woods appeared unchanged, though, and I couldn't see anyone walking toward me. Didn't see much of anything, in point of fact, besides bushes and trees and patches of sunlight that pushed past the thick covering of leaves overhead.

"Niko?" I called warily.

Nothing.

Fear rose, making my heart race with visions of predators creeping closer and all the things humans knew to dread about the forest. But then, I wasn't human anymore. If anything tried to attack me, it would regret it. And for all I knew, this was nothing more than a rabbit hopping innocently around in the—

A shadow moved to my right.

I gasped, only to sag with relief when the shadow rose from the undergrowth to become a swirling cloud of darkness in the form of a wolf.

"Ruhl." I petted his massive head, more to calm myself than anything. "You scared me."

I swore his glowing eyes took on a wry cast.

Giving him a tired look in return, I said, "What are you—"

"Princess?"

I jumped a mile.

Roan held up his hands as he walked closer. "Sorry."

I shook my head dismissively, attempting to calm down again. Gods, I was on edge, and I could only assume the argument earlier was to blame. "No, it's fine. Just nerves."

Roan made an understanding noise, though a heartbeat later, his eyes flicked to the forest. His brow knit for a moment as if something bothered him, but then he looked back at me with a tiny shake of his head like he was dispelling a distracting thought. "About that. I came to see if you were all right?" His hand took mine, our fingers lacing together.

"I'm fine. I was just looking for Niko."

Roan nodded, though he didn't appear totally convinced by my claim I was okay. "Sometimes he just needs space."

I suspected he was probably right, if only because Niko hadn't come back or responded to me. To be fair, he might not have heard me either.

I glanced at the forest. It was so quiet, though. The sounds of little woodland creatures were almost gone, leaving only an eerie emptiness that made my skin crawl. In all of that, for Niko not to have heard me...

Space, Roan said. It must be that.

"Maybe we should go back, then. Give him time." I bit my lip briefly. "It's kind of creepy out here."

Roan nodded. Still holding my hand, he drew me with him as he started back the way we'd come. Like a low-lying cloud of black smoke, Ruhl flowed after us, only barely looking like a wolf anymore.

"What about you?" I asked Roan. "Are you okay?"

His brow rose and fell. "As much as I can be."

"I'm so sorry. That really could have gone better."

"Or worse, considering the demon *did* take you away from them." He released my hand, but only to put his arm around my shoulders. "I don't blame them for how they reacted. When that vampire—" He paused and then continued as if correcting himself. "When *Casimir* stole you from me, I..." A soft scoff left him like words couldn't cover it.

I bit my lip. "Only briefly."

His head shook, ironclad certainty in his expression. "Not briefly. Not to me or the demon. We both were mad with fear for you that day, and this whole time, I've never forgiven him for that." Roan was silent for a moment. "I think maybe I should have."

I leaned my head against his side. "I'm here now."

His arm tightened on me gently, but then he cast a glance over his shoulder.

Apprehension bubbled through me again for no reason I could name. "What is it?"

He shook his head like he wasn't sure, and when he turned back, he gave me a reassuring smile. "Just creepy, like you said."

Despite his words, his eyes flicked to the forest behind

us again, and I didn't miss the flash of distrust that passed over his face.

My nervousness grew. "Are you picking up something out here? Because I—"

A sudden surge of worry and rage flooded through my connection to Ozias, stealing my words and making me gasp. In an instant, I could feel him running this way.

"Princess?" Roan turned me toward him, taking both my shoulders. "What's wrong?"

I shook my head. "I don't know. Ozias is—"

Suddenly, Roan thrust me away from him without ever letting me go.

A thin object shot past, whipping straight through the space where I'd been. Gasping, I threw a panicked look after it.

A crossbow bolt quivered where it impaled a nearby tree trunk.

All emotion vanished from Roan's face. His gaze snapped to the forest behind us, his expression turning deadly cold.

My breath caught. I'd seen that look before. A few hours ago in the city, in point of fact.

His demon was coming back to the surface.

"Run," he ordered me.

Without waiting for my response, he took off, his grip on my arm pulling me with him. Rustling erupted behind us both. More metal bolts shot through the air. I shrieked as one of them whipped past so close it tore a few strands of hair from my scalp.

"Ruhl!" Roan snapped.

I had no idea what he expected, but it didn't matter.

The wolf seemed to know. Whipping in a tight turn, the shadow creature raced toward the invisible attackers.

Screams came from behind us. I looked back, still running at Roan's side.

People stumbled from behind the trees only to fall as Ruhl ripped them down into the undergrowth and their panicked cries cut short with vicious speed. Sunlight glinted dully from burnished metal chest plates and helmets. They were obviously soldiers of some kind, but I couldn't tell what nation they were from or why the hell they were attacking us.

But for all his power, Ruhl couldn't be everywhere. One of the soldiers swung his crossbow around, unleashing a bolt straight at us.

I shifted instantly and slammed into Roan, shoving him out of the way.

But I didn't move far enough.

The bolt ripped through my shadowy form.

Pain screamed through me, blinding with its sheer agony. I tumbled down and crashed into the forest floor, my body instinctively shifting back to human form as if that would help something.

Gods, it didn't. Agony throbbed through my middle, like the bolt had torn straight through my insides when it passed.

"Gwyneira!" Roan crouched before me, the icy look in his eyes becoming panic as he checked me over frantically.

"I'm okay. Get to the others."

"Like fuck I'm leaving you."

Past his shoulder, I saw another soldier take aim. I gasped. "Get down!"

The bolt sliced through the air. Roan grunted as it grazed his side, but still he tried to hold himself between me and the soldiers.

But more were coming.

"Shift," I told him.

Horror joined the agony in his gaze.

"He won't kill us." I stared into his eyes, praying the demon could hear me—and that I was right. "Will you?"

Roan shuddered. But thread-thin fissures of flame cracked through the skin around his eyes.

And then he grinned.

The demon was back.

Shifting as he moved, Roan rose to his feet and spun. Crossbow bolts tore the air. With clawed hands, he batted them away. The soldiers drew their swords.

He lunged.

Screams rose. Blood splattered the undergrowth, and not a drop of it looked as if it came from Roan. Like a living nightmare, he took to the air and yanked soldier after soldier up with him, and his claws made short work of any who tried to stop his attack.

A dark blur shot through the forest to my right, and suddenly Ozias joined the fray. Snatching a soldier who'd started to aim his crossbow my direction, he flung the man through the air and paid no attention as he hit a tree at an angle so sharp, his neck snapped in an instant. Whirling, Ozias merely snagged another, and more blood splattered the ground as he tore the soldier's throat out with his teeth.

I swallowed hard.

Shouts came from behind me, and suddenly, Dex and the twins arrived. Racing into the battle with their swords drawn, they swung at the soldiers, and the sounds of metal against metal filled the air.

"Well, hello, my little fucktoy," Casimir said congenially, his tone utterly at odds with the chaos nearby. Crouching at my side, he flashed me a fanged grin. "Time to go, yes?"

Not waiting for my answer, the vampire scooped me up from the forest floor and took off running in the other direction. Several yards back, Byron was waiting behind a thick tree trunk. When we raced past, he followed, one eye on the battle behind us as if to gauge how close the soldiers were coming.

"What about the others?" I asked, wincing as my insides ached.

"You're injured," Byron replied as if that settled something. "We saw what happened. You need to get out of here before they can shoot you again."

"But—"

Casimir made a chiding sound. "Do not worry, princess. I believe your giants have this well in hand."

That much was definitely true. Over the vampire's shoulder, I could see Dex taking on two soldiers at once, while Clay and Lars dispatched several others in quick succession. Blood soaked Ozias's muzzle and chest, but our connection told me immediately that none of it was his. Diving through the trees, the demon tore soldiers away from the ground faster than they could flee while Ruhl circled the battle, picking off the stragglers as nothing but smoke with glowing green eyes and vicious teeth.

I held onto Casimir. "Have you seen Niko?"

The vampire's arms tightened on me, and worry flashed over Byron's face.

But neither man answered.

My heart started pounding harder. If they didn't know, then that left three options, because I couldn't bring myself to believe Niko simply wouldn't come back to help us in a fight. So that meant captured, injured...

Or dead.

I trembled. No, it wouldn't be that. If he was injured, we'd find him and help him. If he'd been captured, then we would rescue him.

I wouldn't let myself imagine the other possibility.

33
THE DEMON

My treluria had asked for me to return.

Even the broken one could not fathom it, but his shock was nothing compared to my own. No, the princess did not want me as a lover. Did not crave me as I craved her. She let the others touch her, let the broken one have her, and it was hell itself for me to know I would never do the same.

But she had faith in my ability to protect her, and so protect her I would.

By making sure everything that threatened her died.

I caught one of the fools who thought to attack her, lifting him from the ground and then tearing him to pieces faster than he could scream. Another believed he could fire a weapon at her, only to find himself flying into the trees where he was impaled upon impact. More shouted, charging at me, as if their mere numbers could be intimidating enough to stop me from destroying them all.

But if this was the only worth I could have to the princess, then I would bathe this forest in the blood of those even less worthy than I.

The moments became a blur of blood and screams, a crude balm for the ache inside. I'd felt it when the broken one had been with her on that tower after all my plans had gone so horribly wrong. Even though I'd buried myself so deep that his time with her had been nothing but distant sensations, the way he touched her, sank deep into her, made her cry out and moan with need had still been excruciating.

And neither of them had wanted me to take part in that. At the time, I'd believed neither wanted me to exist at all. I'd sworn then that I would stay as far from them both as I could manage. Let him forget me. Let her do the same. I would become nothing but a ghost in the back of his mind, and maybe then he would know peace.

Maybe I would too.

But when these bastards *attacked* her... when she reached out and summoned me back from the darkness, back from my exile, calling for my aid in defending her...

Even a ghost could wreak havoc for the one he loved.

I flew at the last of the attackers. Three were left. One for each hand, another for my teeth, and then this would be over. None would threaten her again.

"Roan!"

I snarled at the shout from the giant with light-brown skin. The leader.

Dex, the broken one snapped at me from inside my mind, struggling to rise from the darkness into which I'd shoved him. Now that the battle was near its end, he wanted to reclaim control.

But he was a fool. My treluria wanted my protection.

I was not finished protecting her.

Whirling around, I hovered above the forest floor. Without bothering to restrain my scorn, I met the eyes of the one called Dex. "I am not *Roan*."

The man paused, but there was no fear in his eyes. Even as I hung in the air above him, my naked form coated and dripping with the blood of my treluria's enemies, he showed no hint of being intimidated. No, there was only assessment in his level gaze, as if he was merely fitting me into a plan in his mind. "Then what do we call you?"

"I am the demon."

He nodded slowly. "Okay. Will Roan return soon?"

I growled. His question only confirmed what I already knew. Only the broken one had value to them.

But that only made them fools too.

I dove swiftly and snatched the nearest of the remaining attackers from the earth.

"Demon!" Dex snapped. "Stand down."

I turned an incredulous look upon him. "Why? They shot my treluria. Now they must die."

Again, Dex paused, his brow flickering lower for a heartbeat, and since he already knew she'd been hurt, it could only have been the fact I'd called her my treluria that stopped him.

But whatever he thought of that was immaterial, and reading the expressions of others was a pursuit I scarcely bothered with, so I simply turned my attention back to the man hanging from my fist.

"Niko's missing," Dex said. "We need a few of these bastards alive in case they know where he is."

I disagreed. The one called Niko had hurt her. Been cold and angry with her. He deserved nothing.

He was hurt too, the broken one whispered in my mind.

Like that mattered.

Scorn came from the broken one. Scorn for my thought, for my rage on her behalf, and it burned. I only wanted to protect her, and the boy had caused her pain. Why was that math not simple?

Because it will hurt her if he dies, the broken one replied.

Growling, I raked my eyes over the forest, finding no trace of the boy. The princess was unpredictable, it was true. She *would* want the one called Niko to be unharmed even though he'd caused her pain.

Fine.

"Put the man down, demon," Dex said.

"Only one needs to be alive," I snarled. "The others can die."

"Unless the survivor lies," he pointed out.

His words were infuriating.

Especially since they contained logic.

"Very well." Letting the air spill from my wings, I dropped to the earth and dug my clawed feet into the loam. Pulling the soldier in my fist closer, I bared my teeth and stared into his watery blue eyes, ignoring the giants as they made protesting noises. "Do not lie or I will eat you."

In my grip, the man trembled, incoherent sounds of fear coming from his lips.

"Where is the boy?" I demanded.

The man whimpered. The stink of piss seeped out into the air, and I glanced down to see the front of his pants becoming wet.

With a disgusted noise, I tossed him to the earth and reached for the next soldier.

Dex stepped in front of me. "If we may?"

His voice was controlled, and despite the fact he stood only inches from my claws, he still showed no trace of fear.

Why did this giant trust I wouldn't kill him? The broken one had told them of what we'd done. Of our shame and all those we'd killed. Even now, I wore the blood of his enemies like a second skin.

Yet this man showed no sign of believing I would add his blood to the mix.

Seeming satisfied with my silence, Dex returned his attention to the three men on the forest floor. With his boot, he rolled one of them over.

The man stabbed at him with a blade he'd hidden beneath his body.

Instantly, my claws sent the attacker's hand flying, the knife going with it, and his head followed. Both tumbled away to be lost among the underbrush, food for whatever creatures feasted upon fools.

"Holy shit!" one of the blond twins exclaimed.

I ignored them. "One less to lie now."

The remaining two soldiers were shaking so hard, I could see their chest plates quivering in the shadows.

For a moment, Dex didn't move, his eyes on me, and then very carefully, he bowed his head an inch. "Thank you."

I froze. He... thanked me? Yes, I'd saved him. But I was the demon.

Nobody thanked the demon.

Nothing in his expression changed to hint that it was a trick. None of the giants around me showed any disgust for his words or for how he'd expressed gratitude to something like me.

I didn't know what to do.

"Clay," Dex continued to one of the blond twin giants. "You think you could..." He nodded at me, not explaining, and instantly I was on alert.

"Yeah," the blond man said as if agreeing. "How, uh... how about we get you something to cover up with a bit, eh, buddy?"

My alarm grew, but before I could demand to know something as foolish as clothing could be more important than the bastards who'd attacked my treluria, the man called Clay gestured and muttered something under his breath.

Clothing materialized on my body.

I snarled, twisting this way and that at the sudden sensation of being trapped within leather and fabric. But the pants and shirt remained, both of them cut with holes to allow my wings and tail to pass through.

And nothing else happened. The clothing did not attack or attempt to poison me. It was just... there.

I stared at the blond man, speechless with confusion. Why had he done that?

"Let's get this over with," Dex said.

My gaze snapped to him, but he wasn't referring to anything about me. Instead, his focus was on the soldiers. Surveying them briefly, he twitched his chin at Clay and the blond man's twin. Both men started toward the soldiers.

I rolled my shoulders, made uncomfortable by more than the sensation of fabric and leather on my blood-covered skin. These giants were odd. They behaved unexpectedly over and over again. I didn't know what to make of them.

The twins drew their weapons as they neared the soldiers, and I cursed at myself silently as I shoved my perturbed feelings down where the broken one stayed. Clothing was a distraction. So were these giants. These soldiers had attacked my treluria, and for that they would pay.

Let the broken one deal with these irritating *emotions*. I had a greater mission.

Inside my mind, the broken one didn't react. But Dex's words and the blond man's actions had thrown him, that I could tell. Plenty of times over the years, his friends had thanked him for things. Helped him with things. But back then, they hadn't known the truth about him. About us. He'd been as certain as I was that scorn and fear and hate were the only responses I would ever elicit from others.

Yet now I had thanks, and he didn't know how to feel about that.

Growling low, I shoved my awareness of his shock away too.

The twins aimed their weapons at the soldiers, one pointing at the piss-covered man on the left, while the other leveled his sword at the guy on the right. Clay grinned, his expression like a mockery of humor, as cold and sharp as a blade of ice. "What do you say, eh?" he asked the soldier on the right. "You answer our questions, or we hand you over to the big guys." He jerked his head back toward me and then again at the furred beast.

I approved of this threat.

The soldier stared up at him, clearly trembling but with a proud glint in his beady eyes that spoke of an arrogance that likely meant I'd be wearing his blood in several more minutes. His bulbous, misshapen nose sat in the middle of a weathered, pockmarked face that looked like doughy leather.

He's not going to break, the broken one murmured, rising so close to the surface in my mind now, it was as if he was riding just behind my eyes, on the verge of returning.

I cracked my neck and ground my teeth, fighting him. He was the broken one. He wasn't strong enough to protect the princess. I needed to stay in control.

Nearby, I caught sight of the furred beast. His eyes went from me to the soldiers and back as if watching both to see what we'd do.

I ignored him. In a contest between us, I had no doubt I would win. The beast would be a fool if he attacked something like me.

Dex stepped closer to the soldier with the round nose. His eyes ran over the man, pausing on the emblem embossed on the breastplate over his heart. "You're a general in the queen's forces. Did she send you here?"

The man spat at Dex. The spittle fell far short of him, a pointless gesture, but still I snarled while angry murmurs passed through the giants around me.

Dex didn't react in the slightest. "Surrender and answer our questions, General, and I swear by the crown and the apple I'll have these men spare you."

I did *not* approve of that.

The general sneered. "I know what you are, stoneskin. You're no soldier of Aneira. Save your false oaths."

Dex's brow arched. "I stood beneath the royal tree and offered my lifeblood to the sword of the king at the start of the Erenlian war. I serve the rightful ruler of Aneira still."

Contempt twisted the man's face, but the piss-covered soldier next to him glanced between Dex and the general with growing doubt and confusion in his eyes.

Ah, I understood now. Divide and conquer. Perhaps I *did* approve of this plan.

Assuming I could still kill the bastards in the end.

"The rightful ruler of Aneira is Queen Melisandre," the general retorted, "and she will make all you disgusting stoneskins burn for your—"

He cut off with a strangled gasp as my clawed fingers wrapped around his throat.

"Demon."

I looked at Dex, incredulous at the interruption. "He offers nothing but insults. I will kill him so the other one may speak."

"Demon guy's got a point," Clay commented.

I grinned. I liked this twin.

"We don't kill people for insulting us," his brother replied.

An irritated sound escaped me. I did not like that twin as much.

"Niko is missing," the annoying twin continued. "What if it turns out we need this guy to find him?"

My fingers tightened on the general's throat. "We do not need one who offers filth, only one who offers information."

"Enough," Dex cut in before the others could respond. "We don't kill him... yet."

A rustling sound came from behind us, and I glanced back to see my treluria standing with the vampire king and the redheaded giant. The wound I'd carved on the vampire's chest glimmered to my eyes, my power laced through it.

But it was irrelevant compared to how my treluria stood with one hand clutched to her middle as if the injury the soldiers had given her still caused pain.

Choking sounds came from the general. His fingers clawed at my own, trying to liberate his throat from my grip.

"Release him," my treluria said to me.

I stared at her, baffled.

"Now."

The man fell to the earth, gasping, his throat intact but bruised from my grip.

My treluria gave me a tight nod. Still holding one hand to her middle, she walked closer, her eyes on the general and the soldier. "Do you recognize me?"

Her voice was cold. Imperious. She'd turned that tone on me at the tower where everything went wrong, but it still made pride rise up in me to hear it leveled at this man now.

My treluria was a queen. Yes, an imposter sat on her throne and dared to pretend to deserve her place, but it changed nothing of what my treluria was born to be.

The general and the soldier stared at her, and it was the stupid general who recovered first. Rage and contempt filled his face, and he looked at her like she was scum he'd found beneath his boots. "I recognize the cowardly snake who murdered her own father. Execution was too good for you, bitch. Your stepmother should have rid the world of an ungrateful whore like you—"

His words cut off with a squelch.

My treluria blinked at me as I drew back, my hand coated in the man's blood and his heart in my fist.

"He should not have spoken to you that way," I explained.

Silence reigned.

Unbothered, I sniffed the organ, debating whether to taste it, but it reeked of fried foods and too much drink. Disgusted, I tossed it aside.

"Well, um…" Clay coughed awkwardly, and his voice was tight when he continued to the soldier, "Looks like you're the only one left, buddy. Care to answer our questions now?"

The smelly man's eyes darted across all of us, and a terrified whimper escaped him. "Please don't eat me."

"Better tell us what we need, then," Clay replied.

I liked this twin indeed.

"There was a young man in these woods," Dex said. "Dark hair, brown eyes, tall but slightly shorter than the rest of us. Have you seen him?"

The soldier's mouth moved for a moment before he found his voice. "I-I can't. Please. She'll kill me."

"Who?"

"The queen."

Clay chuckled wryly. "Yeah, uh, she's not here, so..."

Apparently, that did not matter to the soldier. He only trembled harder.

"Whatever it is," my treluria said gently, "I will protect you. My allies will too."

The man's eyes darted to me as if incredulous she would offer such a thing when I'd just killed his companions.

"Just answer us," she continued. "Please."

Trembling, the man moved just enough to lift his wrist. A thick band of metal clung to him like a skin-tight bracelet. The outward-facing portion was rounded and made of iron with brass trim on the edges. The entire surface was covered in engravings that looked like they were carved in brass as well.

My lips peeled back in a snarl. Those markings were wrong, somehow. They did not move and yet my mind swore they were crawling around the metal like worms.

"Uh, nice jewelry," Clay said, but his tone held more discomfort than sarcasm. Seemingly without realizing it, he and the other giants were recoiling from the band.

"What exactly does that do?" Dex asked.

The soldier trembled and said nothing.

My treluria leaned closer to the man, which sent a jolt

of alarm through me. If there was danger, she should not be risking herself by coming anywhere near it.

"What problem could a mere part of your uniform present?" she asked cautiously.

"It's not just that." The soldier lowered his arm. "It was made by the queen years ago. A new way to stop traitors like the one they found in Orlindria during the war."

A sickened look crossed Dex's face, and the broken one's memories supplied the reason why.

The so-called traitor had been him.

"This prevents solders from betraying Aneira," the soldier continued. "And now from betraying *her*. It also keeps giants from using their magic on us or knowing where we are." Once again, he glanced at me, and pride swelled. I was not a giant. He could not stop me and he knew it.

This is why he spoke.

"It does *what* now?" Clay threw an incredulous look at the others and then extended his hand at the man. Twisting rivulets of moisture swelled from the earth and then flung themselves at the soldier.

The water dissipated long before it reached him, each rivulet falling apart like the magic holding it together simply ceased to exist.

Alarm shimmered up to me from the broken one, and he wasn't alone.

"Lars?" Clay prompted. "You, uh..."

The irritating twin lifted his hand. The air ahead of him shimmered with heat, turning to flames only to have them vanish into useless smoke long before they came anywhere near the man. Appearing perturbed, the redheaded scholar held up a small nugget, bringing it closer and closer to the soldier until suddenly the silvery gleam upon the mineral became dull. He drew back sharply and then froze as the silvery gleam returned.

At the edge of their group, the beast suddenly shifted back to his other form, bare-chested with no boots on his feet, but his pants remained in place.

Clothes were so strange.

"The earth cannot feel him," the beast-man said as if this should mean something.

Dread came from the broken one.

With a grim expression, the vampire walked closer to the soldier. His hand extended, and magic tingled across the air.

I hissed, recoiling. It felt too bright. Burning but not like my flames.

Angels, whispered the broken one. *He's descended from angels.*

I knew nothing of angels, except now I knew I hated them.

But the vampire paid me no attention, the idiotic creature. His power wrapped around the soldier, making the man gasp in terror. Holding it there for an eternal, awful moment, the vampire narrowed his eyes thoughtfully. Finally, he lowered his hand, letting the wretched magic dissipate. "Only Erenlian powers are muted, then."

"All the soldiers have this?" the irritating twin known as Lars asked. His voice held strain and more than a little apprehension.

Jerkily, the man nodded.

The broken one's dread deepened, and it was

mirrored across the faces of his friends. They had known crossing Aneira would be difficult. They'd expected risks and dangers.

This was something else entirely.

But they were not thinking clearly. *I was not muted by this strange bracelet.* They had nothing to fear—nor did they need that vampire.

Yet they did not realize this, and thus they were not reassured.

"How the hell did we miss this?" Clay asked.

The redheaded giant shook his head. "We were in the mountains beyond Aneira. We only had the magic mirror to watch them with for years. How would we have known the queen crafted such a thing?"

While worried looks passed among the others, my treluria stared at the band on the soldier's wrist, her head shaking.

"What is it, princess?" Lars asked her.

"He never told me. My father. I once asked what those were, and he only said it was part of the uniform now."

"Perhaps he didn't know."

She glanced up at him, clearly trying to find comfort in his words.

Even if she didn't appear to fully believe them.

"So what do we do?" Lars continued, turning to the group at large. "We'll never even know the bastards are coming."

The men cast worried looks to one another.

"We'll deal with that when and if we have to," Dex said tightly. "But first things first." He turned to the soldier. "Is our friend alive?"

None of the people around me breathed.

The soldier's mouth moved again, seeking speech and finding hardly any. "I-I don't know. They took him, but..." He gave a weak and cowardly shrug, as if somehow that should be a sufficient answer.

Nausea crossed my treluria's face, and I growled in rage. We would kill anyone who had harmed the boy. We would make it slow because they had brought that anguish to our treluria's eyes.

"Okay," Clay said. "Then where did they take him, you piss-soaked fucker?"

The man's eyes darted around as if seeking an escape.

"Answer us," my treluria demanded of the soldier, but now a thrum of power carried through her voice. "Now."

Terror painted itself across the soldier's face, but still her command dragged the words from him. "I-I'm not sure. We were supposed to take him to the mines, but... lots of times the prisoners don't make it that far. They... they have accidents instead."

A growl rumbled from the beast.

"Which way did they go?" my treluria asked.

Trembling, the soldier lifted a hand to point. "Along the northern road to Lumilia. Queen's orders."

The nausea and agony on my treluria's face deepened, and all of it was laced with fear. I would not abide it.

"We will find him," I growled. "The boy will be alive."

Her gaze found me, and I froze at the new emotion I saw tangled up with her pain and terror.

Gratitude.

Swallowing hard, she turned from the soldier. "We

need to go," she said to the giants and the vampire. "We can't let Niko end up in my stepmother's hands."

Dex nodded. He bore a cold expression that even the broken one wasn't sure he had ever seen on the man's face. One that said the world might have finally gone too far.

And now everything that stood in his path would pay.

A strange feeling rose inside me, and it wasn't from the broken one. I'd never felt it for anyone before.

These men were predators in their own right. Protective ones who would carve a path through the world itself for those they cared about.

And I... I could *respect* that.

"Take that one with us," Dex said with a jerk of his chin at the piss-covered soldier. "We might need him."

Clay and his brother hefted the man from the earth while the others followed the princess from the forest.

Dex turned away. "Let's go save Niko."

Want to know what happens next? Order OF NINE SO BOLD today!

TITLES BY SIERRA ROWAN

ABOUT THE AUTHOR

Sierra Rowan is the USA Today bestselling author of action-packed reverse harem paranormal romance and urban fantasy novels. Sierra loves to write stories filled with steam, heart, and adventure where a happily-ever-after is guaranteed, even if it takes a few magical battles and wild escapes to get there.

Get updates about all of Sierra Rowan's books at sierrarowan.com.

- amazon.com/author/sierrarowan
- bookbub.com/authors/sierra-rowan
- goodreads.com/sierrarowan
- facebook.com/authorsierrarowan
- instagram.com/authorsierrarowan
- tiktok.com/@sierrarowanbooks
- x.com/SierraRowanBook